FRACTURED

GUARDS OF THE SHADOWLANDS
Book 2

FRACT

URED

SARAH FINE

SKYSCAPE

Published by Skyscape, New York

www.apub.com

ISBN-13: 9781477817292
ISBN-10: 1477817298

Source photos courtesy of Shutterstock

Library of Congress Cataloging-in-Publication Data available upon request.

Printed in the United States of America

First edition

For Alma, my very own warrior girl.

ONE

MY CAPTOR PACED THE entryway with heavy footsteps while I sat in a wooden chair backed against the wall. My heart beat hard against my ribs, keeping time with my primitive, animal thoughts: *escape escape escape*.

My rational side, dwarfed by instinct, somehow managed to whisper, *It's not like this is a life-threatening situation. I'll get out of it alive. I hope.*

I leaned forward and planted my feet on the floor, estimating the number of seconds it would take to reach the exit.

The fierce stare of my jailer told me she was thinking the same thing. She halted in front of the door and crossed her arms over her chest. "Don't even think about it, baby. I'm responsible for you. This is a big deal."

I leaned my head back and banged it softly against the wall. "Only because you made it one."

Diane made her all-purpose *mm-mm-mm* sound of disapproval. "You've just gone through something big, and now—"

I was saved from a lecture by a knock at the door, but the knowledge of who it was sent my heart rate skyrocketing. I stood up on shaky legs as Diane turned the knob and swung it wide.

I was still getting used to seeing him in regular clothes rather than armor and fatigues. A week ago he'd shown up at my school, looking like an ordinary high school student instead of a deadly Guard. Well, "ordinary" probably wasn't the right word. He couldn't look ordinary if he tried. And he was trying. Tonight, he wore jeans and a zipped-up gray hoodie. His face was angular and stark, with olive skin framed by ink-black hair; his eyes, which were so dark they looked like solid ebony circles, held an expression I'd seen before.

He was doing his best to look harmless, but he wasn't very good at it. He still looked like he could kill someone without breaking a sweat.

Probably because he could.

"Ms. Jeffries?" Even though he spoke perfect English, every consonant was harder, every vowel deeper, resulting in this clipped, precise accent that perfectly matched his appearance. He held out his hand. "Malachi Sokol. So nice to meet you."

I drew up alongside Diane in time to see her eyebrows nearly hit her hairline. She'd spent her entire career working as a corrections officer at the medium-security prison, so she had a pretty keen sense of danger. Malachi had obviously triggered her alarm. She shook his hand and stepped back to allow him into the entryway. "Nice to meet you, too. Lela said you just arrived here in the States?"

"Yes, it's a brief exchange program. An opportunity to experience American culture before I graduate," he replied, but his focus had already shifted from Diane.

To me.

His smile was a devastating curl of his lips as his eyes met mine. From behind his back, he produced a small bouquet of flowers, a few yellow-and-white blooms and several pale-green buds, wrapped in cellophane. "These are for you."

It took me a few seconds, but I managed to get my hands and fingers to work together to take the flowers from his hand. "Thanks," I said, but it came out as a choked whisper.

Malachi's brows lowered and concern flashed in his eyes before he turned back to Diane. "I'd like to introduce my host father." He gestured toward the front steps.

Raphael, dressed in khakis and a sweater, stepped into the entryway and held out his hand. "Ms. Jeffries. I'm John Raphael. Thank you so much for inviting us to dinner. I was so pleased to hear Malachi had already made a friend."

As he smiled, his face transformed from forgettable to indelible, from ordinary to . . . well, angelic. Whenever Raphael smiled, I wished I had my camera to capture it.

The tension melted from Diane's body as she shook Raphael's hand. Her face relaxed into a warm smile. "I was happy, too, for Lela," she said, which nearly made me laugh, because we'd had a raging argument this afternoon about whether I could go out with Malachi tonight. It was the first time I'd ever asked to go out with a boy, the first time I'd ever mentioned one, actually, and judging by the way she'd clutched at her chest when I did, it really caught her by surprise. Especially because things had been so miserable since Nadia killed herself. Diane couldn't understand how I'd "snapped out" of my grief in the past week.

She didn't know I'd followed Nadia into death. That I'd seen my best friend again. That I not only suspected Nadia was in a better place—I knew it at a bone-deep level. I'd made sure of it, in fact.

I'd sold my own freedom to make it happen.

While Diane and Raphael chatted about the joys of parenting teenagers, I went to the kitchen with the flowers, staring at those thinly veined buds as my throat tightened. I opened a cabinet to pull out a plastic vase, and when I closed it, Malachi was standing beside me.

"You don't like them?" he asked.

I shook my head. "I love them. It's just . . . no one's ever given me flowers before." I turned my back, rolling the delicate stems between my fingers. It was one of those cheap grocery-store bouquets. Tegan, the new queen bee of Warwick High School since Nadia's death, would have scoffed at the already-wilting necks, the scraggly little petals. But to me . . .

Malachi's fingers skimmed along my shoulder. "I have never given a girl flowers before." He laughed quietly. "I hadn't actually seen a flower up close in a long time."

He'd spent the last several decades in a walled city of cement and steel and slime, where the only things that grew were the festering wishes of the dead, sorrowful people trapped there. Because it was always dusk or midnight, never day, nothing green or lush or *real* could grow. Well, that wasn't exactly true. Something had grown between *us*.

I turned back to him and reached for his hand. I wasn't used to this yet, this permission to touch. His skin was so warm. Real. *Here.*

"Unbelievable," I whispered.

He grinned and pulled me toward him, but at that exact moment Diane entered the kitchen. Malachi let go of me and stepped back, clearing his throat.

"I hope you like pasta," she said to him. Her tone was light, but she shot him a look. He'd been warned.

"I suspect I will love anything you cook," he replied. I had no doubt that was true. Malachi hadn't eaten a decent meal since well before his death, sometime in the early 1940s.

Malachi and I set the table while Raphael poured us each a glass of lemonade. Dinner had been Diane's idea. She had insisted on meeting both Malachi and his "people" before she would allow me to go out with him. She kept narrowing her eyes, like she was wondering if he'd come armed. I was wondering the same thing. And while I'd seen Malachi kill Mazikin with deadly accuracy and powerful grace, I'd rarely seen him do anything as mundane as setting forks on a table. By the way he watched his own hands and carefully placed each piece of cutlery, he was probably thinking about it as well. I was dying to ask him what was going on inside his head, to finally get to know the real him better. Maybe there would be time to do that now that we were here, on Earth, and not trapped in hell.

The past week hadn't given us many opportunities, though. We'd spent what little time we had together focused on making sure Malachi had the basic skills he needed to function in the modern world, like operating a microwave and using a cell phone. I'd spent the rest of my after-school hours dutifully attending a series of doctor appointments Diane had set up to make sure I wasn't in need of psychiatric hospitalization. As soon as I'd walked her back from that cliff, I asked if I could go out with Malachi. We couldn't afford to wait any longer.

"Where exactly are you from?" Diane asked him as we sat down to eat.

"Bratislava," he said. "Slovakia."

"What do your parents do?"

My throat tightened again as I watched him give Diane a small, sad smile. "My father owns a shoe store," he said slowly. "My mother, she stays at home. She's a very good cook." He bowed his head for a second. "I miss her cooking."

The sharp edges of Diane's expression and voice immediately softened. "You're homesick, poor baby."

Malachi swallowed and took a breath. "Always. But I am happy to be here. And happy to have met Lela."

"Thank you for agreeing to let Lela drive," said Raphael, passing the garlic bread to Diane and drawing attention away from Malachi, allowing him a chance to recover from the mention of his parents, who had died at the hands of the Nazis.

"Actually, I think it's good for Lela to do the driving," said Diane. She'd told me she wanted me to be able to dump Malachi and drive away if he got "handsy."

Raphael was a charming dinner companion and had no trouble getting Diane to talk about herself, her family, her pride that I was college-bound. As he kept her going, I watched Malachi eat. Every bite looked like an act of worship. He told Diane how delicious it was at least ten times. She probably thought he was kissing her ass, but I knew it for what it was—the absolute truth. The food in the dark city sucked.

"We need to leave soon if we're going to make that movie," I said as we finished up. I was more than ready to make a break for it and be alone with Malachi.

"Which theater are you going to?" asked Diane. "Not Providence Place, all right?"

Here we go. "No, but it's really not a big—"

She gripped her fork like a weapon and glared at me. "Those crazies were caught on video only about ten miles from here. You're not going anywhere near that city until they catch them." She wasn't the only one freaking out. We lived in Warwick, but Rhode Island was the size of a teacup, and the entire state was in an uproar about the sightings.

Raphael wiped his mouth with his napkin. "I saw the news report. The footage was so grainy that it could have even been a rabid dog."

Diane looked at Raphael like he'd betrayed her. "A dog wearing jeans and sneakers?" She took a bite of pasta, her jaw working harder than necessary. When she swallowed, she said, "I'm not saying it's a werewolf or something. I'm not crazy. But a guy running around on all fours? Probably a meth head. Take it from me: those people are unpredictable. Either way, these two are staying away."

"The theater is here in Warwick, Ms. Jeffries," Malachi offered, earning him a nod from Diane. We'd rehearsed this part, and he looked relieved that he'd gotten it right.

"What are you seeing?" she asked, finally relaxing.

"*Night Huntress*," he recited. "It's received great reviews."

"I heard it was a gore fest," she grumbled as she began to clear the table.

I held in my half-hysterical giggles as I helped get the dishes into the sink. "Thanks for dinner. And for being cool."

She shrugged and *hmph*ed. "You've earned my trust, baby. Keep it, all right?"

"No problem," I said. "You don't have to wait up."

"Nice try. It's a *school* night. You're lucky I'm letting you out at all. Be back by ten." Diane leaned out of the kitchen and fixed Malachi with a suspicious look. "You'd better take care of this girl, young man."

Malachi closed the distance between us and took my hand. "Ms. Jeffries, I swear to you, I will protect her with my life."

Diane laughed. If she only knew he'd already done exactly that at least a dozen times.

She let us go with a minimum of fuss, even though she wouldn't let Raphael escape without a hug, which he seemed happy enough to give her. No matter what she thought of Malachi, it was obvious she thought Raphael was all right, which would help a lot. As soon as we were a safe distance away, Raphael turned to us and said, "Mission accomplished.

Have fun tonight, you two. I'm needed elsewhere. Summon me if you require my assistance."

"We won't," said Malachi, squeezing my hand. "But thank you."

"Actually," I said, "can you help me out with Diane? I'm lucky she's letting me out at all, but this curfew..."

Raphael nodded. "When she's not on the night shift, which should suit your patrol schedule nicely, Ms. Jeffries will be sleeping very soundly."

I bit my lip. I hated to do this to Diane, but I didn't have a choice. "Thanks."

As soon as Raphael pulled his generic gray sedan away from the curb, Malachi and I got into my beat-up, old Corolla. I sat there for a second, my heart skipping, unable to believe I was in a car with Malachi, overwhelmed by the complete ordinariness of the moment, no matter how bizarre the circumstances. I glanced over to gauge his reaction, only to find him staring at me.

"What's wrong?"

The corner of his mouth lifted. "I want to kiss you."

And with those simple words, the temperature inside the car rose by about a thousand degrees. "Yeah?" I asked, stupidly breathless.

He leaned forward slowly. "May I?"

"We shouldn't... we should go... and maybe Diane is—"

Then his fingertips skimmed along my jawline, destroying my resistance.

"Just one," I whispered.

I didn't have time to say anything else before his lips met mine, setting me on fire, making me feel like the earth was falling out from under me. My hand slid up to his neck, to the smooth, silver-swirled scar that was a souvenir from Juri, a deadly Mazikin and the first person—no, *thing*—I'd ever killed. Malachi's tongue traced mine as our kiss deepened and my thoughts scattered, leaving me with only the taste of him, the halting rhythm of our breaths, and a bone-melting hunger. His fingers tangled in my unruly curls as he scooted closer. I put my hand on his chest to feel the thunder of his heart against my palm. But when my fingers drifted to his stomach, they did not find the hard ridges of muscle I'd expected. Malachi felt the tremble of laughter run through me and pulled back from my mouth. "I had to put them somewhere."

I looked toward the front of the house, expecting to see Diane peeking at us through the curtains, but there was no sign of her. Plus, the sun had already dipped below the horizon, so I figured it was dark enough. I tugged his hoodie up, revealing the six throwing knives holstered against his torso.

"I knew you'd come prepared," I said.

"I brought you some as well." He pulled a pack from the backseat. "Michael dropped these off for us this afternoon, and Raphael tucked them in here when we arrived this evening."

I unzipped the pack a few inches and peered inside, taking in the knives, two batons, and—good God: "He gave us *grenades?*"

"It will be up to you whether we use them or not. You are the Captain, after all," he said as he moved back to his side of the car and watched me take a few shaky breaths. "You're going to be fine, Lela. I'm here to help you."

I jammed my keys into the ignition. "My first real patrol as a Guard," I said quietly, wishing that saying it out loud would make it sound real instead of crazy. Wishing it made me feel brave instead of petrified, proud instead of furious at the Judge of the Sanctum, who I was pretty sure had coldly manipulated me into leading her "field unit" here on Earth. Worse than that, she'd demoted Malachi and sent him along instead of giving him what he'd earned through decades in her service: a peaceful eternity in the Countryside. Of course, I wasn't totally mad he was on the mission—I got to be with him—but I still felt guilty. He'd done it all for me.

Malachi set the pack at his feet, and then leaned back and smiled at me. Like he didn't regret his circumstances in the slightest. "Let's go hunting."

TWO

I LEFT MY NEIGHBORHOOD and drove toward the highway. Malachi shifted in his seat as I accelerated along West Shore Road. "Are you all right?" I asked.

"Yes. It's just . . . fast."

I glanced over at him. He was holding the *oh shit* handle with a white-knuckled grip. "Still not used to riding in cars?"

"Not yet. I did a few times in Bratislava, but they were not like this." He scanned the road, the sidewalks and stores, the gas stations and office buildings. "Nothing was like this."

"I'm sorry." I touched his hand as I stopped at a red light. "It's easy to forget how new and different everything must be for you. You've done really well so far."

He rewarded me with a sexy smile. "Because I've got you to show me around. Speaking of—where are we going?"

My grip tightened on the steering wheel. "To the East Side of Providence. The camera that caught the Mazikin on video was north of the Brown University campus, and the two people who saw it were students." If anything happened to a Brown student, it would be national news, so the police would be out in force. It made our job that much harder.

Malachi nodded. "It's a densely populated area?"

"Providence is more urban than Warwick, but not as crowded as the dark city. You've seen that the land of the living is different, though. People notice things—and each other. They don't wander around with their heads down, absorbed completely with themselves." My gaze drifted to the sidewalk, where several people were walking along, faces lit from the glow of their cell phones. "Okay; they do sometimes, but not all the time."

The light turned green, and I accelerated again, this time a bit more slowly, and turned onto the ramp to I-95 North. "It's strange," Malachi said as he watched the scenery go by, "that this is the exact place you lived before, and it happens to be where the Mazikin arrived."

"No kidding. Figures that the portal from hell would open up in Rhode Island." I hesitated, and then decided to say aloud what had been bugging me. "I think the Judge knew where they would pop out once they went through the wall next to the Sanctum. I think she might have . . ." I stopped, feeling stupid and paranoid.

"You think the Judge intentionally lured you to the dark city, to be pressed into service." He didn't sound like he thought it was a ridiculous idea.

"Yeah. If it's true, she has funny ideas about what makes a good Guard."

Malachi chuckled. "You sell yourself short, Lela."

"Let's hope so," I muttered as the lights of Providence came into view.

I exited the highway and headed up Wickenden, past the tattoo parlor where I'd gotten Nadia's face inked onto my skin as a memorial. I made my way up the narrow street and turned left, onto the road that would take us deep into the East Side. Malachi squinted out the window, inspecting the shadows. I found a place to park off the main road, beneath the low-hanging branches of a tree and out of the glow of the streetlights. Malachi immediately pulled the pack into his lap.

"We're going to have to talk about this weapons thing," I said.

He gave me a puzzled look.

"You can't stroll down the street with a couple of grenades strapped to your chest. Besides . . . I'm not so keen on carrying that stuff."

Malachi nodded. "Because you're not comfortable with

them yet. You will be, once you're properly trained."

"I know, but—"

He reached into the pack and pulled out a familiar-looking belt. It was part of the set of armor, black leather and badass, that Michael had made for me when I was behind the Suicide Gates.

"Wear this, and take one knife." He held one to the light. It had a subtle curve instead of a straight edge. "This one isn't meant for throwing," he explained. "It has a forward drop, better for slicing than a straight blade, but not curved enough to interfere with stabbing. I had Michael make it for you."

"Um, thank you." I took the belt but eyed the knife in his hand. I could just as easily stab myself as anyone else. "But we might not find anyone—"

"There is no reason not to be cautious." He clipped the knife, complete with a sheath, onto the belt, and then tipped my chin up with his fingers. "If the Mazikin ever did catch you, it would be quite a prize for them. Even before Sil and Juri knew how much you mean to me, even before you were appointed our Captain, they wanted you. And I don't want to think about how they might celebrate if they did get you. *Please.*"

Without further argument, I wrapped the belt around my waist, pulled my fleece jacket over it, and got out of the car to join Malachi on the sidewalk. "So . . ." Now that the moment had arrived, I didn't have any idea how to actually patrol.

Malachi swung the backpack onto his shoulders. His attention was already traveling up and down the street; his body was already tense with awareness. "It's all right, Lela. In the dark city, we often had to roam the streets, looking for suspicious activity. Sometimes we went days without seeing anything. This is as good a lead as any."

"Should we split up?" I knew he'd often patrolled by himself, and I didn't want to be deadweight.

Malachi sighed. "As Captain, you will make this decision. We could cover more ground separately. However," he said, stepping close enough to touch, close enough to make my heart speed, "I'd feel much better if you let me stay with you." He kissed my forehead, the feel of his lips on my skin causing heavy warmth to curl low in my belly. "And as your suitor, I'd appreciate being able to keep my promise to your foster mother."

"My . . . *suitor?*" I couldn't hold back a giggle.

Malachi looked really confused and kind of embarrassed. "I'm sorry. I know I'm your Lieutenant, but I—I just thought we were—"

"No! No. That's not what I meant. Malachi, are you saying you want to be my boyfriend?" I'd never had one before. But . . . I kind of liked the idea.

"*Boyfriend?*" His WTF look only intensified. "I would

never presume . . . but we haven't . . . I wouldn't want people to think you were a . . ." He cleared his throat and stared at the sidewalk, and I realized we might be having a bit of a translation problem. Or a growing-up-in-different-centuries problem.

"That I'm a what? I don't know what you're thinking, but 'boyfriend' just means we're . . ." Crap. This was like the blind leading the blind. "It means we're together. That we're, um, going out. With each other. And . . . not anyone else. But not seriously," I added quickly, my cheeks hot.

Malachi gave me a smile laced with uncertainty. "You can call me anything you'd like, as long as it means I can touch you." He brushed my cheek with the backs of his fingers.

"Okay." I had to tear my eyes away from his mouth. *Focus, Lela. This is your job now.* "The sightings were about six blocks that way," I blurted, pointing toward Hope Street. My body temperature dropped to a slow burn.

"So what do the Mazikin want?" I asked Malachi as we set out. "If we know that, we might be able to predict what they'll do here, right?"

"I don't think their desires are very complicated," he replied. "In my interrogations of the Mazikin we captured in the dark city, they all said the same thing: they wanted out of their realm. All of them. They consider their homeland a prison."

"You think they're trying to relocate their entire population?" The shudder that rolled through me wasn't caused by the cold, but I hugged myself anyway. "How many of them do you think there are, in all?"

"I asked Raphael once. He said that there were originally only two, so it's clear they are breeding, and by now there could be hundreds of thousands of them. Maybe a million. And that was many years ago. He wouldn't tell me much else."

"Huh. He's usually so forthcoming."

"Indeed," Malachi said with a laugh. He gave me a side-long glance as his smile fell away. "Lela, in the dark city they were still enclosed by the city walls. But here—"

"They have the whole world," I said, the idea sitting in my stomach like a boulder. "They could split up and go anywhere. The only thing stopping them from stealing the bodies of a million living humans . . . is us."

Malachi took my hand as we walked by a group of guys coming out of the Brown athletic facility. As he stroked his thumb over my fingers, I had to force myself to focus on his words instead of on his touch.

"We may have a bit of time," he said. "Mazikin are like pack animals. They like to stay together. Only once during my time in the dark city were there two nests at the same moment, and that was because their population had gotten so large. At all other times, they chose one location, one base, and operated from there. It's likely they'll do that here while they figure out the quickest way to grow their numbers. Like me, they have much to learn."

I squeezed his hand and hoped they didn't learn as quickly as he did. "What do you think is the quickest way to grow their numbers, then?"

"I don't know yet, but Sil came through the wall in the dark city, so he'll be in charge of their decisions here. And he is, unfortunately, the smartest Mazikin I've ever encountered. There is a reason he is their leader. Ibram and Juri are also likely to be brought in, to function as enforcers. As a group, they'll need food and shelter and a safe place to possess their victims. They will try to establish a nest right away."

"If there are so many of them, how do they decide who to bring in to possess the humans they capture? Did you ever figure that out?"

"I think they actually have some kind of system." He shook his head in disbelief. "The strongest Mazikin, and especially their leaders, have cycled through several human bodies and are quite good at acting human. Some of them even develop preferences—you'll remember that Juri prefers Eastern European males, for example." He scowled, and his grip on my hand tightened. His conflict with Juri went beyond Guard versus Mazikin. It was personal, and after what Juri had tried to do to me in the dark city, I suspected Malachi was looking forward to fighting him again.

"So some of them have preferences," I said, eager to move the conversation away from Juri. "What about the others?"

"A Mazikin inhabiting its first human body is likely to act more like an animal, and the weaker or older the body, the more likely it is to move like a Mazikin in its true form."

"Ana said she thought they were more animal than human."

He nodded. "It takes practice and intention for them to behave like humans."

That's why they were getting noticed. In addition to surveillance camera footage, at least one cell phone video had popped up on YouTube. "I guess it's good for us that they aren't practiced yet, and that some of them are acting weird." We both paused as a guy ran across the street, carrying a girl on his back. His hands were curled around her knees, and her arms were around his neck. She kissed his cheek and let out a shriek, laughing as her scarf unfurled like a banner behind them.

Malachi stared at the couple. "Yes," he said quietly. "Weird."

We walked along, discussing ideas, covering block after block, passing by the party houses and bars, hiking up the crowded main drag and down narrow residential streets. I counted the times the city and campus police cruised by, wondering what they thought they were looking for, knowing they had no idea what it really was, wishing I could leave them to it and actually head off to a movie with Malachi.

My Guard partner did not seem burdened with such petty thoughts. He nailed every passerby with a look so fierce that some of them pressed themselves closer to the edge of the sidewalk as they walked by. He was the perfect Guard, ready for anything, utterly professional. I tried to do my part and stay vigilant, but as the hours dragged on, a late March chill descended on us with silent brutality. My toes got numb, and I started to stumble over the broken, uneven brick sidewalks on the west side of campus. When I rubbed my hands together and blew on them in an attempt to drive away the cold, Malachi's hand closed around mine, and he tucked it into the pocket of his hoodie.

"We should have brought gloves," he said, flattening my palm against his body. "Your fingers are like little icicles."

I closed my eyes for a second, savoring this strange, unfamiliar sensation, this tender touch and what it meant: that he *worried* about me. And when I opened them, he was watching me so intensely that it sent electric bolts of heat along my skin. "I . . . should have planned ahead," I stammered. Suddenly, I didn't want to be there. I didn't want to be at a movie, either. I wanted to be somewhere private and cozy with Malachi, where I could explore this crazy hunger, where I could maybe get control of it.

Because right now, I wasn't in control. Malachi's eyebrows rose, questioning, as I pulled my hand out of his pocket, and then his eyes grew wide as I slid my fingers up under his shirt instead. Both of us exhaled sharply as skin met skin. He bowed his head and closed his eyes. "Your hand is so cold," he whispered, curling his hand around the back of my neck and pulling me close.

"I'm sorry." I wasn't really, but I started to pull my hand out.

"Don't stop." He laid his forehead on mine.

"Malachi . . ." My heart was beating so fast that I was having trouble catching my breath.

"Lela." He looped an arm around my waist. "It's late, and it's very cold out here. We have school tomorrow, and we haven't seen any suspicious activity. Maybe we could go back, and . . ."

He trailed off, and we both stepped aside, getting out of the way of two guys in puffy coats and backward baseball caps trudging up the sidewalk toward us. I heard snatches of their animated conversation about the Red Sox as I turned back to Malachi. "Go back . . . and what?" I asked, staring at his parted lips. An inch or two from mine. Not close enough.

His fingers burrowed into my hair, as mine flexed over his back, under his shirt, where I could feel the striping scars made long ago by Juri's jagged claws. They were hot beneath my fingertips. Malachi groaned softly and—

He raised his head abruptly, jaw tensed.

"On your knees, shithead. *Now.*" The voice came from behind him. From one of the two guys in puffy coats. I wanted to kick myself for not staying alert to *all* the dangers of the street, not just rampaging Mazikin.

Malachi stood very still for a moment, his eyes never leaving my face. The second guy took a step to the side, watching me with a smug half smile that sent a jolt of pure adrenaline through my body. I took a step back, and he shook his head. "No, no, don't move," he said to me, waving a knife in my direction. "We'll get to you in a second."

Malachi's nostrils flared. "We'll give you whatever you want." His voice was shaky and high, saturated with fear that didn't show in the smooth, steady arc of his hands as he raised them in the air. "Whatever you want. Just don't hurt—"

He spun, looping one of his arms under his attacker's, revealing the gun the guy had been holding to his back. With the guy's arm locked tight against his chest, Malachi jerked to the side so that the weapon pointed away from me. He wedged his elbow against the guy's throat and then kneed him in the balls, belly, and thigh before head-butting him. Wet squeals and whimpers punctuated every heavy thud. The second guy jumped on Malachi's back but instantly went careening backward as Malachi drove the kid's lungs through his spine with an elbow, and then crushed cartilage and bone with a devastating kick to his knee.

It was all over in less than five seconds.

Malachi snatched the gun from the thug's limp hand. The guy was crumpled on the sidewalk, his nose gushing blood. The guy's friend scrambled up on his good leg, clutching at his abdomen, wheezy sobs bursting from his throat. He hopped-ran-hobbled away, all crooked and broken and panicked, like a cockroach that had been sprayed.

With a look of absolute disgust and hatred, Malachi tossed the gun into an alley next to us and drew one of the knives from beneath his shirt. I managed to recover from my shock quickly enough to grab him as he cocked his arm to throw it.

"No, Malachi, let him go!"

"He threatened you," he said sharply, his muscles tensing as he prepared to let the blade fly.

"No! You can't do that here! It's murder!"

Malachi paused, his face a rigid mask of rage. He lowered his arm and watched the guy running up the street, leaving his bleeding friend behind. Still holding the knife, Malachi sank to his knees next to the mugger, who was really just a skinny kid, probably a banger, trying to be a big man, lost and stupid and scared. But that wasn't how Malachi was looking at him. His eyes were blank, like a shark's, as he grabbed the kid by the hair and wrenched his head back.

"Oh shit, man, I wasn't going to hurt you. I fuckin' *swear*," the kid babbled, all nasal and snotty, refusing to look Malachi in the eye. I couldn't blame him for that.

I put my hand on Malachi's arm. "You have to let him go, too. He won't call the police—he doesn't want to draw their attention." I tried to keep my voice even, but it was hard. I'd never seen Malachi look so predatory.

He leaned down slowly, speaking directly in the kid's face. "If I see you again, you will not live long enough to regret it." He held his victim in a punishing grip until the kid's eyes darted up to meet his and widened when they registered the absolute raw truth in those words. Then he let the now sobbing kid slump back onto the pavement. "*Run*," he whispered, baring his teeth.

The kid hesitated, like he thought Malachi might take him down as soon as his back was turned, which did appear to be a distinct possibility.

"Dude, you need to go," I snapped at the thug, keeping a firm grip on Malachi's arm as he knelt beside me. "Do as he says."

The kid looked at me with terror in his eyes, but he lurched to his feet and took off, his feet clunking unevenly against the sidewalk, his arms pumping. Malachi watched him go, and judging by the tick in his jaw, it was taking a lot of effort for him not to nail that kid with a knife to the back. After a few seconds that felt like an eternity, the kid turned a corner and disappeared. Malachi bowed his head. He put his hand over mine, holding it to his arm, like he needed the contact as badly as I did.

"Are you all right?" I asked, my voice trembling. Malachi hated guns, having watched as Nazis shot and killed his brother, Heshel. It was one of the many reasons I wasn't even going to suggest that Michael supply them for us to defend against the Mazikin.

Malachi nodded. "I'm all right."

I stared at the dark smear of blood where the kid had been. "We need to get out of here."

Silently, Malachi rose to his feet and sheathed his knife.

"Come on," I said, already walking. "We're going home."

I got us back to the car, nearly jogging in my desperation to get away from the scene of the attack. Malachi didn't say a word until I had the key in the ignition.

"I disappointed you," he said, barely loud enough for me to hear.

I sagged into my seat. "No. You scared me. You have to understand how things work here. This isn't the city you're used to."

"I know."

I started the car and pulled away from the curb. "People here aren't like they are in the dark city. The Mazikin aren't the only ones who'll talk back to you. They aren't the only ones who hurt people." I knew this all too well. "And Guards don't have any authority, so you have to be careful. You don't want to be arrested. Trust me." I knew that all too well, too. "You're used to doing whatever you need to do, but you can't. You're used to being the law, but you aren't."

"Yes, Captain. I understand." His voice was as distant as his expression. He folded his arms over his chest and turned his face to the window. Neon signs and streetlights painted him pink and yellow and green, and I wanted to stop the car and hold on to him, but I couldn't. He'd made me nervous, and I needed him to *get* that, for our safety and for our mission.

But still, it felt so upside down. Malachi was the leader between us, not me. I wanted him to be in charge, but at the same time I realized he couldn't be. Not here. Not on my turf, where everything he'd learned over the last seventy years would get us in a crapload of trouble.

I pulled into the driveway of a pretty little Victorian tucked into a secluded lot, which happened to be less than a half mile from the waterfront mansion where Nadia's mom still lived, alone. I had to wonder if Raphael had chosen this place as a joke: it looked more like a gingerbread house than a Station for Guards.

I walked with Malachi up to the wraparound porch, my chest aching. What had happened back there on the street still lingered between us. I had no idea how to be in a relationship, but I knew *this* didn't feel right. "You've got to say something," I finally said.

He turned to me quickly, like he'd been waiting for permission. "I never expected to be a liability, Lela." He opened his mouth and then closed it again, like he didn't know if he should have said that or not. "I want to be an asset to you. I want to destroy anything that threatens you."

All the tension in my body evaporated. I slid my arms around his waist and pressed my head to his chest, where his heart beat solidly beneath my ear. It was the feeling, the sound, the scent that made me feel strong. No one else in the entire world could do this for me. In fact, I shied away from most other people, hating to be touched after so many years of not having a choice about it. But Malachi . . . was different. He let me choose, he sought permission, he waited for me, he gave me control. And when I showed him I was ready, he was there. He wrapped his arms around me, his hand skimming up my back and settling in my hair. The feel of it was like this glowing ball of light at the heart of me, sending waves of honey warmth along my limbs.

"You *are* an asset to me," I said. "And you did protect me, okay? But I want to protect you, too, which means we have to be careful."

"Agreed." He bowed his head and kissed my temple. "Lela, anger is something I've worked to master for many years, and tonight I was nearly its slave again. If not for you, I might have done something I would have regretted always. Thank you."

His lips were on mine when the front door swung open, momentarily blinding me with the light from the entryway.

"This looks like a *hell* of a lot of fun," said an unfamiliar voice. "Can I have a turn with her when you're done?"

THREE

MALACHI DREW A KNIFE and shoved me behind
the solid wall of his body.

"I'm pretty sure we're on the same side," said the voice.
The porch light above us clicked on. "Put that away."

I jerked myself away from Malachi and stepped around
him. Standing in the doorway was a guy about our age. He
had messy pale-blond hair and dark-blue, slightly bloodshot
eyes. His face was masculine but kind of rounded at the
edges, like he was just growing into his looks. But his body
was already there—I could see through his T-shirt that he
was packing a hell of a lot of muscle. He seemed completely
relaxed about the fact that Malachi had a knife pointed at
his throat.

"Tell me who you are and what you're doing in my house, please," said Malachi. He always sounded so calm when he was about to hurt someone.

The blond guy leaned away from the knife and held out his hand. "Jim. I've been assigned to this unit. You are?"

Malachi lowered the knife but did not shake Jim's hand. "Malachi."

Jim looked down at his palm and then wiped it on his jeans. "You in command?"

"No." Malachi looked down at me. "She is."

Jim's gaze moved from my head to my toes, lingering on all the places you might expect. I wanted to punch him. He grinned and held out his hand. "Okay. Captain . . . ?"

"Lela Santos." I shook his hand, which was kind of clammy. "Where did you come from?"

Jim's leer melted. "The Blinding City."

"The . . . *Blinding* . . . City? Who ends up there?" I knew there were other hellish realms in the Shadowlands where the dead were sent; that it wasn't just the dark city, the realm for people who had committed suicide, and the Countryside, which I understood as heaven.

Jim gave me a rueful glance. "The insatiably greedy, I guess you could say. The addicts, the gamblers, the cons, and the thieves."

"Which are you?" Malachi asked.

"Now, that's kind of a personal question, isn't it?" Jim

raised an arm and leaned on the doorframe, either not rec-
ognizing or not caring about the waves of danger still rolling
off my Lieutenant. I made a mental note to watch Jim very carefully. "How
did the city get its name?"

"Brightest place you've ever seen," he said, but he didn't
sound like he missed it. "So much light, it hurts. Spotlights
and streetlights and signs and sun, all on at the same time.
Hard to hide anything in that kind of light." He winked.
"Not that it stops people from trying."

"And you were a Guard there? For how long?"

"I try not to think about it. Where are you from, then?"

I thought about that for a second. "Here."

"Ah." He nodded, and then frowned. "Huh?"

"It's a long story," Malachi and I said in unison.

Jim shrugged. "Yes, ma'am." He leaned back into the
house. "Hey! Henry! Come meet our new leader. You'll love
this." He stepped onto the porch, making way.

A lean, stooped man appeared in the entryway. He had
a pouchy, grizzled face and the saddest eyes I'd ever seen,
weighed down by dark circles and a lifetime of tragedy.
Then again, if he was a Guard, that was pretty much a given.

Jim gestured at me. "Captain Lela Santos, meet Corporal
Henry Travis."

Henry nodded solemnly at us. Jim was standing there
like he expected a big reaction, but Henry didn't look sur-

prised or disappointed or angry. Just resigned.

"Where are you from, Henry?" I asked, trying to sound friendly.

He didn't answer for several uncomfortable seconds, and then, his lips barely moving, he said, "The Wasteland."

I don't know whether it was the hopeless look in his eyes or the desolate sound of his voice, but I decided that, for the moment, I didn't really want to know what kind of person ended up in a place like that.

I looked up at Malachi. "Why didn't you tell me there would be others?"

"Because I didn't know."

Jim smirked. "I guess the Judge thought you needed some help. What are we up to here? What's the mission?"

"Mazikin found a way to breach the wall of the dark city and enter the land of the living," I began.

"Wait. Who's Mazikin?" Jim asked.

Malachi's brows shot up. "You . . . do not know what a Mazikin is?"

Jim shook his head. "Never heard of it."

"Me neither," said Henry, taking in Malachi's expression. "Maybe the two of you should come in."

I touched Malachi's back gently because the stiffness in his shoulders told me exactly what he thought of being invited into his own Station by a newcomer. The old wooden floors creaked beneath our boots as we followed Henry and

Jim into the parlor, which contained a few mismatched easy chairs and a couch covered in embroidered flowers. Henry sat on the arm of the couch, looking a bit like a praying mantis. I sat in a carved wooden chair, and Malachi stood next to me. I almost reached up to take his hand, but then remembered I was the Captain—of all these guys—and I needed to act like it. "How were you two chosen for this mission?" I asked.

Jim, who'd settled himself in a leather recliner, looked down, suddenly fascinated by his own feet. Henry turned his dust-colored eyes to me. "We were called to the Sanctum, and the Judge offered it to us."

"But she didn't say why?"

"*He* didn't." I guess the Judge appeared to him as a male, but the Judge *I'd* seen was a woman. Apparently, she could appear however she wanted to. "He told us we would be joining a new field unit, and that we would get everything we needed when we arrived."

"But you have never faced a Mazikin." Malachi's voice was flat with anger.

Jim rubbed his hand down his face. "Maybe you should give us the benefit of your wisdom."

Malachi's jaw clenched. I could almost read his mind— he was pissed that we had been given this tiny misfit army and was wondering if we might have been better off on our own. I was wondering the same thing.

"Mazikin are not human," I explained. "They're spirits, and they can possess people. Inhabit their bodies. Access their memories and skills."

"The Mazikin infest the dark city where I was a Guard," Malachi said. "I find it hard to believe they did not inhabit your cities as well."

"I don't," said Henry. "The Wasteland is a place where no one would choose to go." He looked thoughtful for a second. "You know, part of the Wasteland is taken up by a huge desert, and there's a domed city at its far edge. Rumor is that it's full of monsters."

A hard chill rode straight down my spine. "Malachi, could that be their realm?"

"It's possible," he replied, "but if they're *not* in the Wasteland, there must be something preventing them from escaping their city, except through possession of bodies in other places."

"You said they described it as a prison."

He nodded. "One of them told me that his home was a place of fire and death."

"If they're under the sun in the Wasteland's desert that sounds about right," said Henry. Listening to his desolate voice was like walking through a cemetery. "Not many residents of the Wasteland journey into the desert. The climate is too extreme."

"Wait," I said, "Jim, you told us the Blinding City was full of light, too, right?"

"Yeah."

I turned back to Malachi. "I wonder if the Mazikin prefer the dark."

He rubbed the back of his neck. "It's possible. That may be one of the reasons they were so fond of my city." His shoulders relaxed slightly. "Maybe they'll be more active at night."

"Active like how?" asked Jim.

"They'll be recruiting," answered Malachi. "In the dark city, they snatched people off the street, sometimes out of apartment buildings. They tie their victims to a table and perform a ritual where they burn incense and chant in their language. It calls up a Mazikin spirit from their realm to inhabit the body."

Henry grimaced. "You mean, like demon possession or something? I've heard of that. Can they be exorcised, then? Is that what we're supposed to do?" The expression on his stubbly face showed how uneasy he was with that idea.

Malachi shook his head. "There's no going back once a Mazikin spirit takes hold. The body must be killed. It's the only way to deal with them."

"Not the only way," I said quietly, remembering how Mazikin could be imprisoned in the dark tower. It forced all trespassers to relive their worst memories, and Mazikin got a double dose of that, having to endure both their own traumatic recollections and those of their human hosts.

"Killing them is the *only* way," Malachi snapped. "Unless you want to leave human souls trapped in that place of fire and suffering." He had been told by a Mazikin that killing the host body sent the Mazikin back to its homeland *and* liberated the human soul that had been exiled there by the possession.

I put up my hands to show I wasn't going to argue with him. "Fortunately, it's not as simple as grabbing someone off the streets here," I said to Jim and Henry. "Most people would be missed by their families and reported to the police, which means the search would be on for them, making it more likely that the Mazikin will be found and exposed. But at this point, they must have possessed a few because every night there are more sightings."

"At least a few?" Henry asked. "How many of these things are there?"

"A lot," I said. "Maybe one of them for every person in this state."

Henry blinked. "And what's stopping them from taking over right now?"

Malachi shifted next to me. "It's not that easy. It requires some coordination with Mazikin in their home realm, which is why they collect victims and possess them in batches, though they must perform the ritual with one person at a time. And based on what I have witnessed, it is a lengthy and painful process. The ones who are here now will be preparing to accommodate more, and they're possibly gathering a specific type of victim in some cases." He glanced at me, and I knew he was thinking of Juri.

"Between that and the fact that they need to be careful to avoid getting caught," I added, "as well as the likelihood that people will fight back, we have some time before there are too many of them to stop." *But probably not much.*

"They'll create a nest for themselves," said Malachi. "A secluded place where they'll take their victims and perform the ritual, where they'll live. We have to find and destroy it."

"And from what you're saying, the nest could be anywhere." Jim sat back again, looking skeptical.

"Hang on," said Henry, getting up and walking over to a large pile of newspapers. He shuffled through the stack, finally finding the section he wanted, and then flipped through a few pages with black-tipped fingers. "It's been a while since I was on Earth. Not since the fifties. I asked that Raphael guy to get me something to catch me up." He handed the folded paper to me. "You said they'd recruit. Gather victims. This kind of thing unusual around here?"

I read the headline: "Homeless Fight to Keep Winter Shelters Open." It was buried deep in one of the back pages.

Homeless advocates are asking the city to postpone the April 1 closing date of Providence's four emergency winter shelters, but not because of the weather. Police have received several complaints in the last week about attacks on the city's two largest homeless camps. "They come through quick and take our food, our supplies. A couple guys got beaten up bad," said Orián Velasquez, a resident of one of the camps currently seeking refuge in the shelters, scheduled to close next Friday. "We're not criminals. The city owes us some protection." City officials responded today by saying police are investigating the disturbances, but that it is unlikely the city will extend the deadline for closure due to deep budget cuts in the past year.

"You could be right," I said to Henry. I handed the paper to Malachi. "Do you think the Mazikin could be responsible?"

He took a moment to scan the article. "It's possible. Though I would expect them to kidnap people, not beat them up."

"How do you know they didn't try?" I asked. "The people in those camps probably fought back. They wouldn't just take it like the citizens in the dark city. We should check this out."

"So how *do* you fight a Mazikin?" Jim asked.

"Like anyone else," said Malachi. "But you must be careful of their teeth, as their venom is deadly. And of their fingernails, which the Mazikin allow to grow long until they resemble claws. If you are scratched, it will kill you more slowly but just as effectively, if you do not have access to Raphael."

He glared at me for a moment. I had three slashing scars across my stomach, a reminder of how deadly Mazikin claws could be. They'd come courtesy of Sil, the Mazikin leader who had successfully breached the walls of the dark city to overrun the land of the living. From the look in Malachi's eyes, he was once again worrying about what Sil would do if he got ahold of me.

"Tooth and claw. No problem," said Jim.

Malachi's face twisted with contempt. "Some of them are very skilled fighters. And all of them are vicious. Do not underestimate your enemy."

Jim rolled his eyes. "Wouldn't dream of it. So what do we do, just kill them all?"

This time I answered because it looked like Malachi wanted to punch Jim for being so casual. I couldn't blame him; that attitude could get a Guard killed. "We have to terminate every single one of them, yes. Because as long as there's one Mazikin here on Earth, it can bring in others. We won't be done until we eliminate them completely."

"We have to find them first," added Henry, reminding me of how I'd failed so far.

"We're going to patrol tomorrow tonight, starting with the area where the latest sightings have been, because the nest might be nearby. Then maybe we can check out those homeless camps," I said. "Also, Malachi and I have school tomorrow. I have to go or else my . . ." Or else Nancy, my

PO, would cheerfully cart me back to juvie for violating my probation, but I didn't feel like explaining that. I turned to Jim. "Are you coming to school with us?" There was no way Henry would pass as a student, but Jim looked like a teenager.

Jim stretched and yawned in this exaggerated way. "If you don't mind, I'd like to sleep in."

Malachi's eyes narrowed.

We sat there in silence until I remembered that I was supposed to be in charge. I drew my shoulders up and tried unsuccessfully to ignore the burning in my cheeks as I pretended to know what I was doing. "Rest up, then. I'll pick you up tomorrow night."

Henry nodded as I rose from my chair, and Jim's eyes bounced between my face and my chest. Malachi glared at him and stepped between us, blocking Jim from sight. My Lieutenant kept a respectful distance between us but gave me a lingering look, full of wish and want. It took everything I had not to touch him. With Henry and Jim there, though, it wouldn't be very Captain-like of me to fling myself into Malachi's arms.

So I headed home.

I let myself into the house as quietly as possible, but as soon as I closed the front door, I could hear the heavy, even breaths that told me Diane was deeply asleep, as Raphael had promised. I padded down the hall to my room and closed the door. My books and papers lay scattered across my desk. My backpack was propped against my chair, my camera tucked into one of its side pockets. A pile of dirty clothes in the corner, a pair of sneakers under the bed.

Life as it had been.

I lifted my fleece jacket and looked down at my waist, at the black leather belt and sheathed knife.

Life as it was now: a weird intersection of normal and crazy, of life and beyond-life, afterlife, undead, whatever. I put my hand to my heart and felt it beating, remembered feeling Malachi's pounding through his shirt as he kissed me. Were we alive? Were we here on borrowed time? Did we have a right to *live* or only to serve as Guards? Did we have a future, or were we headed back to the dark city when we were done? Did *anything* we did here, apart from eliminating the Mazikin, matter? Could we keep anything for ourselves? I hadn't exactly signed a contract that spelled that out for me.

Raphael had told me I should finish high school, that I should "go be a normal American teenager." But this wasn't the dark city, where all the Guards had a Station, a base from which they patrolled. Where they had authority. Where they could get things done.

Nope, this was freaking Rhode Island. And I was freaking Lela Santos. *I* was stuck in this house with my overprotective foster mother—the department of child welfare had custody of me for another three months and sixteen days. *I* had to attend school so that my probation officer didn't come calling, and so that I could stay away from an all-expenses-paid trip back to the Rhode Island Training School, or the RITS, the state's glorious juvenile facility. *I* had to keep my grades up so that I could stay eligible for that scholarship to the University of Rhode Island. If we could get rid of all the Mazikin, maybe the Judge would let me have that chance. Maybe she would let me have a future.

"And in the meantime, I have to save the world and be home by ten," I whispered.

The Judge had said this would be hard. From where I was sitting, it looked impossible.

FOUR

AFTER WAKING IN A panic from nightmares of battling a million Mazikin who closed in on me with grasping hands and crazed, hungry grins, I drove to the Guard house early, only to find Malachi waiting on the porch swing. He slid into my front seat and gave me a concerned once-over.

"Did you sleep well?" he asked, stroking his fingers down my cheek.

"It could have been better." I pulled out of the driveway and steered toward the school.

"What's wrong?"

"Four against a million," I said, feeling the sense of dread in the pit of my stomach.

"Only if we sit back and do nothing, Lela. It will take the

Mazikin a long time to bring that many into this realm, and that's even if they were unopposed."

"But the odds—"

"Were never in our favor. This is not new." He sighed. "In the dark city, we were given enough to fight them and no more. My requests to double the number of Guards and outposts were refused on many occasions."

"And did Raphael tell you that you *wanted* more but didn't *need* it?" I asked with a laugh that died quickly as I glanced over at him. He was staring at his empty hands.

"Sometimes I wonder if they don't want us to win or if it's more entertaining to watch us struggle," he said quietly, and then shook his head. "But if I dwell on that, I only feel angry. So I choose to believe that we are not given more because we have to find the rest inside ourselves."

"I'd rather have an army."

He chuckled. "So would I, but it helps to believe there might be a reason we don't."

We spent the rest of the ride in silence as I mulled that one over. Was this whole thing a game the Judge had set up to amuse herself? Or was it some kind of "growth experience"—as my probation officer had once described the RITS—for a lucky few? Either way, it seemed like a lot of effort and hassle. And I wasn't sure I believed either was true, but I didn't feel like arguing about it, either. If it helped Malachi to believe his own inner strength could make up for miserable odds, who was I to take that hope from him? Especially when I'd never met anyone as strong as he was. I couldn't be sure he was wrong—about himself, at least.

We made it to school with time to spare, so I headed to the vending machines to get myself a granola bar. Standing close beside me, Malachi was alert and scanning the hallways, always the Guard looking for danger, but his eyes got snagged on the selection of goodies behind the Plexiglas.

"You didn't eat breakfast, did you?" I asked.

"I'm still getting used to being hungry," he said as I popped another three quarters into the slot and got a bar for him, too.

Nutrition in hand, we headed into the open cafeteria, past the Goths sleeping on their backpacks, past the skinny, wannabe-gangsta kid in dirty jeans completing his oh-so-sneaky drug deal behind one of the wide, round pillars around the perimeter of the room, past the procrastinators hunched over their homework, and past the cheerleaders crowded around . . .

Tegan.

She sat behind a table, underneath a banner that said NADIA VETTER MEMORIAL FOOD DRIVE.

"Is that for *your* Nadia?" Malachi asked.

I rolled my eyes. "Yes, indeed. I have no idea what she's up to."

I set down my backpack at a table and slid into a chair,

watching Tegan accept cans of food and cash donations from the rest of the student body. Her short brown hair was stylishly messy around her pixie-like features, and her attire carefully treaded the line between painfully fashionable and outrageously slutty. She had this holier-than-thou look on her face, and I had to turn away because it was pissing me off.

"Are you going to eat that or merely crush it to dust?" Amusement laced Malachi's voice as he sat down in the chair next to mine.

I looked down at my now manhandled granola bar. "This is how I like them."

At that exact moment, Tegan spotted us. She waved me over, first happily, and then frantically when I didn't move fast enough for her.

"If I want to avoid drama, I should at least go say hi. She's trying to be nice."

Malachi stared at her with curiosity. "Do you want me to go with you?"

This was our fifth day of school together, but we'd spent morning and lunch times discussing everything from the finer points of knife wielding to the art of sending a text message, leaving us little time for socializing. Which was fine with me. Especially as I took in the hungry expressions on the faces of the cheerleaders, all eyeing Malachi like they were hoping to have him for dinner.

"Um . . . maybe let me handle this one alone." I got up from my chair. "I won't be gone long."

Tegan came out from behind her table to greet me. "I left a message for you last night. You didn't call back."

Ah, the smell of entitlement in the morning. "I haven't checked my messages. I was kind of busy."

Tegan's eyes lasered past me and zeroed in on Malachi, who was perusing his history textbook in a way that told me he was completely aware of his environment and ready for anything. She made a suggestive noise that made my fists clench. "I heard you had gotten together with some guy. I sincerely hope the rumors are true, for your sake."

My cheeks were on fire. "People exaggerate. You know that."

Her shell-pink lips curled into a lazy, speculative smile. "Too bad."

I didn't know whether to be flattered or to tell her to step the hell off. I was gravitating toward the latter when her smile fell away like a mask that was too heavy to wear for another second. "I wanted to talk to you," she said quietly. "I've been thinking. You know. Since she died. About stuff. And people."

I looked around, at the entire cheer squad staring at Tegan like she was crazy for speaking to me, and at the Goths, who had raised their heads to watch us like they wondered if they were about to witness a girl fight. Had she really chosen *me* to be the recipient of her thoughts about stuff and people?

"Tragedy has a way of making people think about life," I said, offering the same empty statement I'd heard from one of our teachers after Nadia died. I waved my hand at her banner. "I take it this . . . whatever *this* is . . . is the result of your thinking?" I opened my mouth to suggest suicide prevention might have been more relevant, but her haunted expression stopped me. "This is . . . nice. A nice thing to do. Nadia would have approved." It was the friendliest thing I could manage.

Tegan gave me a fragile smile. She'd always been an organizer. She liked bossing people around. But it was usually team fund-raisers and running for student council and stuff. Charity wasn't really her thing.

"I wanted to do something real," she said, staring down at her french manicure. "For her. Something that wasn't bullshit. So I'm collecting food to take to Anchor House. It's like a homeless shelter and soup kitchen kind of place. Nadia's mom is on their board, and so is mine." She bit her lip and looked at my hands, at my broken, unpolished fingernails. "I wondered if maybe you wanted to come with me tomorrow when I take it. We could work the lunch shift at the kitchen. They need volunteers."

Tegan's therapist must have put her up to this. "Where is it?" I asked.

"Pawtucket. You know, in the sketchy part?"

I did, having lived in that area at one time. It also happened to be pretty close to where the Mazikin had been caught on video, north of Providence's East Side. And if Henry was right about the Mazikin targeting the homeless specifically . . . I groaned inwardly. Nadia had considered Tegan a close friend, and I didn't dislike her enough to wish Mazikin possession on her. I also didn't feel like carrying the guilt if anything happened to her. "Yeah . . . I'll tag along."

She flashed me a winning smile that screamed *mission accomplished.* "Cool. Aden's coming, too."

I snorted. Aden, Tegan's boy of the month, was the starting pitcher for the baseball team and, as far as I knew, a first-class jackass, one of those golden boys who believed the world owed him something special. He seemed more likely to shout, "*Get a job!*" from the window of his car than to work a shift at a soup kitchen. "I have new admiration for your powers of persuasion."

Tegan arched an eyebrow and gave Malachi another speculative look. "How about yours? You can bring *your* boy toy if you want. Or do you need me to help you convince him?"

The idea of Malachi being anyone's toy made me want to laugh. And the idea of Tegan going anywhere near him made me want to kidney-punch her. "I'll ask him."

Then Tegan reached forward and grabbed my arm, which

made my muscles tighten. I hate being touched without permission, but she didn't seem to take the hint. She also didn't seem to notice that Malachi was on his feet as soon as her hand moved. He was watching us with total concentration, like he thought Tegan might attack me or something. As if I couldn't kick her ass without blinking. Still, his concern felt nothing short of awesome.

"Lela, I was thinking maybe it would give us a chance to talk."

The way she said the word *talk* made me queasy, and I suddenly craved the opportunity to give her therapist the finger. But her trembling bottom lip and her waifish fingers on my arm reminded me of Nadia. Maybe Tegan was over-achieving on the outside while she caved in and shriveled up inside. "We should do that," I forced myself to say.

She grinned as the bell rang. "Later, then," she said, and she headed back to her table.

"Later," I mumbled, wondering if I would live to regret this.

The school day raced by. The teachers were outdoing themselves with final project assignments and homework, and all I could think about was how I'd never get any of it done because when I got home, I had to figure out how to prevent a full-scale Mazikin infestation.

When I passed Aden in the hall, he actually nodded at

me, as did Ian Moseley, his best friend and the star slug-
ger on the baseball team, and the five teammates crowded
around them. Had Tegan told them to be nice to me?

Or was it that I was holding Malachi's hand?

After all, he was the hot foreign guy who, within an hour
of arriving at our humble school, had nearly strangled Evan
Crociere—who would forever be known as "Dirty Jeans" in
my mind—our school's resident drug dealer. And not only
that, Malachi had performed said strangling defending the
honor of Lela Santos, who, it was rumored, had killed someone, and who, it was also rumored, was either a lesbian or
a stone-cold bitch more likely to shank a guy than let him
touch her . . . or both. Our reunion by the fence behind the
school had been the source of gossip that had been building
for a week.

I had only two classes with Malachi—Pre-Calc and
Senior Lit—which wasn't nearly enough for me. Apparently,
Raphael didn't think we needed to be together all day. And
. . . maybe he was right. Sitting next to Malachi was a full-
on distraction, and I wasn't the only one who seemed to
think so. But if everyone else was distracted, he was totally
focused, his eyes on his work, his pen in constant motion,
taking scrupulously neat notes.

I watched him like a movie. The way he put his elbow
on his desk and pressed his thumb between his eyebrows,
propping his head up with his knuckles as he wrote. The

way his eyes scanned the hall, not just on guard, I realized, but taking everything in. Every flyer, every person, the lockers and the trophy case—his gaze slid over all of it, tracing and memorizing, and the whole time, his lips were curved up into this tiny smile, easy to miss yet impossible not to stare at once you knew it was there. If I had been tossed into high school cold, I couldn't have pulled it off. But Malachi looked like he'd won the lottery. It made me want to ask him about it, to hear what kind of future he hoped for now that he was here. And I wanted to be a part of it.

At lunch, we loaded our trays and threaded our way toward an empty table in the corner. As we were walking, Tegan waved us over to hers, where she sat with Aden and a bunch of her friends.

Malachi nudged me with his shoulder. "They want you to sit with them very badly."

I laughed. "I think it might be *you* they want to sit with."

His brows lowered in confusion. "Me?"

"You really don't know how you look to people, do you?" Tegan and Laney Fisher were staring at his chest. Jillian Flemming and Alexis Campbell were staring at his face. And the guys were all kind of sizing him up, like they wondered if he was as much of a BAMF as they'd heard.

Malachi looked down at his jeans and white thermal shirt

and frowned. "Raphael said this was what people wore. He told me that I would blend in. You should have said something if—"

I leaned my head into his shoulder, working hard not to crack up and sneaking in the opportunity to inhale his scent. "It's not your clothes, my friend. Look, don't worry about it; all right? You're just kind of mysterious to them. If you're ready to answer a bunch of questions about where you come from and what it's like there, I'm fine with going over to sit with them."

Malachi's eyes darted over to Tegan's table. "That boy, the one named Aden, is in my physical education class."

When he saw Malachi looking, Aden stood up and made this exaggerated get-over-here wave. All eyes at that table were on us.

"Holy cow, dude, I do believe Aden Matthews is bro-crushing on you," I said with a laugh. "At least he has good taste. Look—we've got to go over there now."

Malachi gave the empty table in the corner a look full of longing. "Is that an order?"

I nodded solemnly. "It's in the high school code of conduct, clause H-twenty-three-point-one-five, that if the two most popular people in school invite you to their table, you have to answer their summons. Plus, it will increase your pain tolerance."

Malachi's expression told me he actually thought there might be such a code. "Very well, then."

As we approached the table, Aden and Tegan scooted down, and Ian and a couple of other guys made way on the other side. Levi, another of their close friends, moved around the end of the table to sit next to Jillian, his girl-friend. I ended up sandwiched between Ian and Malachi. They were built similarly, with lean hips and broad shoulders, leaving plenty of room for my ass but no room for the rest of me. I wondered if I might drown in testosterone and Axe body spray before I finished my sandwich.

I was taking my first bite when Greg, Nadia's ex and one of the baseball team's relief pitchers, approached the table, tray in hand and clearly irritated that I was seated there. He was one of the hangers-on, a kid who desperately wanted to be a part of this clique. But like me, he drove a crappy sec-ondhand car, and his clothes were more likely to come from Walmart than J.Crew. One would think I'd feel some sym-pathy for him . . . but I didn't. He hadn't treated Nadia very well, and I'd come to the conclusion that he was a wannabe user who latched onto her because it made him look good.

I refocused my attention on the conversation as Ian scooted even closer to me to make room on his other side.

Laney flipped her auburn hair over her shoulder. "How are you liking our school?" she asked Malachi in a loud voice, enunciating every word and speaking slowly.

Aden and Ian snickered, but Malachi gave her a polite smile. "I am enjoying the classes very much, and particularly literature. I had only read Rilke in the original German, so I am happy to have the opportunity to read it in English as well."

Laney's eyes went all dreamy, and her tongue traced her bottom lip. "Wow. You speak beautiful English," she said breathlessly. And then she made this weird, little yipping noise and glared across the table at Tegan. "It's true," she said, all pouty as she reached under the table to rub her shin.

I reached for my fork, not sure whether I wanted stab Laney with it or use it to eat my salad. I was still trying to decide when Ian's elbow collided with my arm. "Oh, jeez, sorry," he said, giving me a surprisingly sweet, apologetic smile that revealed deep dimples. His shaggy brown hair hung over his forehead as he looked down at me. "I'm a lefty. No one should ever have to sit on that side of me." He tucked his elbow against his body.

"You should see him in the batter's box," said Greg, obviously trying to make nice. "Pitchers don't know what to do with him. It's one of the reasons we're gonna take state this year." He lifted his chin at Malachi. "You must have played some sports in school, right?" He looked like he was ready to recruit Malachi on the spot.

Malachi shook his head. "I never had much opportunity to play sports."

Aden looked completely baffled, probably because he'd seen Malachi's abs in the locker room. Tegan, who had been poking at her plateful of iceberg lettuce, set her fork down and put her arm around Aden's waist. "What are we doing tonight?" she asked him.

Aden leaned in to kiss her cheek. "We were actually planning a guy thing, Teg. Sorry."

Tegan flushed, but she smiled up at him anyway. "Maybe Saturday."

He raised and lowered his eyebrows a few times. "Definitely Saturday." He turned to Malachi again. "You want to come out with us tonight? We could show you how we have fun around here."

Ian, Greg, and Levi smiled while the girls looked sullen.

Malachi wiped his mouth with his napkin. Under the table, the fingers of his other hand brushed against my thigh. "Thank you for the invitation. Perhaps another time. Lela and I have plans tonight."

Now my cheeks were pink, for sure. It had been such a soft-spoken, casual statement, but he might as well have shouted it. Everyone's eyes were on me, conveying everything from resentment to curiosity to admiration. Greg stared at me like he'd never before realized that I was a girl. Laney looked like she wanted to flee to the bathroom and burst into tears. And Ian . . . I was stunned to see the glint of interest in his green eyes. For a year now, most of these guys hadn't even thought to glance in my direction, and I definitely hadn't looked in theirs. Apparently, all it took was for one hot guy to like me, and the rest of them were suddenly taking notice.

Aden shrugged. "Maybe we'll hang out after the volunteer thing that our women are dragging us to. Ow!" He rubbed his arm, which had been on the receiving end of one of Tegan's sharp little elbows.

"Stick to the left side," instructed Greg. "His throwing arm is school property."

Tegan smiled at him sweetly, but her dislike for Greg was one thing we had in common. "I'll remember that," she said icily. Then she looked at me and Malachi. "You two *are* coming tomorrow, right? The rest of these losers turned me down."

I forced myself not to roll my eyes. "Yep, wouldn't miss it."

"You're such a good friend, Lela," she said. "Oh, and can you drive me? My dad would kill me if someone snatched the emblems and rims off my Beamer."

Malachi's hand closed over mine and squeezed. It was enough to keep me from telling her where she could shove her BMW emblems, but not enough to keep me from wondering if I'd added one more thing—a friendship with Tegan—to my impossible to-do list.

FIVE

I WENT HOME AFTER school, tried to catch up on my homework, and ate dinner with Diane. She grilled me about the movie and whether Malachi had been a gentleman, and I told lies about the former and the absolute truth about the latter. Well, except for the part about how he nearly killed some muggers.

After dinner, we watched the news, and I listened to Diane freak out about the new sightings of the Animal Guy . . . and at least one sighting of an Animal Gal. Equally unnerving were reports of vigilantes on the streets, determined to capture Animal Guy, either on camera or for real. The city had announced it was upping patrols to the East Side and southern Pawtucket. Police had issued statements reiterating that anyone with a weapon had better have a permit to carry it, and that they would have zero tolerance for rule breakers. It seemed like they were less worried about the Animal Guy and more concerned about regular citizens getting their crazy on. Part of me was relieved, and part of me was cursing. The more people were on guard, the less likely someone was to be dragged away. On the other hand, some people were going in search of the Mazikin. The whole thing had the potential to get seriously out of control.

After Diane left for her night shift at the prison, I picked up my motley crew of Guards and drove us through Providence, along the narrow streets of the East Side, toward the area where several of the Mazikin sightings had taken place. It was less than a mile from the place where we'd be tomorrow morning, helping Tegan serve up soup to the homeless, which made me both eager to find the nest—and hopeful that it wasn't anywhere near this part of town.

Jim looked vaguely sick as we got out of the car, and I had to wonder if, like Malachi, he didn't have much experience riding in one. Either that or he was hungover. Henry claimed he didn't know where Jim had gotten the bottle, but while we were at school, the younger Guard had been getting trashed. Malachi had returned home to find him vomiting into the bathtub. Judging by the stony silence on the ride over, the last several hours had been rough for all three of them.

Jim was freshly showered and dressed in new clothes that made him look like an all-American high school kid. Like the rest of us, he was armed, but not obviously so. He carried a baton in the backpack slung over his shoulder and had a knife in his pocket. "Now what?" he asked, sounding like he'd rather be at home sleeping it off.

"Now you wait for your orders," Malachi barked, making Jim wince and rub his temples.

I touched Malachi's arm, but pulled my hand away when I realized Henry was watching us closely. "Jim and I will patrol north and west. Malachi and Henry, head south and east, toward some of the homeless camps along the Blackstone River. We can meet back here at midnight."

Malachi looked like he wanted to argue, and I couldn't blame him. I would so much rather patrol by his side, but I'd already thought this through. Henry and Jim didn't even know how to spot a Mazikin, and I suspected Malachi would end up throttling Jim if I paired them up. "What is our course of action if we discover a Mazikin?" Malachi asked.

"Unless it attacks you, I want you to stay out of sight. Text me your location, and follow it. We need to find the nest, and that's more important than eliminating a single Mazikin."

Malachi smiled. "I think those are excellent orders, Captain."

His words brought warmth to my chest that I badly needed—because I could tell he meant them. "Thank you. Be careful, okay?" I said it to him, but then shifted my gaze to Henry, who eyed me for a second before nodding.

Jim and I trudged up the block and turned left onto a smaller side road. It was about nine, still early, but already dark enough to make me grateful for every streetlamp. We zigzagged through the neighborhood for over an hour, but saw nothing more suspicious than a group of teenagers heading into a duplex that was practically shaking from the bass pumping inside. I was about to suggest that we return to the street where our car was parked when I heard running footsteps and male laughter. I sniffed at the air, trying to detect a hint of incense that might tell me whether they were Mazikin, but all I smelled was the garlic and spices coming from someone's kitchen nearby. "Let's get a little closer and see what's happening," I said to Jim as the laughter was punctuated by shouts and crashes.

"Sounds like someone's having a good time. That's a crime around here?" Jim asked.

I ignored him, tensing when I heard a familiar voice say, "Dude, don't point that at me. Aden, I'm serious!"

It was Ian Moseley, our classmate. My stomach churned as four guys rounded the corner several yards ahead of us. Aden, Ian, Greg, and Levi. Dressed in jackets, with beanies pulled low over their ears, they had the loose-limbed grace of privileged boys who thought the world was a giant amusement park. Aden was in the lead and holding what looked like a paintball gun, with a long, narrow tube for a barrel.

"Don't worry. I know what I'm doing," he slurred to the others, shaking the thing and sending several pellets splattering onto the concrete in front of him. "Oops."

Ian, his hair concealed by his cap, was reaching out to take the gun away from his friend when he noticed Jim and me watching them. He squinted at us like he couldn't quite believe it. "Lela?"

"Hey." I waved spastically, realizing in that moment how awkward these next few minutes would be.

His eyebrows shot up as he zeroed in on Jim and then looked back at me. "Didn't Malachi say you two had plans?"

"Uh . . ."

"Those plans changed," said Jim, throwing his arm around my shoulders and yanking me close.

I elbowed him in the side before I could stop myself, and he grunted and stepped away as Levi, Greg, and Aden guffawed. Ian, who appeared to be the only sober one among them, stepped forward like he thought I needed protecting, so I tried to smile. "I'm catching up with Malachi later," I said.

Aden was laughing so hard that he could barely stand up straight. "You're a busy girl," he said, but barely got the words out before Ian shoved him. He lost his balance and staggered into a mailbox, which he draped himself over, still chuckling.

"Sorry about that," Ian said. "He's an idiot, obviously."

"What are you guys doing out here?" I asked, eyeing the paintball gun.

Greg held up another weapon, one I sincerely hoped fired pellets or paintballs and not bullets. "We're hunting the Animal Guy!"

"Huh," said Jim. "So are we."

Ian's eyes grew wide. "You are?"

"He's just kidding," I snapped, wanting to punch Jim in the throat. "We're visiting some of my friends in the neighborhood."

Aden raised his head from the mailbox. "In this neighborhood? What are they, Kings or MS-13? Come on, Lela. You can tell us." He rested his head on his arms and continued to giggle.

"Are you serious?" groaned Ian. "Dude. Shut. *Up.*"

I let out a slow breath through my nose. "You guys really think you're going to find one of those Animal Guys around here?"

Ian rolled his eyes, but the others nodded.

"And you're going to . . . what? Bring it down with a paintball gun?"

While the other three shouted things like "Fuck, yeah," Ian dropped his face into his hands, his fingers tugging the front of his beanie down like he wanted to hide inside it.

"Listen," I said to Ian. "Aden's right about one thing: this isn't a great area if you don't know it well, and right now you guys are drawing a lot of attention to yourselves. The cops are out looking for vigilantes, too, so maybe you could go hunt somewhere else. Like back in Warwick."

His hands fell away from his face. "She's right, guys. This was a dumb idea. Come on. Car's this way." He grabbed the back of Aden's coat and hauled him off the mailbox. As he herded his drunk friends back toward the corner, he looked over his shoulder at me. "Are you going to be okay?" His gaze flicked to Jim.

I forced myself to step closer to my Guard partner. "Yeah, totally. See you on Monday."

He sighed. "See you."

As soon as he turned his back, I grabbed Jim's sleeve and marched in the opposite direction, cursing under my breath.

"You didn't even introduce me," said Jim, amusement in his voice. "And I think the tall guy was jealous."

"Shut up," I barked. "And don't ever touch me again."

He chuckled. "Hey, I was only trying to help."

I clenched my teeth and kept walking, barely looking where I was going, nearly twisting my ankle as I stepped off a curb and into a cross street. Jim watched me stumble with a smirk, and I was about to snap at him again when he said in a low voice, "There's someone in that park up ahead," pointing toward the end of the street.

We quickened our pace and headed for the park. Once again, I sniffed deeply, and this time, I caught the faintest scent of incense, so faint I thought maybe I was imagining it. "Where did you see—" I started to ask but then heard hooting laughter coming from a stand of trees about ten yards away. The sound made everything inside me tense; I'd never heard any human make a noise like that. It sounded more like a hyena . . . and *exactly* like a Mazikin. I touched Jim's shoulder and held my finger to my lips.

We crept toward the laughter, which was intermixed with the sound of crinkling and thuds. I pressed myself against a tree and tried to catch sight of the creature, but all I could see was a pair of legs surrounded by debris. I leaned forward as much as I dared and caught the slope of a spine, with a long braid trailing down its center. Someone was squatting next to the legs. Hooting and grunting as she rummaged, tossing dented cans and paper packages over her shoulder.

Jim moved in close behind me, making me want to elbow him again. "Is that one of them?" he whispered.

"I think so," I breathed.

"How do we find out?"

"We wait and watch."

The creature continued to paw through the junk. Jim

sighed impatiently. "Or we could just ask." He stepped away from me before I could grab him. "Hey!" he called. "Are you a Mazikin?"

The woman with the braided hair pivoted sharply as she heard that last word, bringing her into full view. Her face was streaked with dirt, and her chin was smeared with blood. She growled as Jim jogged forward. "Mazikin," she said in a harsh voice.

"Jim, stop!" I yelled. He ignored me.

Before I could decide which of them I'd rather kill, they both took off, Jim sprinting after the woman.

"I'll get her!" Jim shouted.

"No!" I yelled, running after them. The woman was headed for an intersection with a traffic light. Well lit. Full of witnesses if Jim tried to take her down, witnesses who would only see a woman being attacked. Just past that intersection was a gas station, with a few cars filling up. The female Mazikin looked over her shoulder and smiled a gap-toothed, chilling smile.

"Jim!" I cried out, right as the Mazikin screamed, in a very human voice, "Help me! Don't let him hurt me!"

A middle-aged bald guy and an older guy in a red scarf, who had both been standing by their cars beneath the gas station overhang, looked up and noticed our little drama unfolding in front of them. The Mazikin darted into the intersection as both men started forward.

Jim slowed enough for me to tackle him from behind. It didn't knock him off his feet, but he finally stopped running when I landed on his back. "You idiot," I said into his ear. "Come on. We have to—"

"Get *off* me." He shoved me away so hard that I nearly fell on my ass. "I almost had her!" He began to run again. Stunned at his complete disregard of my orders, I followed but couldn't close the distance before he made it across the street.

"Hey!" shouted the bald guy as the Mazikin sprinted toward the older man who protectively opened his arms to receive her. She sobbed loudly while he examined her bloody mouth and wiped at it with his scarf.

"Did you hit her?" he barked at Jim.

"No," he replied, stopping a few feet away, "but I'm about to."

"No, you won't!" I shouted, finally catching up. The bald guy was dialing his cell phone. This was so far out of control that my head was spinning.

"Miss, I've got this handled. You should probably stay away from him," the old man said to me. "I'm going to take this young woman inside and help her get cleaned up."

"The police are on the way," called the bald guy, waving his phone at Jim.

Jim paid no attention. He lunged, clearly intending to attack the Mazikin. I threw myself in front of him, planted both hands on his chest, and pushed him backward. He made a move to shove me off again, and I lost it. I looped my hand around the back of his neck and jumped up, kneeing him in the stomach. "Stand down!" I yelled.

He let out a grunt and grabbed his abdomen, but straightened quickly. A siren wailed. Jim startled, looking around, and I slapped him across the face, desperately needing his attention. When his eyes locked on mine, I said in a low voice, "Jim, we have to go, unless you want to spend the night in a tiny holding cell."

"Where you belong," snapped the bald guy, still gripping his phone and watching us warily.

The violence in Jim's eyes evaporated, replaced by fear. "A cell?"

Knowing the cops would arrive in mere seconds, I said clearly and slowly, "That's what I said. Unless you run as fast as you can back to the car."

It was the first order of the night that he actually followed.

As the bald guy shouted after us, we sprinted across the road, back through the scraggly trees and leaf-strewn brittle grass, past the pile of cans and packages the Mazikin had been going through. I slowed when I saw a homeless guy motionless on the ground. His hands and neck had been severely bitten, probably as he tried to keep the Mazikin from stealing all his worldly possessions and dragging him back to the nest. His cheeks were striped with claw marks, and his eyes were wide and fixed. He was dead.

I took off running again, catching up to Jim, and we fled through the side streets, block after block, until we made it back to the car. I pulled Jim down as a cop car streaked by, headed north, lights flashing and sirens blazing. Then I unlocked the doors and dove into the front while Jim climbed into the back. I caught my breath for a second and then fumbled with my phone, texting Malachi a rendezvous point several blocks south of our location. I trusted him to have a map of the area memorized already—at least I could depend on *him*.

"Wait, are we going back to the Station?" Jim said. "That's so stupid! I thought we were supposed to be killing all of these Mazikin things. You let that one go!"

"Shut up!" I yelled, banging on the dashboard. "My God, do you not realize you could have gotten both of us arrested? Are you still drunk? Chasing a screaming woman through a populated area? Threatening to hit her in front of a bunch of witnesses? In complete violation of my orders! Don't say another word, Jim. I fucking swear I'll stab you if you do."

The realization seemed to have sunk in. Jim wisely stayed silent as I drove us to the pickup spot. Malachi texted that he and Henry would be there, but it was still the biggest relief to see them standing at the curb. Henry slid into the backseat while Malachi folded himself into the front passenger seat. He sat back and put his seat belt on as I lurched onto the street, cutting off another car.

"What happened?" he asked.

I shook my head, knowing that I'd start yelling again if I tried to explain.

"We saw one," Jim said from the back. "In a park. It had killed some old guy."

I slowed down and drove more carefully, feeling Malachi's eyes on my face. "But you didn't follow the protocol," he said.

My nostrils flared as I squeezed the steering wheel . . . much like I wanted to be squeezing Jim's neck. Malachi touched my arm. "Are you hurt?"

"No." I had a feeling if I mentioned the way that Jim had shoved me, Malachi would gut him.

My Lieutenant pivoted in his seat. "You violated her orders, didn't you?" he asked in a deadly calm voice.

"I chased it," Jim said defensively.

"That's insubordination," Malachi snarled. "You might have alerted the Mazikin to our presence in the area. And you endangered our Captain."

I reached for Malachi's hand, which was clenched in a tight fist. It loosened slightly at my touch.

"She's fine," Jim mumbled.

"No thanks to you, it seems," said Henry. "Jim, your actions affect more than just yourself. We all have to help each other, or else someone's going to get killed."

Jim punched the ceiling of the car. "Shut up!"

"This isn't the first time you've disobeyed orders," Malachi guessed. "I would bet that it is not the first time you've endangered another Guard either."

"Stop!" Jim shouted, a frantic edge in his voice. "You don't know anything about me!"

We were slowing down for a red light when Jim threw the door open and jumped out. I slammed on the brakes. Jim was a mess as he stumbled onto the sidewalk, his eyes red-rimmed, his chest heaving. He hesitated for a moment, staring back at me, and then turned on his heel and sprinted away.

"He may be able to outrun us," Henry said quietly. "But there's no way that kid can outrun all his demons."

SIX

WE SPENT NEARLY FOUR hours driving around town looking for Jim before we gave up and headed back to the Station. Although I'd hoped for some time alone with Malachi, we were all exhausted and down after losing one of our Guards, and I left to go back to Diane's with nothing but a squeeze of his hand and a lingering stare that made me wish we were regular kids without the weight of the world on our shoulders.

I fell into bed at two and got up at seven even though it was a Saturday, eager to shed my dreams of being locked in a car with Jim, who was driving the wrong way on I-95, steering our car toward the headlights of an oncoming semi. I showered and sat at the breakfast table, letting my cereal get soggy as I scrolled through not one but three texts from Ian that had come in after I'd sunk into a heavy, exhausted sleep.

2:17 a.m.: Got yr number from Teg. Aden ran off. Seen him?
Plz lemme no
2:29 a.m.: Still in area? Cant find Aden. Msg me if u have
ideas where to look
3:34 a.m.: Found him. Sry for bothering u

I was glad he'd found Aden, but had to wonder what kind of shape our star pitcher would be in this morning when we all showed up to volunteer at the homeless shelter.

Keys jangled at the front door and Diane walked in, her footsteps heavy. "Hi, baby. You're up early," she said in a weary voice.

"Morning. Quiet shift?"

She made a so-so gesture and shed her jacket; then she headed for the kitchen.

"Hey," I called, shoving my phone in my pocket. "I need to ask you something. I want to go to this volunteer thing with Tegan this morning."

She smiled as she pulled a box of cereal from the cabinet. "She's the friend who planned Nadia's vigil, right?" I nodded. "What are you doing?"

I crossed my fingers under the table. "Going to a soup kitchen. We're helping to serve meals."

She froze. "A soup kitchen here in Warwick?"

I considered lying, but Diane knew the area really well, and she'd figure it out. "No, um . . . Pawtucket."

Her smile evaporated as she closed the cupboard and turned to face me. "Haven't we talked about this? I don't want you in that area. Every night there are more sightings. I just heard that a homeless man was *mauled* to death by something last night, right around there!"

I shrugged even though my heart was beating really hard. "But all that stuff's going on at night, and we'll be there in the middle of the day. With a lot of other people. Doing good." *And maybe spotting a Mazikin or two.* If they were really attacking the homeless, whether to possess their bodies or to steal their supplies, maybe a homeless shelter was the best place for the Guards to be.

Diane folded her arms over her chest. "Can't you do good somewhere else?"

"Diane, I'm going to be with a group of other kids, surrounded by responsible adults. This shelter serves meals to people who are homeless." I cleared my throat. "If it hadn't been for you, I might have been on the streets, too. So maybe I'd like to give back."

It was absolutely true, but even so I worried I was laying it on a little thick. Then I saw that her eyes had gone all shiny. She turned away and wiped at them. "You can go, baby. Just be careful, okay? I couldn't handle it if anything happened to you."

Now *my* eyes were probably getting shiny. I swallowed the lump in my throat. "Thanks." I got up and set my cereal bowl in the sink. "You don't have to worry about me," I said quietly.

Her laughter was brief and raspy. "The hell I don't." She waved at the door. "Have fun. Do good."

I didn't need to be told twice. I was pulling into the driveway of the Guard house about fifteen minutes later. I tromped up the steps and knocked, but no one answered, so I let myself in. Malachi had left a note for me on the kitchen table. I smiled at the tiny, neat script. And then I processed the words: *Jim has not returned. Henry and I are training in the basement. Come down.*

I groaned. We were supposed to pick up Tegan in an hour, and one of my Guards was still missing. And, with a twinge of guilt, I realized I wasn't that broken up about it. Maybe we'd be better off without him. Not the most charitable thought I'd ever had, but there it was. Jim was a problem, and I had too many of those already. I could only hope Raphael and the Judge would realize that assigning him to this mission had been a mistake.

I paused at the top of the stairs, listening to the sharp breaths and grunts of my Guards sparring. The basement of the Guard house was a near-perfect replica of the training room used by the Guards in the dark city, except the light was provided by halogen bulbs instead of gas lamps, and it was about a third the size. Malachi had told me that Raphael sometimes opened some kind of door to the Shadowlands down here, and that the morning after we'd arrived on Earth, Michael, the Guards' weapons supplier, had done the same. I guessed it was something only angels could do because the foul-tempered fat man had magically appeared, along with his entire blacksmith's forge and a respectable arsenal. Along the far wall, staffs, knives, and sharp things I didn't even recognize hung in orderly rows. Cloth dummies were clumped together in a corner. The floor was covered with a thick rubber mat, soft enough that we wouldn't break bones when we hit.

And that was good because Henry crashed to the mat with a loud thud right as I reached the bottom of the stairs. His face was twisted in a grimace, showing all his crooked teeth. A weird wheezing sound was coming from his throat. I was about to ask him if he needed Raphael, but then realized he wasn't in pain.

He was laughing.

Malachi leaned down and offered his hand, which Henry accepted. Once Henry was on his feet, the two of them stepped apart, both breathing hard. Malachi gave Henry a genuine smile as the older Guard wiped his face on his sleeve.

"Henry's a very crafty fighter," said Malachi.

Henry grunted. "Doesn't matter much when your opponent

is both stronger and more efficiently brutal. You have some things to teach me. I've always been better at a distance. In the Wasteland, I used a crossbow."

"What do the Guards in the Wasteland do if there aren't Mazikin to fight?" I asked.

Henry turned to me, his face serious. "We protect anyone who needs it. There are creatures there. Wolves as tall as a man and twice as broad. Vultures with twenty-foot wingspans. Humans who have lost touch with anything that made them human. In a place where everyone's a murderer, there are still different kinds of evil. Lots of 'em." It seemed like he was avoiding my eyes.

I looked him over. Henry'd basically just confirmed he was a killer, but then again . . . technically, all of us were. And he'd been chosen as a Guard and then chosen for this mission—where he had yet to disobey an order, unlike Jim. I was beginning to believe Henry might prove useful. "What's the range of your crossbow?" I asked.

Henry's eyebrows rose, like that wasn't the question he expected me to ask. But then his thin lips formed the faintest smile. "Sixty yards, maybe?" His gaze flitted cautiously to mine.

"In other words, you can shoot to kill from far away."

He nodded.

"That could be really important," I said. "Maybe you have something to teach *us*, Henry."

He bowed his head. "I'm going to go wash up before we go," he said quietly, and marched up the stairs, that faint smile still on his face.

"That was good, Lela," Malachi said when the door to the basement clicked shut.

"What?" I tore my eyes from the stairs to look at him. He was wearing warm-up pants and a sweaty T-shirt that clung to his lean torso.

"Henry thought you would judge him for his past crimes. But you showed him that you value what he can do now. You're earning his loyalty. It's a good thing to have as his commander."

"If only I could do the same with Jim," I said.

He nodded, his jaw tightening. "I don't think Jim has been a Guard for very long."

"What makes you say that?"

His eyes met mine. "Because when Guards are first sentenced, they often don't . . . accept it."

"Did you?"

He rubbed his hand over the hair on the back of his head. "I tried to escape at least three times before I realized it was impossible. Worse than that, I attacked my Captain at the time, Philip, and Takeshi, who was my Lieutenant, on numerous occasions, unable to control my anger about the situation."

"How long did it take you to adjust?" I asked.

Malachi considered this. "It took me over a year to resign myself to my new existence."

"A year?" I asked in a choked voice.

Malachi folded his arms over his chest. "Hopefully, Jim will learn faster than I did." The corner of his mouth lifted slightly. "You certainly have."

"I'm trying, but I'll be honest: part of me wants to blow off my responsibilities and go to a movie or something."

He smiled and closed the distance between us. "Could I go with you?"

"Of course," I whispered, suddenly breathless as his fingertips skimmed along my neck.

"There are so many things I'd like to experience here," he murmured.

"What would you do if you could do anything?" I asked, remembering how he had looked when he was at school: like he'd hit the lottery. "If you were free. If you weren't a Guard."

He pondered that for a few moments. "I think I'd travel. I want to see the world as it is now. I'd go to Bratislava, maybe. I would walk the streets and breathe in the scents of the city and not worry about who was at my back."

"And after that?"

"I think I'd like to go to university," he said, and then

gave me this adorably sheepish look. "I would perhaps study to be a teacher. Or maybe do something with computers. I like them."

My voice was husky and strained as I said, "So basically, you're saying you would be an ordinary guy. With a normal kind of life."

He slid his arm around my waist. "I would love nothing more than that. To have a job. A home. A family. To wake on a Sunday and choose to stay in bed with my love warm beside me. To chase my children around the backyard. To watch them grow and know that they would have that chance. That it could not be taken from them."

My chest ached fiercely. Suddenly I wanted these things for him more than I wanted anything else. And more than that, I wanted to be part of it. I touched his face, smoothing my fingers along the plane of his cheekbone. "Maybe you could have that someday. Maybe it's possible."

Our eyes met. "Maybe it is," he whispered.

The door at the top of the stairs creaked open. "Hey, Captain," Henry called from the top of the stairs.

I jerked away from Malachi. "Yes?"

"You want me to leave early? Maybe go scope the place out?" Unlike Jim or Malachi, Henry actually knew how to drive, and Raphael had gotten him a driver's license. The plan had been for him to drive with Jim to the shelter in the generic gray sedan, but now he'd be going alone.

"Sure," I said, sounding winded. "We'll see you there."

The door closed again, leaving Malachi and me staring at each other.

"We have some time before we need to pick up Tegan," he said. "Do you want to train for a bit?" He moved closer and wrapped one of my curls around his finger. "Or do you want to . . ." He lowered his head and brushed his lips over mine, and it sent the most powerful jolt of *want* through me that I took a full step back, shaky and overwhelmed.

"We should train!" I squeaked, not sure I could trust myself. Beneath the weight of all the new things I wanted to share with him, I was tempted to forget what we were actually here to do.

"Come on then, Captain," he said, stepping back and arching his eyebrow. "Show me how much you've learned." He beckoned me forward. A challenge, for sure.

He probably had no idea how much it felt like a seduction.

I planted my feet on the mat, breathing like I'd been sprinting. My thighs and calves ached; I'd done about a thousand knee strikes in the last half hour. The muscles of my abs and arms were screaming, too, courtesy of palm and elbow strikes aplenty. I had knotted my unruly hair to keep it away from my face, but tendrils of it had escaped and were sticking to the sweat beading on my temples. I'd shed my hoodie and was down to my T-shirt.

Malachi had stripped off his shirt entirely. It was miserably distracting.

He stood across from me, a spider waiting for a vibration in his web. The only part of him that moved was his eyes, following me as I moved closer.

"Are you waiting for some type of signal from me?" I asked.

A shadow of a smile crossed his face. "Always."

"It would feel less weird if you attacked. You know, like a Mazikin."

"Maybe I need practice, too."

I laughed as I took another step toward him. "You're hilarious."

I faked toward his left and then skipped back out of his reach as he blocked and recovered.

His dark eyes never left mine. "And you're dangerous."

"I'm trying."

"Keep your weight on your rear leg so that you can propel yourself forward. You cannot rely on your upper body strength alone . . ."

Before he finished his sentence, I threw myself into an attack. He blocked most of my strikes easily with his forearms, but I landed a palm strike against his chest that resonated with a deep thud and left an angry red mark on his skin.

I dropped my arms immediately. "I'm sorry!"

His shoulder hit my chest before I could draw another breath, driving me backward until my back smacked against the wall. "Don't you dare lower your guard!" he said as he released me. "You *need* to break that habit, Lela. Do your damage, drop your opponent, and don't stop fighting until it's done."

I shoved off the wall and got my fists up before he could hit me again. Malachi was all severe angles and barely contained ferocity, the way he always looked when we trained—so intent, so determined to make me better.

I ducked to avoid his palm strike and gritted my teeth when his knee hit my side and sent me flying. Instead of pain, all I felt was a grim resolve, this desperate desire not to let him down. And also . . . that bone-deep hunger for him I couldn't shake. It was too big to understand and too scary to analyze, but it was there, always. Low in my belly, clawing at me.

I scrambled to my feet, keeping low to avoid another kick, and leaped on his back. I wrapped my arm around his neck in a choke hold and hung on as long as I could before he flipped me over his shoulders and onto my back. In a flash he had me pinned to the floor. The weight of his body sent shockwaves of heat through mine. It should have scared me. It *did* scare me, but it was also exactly what I wanted.

Instead of punching or choking me, which was what he was supposed to be doing, Malachi stared down at me, his chest heaving, his eyes dark and intense. They held me fast, quickening my pulse. My hands slid up his arms, over the raised welts of his battle scars, over sweat-slicked skin and the rigid muscles of his shoulders. I took his face in my hands. "You win," I whispered, pulling him down, giving him the signal I hoped he'd been looking for.

Malachi stilled as my lips touched his, but only for a moment. Then, like a switch had been flipped, he crushed me to the ground and fisted a hand in my hair. His mouth on mine was merciless, tongue and teeth and total possession, like this had been building inside of him forever, and he'd just been waiting for permission to let it out. He kissed his way down my neck, nipping at my skin, drawing a choked moan from my throat and a low growl from his. It was like a boulder rolling downhill. An avalanche. I could not control what I had unleashed . . . and wasn't sure I wanted to.

The sensation of Malachi—the unyielding weight and smooth, hard contours of his body, the earthy scent—upended me completely, unlocking doors that had never been opened, shaking loose feelings that had been bolted down. Need and terror. Now and *then*. Every time we'd kissed in the past, he'd let me be in control, let me set the pace.

Not this time.

His hand stroked firmly down my arm and ribs, his thumb skimming the edge of my bra and sending bolts of pleasure through me while at the same time awakening old fears: I couldn't stop him. He was too big. Too strong. Too—no. This was what I wanted. I arched up as he tugged the neckline of my T-shirt aside and ran his tongue along my collarbone. The searing heat of my desire for him made it easier to shove all my memories down a deep hole in my mind. This was *my* choice. This was mine.

His fingers traveled down my hip and curled around my thigh, hungry and searching. I kept my arms around his neck and my hands in his hair, holding on for dear life as our need for each other took over. And just as I was reaching that equilibrium—that reassurance that this was all right, that I was safe, that Malachi would not hurt me—he shifted his hips and settled himself between my legs. I couldn't contain the whimper.

Malachi froze, his mouth locked on to the junction of my neck and shoulder. And then, quick as a viper, he scooted away from me, leaving me lying on my back, stunned.

"I shouldn't have done that," he panted. "I shouldn't have—"

"Stop," I said, staring at the ceiling. "Please." I summoned all my courage and turned to look at him.

Malachi had drawn his knees to his chest and had one hand over his mouth. He was staring at me like he'd just stabbed me. "I forgot myself," he said. "I forgot that you— that . . . I forgot."

I covered my eyes with the heels of my palms and pressed hard, trying to scrub his expression from my memory banks. Because here it was, that look I'd never wanted to see. The one that said he thought I was broken. And inside me, the echoing fear that I actually was. I should have been thankful he was so sensitive. I'm sure a lot of other guys would have ignored that whimper. But instead it pissed me off, because I didn't want to have to deal with it. I wanted to be normal. "Since you're feeling forgetful, can we forget this happened?"

"No," he said in a hollow voice. "Please look at me."

I finally complied. He'd moved a bit closer and didn't look as shell-shocked, but I had to wonder if it was just beneath the surface. "Okay. I'm looking at you."

And God, it felt wonderful and terrible at the same time. Everything I wanted was wrapped up in that moment, along with everything I couldn't have because it had already been taken.

"I'm sorry," he said, "for scaring you."

"You didn't—"

"Don't lie to me, Lela. I heard you. I *felt* you. And—" He closed his eyes and raked his hand through his short hair. "I scared myself, too. Sometimes the things I feel for you are so . . . big. I'm not used to that. Over the past seventy years, I've become very good at feeling nothing at all."

"I don't believe that," I rasped. "You loved Takeshi. And Ana."

He nodded. "But this is different. You are different. And I don't know how to do this. I'm trying very hard, but sometimes—"

"I'm sorry I'm so complicated."

He let out a huff of laughter. "I'm sorry I'm so inept. Most of me wants to protect you. From everything. I hope you know that."

I took in the stark lines of his face while my heart beat triple time. "And what does the rest of you want?"

He raised his head, and his eyes looked nearly black. With every muscle taut, he studied me. "The rest of me—"

My phone buzzed, and Malachi's mouth snapped shut. He rose to his feet as I pulled it from my pocket. Tegan, of course. Texting to find out if we'd bring her coffee.

I looked up from the screen to see Malachi striding for the stairs. "Hey, wait!"

He didn't stop walking. Instead, he said over his shoulder, "I have to shower so that we can go. We can talk later?"

"Okay," I whispered, hating Tegan and her caffeine addiction with the fire of a thousand suns as I watched Malachi flee up the stairs.

SEVEN

THE SOUP KITCHEN WAS just north of that gas
station where we'd chased the Mazikin. The streets were
lined with duplexes—these enormous, dilapidated houses
with big porches and balconies, all sagging wood and peeling paint. Decayed leaves had collected in piles at the bases
of spindly trees. Wobbly chain-link fences enclosed tiny,
cluttered yards full of children's toys, the bright colors fading to pastels after a long winter of snow and thaw.

For the umpteenth time since we'd picked her up,
Tegan sighed from the passenger seat. I glanced over
at her, forcing myself not to comment on her outfit of
ripped jeans and an old flannel shirt that screamed *trying
too hard*. From the neck up she looked expensive as always:

flawless makeup, perfect highlights, tiny diamond studs in her ears.

"Are you going to tell me what's up?" I asked.

"Aden's not coming. He texted me this morning to say he'd been out late and was going to crash. It's fine. I think I'm done with him."

I was relieved to hear Ian had gotten him home safely but realized that was probably not what Tegan wanted to hear. "That sucks. Are you all right about it?"

She shrugged, tossing a glance at Malachi, who was sitting silently in the backseat, gazing out the window, searching for threats. "I was up and down with him even before . . . all this. It's fine. We can talk about it later."

"Um. Sure," I said, feeling a twinge of guilt as I thought about how much I'd rather spend time figuring things out with *my* boyfriend instead of talking to Tegan about hers. We pulled up outside the shelter. "We better get inside, right?"

Tegan nodded as she stared at one of the more ramshackle houses on the block. She shuddered like a wet cat and got out of the car, clutching her donation envelope to her chest like she thought someone was going to pry it out of her hands.

Rolling my eyes, I opened the trunk and braced myself to lift a big box of canned goods to carry in to the shelter.

"I'll take it," Malachi said, stepping close and sliding his hands over the box. *Over my hands*, lighting me up with hope and a billion other things. Maybe he was over what had happened in the basement. He looked at me out of the corner of his eye and gave me a hesitant smile. "You can take the dry stuff."

He lifted the heavy box with ease and followed Tegan toward the shelter, leaving me trailing behind. A red SUV pulled up to the curb as I neared the front door, and Ian got out a second later, a worn baseball cap crammed over his messy hair. He smiled wearily at Tegan, who jumped up and down and clapped her hands when she saw him. "The guilt trip worked!"

"I knew Aden wasn't going to make it." He shook his head as he stepped onto the sidewalk next to me. "He was kind of messed up last night."

Malachi tilted his head as he looked at Ian. After all the crap with Jim, I'd forgotten to tell him that I'd run into the star players of our baseball team while they hunted for the Mazikin with paintball guns.

"But you got him home safely?" I asked.

"Yeah. We actually picked up the asshat a few blocks away from here." He whipped off his cap and ran his fingers through his hair before jamming it back on his head again. Then he gave me a nervous glance. "And sorry about the, um . . ." He gestured at the phone-shaped bulge in the pocket of my hoodie.

"Sorry about the *what?*" Malachi turned sharply toward me, the contents of the box in his arms sloshing and clanking. Ian obviously sensed his back-the-eff-up vibe. "Aden ran off last night," he said slowly, considering his words. "And I . . . um, knew that Lela is familiar with the area, so I texted her a few times. I thought she might have some idea where we could look." He motioned at the entrance to the soup kitchen. "Anyway, I'm here, Teg. What do you want me to do?"

He didn't mention that we'd seen each other. And he didn't mention Jim. He probably thought he was protecting me from Malachi's jealousy. It wasn't necessary, but it was kind of . . . nice. I gave him a quick smile as we entered the shelter, and he returned it with dimples.

The shelter was already buzzing with activity. Waves of heat poured from the kitchen, where the volunteers were readying giant pots of soup and stacks of neatly wrapped sandwiches. A ruddy-faced woman in a hairnet waved a spoon at us. "Volunteers?"

When we nodded, she gestured to a bunch of people standing by a long table. "Go sign up if you want credit for community service. And you," she said, pointing at me. "Get your hair back or put on a hairnet."

I pulled my all-purpose elastic off my wrist and lashed my hair into a tight ponytail. We joined the group of volunteers, mostly other teenagers and a few parental-looking grown-ups. Henry was there, too, doing an excellent job of pretending he didn't know us.

We signed in and got a little tutorial on how much food to dish out and how to handle requests and complaints. As soon as the shelter worker was finished talking, a few people filed in from the street, wearing mismatched layers of clothes and wary expressions. Some looked like they'd just stopped in on the way to a day job, but others looked like this was their last chance. There were kids, too, with hollow eyes and solemn faces that reminded me of me, not too long ago. I looked away.

Following the kitchen staff's orders, Henry, Malachi, and Ian helped bring the pots of soup to the warmers while Tegan and I grabbed bowls and spoons. It didn't take long for the room to get crowded. The long cafeteria tables that took up half the room were filled to capacity, and several people came in and asked for their food to go. A staff member told us to keep our pace up, that they served over seven hundred meals during every shift. It was barely controlled chaos.

I glanced over at Malachi, who was scanning the mob, frowning. I knew what he was thinking: there were too many people here. And only three Guards when there should have been four. It would be hard to spot suspicious activity . . . and it would have been nice to have an extra pair of eyes.

Even though frost glazed the windows and coated the

grass outside, inside the shelter it was hot as hell and reeked of tomato soup, sweat, minestrone, rum, burnt toast, cigarettes, and unwashed bodies. When a garbage can next to me began to overflow with paper plates and plastic bowls, I seized the opportunity to get some air.

"I'll be right back," I hollered to Tegan as I gathered the giant plastic bag and lugged it toward the back exit. She waved absently in my direction.

A blast of frigid air greeted me as I swung open the door, and I inhaled it greedily.

And immediately dropped my garbage bag.

Was I imagining it? Was it some sort of weird hallucination after the crazy scent overload of the soup kitchen?

No. As I stood in place and breathed, it was definitely real. The cloying, sick smell of incense. A scent I associated with only one thing: Mazikin.

I took a few steps into the back lot, my breath fogging in front of my face. The scent was carried on the wind, beckoning me forward. I walked around to the front of the shelter, wondering if there might be Mazikin right here, trying to get a bowl of soup or lure new recruits. The line of hungry people was out the door, but the smell was definitely fainter, so I returned to the lot, which backed up to a row of houses. I skirted the Dumpster and followed a narrow lane between the houses that was littered with old tires, discarded ride-on toys, and garbage bins. The smell was getting stronger, and my heart beat faster each time I inhaled. I turned left and walked a block up the street before I realized the smell was fading, so I jogged back the way I had come.

I was passing the lane that would take me back to the shelter when a guy with greasy, dark hair and a gaunt, stubbly face loped out from between two houses up ahead, not even twenty feet from me. He was wearing a padded flannel shirt and gloves with the fingers cut off, and I caught a glimpse of grimy, jagged fingernails just before he turned his back. Carrying an oil-spotted paper bag in his arms, he made his way briskly up the road away from me. I followed, sniffing at the air, probably looking a little crazy. Fortunately, the guy didn't seem aware of me as I trailed him.

I walked up the street, block after block, scanning every side yard and window for movement, looking for more suspicious characters. The scent only got stronger, so I knew I was heading in the right direction even if the guy I was following was just a regular human with really poor hygiene. The street finally dead-ended with an empty lot bounded by a chain-link fence. On the other side was a cemetery, which separated the neighborhood from a busy state highway. The incense smell was so heavy that it was making my head swim. Just as I was wondering if the guy was about to climb the fence and cut through the cemetery, he scrambled up the front steps of a huge old colonial next to the empty lot and ducked inside, closing the door softly behind him. I paused a few houses away, assessing. Boarded-up windows. Graffiti on the sidewalk. Abandoned? This whole street had that feel, like blight had eaten it away and chased families and normal residents elsewhere. Sure enough, there was an eviction notice taped to the front door.

It could be a crack house. Or a meth lab. Or a hangout for a bunch of homeless people burning whatever they could find to keep warm. Or . . .

It could be the nest.

EIGHT

WITH SHAKING FINGERS, I extracted my phone from my pocket and texted Malachi the address of the colonial. I was nearly ten blocks from the shelter, but maybe he could get Henry to drive him here, and then we could figure it out together.

While I waited for a reply, I crept around back to get a sense of what we were dealing with. Though most of the windows were boarded, some of the plywood was rotting in places and sagging away from the sills. A few of the low basement windows hadn't been covered. I lay down on the ground and peeked through an open frame that still held a few shards of glass. The white winter sun was high enough to give me some help, its beams revealing an open room full of boxes and junk of all types. Nothing moved inside. My hand drifted to my waist, where I'd clipped a knife before we'd left the Station, once again at Malachi's quiet insistence.

As I stood up, I heard it. A soft mewling sound from inside the house. Wishing my heart wasn't beating so loudly in my ears, I skirted down an incline and around the back; then I crawled past the shattered windows of the walk-out basement to the other side. The whimpering was louder near the front of the house, wrenching sobs that penetrated the walls and dissipated like smoke in the chilly air. I squatted beneath the boarded window where the noise was loudest.

"I said, *shut up!*" someone growled, deep and vicious.

"Please please please," cried the voice. It sounded male, but young. And so, so scared. "Please let me go. I won't tell anyone!"

Then he screamed, a sound that tore through me like a blade.

"I'll do it again if you don't shut up," said the boy's snarling captor. "My brothers and sisters are trying to sleep up there. You wake them, I get in trouble."

I gritted my teeth and wrenched myself away from the window, pulling my phone from my pocket again while I jogged toward the back of the house. This time, I called Malachi. What was taking him so long? It rang until it went to voice mail. I called Henry. Same thing. I almost called

Jim but then realized that even if he picked up, he either couldn't or wouldn't help.

I had a choice. I could try to get the boy out now, or I could go all the way back to the shelter and try to round up my Guards, who seemed unable to operate their cell phones. I could also call the police, but all that would do was clear out the Mazikin, who would be free to find a new home. We couldn't exactly mow them down in front of the authorities. What we needed was for the Mazikin to stay put so that we could burn this place to the ground with them inside. The last people we wanted paying attention were the cops.

The boy screamed again, and my decision was made.

The Mazikin had said his brothers and sisters were sleeping "up there." Since he was on the first floor, he must have meant they were on the upper floors. Maybe I could get in there and free the boy without alerting them to my presence. Maybe by the time I had, Malachi would have arrived.

I texted Tegan: *Tell Malachi to check his phone.* Then I wiggled through a broken window at the rear of the house and let myself into the basement, my knife out and ready. The stale air reeked of mildew. I went over to the basement door and unlocked it, giving myself a quick escape route.

The stairs to the first floor were rickety but passable, and my boots made no sound as I inched my way up. The door at the top of the steps was hanging open, and I kept low as I poked my head out, taking in the dim hallway, lit only by fingers of light from the few windows not covered with boards. The silence was broken only by the muffled sobs of the boy, and I stayed close to the wall as I passed by a living room jam-packed with ugly couches and ripped cushions, their fluffy guts exposed. Discarded clothes lay in piles along the edges of the room. Someone had barfed all over the carpet, and the stench almost overpowered the scent of incense and mildew.

I froze when I heard clonking footsteps on the stairs to the second floor. The ceiling above me creaked, and then came soft, hooting laughter. Maybe the Mazikin had gone upstairs to join his brothers and sisters. Luckily for me—it meant I wouldn't have to find a way to kill him quietly before I rescued the boy. After a few moments, the laughter quieted and the creaking stopped. I continued my slow progression toward the front of the house.

I tiptoed my way up the hall, careful not to touch the walls, some of which dripped with what I was pretty sure were various bodily fluids, viscous and cloudy, drying in raised beads and thin smears. A row of holes had been punched in the plaster, and at the end of the hall lay a clump of brown, curly hair, held together by a black-crusted, shriveled hunk of flesh. I swallowed my disgust and turned the corner to the parlor.

My stomach dropped.

There, illuminated by the light filtering in through

tattered lacy curtains from one of the unboarded windows, sat a low, heavy table.

Four pots full of ashy, smoking incense surrounded it. To each of its legs was tied a length of rope. The frayed ends of each rope were stained reddish brown. This was their altar, the place where they tied their victims to perform their possession ritual. "My God," I muttered.

"Who are you?" someone whispered.

He was close. I blinked, venturing past the stairs that led to the second floor. My knife at the ready, I glanced up to see nothing but darkness at the top of the steps, and so I returned my attention to the parlor. Crouched by the window, his hands tied to the radiator, was the boy, maybe a year or so younger than me. He was trembling, stripped to a filthy, formerly white T-shirt in the cold air of the unheated house. His arms were covered in claw marks, nasty, oozing red gashes. His bright-green eyes, round with terror, peeked out from under matted dark-blond hair. Tears streamed down his cheeks and cut narrow paths through the grime on his face.

A voice from my past echoed in my ears: Ana, a Guard in the dark city, telling me how she knew Nadia hadn't been possessed by the Mazikin yet: Nadia had been crying.

"I won't hurt you," I mouthed, and then put my finger to my lips. I slowly moved forward, conscious of the tiniest groan in the floorboards that would alert the Mazikin upstairs to my presence. Squatting next to the boy, who reeked of piss and sweat, I used my knife to carefully cut through the ropes binding his wrists, which were bloody from his frantic attempts to free himself. The boy fixed his attention on the stairs. We both knew that was where the threat would come from if we were discovered. While I worked, I noticed his arms were covered in more than claw marks . . . they were covered in track marks, too. Recent bruises and scabs in the crooks of his elbows and down his inner arms. This kid was so young, but he was already an addict.

"They told me they had some good stuff here," he whispered when he saw me looking at them.

I put my finger to my lips again and shook my head. He could tell me all about it *after* we were safe. But my insides knotted with anger. So that's how these Mazikin were recruiting. They were luring messed-up kids into this house . . . and sending their souls straight to hell.

With one final slice of my knife, the ropes fell away from the boy's wrists. I caught him as he collapsed onto the spongy, damp carpet. He cradled his raw, torn wrists and sank into me, his shoulders shaking and his face twisted with pain. I wrapped my arms around him, whispering as quietly as I could, "It's okay. You're okay. I've got you."

As much as I didn't like being close to most people, I wanted to comfort this kid. I knew how he felt, and I wanted to make him promises. I wanted to tell him that he wasn't disposable, that better things were ahead, that he wasn't alone. I could have been just like him if not for Diane. So I held him like the mother he needed in that moment and silently fought my own memories of being broken and having *no one* to do this for me.

He finally pulled himself together and swiped his hands across his face, smearing tears across his dirty cheeks. He looked up at me from underneath his mop of greasy blond hair, cautious and shy. "My name's Nick," he said.

I shook my head, pinched his lips together, and then tried to smile in a reassuring way. He nodded, smiling back even though I was holding his mouth closed. It was the sweetest, most hopeful little smile, and I was determined to earn it. I put my face close to his dirt-rimmed ear. "Can you walk? We need to get you out of this place."

He nodded, and I pulled him up and held him by the arm as he steadied himself. I pointed toward the hallway that led to the basement. Together, we inched past the staircase, through a few beams of light piercing through the cracks in the boards, revealing the swirling dust in the entryway.

The floor over our heads squeaked. Nick trembled against me. I took his hand, holding it firmly as I tugged him into the hallway. We tiptoed past the kitchen. Past the living room. From above came a growl, followed by a series of grunts. Someone was awake. Another series of snarls and coughs followed. "What are they doing up there?" Nick breathed in my ear.

I was pretty sure the Mazikin were talking to each other, but I was afraid that would scare him, so I shrugged and pulled him to the basement door as the ceiling began to groan and squeak. Someone was moving. Fast. They'd heard us.

We'd just made it onto the rickety basement steps when Nick cried, "Oh, God!" His panic nearly drowned out the sound of heavy footfalls nearby. A harsh curse from the parlor told me we had only seconds before we were caught. Before I could get him in front of me to protect him, Nick shoved me hard, trying to get past. I crashed down the steps, off balance and out of control, smashing my elbow and knee. The side of my head collided with the handrail, and I landed on my stomach on the cold cement floor. Nick was right behind me, so I pushed myself up and lunged for the basement door.

It flew open. A form stood silhouetted in the light, and I recognized the shape immediately. "Malachi," I gasped.

The next few seconds split apart into disconnected sounds and sights, a moment torn at the seams. Malachi's dark eyes narrowed. A roar from the top of the steps jolted my heart. The tips of Nick's fingers brushed my back as we ran toward my Lieutenant.

Malachi's knives flashed as he drew them from beneath

his shirt. His face was fierce as he cocked his arms and let the blades fly. The knives spun past me, lifting a few strands of my hair as they flashed within inches of my temples.

They hit home with the solid *thunk* of metal penetrating flesh.

I spun around to see Nick fall back, Malachi's blades buried to the hilt in his chest. Nick's gaze met mine, pleading, questioning. His fingers spread wide, reaching for me as he sank to the floor. His mouth opened, but he never made a sound.

NINE

BY THE TIME NICK landed, his glazed eyes told me his soul was already headed to its next stop . . . wherever that was. I stared into them, willing him to come back, to be okay. I had promised him he'd be okay. Without thinking of the danger, I dove for him, disbelief making me stupid and slow.

Malachi jumped forward and wrenched the knives from Nick's body in time to bury them both in the stomach of an oncoming Mazikin—the guy I'd followed to this house. With a groan, the Mazikin dropped to the ground, curled in on himself. Malachi sheathed the bloody weapons, grabbed my arm, and wrenched me away from Nick. "Go. Henry's out front with the car."

I was still glued to Nick's empty eyes. "But he was—"

"Go!" Malachi shouted in my face, spinning me around and shoving me toward the door.

My eyes stinging, my chest aching, I stumbled out of the house. "We have to—"

"We have to get out of here," said Malachi as he dragged me toward the street.

I forced myself not to look back as we climbed into the back of the gray sedan. Henry took off immediately, steering competently through the maze of the run-down neighborhood. "That was the nest," I said between breaths.

"And you went in without waiting for me. For us," said Malachi in a hard voice. "You failed to follow your own protocol."

"Those Mazikin will know someone was there," said Henry. "They might clear out."

"We can go back tonight and burn it out," Malachi replied, looking me over. "A daytime assault is inadvisable now, considering we're one Guard short and our Captain is wounded."

The injuries from my fall down the steps jabbed splinters of pain up my arm and down my leg. The side of my head throbbed. I buried it in my hands, wishing I could erase Nick's face from my mind. "We have to be more careful," I murmured to no one in particular.

"We?" snapped Malachi. He pulled me to him, clearly

past caring whether Henry noticed that we were a little more than Captain and Lieutenant. He tipped my chin up and made me look at him. "How badly are you hurt?"

"I fell down the steps. I'll be okay." Honestly, I wasn't sure, but it didn't seem to matter right now.

"You shouldn't have gone in alone." His words barely made it out from between his clenched teeth. "That was reckless."

A tiny whisper of anger coiled in my belly, but I tried to keep my voice calm. "I texted you. Then called you."

His cheeks darkened. "I didn't hear the ring. The shelter was too loud. Tegan felt her phone vibrate in her pocket, and she alerted me. That was my mistake. But it doesn't excuse yours."

I swallowed, but it did nothing to remove the lump in my throat. "There was a kid in there, Malachi. They were hurting him."

Malachi shook his head. "They don't hurt their recruits. Not unless—"

"This isn't like the dark city where their prisoners are passive and cooperative! The kid wouldn't be quiet, and he was trying to escape. They'd scratched him." Tears burned my eyes. "I saw a chance to get him out. I couldn't leave him there."

Confusion softened Malachi's steely glare as Henry called out, "You freed a prisoner? Where is he now?"

I have no idea. I bit my lip as a tear leaked from the corner of my eye. Malachi cupped my face in his hands, and I shuddered as I noticed a smear of blood on his fingers. When he spoke again, his voice was soft. "Is he still trapped in there?"

I shook my head, the dread suffocating me. Malachi searched my expression for clues. "Did he escape before I arrived?"

I shook my head again. "He was right behind me."

Malachi went utterly still as the color drained from his face. "No. No, that was a Mazikin," he stammered. "He was chasing you—trying—he was trying to grab you. I had to . . . to protect you."

"You did," I choked out. "The other man *was* a Mazikin."

"But the boy—"

"Wasn't."

Malachi's hands shook as they fell away from me. He stared down at them and finally seemed to notice the blood on his fingers. "Are you sure?" he whispered.

Before I had a chance to respond, he was already wiping his bloody hands on his pants with desperate movements. But the smears had dried, so he started to rub them fiercely and scrape at them with his short, blunt fingernails. In seconds, his skin was red from the friction, and I reached over to stop him. He ripped his hands away from me and folded them beneath his arms. I sat back, completely at a loss. He looked like he was about to explode, and I had no idea how to defuse this kind of bomb. We lapsed into an uncomfortable silence.

As Henry got onto the highway, I realized I'd forgotten all about Tegan. I reached for my phone so that I could text her. But it wasn't in my pocket. I patted myself down and realized that, somewhere along the line, I'd dropped not only the phone, but also my knife. Sucking in a breath, I touched Malachi's arm. "Can I borrow your phone?"

He dropped it into my hand without looking at me. Pretending to be Malachi, I texted Tegan, telling her he'd found me and asking her if she could get a ride home from Ian. I got an answer immediately:

Where the hell did Lela go?!

So I responded: *Had to deal with something*

Tell her shes on my shitlist

I sighed. *If you insist*

I nudged Malachi's arm. He quietly took the phone back and tucked it into his pocket; then he returned to rubbing at his skin. The blood had fallen away in dry flecks, but his hands were raw. I sat very still and watched my Lieutenant, who I ached for . . . who'd just killed a boy. An innocent one. One I'd promised to save.

Sorrow swelled in my chest, crushing me from the inside out, filling my lungs and lodging in my throat. Was Nick in the Countryside now? Or had he gone somewhere like the Blinding City? Jim had said it was a place for addicts. But

Nick had seemed so young. So in need of gentleness and mercy. I wanted to believe that's what he would get, but I'd seen enough to know it might not turn out that way. It made me want to scream with grief, even though I'd only known him for a few minutes. It had been long enough to feel him tremble in my arms, to see how hurt he was, and to have his hopeful, shy smile burned into my memory.

He was the reason we had to succeed against the Mazikin. They were taking the homeless, the street kids, the ones no one noticed or cared about. They were using people who had already suffered so much, and they were condemning them to hell.

"Henry," I said, "I need you to drop us off at the Station, and then go back to the nest and watch it. If they try to clear out, you have to let us know. We'll hit it tonight, but you're right—they could move before then if they know we're after them." And considering how we'd left two corpses in the basement—along with my phone and my knife—it seemed like a distinct possibility. Especially if that female Mazikin had reported to Sil that we chased her last night. Like an idiot, Jim had actually *asked* her if she was a Mazikin. Which meant that at this point, they probably knew that the Guards of the Shadowlands had followed them to the land of the living.

"I can go with Henry," Malachi said as he stared at his hands. He'd stopped rubbing them, but was now grasping his knees so tightly that his knuckles had turned as pale as his face.

"No, you can't," I replied. It was the easiest decision I'd made all day.

Malachi closed his eyes. The sorrow inside of me expanded, and I couldn't stop myself from reaching for him. I knew we'd have to deal with this, have to talk about what he had done, have to make sure it didn't ever happen again. But Malachi was obviously devastated, and seeing him this way hurt me almost as much as Nick's death. My fingers skimmed along his brow, an offer of warmth, of myself. Not as his Captain, but as his girlfriend.

Henry pulled into the driveway of the Guard house. "Do you need a minute before I leave?" he asked, watching in the rearview mirror as I waited for Malachi to lean into me like he sometimes did, to seek more from me like I knew he needed.

"Yes," I said at the same time that Malachi said, "No," and then flung open the car door and bolted. My hand was still hovering where his head had been when he disappeared into the house.

I swallowed, my throat aching. "Henry, do you have what you need? You understand what I want you to do?"

He nodded, regarding me in the mirror.

"All right. See you later, then. Be careful."

I got out of the car and trudged into the Guard house.

It was slowgoing because every step sent crunching, vicious pain from my ankle to my knee. Clinging to the railing, I climbed the stairs to the second floor and heard the shower already running. By the time I got to the top, steam was billowing out from under the door of the bathroom. I rested my head against the wall and stared at the swirling cloud. Malachi was trying to wash himself clean. I'd done that a few times before. Maybe more than a few times. I knew how it felt to sit under scalding water and wish it were enough.

Knowing I needed to give him time, I carefully descended the steps.

And found Jim sitting in the parlor. Like he was waiting for me to find him there. His shirt was ripped, and his blond hair was a mess, but he looked sober enough as he watched me sink into the nearest chair.

I rested my elbows on my knees and let my head hang. Every part of me hurt. "So. You decided to come back."

"Raphael found me and brought me in a little while ago. He said I needed to decide what I was going to do and to let you know."

"And what are you deciding?"

"Whether I'm going to stay."

I raised my head. "And?"

Jim's face twisted with pain. "I'm not . . . I'm not a very good Guard."

No kidding. "Then why did you get assigned to this field

unit?" I asked, working hard to keep my voice gentle rather than accusatory. "Did you mess up or something? Is this, like, a second chance?"

"More like a *last* chance," he said, rising abruptly to pace.

"What do you mean?"

"It was here or the Wasteland," he mumbled.

Thinking of how Henry described the place, I said, "Are you telling me that if you choose not to be part of this field unit, the Wasteland is your alternative? Dude, why would you quit if *that's* where you'd go?"

He crossed his arms over his chest and held onto his biceps. "Because I realized Henry was right last night. You guys are depending on me. And that . . ." He set his shoulders and turned to me. "I'm not good at keeping my Guard partners alive."

I stared up into his deep-blue eyes and saw the pain there. The guilt. The regret. "Tell me?"

He grimaced and shook his head.

"Consider that an order."

He closed his eyes. "His name was Bomani. He's dead because of me. That's why I'm here."

I waited to speak until he was looking at me again. "So maybe this is your chance to redeem yourself."

"I don't deserve a chance," he blurted. "You *really* don't understand. Bomani was a good Guard. A great one. He was about to be released into the Countryside. He'd gotten rid of all his possessions and lived on simple rations, bread and water and nothing else. In the Blinding City, where everyone's addicted to something, where everyone's trying to get stuff so that they can have more than everyone else, where everyone's chasing a high, that's the sign you're ready to get out. We all knew Bomani was about to go.

"And I . . . I hated him. He was always in my way. Always trying to stop me from going out, from getting things I wanted." He started to pace again, like a caged animal. "One night, I got in over my head. I snuck out of the Station to meet up with a girl, and it turned out to be a setup. I thought she could give me what I wanted, but it turned out she and her gang wanted something from *me*. Like the patrol schedules and routes of the Guards, so they could take us out one by one, keep us from interfering with their plans or whatever." He bowed his head and chuckled, a choked, sad sound. "Bomani was too clever for his own good. He tracked me to the apartment and tried to get me out. But I knew . . . I knew he would tell my Captain that I'd sneaked out, and then I'd be punished. That they'd lock me in the Quiet Room, this tiny cell with nothing in it, where I'd be alone with—with—just . . . *me*." He shuddered, and suddenly his crazed fear at the mention of a holding cell the night before made a lot more sense.

He rubbed a hand over his face. "It shouldn't have mattered. It was what I deserved anyway. But I was so selfish, and when they attacked Bomani . . ." He trailed off, and then met my stare. "I let them kill him. That's why I'm here, Captain." He swiped his sleeve over his eyes. "Happy now?"

I stared at him, somehow knowing everything rode on my reaction to this horrible revelation. He'd stood by and let another Guard die, which made me feel sick. But I remembered what Malachi had said about the importance of forgiving Henry for his past and believing in him now. And hearing the agony in Jim's voice . . . I knew I needed to at least try. "Jim, I need you to tell me the truth, not what you think I want to hear, okay? No bullshit."

He shot me a wary look.

"If you could do it over again—knowing you'd be punished—"

"In a heartbeat," he whispered. "I relive it every night, every day. I'd stop them. I'd let them kill me if that's what it took."

"Then take this chance, Jim. Stay sober. Follow orders. Help us keep more people from dying. You were chosen for this mission for a reason. I have to believe that. I don't think the Judge makes decisions randomly, and this is no exception. Which means we need you, or we're going to lose."

He hadn't looked away. In fact, he was staring at me with this desperate look in his eye. "But what if I—"

"We all make mistakes. And some of them are really bad," I said in a husky voice, hearing the shower switch off upstairs. "But that doesn't mean we're allowed to use those mistakes as excuses. In fact, doing that makes them even worse. If you want to honor Bomani, then you need to do your job here on Earth. If you want his death to mean nothing, then go to the Wasteland. It's up to you."

He sat down quickly like he had no more energy to stand.

"You actually want me to stay?"

"Honestly? I don't know. You could have gotten us both into a lot of trouble last night. And I'm pretty sure you tipped off the Mazikin that we're here, hunting them. But like I said, I have to believe you're here for a reason. Otherwise, the Judge would have sent you straight to the Wasteland, right? Why give you a choice at all?"

He frowned.

From upstairs, I heard the sound of Malachi's door closing. I sighed. "If you're willing to do this job, I'm willing to give you a chance, but expect your leash to be short. Let me know what you decide. I have to go upstairs and talk to the Lieutenant."

As I limped from the room, I could have sworn I heard Jim whisper, "Thank you."

TEN

I WALKED UP THE stairs, practicing a little speech in my head, very similar to the one I'd just given Jim, since it had seemed to work out well. Not only for him but for me, too. It had helped me realize where my focus needed to be. What Malachi had done was shocking and tragic. It couldn't happen again. We'd have to plan and train so that it didn't. But . . . it was also an accident. He'd burst in on a dangerous situation and had made a mistake in the heat of battle. It was an error any of us could have made. He needed to know I understood that.

Two of the bedroom doors on the second floor were open. One room was messy, the other neat. Probably Jim's and Henry's, in that order. And the third door was closed. I went over to it and knocked.

"Not now, please," he called.

"It's me."

Silence. For, like, a whole minute. Enough to make my heart pound harder. Then, "Come in."

I opened the door. He was sitting at a desk. He had changed into track pants and a T-shirt, and his damp black hair was sticking up every which way, like he'd just been rubbing it with the towel that was draped over his shoulder. His face was still pale. His arms and hands were red and raw. And there were little lines etched around his mouth, like he'd aged a few years in the last hour.

"You should call Raphael to heal you," he said. "That bump on the side of your head looks quite bad. And you're limping."

"I might, later. Talking to you was more important."

He winced and looked away.

"Malachi," I said, reaching out to him. "I know you must be feeling really bad—"

"You have no idea," he said in a strained voice, rising from his chair. "*No* idea."

"Okay, but I can imagine. And I can see it on your face."

His nostrils flared as he let out a breath. "It won't happen again. That I can promise you."

My fingers stretched out to touch his, but he laced them behind his head and stared at my hand like it was a poisonous snake. I cleared my throat. "I know you don't want it to hap-pen again, but we need to talk about how to prevent it—"

"I already know how to prevent it," he said in a quiet voice.

"You do? That's, um, good." I'd expected to have to give him a pep talk, and he seemed to have already managed it for himself. "Can you tell me your plan?"

His dark eyes met mine, and he let his hands fall to his sides. "Yes, I need to." He stared down at me for a long moment, and then squared his shoulders like he was facing an opponent in battle. "I can't do this, Lela. I was arrogant and stupid to believe I could."

It took me several seconds to process his words, and when I did, my mouth dropped open. "You're quitting? Jeez! Jim might be doing the same thing, and that's bad enough. You *can't* quit, Malachi. I'll never be able to do this without you."

Pain flashed in his eyes, and then it was gone, smoothed over. "No, that's not what I meant. I'm not quitting. Even if I could, I wouldn't, because you need me."

"Exactly." I shuffled forward on my aching legs, needing to feel him, to be in his arms. "You scared me for a second there."

He caught my wrists before my hands reached his body and whispered, "But I can't do *this*."

My heart picked up a frantic, uneven rhythm. I stood, with my arms out to my sides, held there gently in his hands.

"You can't do . . . *what?*" I mouthed it more than said it. My throat had closed.

"If I am your Lieutenant, I shouldn't be anything else. I can't touch you like I have." His gaze dropped to the floor. "And you can't look at me like that."

"But you said—when we were in front of the Judge, you said . . ." He'd said he loved me. He'd said it. I'd heard him. The moment was etched onto my heart in vivid detail.

He closed his eyes. "Regardless of what I said, this is over between us. I can't do my job like this. What happened today proved that. I was so consumed with fear of you being hurt that I killed an unarmed *boy*. Someone who needed my help. A person you were trying to save."

"Anyone could have made that mistake," I argued, my voice cracking. "You had a split second to assess the situation."

"I have been a Guard for seventy years, and I have never made a mistake like that." His eyes opened, and in them I saw myself, pleading and desperate. "Even if I had, it's different here. We are in the land of the living. That boy was innocent, and I deprived him of his life." He released my wrists and took a giant step back. "Because of my feelings for you."

I stood there like an idiot, my arms still out at my sides, reaching for the comfort of his body, for *him*. "I know it's taking some time to adjust to this new place. But it's not me—it's not us." I knew how pathetic I sounded, but I didn't care. "Please. We can talk this through."

"It won't change my decision."

I took a step toward him. He backtracked. "You're blaming me for this," I said.

"No. I'm the only one at fault. Ana warned me that I was making mistakes because of you, and I ignored her. But as I think back, I realize how right she was. Especially now."

It felt like he'd landed a rock-solid kick to my gut. I nearly doubled over with pain. "What?" I blinked fast to hold back tears. "You said you were doing the right thing . . ."

"I thought I was almost ready to get out of the dark city," he said roughly. "Then you arrived, and I was stupid enough to believe it was meant to happen, as if this was my reward after all those years of service. So I let go of everything I knew because I thought I didn't need it anymore. I let my emotions rule me completely." He laughed bitterly and raked his hand through his hair. "I actually thought I could be with you, that we could go into the Countryside. And when we were sent here, I was *still* telling myself we could be together, still holding on to all those wishes for a future." He bowed his head, not letting me see his expression. "I have been such a fool."

"N-no. We're not a mistake." It came out broken, little

more than a squeak. "This is a good thing. *We're* a good thing. We can figure this out together. We can fight for that future. We don't have to—"

"Don't," he whispered, holding up his hand. "Please don't."

"You love me," I breathed. "You can't just . . . stop."

"I can," he said softly. "I have. What happened today was too much."

"And you could let it go this easily. Just like that." My vision spotted and sparked as the truth of my words hit me. He *had* let it go that easily. Why would I even question it? It wasn't like this kind of thing hadn't happened before. I'd simply forgotten how little I was worth. I leaned on the desk, needing something to hold me up. "Okay. I get it."

"You obviously don't," he said, so quiet I barely caught it.

"What?"

He shook his head like he was trying to clear it. "This isn't about *you*," he said, an edge creeping into his voice. "This is about me, and our mission. If I'm focused on you, I can't do it. I'll keep making mistakes. I can't be what you need if all I want is—"

"I'll do better," I pleaded, unable to accept what was right in front of me because it was too painful. "I won't go charging into places alone. I won't—"

"Please respect my decision." He crossed his arms over his chest. His knuckles were pale again as his fingers bit into the flesh of his arms. "Things between us will be professional from now on. As my Captain, you have my support and loyalty. I will follow your orders, whatever they are." He clamped his lips shut and swallowed hard. "But that is all I am to you."

A more untrue statement had *never* been spoken. I hugged myself, willing myself to stop being pathetic, forcing every ounce of pride to the surface, needing it to coat me like armor.

Like I was watching from outside my body, I heard myself say, "Of course I'll respect your decision."

He sagged a little as I spoke, but recovered quickly. "Thank you," he murmured. "Now if you'll excuse me, I'd like some privacy."

"Yeah, sure. It's your room." I spun around and fled as my armor melted away, leaving only a raw lump of misery and confusion where my heart used to be.

Blinded by tears, hurting and dizzy, desperate to escape to a place where I could scream and cry without being observed, I took the stairs too quickly. My knee gave out halfway down, and I flew forward, knowing this was going to be bad.

But I never hit. Warm arms caught me and set me on my feet. "That was nearly your second stair calamity of the day," Raphael said, holding me steady as I regained my balance.

"How did you—never mind," I said.

"Come into the living room, Lela. You need to rest." He put his arm around me, and I didn't fight him. I might have fallen without his support. My knee was killing me, my head was throbbing, and my heart was shattered. He guided me to the couch. I fell onto it, pulled a cushion over my chest, and hugged it tight, needing something to contain me, to keep me from falling apart.

He squatted in front of me, dressed in plain khaki pants and a button-down. Perfectly designed to be utterly forgettable . . . like me, apparently. "I won't ask what hurts," he said gently.

"It's been a shitty day," I said, praying he wasn't going to make me talk about it.

His gaze slid up the steps before returning to me. "There is so much pain in this house."

Looking at the slight sadness in his expression, I got an idea. "Can you . . . can you take that away? You take other kinds of pain away." A tiny bubble of hope rose through the horrible, heavy despair inside of me. "You . . . you could just make it black, and when we wake up, we'll be okay. Maybe you could do that. Because I—" My voice cracked as the reality of what had happened broke over me again. "I'm not sure I can—" I ducked my head so that he wouldn't see the tears start to fall. "I'm really sorry. I can't do this."

He nudged my chin up with his fingers. "You can."

"Find another Guard. Put Henry in charge. *Please.*"

He smiled, nearly blinding me. "This conversation is sounding remarkably similar to the one you had with Jim not thirty minutes ago, isn't it?"

"I don't want to think about the fact that you're listening to every freaking word I say," I snapped.

The smile didn't fade, so I directed my attention out the window until he let go of my chin. "You're smart enough to recognize the parallel, Lela. Jim didn't think he could handle this mission, and you told him he needed to take responsibility. Malachi is now confronted with his very worst fear—as a victim of the wholesale slaughter of his people, his family, all of them innocent, he is now himself responsible for the death of an innocent child. And yet he is determined to do his job."

I leaned back, wanting to scream in Raphael's face. Malachi was determined to do his job, all right. And I had interfered with that, and he had pushed me away without hesitation, totally calm as he crushed my heart. "Yeah, his dedication is admirable." And it was, really. It just hurt more than I could bear.

"So is yours, Lela." He pulled a phone out of his pocket that was identical to mine. "I figured you'd need this. And if you give me your keys, Henry and I can fetch your car when he returns."

"Is that my cell?" I asked as I dug in my pocket for my keys. "You got it from the Mazikin nest?"

He shook his head. "But I knew you'd need a new one—"

It buzzed. Raphael handed it to me. My new phone had just gotten a text from Henry:

They set the nest on fire cops here people everywhere no idea who to follow

"*Goddammit!*" I shouted as the phone vibrated in my hand with another text from him.

Orders?

I texted back: *Come home.* Then I tossed the phone onto the coffee table. "Do you want to revisit the notion that I'm actually capable of being the Captain?" I snarled at Raphael. "Because everything I try seems to explode in my face."

Raphael chuckled. "Then you should do better."

Fuck you almost made it out of my mouth, but I clenched my teeth around the words. And for some reason, it seemed to intensify Raphael's amusement. He patted my knee but pulled his hand away at my sharp intake of breath.

"What we need is to be immortal," I said, clutching at my knee and realizing it was swollen to nearly twice its normal size. "If you need us to fight the Mazikin, why can't you make us invincible? Or fight them yourself?"

His smile disappeared. "The Mazikin are not under the authority of the Judge, and haven't been for thousands of years. I cannot interfere with them directly. I am bound by the Judge's oath in this matter."

"Wait, what? The Judge promised the *Mazikin* that you wouldn't—"

"Only what you need, Lela," he said with a tone of quiet warning.

I bit my lip and tried to figure out what I might *need* to know. "They've escaped before, haven't they? Ana told me."

Raphael settled himself on the floor. "They have."

"And the human Guards stopped them."

"They did."

"So we can do this, right? We can win?"

"I can't tell the future, Lela. That's not one of my skills."

I watched his face, looking for clues. "They're stronger now, aren't they?"

He nodded.

I swallowed back the metallic taste of fear. "So I'm in charge of preventing an evil demon scourge from killing who knows how many innocent people, and if I don't do it soon, they'll split up and become unstoppable."

He smiled again, but it had a distinctly ghostly quality. "I'm glad you understand."

"I could do this better if you could numb me up, you know?" I said, my voice breaking. "You said you wouldn't ask where I hurt, but I'll tell you anyway. Everywhere. Not just my knee or my head. I don't want these feelings. It's too much."

He didn't even have the grace to look apologetic. "That's a different kind of battle wound entirely. I can't erase that kind of pain, Lela. It wouldn't be good for you anyway."

I lay back on the couch. "Then you'd better patch me up so that I can get out there again." Not that I was eager to go. What I wanted was the moment of peace Raphael's healing provided. Just for a little while, I needed the world to go the fuck away.

"Now, that I can do," he murmured, and sank me under the weight of dreamless sleep.

ELEVEN

WHEN I WOKE UP on Monday, for once, I found
myself grateful that I had to go to school. It had been a long
weekend of fruitless patrols, broken up only by the hours
I spent alone in my room, crying into my pillow so that
Diane wouldn't hear. Jim had decided to remain a Guard,
and so far was following orders. So was Malachi. Perfectly,
as I would expect. Coldly, which hurt more than I could say.
Firefighters had discovered two bodies in the basement of
that Mazikin nest, burned beyond recognition. Police were
investigating. They suspected the house had been a drug
den. I knew better, but we'd combed the area and come up
empty, so now we were back at square one.

I needed the distraction desperately. And maybe the

chance to grab a nap.

Then I remembered I had two classes with Malachi. At least Henry had agreed to drop him off at school in the mornings, so I didn't have to ride in a car with him. I wasn't sure the fragile stitches holding me together would hold if he were that close to me.

The early morning sun bounced off lampposts and windows and windshields, blinding me as I pulled into the school lot well before school was set to start. I stood outside my car, which was one of the few in the parking lot, wishing my head would stop pounding, wishing I hadn't promised to meet—

Tegan pulled her little black BMW into the space beside mine and got out, holding two coffees. She offered one to me. "I don't know how you like it, so it's black."

I cradled it in my hands, savoring the warmth in the cold morning air. "Thanks."

"Want to go in or sit in my car?"

I didn't really want to be in an enclosed space with her, but when I saw the gray sedan pull into the lot, Henry at the wheel and Malachi sitting next to him, I practically dove into her passenger seat.

"Okay," she said as she settled herself in the driver's seat. "How was the rest of your weekend?"

I took a sip of the coffee and let it sear my throat. "Fine. But you didn't ask me here to talk about my weekend."

She blinked. "You always cut right through the bullshit, huh?"

"I've never had time for it." And I had no interest in preserving her feelings.

"Well, if that's the way it is . . . the purple in your shirt matches the circles under your eyes," Tegan commented.

"I guess you won't bullshit me, either. I haven't been sleeping much lately."

"Because of Nadia?"

"No." Missing Nadia was like a chronic ache inside me, especially at moments like this, because Tegan was trying to be friendly, but she was no substitute for the friend I'd lost. That wasn't what was keeping me up at night, though.

Tegan's gray-blue eyes landed on me hard. "Lela, are you okay? I mean, I thought you were, but then . . . what happened on Saturday?"

I closed my eyes, wishing I hadn't been too wrecked to come up with a decent cover story. "I . . . the smell in that kitchen started to make me feel sick, so I went outside to get some air. I, um, got jumped. By a guy. I didn't have my wallet. So he . . . beat me up and left me there."

Tegan's eyes grew huge and shiny, filled with righteous anger. "You got mugged? You texted me to get Malachi for you and didn't even *mention* that?" Her little fist banged against her steering wheel, causing the horn to let out a high-pitched yip. "Was it one of those homeless people?

Could you pick them out of a lineup?"

I rubbed at my temples, my head feeling like it was going to split open. "Slow down, Tegan. I don't . . . it's okay. Can we drop it? I'm fine, and I shouldn't have been wandering around alone anyway. Serves me right."

She shifted in her seat and tapped her long fingernails on the bottom edge of the steering wheel. "You—you aren't involved in anything illegal, right?"

I shook my head but couldn't look at her.

"You're not taking drugs or something, are you?" she whispered.

"What? Are you crazy? Did Nadia tell you *anything* about me?"

She shrank back in her seat. "All right, I'm sorry." Her face was super pale. She looked like she was about to faint. "Nadia did tell me you thought drugs were stupid and everything, but I thought maybe, you know, when she died . . . never mind." She chewed on her bottom lip. "I . . . went to her grave yesterday."

I sank back in my seat. I hadn't been since the funeral, but that would sound heartless to anyone who didn't know what I'd gone through to make sure Nadia was all right.

"I hated you," Tegan blurted, and then looked straight-up startled at the sound of her own voice. She cleared her throat. "I still hate you, a little."

Once again, I found myself regretting that Tegan's therapist had once told her she should *bond* with me. I leaned forward, all her rude comments over the past year running through my head. "You brought me coffee so you could tell me *that*? I never did anything to you. Except to hate you, too, but that was because you were such a bitch to me."

"I know."

"Why, then? Is it because I don't come from money? Because I wasn't raised like you?"

She looked at me in horror. "No! No. None of that." With shaking hands, she put her coffee in the cup holder, and then picked up a napkin and started to fiddle with it, mumbling inaudibly.

"Come on now," I snapped. "If we're going to have it out, let's do it. Speak. Up."

"Because you were good for her!" she shouted.

I focused on my cup, my fingers squeezing it so hard that the lid popped off. Nadia had been good for *me*, that was for sure. "I'm sure you were good for her, too."

She scoffed. "I thought you were all about the absence of bullshit. Now I see you're full of it."

I shrugged. "You were friends with her for a lot longer than I was."

She ripped the napkin down the middle. "Maybe. I thought I was a good friend, too. I never said no to her when she wanted something."

I took another sip, even though it tasted like tar and

ashes It took me a long time to swallow it. "It was hard to say no to her."

"You did." Her unsteady fingers tore the napkin at the edges, creating a brown paper frill. "I was the one who gave her the pills," she said in a strained voice. "It wasn't the first time, either. She told me she just needed to relax, and my dad had a bottle of oxys left from his back surgery a year ago. I had no idea she'd take all of them at once . . . it's bad, I know."

I raised my head and stared at her. I knew she wanted me to tell her it was okay, but it wasn't. Pills. Nadia'd had a problem even before I met her, and it was what had killed her. Hell, even *after* she died, she was *still* looking for them. I set my cup in the cup holder and jammed my hands between my knees. "Don't tell me that, Tegan. Just. Don't."

She sniffled and pulled a tissue from her purse. "Fuck you."

It struck me as so ridiculous, me and Tegan, sitting here, cursing at each other. I started laughing. "Fuck you, too," I said, and flipped her off for good measure.

She accepted my twisted peace offering for what it was. She raised her prettily manicured middle finger and stuck her tongue out at me. We both needed to step off the hot topic. The ground there was too dangerous, so we could retreat behind this stupidity because it was all we had right now.

We stared out her windshield for a few minutes, watching Malachi walk slowly across the wide sidewalk and up to the looming glass and brick facade of our school. "Laney's pretty determined to snatch your boy," Tegan commented. "Just thought you should know."

Before I could respond, Malachi's eyes swept across the parking lot and landed on my car. I sank down in my seat, praying his eyes wouldn't stray to Tegan's BMW, hoping the sun's glare would keep him from seeing me if they did.

"Whoa. All is not well with the Russian hottie?" she asked. "He looks almost as unhappy as you do."

I slumped in my seat. "He's not Russian. And no, all is not well. And also: I don't want to talk about it."

She leaned back in her seat and slumped a little, too, so her head was level with mine. She nudged me with her elbow. "Fine. But I'm here, all right? If you ever do want to talk."

"Are you serious? You want to listen to my boy troubles?"

"Meh. Not really." She flipped me off again.

I nudged her back, hard enough to make her wince. "That's more like it. Are you ready to go?"

"Yeah. It's going to be awkward today with Aden, but I'll deal with it."

"I sympathize."

We got out of the car and looked over the now crowded lot. A bunch of baseball players were having an animated conversation over by Ian's huge cherry-red SUV. Greg was gesturing wildly, and in his hand was an iPhone. No more crappy flip phone for him—and it looked like he wanted everyone to know it. Ian appeared to be listening to him with good-natured patience, but his eyes kept moving over to me and Tegan.

"He was worried about you on Saturday," Tegan said as she waved at him.

I looked away as Ian's gaze landed on me. "It was nice of him to show up at all. Have you talked with Aden since he no-showed?"

She made a gagging noise as she flashed a death glare at Aden's hapless teammates. "Ugh. Yes. He's such a creep. He came over to my house Saturday night and tried to get me to go out with him. He was so pushy and weird that my dad threatened to call the police if he didn't leave. Dad says I should get a restraining order. Hang on," she said as she fished her ringing phone from her purse. "Oh my God! This is, like, the fourth time he's called me this morning." She held it up to her ear. "I told you to delete my number," she hissed. "I—what? Why would you want to talk to her?" She stared at me.

Then her eyes grew wide, and she turned sharply to look up at the school. I followed the line of her vision, up the side of the building, until it landed on a figure standing on the roof.

"What the hell are you doing up there?" she shrieked into the phone. "What? No—*what*? Don't—no; whatever, sure, here she is! Here she is!"

My mouth dropped open as she shoved the phone at me. Her voice was painfully high-pitched as she said, "He said he wants to talk to you, and if I don't give you the phone, he's jumping."

I grabbed the phone, too stunned to do anything else. From all around me came the voices, laughing first and then more frantic as all eyes fixed on Aden Matthews, who stood on the edge of the roof, four stories up, right over the front entrance, one arm spread wide, one hand holding his phone to his ear.

"Hello?" I said into the phone as my world tilted dangerously, sliding my morning straight into crazyland. "Aden?"

"Lela," he said. "*Lela*." His voice was shaky with energy. Maybe he was high?

"Hey, Aden. What—what are you doing up there? School's about to start." I sounded like such an idiot, but what was I supposed to say? I'd never talked someone off a roof before.

He chuckled. "Lela. Lela and *Malachi*."

I stared at his distant figure, at the toes of his shoes protruding over the edge of the roof. Surely somebody had called school security by now? I glanced over to see Ian staring up at his friend, his own phone pressed against his ear.

"Um. Yeah," I said. "If you come down, I'm sure Malachi would go out with you and your—"

"*Captain* Malachi. Tell him Ibram sends his regards."

Cold fingers of dread snaked out of the cracks in the blacktop beneath my feet and slid up my legs, anchoring me in place. "What did you say?"

"We know you're here." His low, hooting laughter made me pull the phone away from my ear.

I heard the shout through the phone. Aden spun around to look at someone who had joined him on the roof. For a moment, he held both his arms out for balance, but then he pressed the phone to his ear again. "Sil knows you're here. He knows who your friends are. And he'll see you soon."

And then, the body that had once belonged to Aden Matthews stepped off the roof of Warwick High School and plummeted to the cement below.

TWELVE

EVERYONE WAS SCREAMING. MOUTHS wide, tongues vibrating with the terror and shock, the whites of their eyes shining in the morning sun.

But in my head, it was silent. Like I was wearing a helmet of soundproof glass.

I was in motion before he landed, running toward the spot I knew he would hit.

Not because I wanted to save him. It was far too late for that.

Because I wanted to interrogate the Mazikin inside him.

But after the *crack-split-thunk*, I knew the creature inhabiting his body would never be able to answer my questions. Air whooshed from my lungs. My heart jacked up tight and painful, beating itself into a giant bruise.

Then a sound reached me, an animal wail, wretched and broken. I spun around. *There's another one here.* But no. Tegan shoved past me, staggering toward Aden's shattered body. Those horrible, wrenching sobs were coming from her. Beyond her, half the student body had their phones out, probably blowing up the emergency dispatch, calling for a completely unnecessary ambulance. Or snapping pics to post on Facebook. Ian and the rest of Aden's teammates were still huddled by his SUV, all the blood drained from their faces.

A hand closed over my shoulder, and I jerked away.

"Are you all right?" Malachi asked as he shoved his hands in his pockets. "What happened?"

I nodded toward Aden's body, which was now surrounded by a bunch of people, gray-green-faced teachers holding out their arms to shove students back, the weeping school nurse on her knees beside his head, the principal wringing her hands and shouting at everyone to calm down. The red-haired school counselor, Ms. Ketzler, had folded Tegan's waifish body against her own and was rocking back and forth, mascara-laced tears falling from her round cheeks into Tegan's hair.

"Mazikin," I said quietly. "I think it was Ibram." The Mazikin responsible for the death of Ana, Malachi's former Guard partner.

Malachi's expression sharpened. "Say that again."

"They got Aden. He'd been possessed." I jogged out of the way as an ambulance with screeching sirens pulled up to the curb and disgorged two frowning paramedics.

Malachi followed me back to my car. I didn't realize I was still clutching Tegan's phone until it started to ring in my hand. I put it in my pocket and then told my Lieutenant what had just happened.

"You know, Friday night? When Aden asked you to go out with him and his buddies? They were hunting the Mazikin. Jim and I ran into them as we were patrolling in south Pawtucket." I looked over at the baseball team, still hovering around Ian. "I should have had you go with them."

Malachi looked back and forth between the carnage and the pale-faced baseball players. "You think they found the Mazikin?"

I nodded. "If Ibram possessed Aden, he would have had access to his memories. He must have recognized you. And me."

"They sacrificed Aden to make a point," Malachi said.

And what a point it was. They could kill our friends, and from the outside, it would look like suicide. No way to prove otherwise. "What if Aden wasn't the only one they got?" I asked.

The baseball players watched as the ambulance, sirens silent, carried Aden's body away from us. The voice of the principal blared over loudspeakers, announcing that school would be cancelled for the day, but that any student who wished to talk could convene in the cafeteria. Parents were being alerted, which meant Diane would probably be home within half an hour, waiting for me.

"Ian appeared to be himself on Saturday," Malachi replied. He watched the baseball players as they began to walk toward the school. "But it's been nearly forty-eight hours since we've seen him. And there is no way to know about Greg and Levi just by looking at them."

"Do you think you could get close to those guys?" I pulled Tegan's phone from my pocket to see that Ian was trying to reach her. Picking up where Aden left off? "You're right—a lot of time has passed since Friday. Some of them might have been taken, too. And they might be trying to lure others. Aden—Ibram, I mean—tried to get ahold of Tegan on Saturday. If her dad hadn't been home, he might have succeeded."

"Then I'll question them," he said, glaring at Ian's back as he and the others disappeared into the school.

Seeing the fierce look on his face, I reached for his arm but stopped as my hand bounced off the boundary of the no-fly zone I imagined around his body. "Go easy, all right? Act like a curious, concerned guy, not a Guard. I mean, if you smell a Mazikin, let me know immediately, but stay cool. Don't gut anyone in the school cafeteria."

He looked down at my hand still suspended in midair.

"Understood, Captain."

I wished he'd just punch me. It would have been less painful than his remoteness. I drew a shaky breath. "And make sure you have their numbers, okay? We need to start keeping closer tabs on all of Aden's friends because Ibram made sure to tell me that the Mazikin know who they are. I'm going to check on Tegan. I'll touch base later."

I walked away without another word, too fried for politeness, too brittle to look Malachi in the eye. Probably too burnt to talk to Tegan, but it was the right thing to do. After all, if the Mazikin were infiltrating our school and targeting people I knew, she would be at the top of the list.

I ended up taking Tegan home. She was too distraught to drive. Plus, until I knew whether any other students were Mazikin, I didn't feel like leaving her alone. They might know they could get to me through her now.

"This doesn't make sense. He had a scholarship to BU," she whispered after several minutes of silence. "He was so psyched. And he said he was going to travel this summer. To Europe. He wanted to get drunk at an Irish pub. One in Ireland."

I turned onto her pristine street lined with carefully trimmed shrubs. "I'm sorry, Tegan."

"Why would he do something like that? He wasn't depressed. He was, like, the opposite. He had a great life, and he knew it."

I glanced at her. "Maybe . . . do you think he was high or something?"

"It was baseball season, Lela. Hello, drug testing? He would have lost his scholarship."

Damn. "Well, I know that some mental illnesses can kind of come out of nowhere."

She sagged back in her seat. "He was acting really weird on Saturday. And he smelled so bad. I actually did wonder if he'd been smoking something."

My stomach turned when I considered how close the Mazikin had gotten to her. And how they could try again at anytime. "Maybe he was self-medicating." I'd become familiar with the term a few years after I entered the child welfare system, when I was about six years old. Long before I was ready to understand it, I heard some social worker talking about my mom to one of my foster parents, explaining why she hadn't shown up for a scheduled visit with me. I'd stood barefoot in the dark hallway in my pajamas, listening as the lady said that my mom was mentally ill. That she'd drugged herself into oblivion, trying to silence the voices in her head. I'd spent a long time wondering where *oblivion* was and if I could find my mom there.

Tegan sniffled. "Like Nadia was, right?"

I'd never even thought of it that way. "Yeah." I pulled to a stop in front of Tegan's gated drive. She told me the code, and I punched it in; then we drove up her long driveway and parked.

Tegan folded her arms over her chest, shivering like she was cold even in the warm air of the car. "Do you ever wonder where she is now? Do you believe in any of that afterlife crap?"

I let my forehead rest on the steering wheel, not wanting her to see the look on my face: bitterness and awe and rage and wistfulness all rolled up in one. Too painful to share. "I do believe Nadia is in a better place." I gave myself a moment to smooth my expression and turned to her. "I know that for sure, in fact."

Tegan rolled her eyes and wiped a tear from her cheek. "I'm so tired of people saying that."

I tucked some stray curls behind my ear. "I was too. But I *know* this, Tegan. No bullshit, right?"

She stared at me, her shell-pink lips trembling. "No bullshit. I hope you're right."

"It doesn't mean I don't miss her. I will always miss her. And I will always regret that I didn't do more for her when she was alive."

Tegan's face crumpled. "Me too," she choked out as she began to sob. "And now Aden. Oh, God, is it me?" Her whole body shook, twisted up with guilt and sorrow I understood so well.

I knew I was supposed to hug her, but I wasn't sure I wanted to.

Then I thought about all those times I'd shrugged off Nadia's casual, caring touches. I thought about how I craved Malachi's touch, how comforting I found it and how much I missed it now that I couldn't have it. Was this really so different?

I reached out and touched her shoulder. Tegan put her hand over mine and took a snuffling, shuddery breath. When she let it out, it was as a wet, hoarse sort of . . . laugh. "Thanks for trying, Lela. I really appreciate it."

She wiped her eyes on her sleeve and got out of the car. I followed her. "Hey," I called as she trudged toward her house. "Are your parents home?"

She nodded. "My mom's here."

I fingered my keys. "All right. I'm going to call you later. Just to see how you are."

"Since when do you care, Lela? Are we friends now?"

My fist closed over my keys, the teeth biting my palm. She wasn't Nadia. She could never be Nadia. But I didn't want anything to happen to her, and it wasn't just because Nadia had cared about her. Somewhere along the line, I started to care about her, too. A little. "I was wondering the same thing."

She gave a raspy laugh.

"Hey, Tegan. Aden obviously got into something bad. If anyone shows up here acting the same way, don't let them in, and don't go with them, okay?"

"I'm not an idiot."

I handed over her phone. "Later, then."

On the drive home, finally alone, my mind whirled through the events of the last few hours. Aden was gone. Dead. Where was his soul now? Was he trapped in the Mazikin realm, which was supposedly so terrible that the dark city looked like a paradise by comparison? Or maybe his soul had been liberated the moment Ibram had crashed his body into the slab of cement. That's what Malachi believed. That was why he was so determined to kill the Mazikin and the bodies they inhabited. Sure, it gave the Mazikin a chance to come back, but if it freed the souls of their victims, he believed it was worth it.

Which meant that if Levi or Greg or Ian or any of the others had been possessed, Malachi would want to eliminate them immediately. We would end up murdering our classmates, one by one. Well, not really, but as I thought of Ian's surprisingly sweet, dimpled smile, I knew it would feel that way.

As I pulled into Diane's subdivision, I was already making plans to check in with the other Guards and scan the news to see if there had been any additional attacks. But all my plans scattered when I saw the car parked in Diane's driveway. It belonged to Nancy, my probation officer. And parked right next to it was a police cruiser.

THIRTEEN

I PULLED MY CAR to the curb, trying to slow the galloping pace of my heart enough to hit a few buttons on my phone.

Malachi answered immediately. "Where are you?" His voice was knife-edged, sharp and deadly.

I inhaled a shaky breath. "At Diane's. You?"

"The house. Jim and Henry are here. I have information."

Needing to postpone the moment I had to tell him how much trouble I was in, I asked him for a report.

"Ian admitted he saw you and Jim on Friday. He said he tried to get the others to go back to the car afterward, but he was overruled. They were in that neighborhood near the homeless shelter and saw someone running on all fours. So they chased it. Aden was fastest."

I squeezed my eyes shut. I didn't want to think about what had happened to him. How scared he must have been as they tied him to their altar. How badly it must have hurt. I'd seen the Mazikin possess a guy once. It had twisted him up like a pretzel and made him scream for endless, wrenching minutes as the Mazikin spirit—Juri, as it turned out—tore the guy's soul loose from his body and sent it to hell.

"They looked for Aden on foot and tried calling him," Malachi continued. "He didn't answer at first, but just as they were going to drive back to Warwick without him, he called Ian and asked to be picked up. One guess where."

"That nest."

"Ian thought it was a drug house. He said there were a few suspicious characters hanging out on the porch, and Aden was with them. Aden wanted the boys to join him in the house, but they refused. Ian was very angry, because all of them must submit to drug testing, and Aden was acting very out of character. Probably because he was inhabited by Ibram at that point."

Poor Aden. And Ian. "Did the Mazikin try to force them?"

Malachi sighed. "No. Aden went back into the house, probably got his marching orders from Sil, and then came back out and went home with his teammates. They dropped him off at his house. Ian said he was sure Aden had been smoking something."

"Because of the smell."

"Yes. But I can confirm that none of the other boys who went with him that night are Mazikin. I believe their determination to avoid getting kicked off the baseball team saved them."

"Thank God they take it so seriously."

"I acquired the phone numbers of most of the baseball team." He cleared his throat. "Cheerleaders as well. They were all gathered in the cafeteria."

"Good, good . . ." My voice trailed off as Diane poked her head out the front door and looked up the street, right at my car. "Malachi . . . I have to go."

"What's wrong?" He must have heard the hitch in my voice.

"The police are at my house. My probation officer, too."

"Why?" From the whoosh of air into the phone, I knew he'd probably just shot to his feet.

My throat was so tight I could barely talk. "I dropped my phone at the nest on Saturday. My knife too."

He cursed. "Drive away. Come here. We'll figure something out. We'll ask Raphael to—"

But Diane was already walking up the sidewalk, and the police detective, stocky and blond, his badge clipped to his belt, was on her front step. "Too late. I have to deal with this. I'll call you when I can, if I can. I'm sorry."

"Don't apologize—just tell me what you need!" he shouted, so loudly I had to pull the phone away from my ear.

I talked fast. "You're in charge. If you don't hear from me, patrol tonight without me. Look up the city's emergency winter shelters and sniff around there, since they seem to be targeting the homeless. Patrol the parks. The homeless camps—especially the ones mentioned in that news article Henry showed us. And check on Tegan and the rest of them, all right? Monitor statuses on Facebook." I gripped the phone so hard it creaked.

"I could come, now. To you," he said. "I could—"

"Those are my orders," I said sharply, unshed tears stinging my eyes as I watched the police detective descend the steps and come my way. I hung up on my Lieutenant and stashed the phone in my pocket.

Diane pulled my car door open. Her silver hair, usually in a tight bun, was haloed around her head, and her deep brown skin was creased with worry. "I saw what happened at your school this morning. And the school called. Where have you been?"

I got out of my car. The detective had stopped by his cruiser and was watching us. "Sorry. I was taking Tegan home. We saw the whole thing. What's with the cop?"

"We've been waiting for you, baby. The detective said he wants to ask you a few questions."

"About this morning?"

Her expression tightened, making all the wrinkles deeper. "They didn't tell me why. I'm sure they're just trying to check in with all the witnesses. Come inside, so we can sort this out."

It was like my brain had been tossed in a blender as I followed Diane up to the house, passing the car I knew belonged to Nancy, my probation officer. I might be back at the RITS by this evening. Completely cut off. Caged. I wanted to scream. I wanted to run. I wanted Malachi to come bursting through Diane's front door and carry me away. But instead, I sat down in a wooden chair at the kitchen table and folded my hands in my lap, trying to look sad and confused and not at all scared.

"Lela," said Nancy, who had faithfully stalked me since my release from the RITS, just over a year ago, "Detective DiNapoli needs to ask you a few questions." She twisted the rings on her thick fingers.

"Sure," I said softly, trying to make enough—but not too much—eye contact. Open but not defiant. "What do you need, Detective? Is this about what happened at the school today?"

"No, Ms. Santos." DiNapoli walked over to a briefcase he had set next to the table, pulled something from it, and set it in front of me. It was a plastic bag containing my dusty, chipped, sadly unmelted phone. "We found this on Saturday afternoon."

Everything in my world narrowed to a point, focused on that phone. Raphael had my old number connected to my new phone, but it obviously hadn't happened fast enough. I forced my expression into a surprised smile. "You found my phone! Did you get the guy who took it?"

Diane, still standing by the door, looked back and forth between me and the cop. "Took it? What are you talking about, baby? I just saw you talking on the phone in your car."

I pulled my new phone out of my pocket. "Yeah. Mine got stolen on Saturday, so I got a new one yesterday." I prayed Raphael might be able to pull a receipt out of that magical pocket of his, should the need arise.

Diane's eyebrows shot up. "At what point were you gonna tell me about that?"

I shrugged, hoping none of them could hear my heart pounding against my ribs. "I didn't want you to get mad. Or worried. It happened when I went to do that soup kitchen thing." I looked up at the detective and then over at Nancy, who was leaning on Diane's recliner, scratching a spot on her hip. "I was taking out the garbage midshift, and I was right out by the Dumpster. A guy jumped me. He took my phone."

"You were *mugged?*" Nancy asked. She looked shocked. Probably because she'd always thought of me as a perp rather than a victim.

"Yeah, Nancy. It wasn't fun." I looked up at Diane, willing her to believe my lie. "I knew you would freak. I got

Tegan to take me to get a new phone."

"Why didn't you report the crime?" Detective DiNapoli asked.

I let my eyes dart up to his, which were red-lined and wet-looking. "I didn't want trouble. I just wanted to get out of there. I didn't even finish my shift at the soup kitchen. A friend drove me back to her house, and I took some Tylenol."

DiNapoli leaned forward. "You were injured?"

Crap. Yeah, I had been, but I'd also been healed. "Nothing serious. I got knocked against the Dumpster. He took off as soon as he had my phone."

"Could you identify your attacker?"

"I'm not sure. It's been a few days." I thought back, trying to remember the guy in the padded flannel shirt, the one I'd followed to the nest. "He had, uh, really long fingernails? And his face was dirty."

DiNapoli's lips formed a tight line. He reached down and pulled a picture from his briefcase. "This the guy?"

It was a mug shot, but not of the flannel-wearing Mazikin. It was Nick. "No," I whispered, feeling like my chest had been torn open. "That's not him. The guy who attacked me was older."

The detective watched me carefully. As I fought to get myself under control, he pulled out another photo. "How about this one?"

It was the Mazikin. The one Malachi had stabbed. Dark,

greasy hair around a stubbly face. "That might be him," I murmured.

"We found these guys in the basement of that burned-out house on Garden Street, and this one"—he pointed at Nick's face—"was lying on top of your phone, Ms. Santos. We identified him using fingerprints and dental records this morning. The house is only about ten blocks from the shelter you were at."

Diane let out a disgusted noise. "Shouldn't have let you go," she said, making that *mm-mm-mm* of disapproval.

"They died in the fire?" I asked, trying to sound sincerely confused.

DiNapoli stared at me. "No, ma'am, they did not."

CRAP. "Oh," I said in a small voice. "That's what they said on the news."

His eyes narrowed. "No, the news reported that the bodies were found in the building. We did not release cause of death." His fingers spun the picture of the Mazikin on the table as his gaze slid down the hall. "Do you own any weapons, Ms. Santos?" All I saw was red as I thought of the black leather belt under my bed, to which was clipped an empty sheath. I swallowed hard, wondering if the next thing the officer was going to whip out was my knife.

Diane was next to me before I could open my mouth to answer him, moving faster than I'd ever believe possible for someone of her significant girth. "Excuse me, Detective.

Now I'm going to have to ask you to explain your line of thinking."

She put her hand on my shoulder. I looked up at her, my tongue glued to the roof of my mouth with panic-flavored superglue.

"Diane, they found Lela's phone at the scene of a *murder*," said Nancy, stepping forward and crossing her arms across her chest.

DiNapoli raised his hands in a conciliatory gesture and tossed an annoyed look over his shoulder at Nancy. "We're trying to cover our bases, Ms. Jeffries. The victims were indeed deceased prior to the fire. We think the murderer may have set the fire to cover his or her tracks." His watery eyes lifted to mine for a second, and I forced myself not to look away.

"How were they killed, exactly?" Diane challenged.

"I am not at liberty to say," the detective responded. He scratched his chin and sat back in his chair. "We were hoping Lela might have some information about that."

I shot back from the table until the chair hit the wall. Every adult in the room tensed, like they were ready to jump on me if I tried to escape. "Are you saying you think I killed those guys?"

"You do have a history of violence, Lela." Nancy said it like she'd been waiting for this for the past year.

A thick swell of anger rose in me, hot as lava. "You find it easier to believe I offed two guys in some burned-out meth house rather than I'm on the straight and narrow? Thanks for believing in me, Nancy!"

Detective DiNapoli shrugged. "The one guy stole your phone. He provoked you. Maybe the other one got in the way."

"Seriously? You're giving me a lot of credit if you think I could do something like that."

Diane's grip on my shoulder was iron as she pointed to the picture on the table, at the bright green eyes of the kid I'd tried to save. Nick. Smeared black eyeliner smudged beneath his sad, empty eyes. His lips were swollen and cracked.

"Who are these guys, anyway?" she demanded. "You tell me who they are. Or don't. Let me guess. Street people. Into drugs. Prostitution. They've both got that look." Her chin was sticking out. Her eyes were blazing pools of darkness. I was suddenly very glad she was on my side.

The detective looked down at the picture in a way that told us Diane had just hit the nail right on the freaking head.

"*Mm-mm-mm.* That's what I thought. Does it really make sense that a high school girl with a scholarship to URI, who was volunteering at a *soup kitchen*, would attack and murder *two* guys like that? Maybe they killed each other! Or how 'bout their tricks? Dealers? Pimps? Are you telling me *this* young lady is your prime suspect, just because you found her stolen phone on the scene? Detective, I've worked in the corrections system for a quarter century now, so forgive me for being skeptical."

Her finger was up and waving now. Her head bobbed back and forth on her neck as she spoke. To me, she looked like some kind of avenging superhero. "And Lela's not saying another word to you without a lawyer. I know the rules, so with all *due* respect, don't think you can come in here and mess around with us, sir."

"The Department of Children, Youth and Families has custody of Lela, Diane, not you." But Nancy had picked up her purse, and the detective had gotten to his feet.

Diane nodded. "I'm well aware of that. So you get her social worker on the line, and you tell them that the police are trying to violate this young lady's civil rights."

"Ms. Jeffries." Detective DiNapoli was almost at the door, looking a little shaken. "Apologies for any inconvenience. We'll arrange to talk with Lela at a different time."

Diane's finger was still waving. "You do that." She pointed at Nancy. "And you arrange for a lawyer if that's what's going to happen. She's no throwaway, so don't you treat her like one." Her outrage shook her usual honey voice.

I watched, stunned, as Nancy and DiNapoli retreated, probably planning to regroup and form a strategy for their counterattack. As soon as they pulled out of the drive, Diane sank into the chair across from mine. It squeaked under her weight. "I'm sorry, baby. I should have asked more questions before you even got home."

"Thank you." I leaned across the table and took her hand. Her eyes grew wide as I squeezed her fingers. "I didn't do anything to either of those guys, Diane, I swear."

She looked up at me and gave me a fierce return squeeze that might have cut off my circulation. "I know, baby. But even if you had, it would have been justified." Her words were quiet but clear as crystal. "If someone ever tries to hurt or take advantage of you, you fight back, and don't apologize for it. Don't let them hurt you."

I stared into her chocolate-brown eyes. I'd never talked about what had happened to me, had never admitted why I'd nearly beaten the life out of my foster father, Rick, who had been using me as his personal chew toy for months before I'd snapped. But I think Diane had figured it out a long time ago. "I'll try. But this—what are they going to do?"

She shook her head. "I don't know. We'll sort it out. I'm going to call your social worker before Nancy does."

I wrapped my arms around myself. "Can I go to Malachi's, please?" I needed to get back to work.

She pursed her lips. "Baby—"

"Please, Diane. I just—I need to see him."

She stood up and pulled her hand from mine. "You've only known him for a week."

I mentally kicked myself for not asking to go to Tegan's, but I was still too scattered and panicked. "I know. But he's important, and I feel safe with him." *And, oh yeah, he broke my heart, and now looking at his gorgeous face feels like crawling naked over broken glass, but whatever.*

Her expression softened. She was wavering. "Is Mr. Raphael at home?"

"I'm sure he is—all the parents were notified about this morning. He'd want to make sure Malachi was all right."

She nodded. "Go ahead. But you be home for dinner."

"Yes, ma'am." I got up from the table and walked as slowly as I could back to my room. I closed the door behind me.

"Lela," greeted Raphael. He was sitting on my bed.

"Shit!" I gasped out. "*That* is creepy. Couldn't you have sat at my desk?"

He raised an eyebrow in a way that told me he thought I was ridiculous. I took a deep breath and leaned against the door. "I was just thinking I needed to talk to you."

"That's why I'm here. You summoned me."

"I did? All I had to do was think about you? Since when?"

He smiled. "Special circumstances." He pulled his buzzing phone from his pocket. "One moment, please." He held his phone to his ear. "Hello? Ah, Ms. Jeffries. Yes, I'm home. Terrible tragedy, today. Malachi is extremely sad. He knew the boy who died. It would be such a help to him if he could see Lela." His gray eyes rose to mine. "Thank you. I'll be here if you'd like to talk, of course." He hung up. "You are free to go."

I scooted over to my bed and looked under it. "I need you to take something for me. I can't be seen with it."

He shifted his legs as I scrounged through my junk. "Are you looking for this?" He held up the belt and sheath. "We have no intention of allowing you to be tried for murder." He nodded at my desk, upon which sat a receipt for the new phone.

I sank into my desk chair. "Couldn't you have spared me the tense moments back there?"

His look sharpened. "We won't control people, Lela, contrary to what you believe about us. I will intervene as necessary for you to do your job, but I will not interact directly with the Mazikin, and I will not interfere more than is absolutely necessary with the living. The judicial process will have to take its course. But there will not be sufficient evidence to press charges."

"You can't stop them from questioning me, can you?"

He looked entirely unconcerned. "What I can do and what I will do are sometimes two different things. I am not here to give you what you want. I am here to—"

I held up my hands. "To give me what I need. I *know.* Fine." I folded the phone receipt a few times. "Okay, then, I need a few things," I said as a plan formed in my mind.

He tilted his head. "I'm all ears."

"I need camping stuff. Used. Heavily used."

"What, exactly?"

"One tent. Two backpacks. A sleeping bag or two. And a bunch of old clothes. Like stuff you would find in the dark city. But I could do without the . . . you know, stringy, slimy stuff?" I could only go so far in the line of duty.

"Non-slimy but heavily used camping equipment and clothes." He stood up. "They'll be waiting for you at the Guard house."

I stood up, too, not willing to let him get away yet. "Hey, where's Aden's soul now? Can you tell me? Is he in the Mazikin realm, or is he somewhere else? How does that work?"

For the slightest moment, the edges of Raphael blurred and glowed, and I tensed. He frowned. "As that police detective said, I am not at liberty to say."

"Why not?"

The glow disappeared. "Need, Lela. Only things you need." And then he disappeared, too.

FOURTEEN

THE MOMENT I PULLED into the driveway of the Guard house, Malachi was out the door and on the porch, striding forward to meet me. He looked like he was planning to rip the car door off its hinges and scoop me into his arms. His relief and desperation made my heart beat double-time.

But then he stopped dead at the edge of the walkway, like he'd run into an invisible wall. As I got out of the car, his smile faded to nothing. "We've been waiting to hear from you, Captain."

I ground my teeth. "Sorry about that. It turned out to be a minor complication. I hope." I slowly walked past him and up the steps. *Grab me touch me tell me it was all a mistake. Tell me you want to be with me. Tell me you were worried sick and then kiss me and make me forget.*

He didn't. He followed me, keeping a respectful distance as we entered the house. Jim and Henry were in the living room, sitting next to the computer. The empty chair in front of the keyboard was overturned. Malachi leaned over and set it upright. "We were trying to fulfill your orders to check Facebook. And I've called or spoken in person to all the individuals we sat with on Friday. All are accounted for and appear to be themselves." He gave me a weird look. "Ian Moseley asked how you were doing."

"Huh? It was his best friend who died."

"Yes, but he said . . . because of Nadia. Her suicide."

I fiddled with the zipper on my jacket. "Yeah. That was . . . nice of him, considering what he's been through today."

"Very nice," he said in a hard voice, drawing my eyes back to him. His hair was messy, and some of it was standing on end. His jeans were low on his hips and his T-shirt was fitted enough to make me look away.

I thought of what Tegan had said about Laney. "How many of the girls you called invited you over to comfort them?"

He cleared his throat. "I don't think—"

"Three," said Jim.

My gaze slid to Malachi's face. He was staring at Jim like he'd love a chance to rough him up in a dark alleyway.

"It's fine." I motioned for Malachi to move and sat down at the computer. Instead of getting his own chair, he stepped behind me, close enough so that I could feel the heat of him. I combined some research with a lesson in computer literacy for Henry and Jim. We checked YouTube—two more videos of the Animal Guy, except it was obviously two different Mazikin, with different body types and hair color. One was in the cemetery near the burned-out nest, but it had been taken before the fire. The newest video had been taken beneath a highway overpass near the waterfront.

"That's one of the homeless camps," I said, pointing to the tents in the background. "Henry, I think you were right about these being favorite spots for the Mazikin."

I got up and stretched. "Raphael left some equipment for me in the basement. I'm going to get the stuff ready before I have to get back to Diane's. We'll patrol tonight. Henry, you'll be with me."

Henry nodded and silently walked toward the stairs.

I glanced up at Malachi as I edged past him. "Like I said on the phone, you and Jim can go sniff around the emergency shelters."

His footsteps dogged mine as I hit the stairs to the basement. "What equipment did you request?"

I entered the training room to find a pile in the middle of the floor. "Henry and I are going undercover," I explained. "It's supposed to be a little warmer tonight, and that video showed that there are people staying in that camp. We're going to join them. I want to see if we can talk to a few people—and maybe be in the wrong place at the right time."

Malachi stared at the equipment on the floor, which closely resembled a mound of garbage. "You're hoping to get attacked."

"I'm hoping to grab one of them to interrogate." I picked up a checkered sleeping bag that smelled vaguely like canned dog food. "I figure if I layer up and cover my hair, they won't recognize me. And Henry already looks like a street person, so it'll be easy for him."

"Jim and I could set up a perimeter. I can keep watch—"

"You can go to those other places like I told you to," I said firmly. "There are only four of us, Malachi. We need to be in as many places as possible. We keep missing them, and it has to stop."

"Of course," he said, keeping his gaze focused on the equipment. "It was only a suggestion."

I dropped the sleeping bag and picked up a knit cap. Ignoring the smell of all the unwashed heads that had come before, I jammed it over my hair. "See? Don't I look like a vagrant?"

Malachi's lips twitched, which made my heart skip. "Hardly." He blinked and turned his back. "What weapons will you carry?"

"I don't know. Care to advise me?"

He straightened his shoulders. "Knives. You'll want to stay light and agile." He paced over to the pile of old clothes. "Choose your clothes, and put them on." He began to paw through them.

"Now? I have to get back to Diane's by six."

"That's enough time for us to outfit you and practice. Your plan may be to capture instead of kill, but surely you do not intend to enter enemy territory unprepared." He looked up at me and arched an eyebrow, his expression full of challenge.

"Wouldn't dream of it," I grumbled.

He tossed me a thermal shirt with heavily stained pits. "Tight on the bottom, loose over the top."

It took me several minutes to figure out my outfit, which ended up consisting of two sets of long thermal underwear beneath a pair of holey jeans, which Malachi made sure would stay up by fastening a belt around my waist, where he secured two horizontally sheathed knives. He kept chivalrously turning his back as I wiggled into the clothes, and patiently waiting until I gave the all clear to turn around and start helping me again. He strapped a holster around my shoulders and torso that held four more knives. When I protested that it was overkill, he leaned down and looked me in the eye. "Underestimating the danger is a mistake. Do not make this mistake."

"I'm afraid I'm going to end up stabbing myself."

He held up a thick blue-and-yellow flannel shirt, holding it for me like a jacket while I put it on. For a moment, I felt the brush of his chest against my shoulder blades. He was that close. *So* close. I took a step forward to keep myself from whirling around and wrapping my arms around him.

"Now," he said, "to avoid the self-stabbing issue." His hand skimmed up under my flannel shirt, and I gasped. He briskly unsheathed one of my knives and dragged it along his palm. No blood welled on his skin. "These are for practice," he explained, handing it back to me.

He made me draw the knives from the sheaths and strike out. Standing. Sitting. Squatting. Lying down. On my hands and knees. With my eyes closed. After spinning me around in circles to make me dizzy. With all the lights turned off. He made me erect the tent and lie inside while he attacked from the outside.

An hour later, the tent was destroyed. My flannel shirt was ripped. I had a swollen red spot on my cheekbone, courtesy of his elbow, and Malachi had a bump on his forehead, courtesy of my knee.

"One more time?" he invited. A drop of sweat fell from his chin.

"I have to go in a few minutes, but what the hell."

"Do you have a position you'd like to try?" he asked politely.

"From behind, maybe? I need more practice with that."

We stared at each other. Heat suffused my cheeks as I considered the double meaning of our conversation. Was Malachi aware of it, too? Did he care?

He didn't give me any hints. "Good choice," he finally said. "Remember, keep your arms close to your body. If they're out to your sides, that's an invitation for me to strip you of the weapon."

"I know," I said, turning my back to him. "But thanks for the reminder."

The space behind me filled with predatory silence. I closed my eyes, focusing on my hands, my aching muscles, the hairs on the back of my neck, which would warn me of his movement. I strained to hear him breathing, to picture his body behind mine, closing in. I wondered if he was watching me now, and what he was thinking.

And then I heard it, the tiniest *plop* of a drop of sweat on the mat that told me where he was—and that he was moving. I didn't wait for him to attack me. I attacked *him*. I whirled around, dropping low, and plowed into his legs, drawing a knife and sliding it along the backs of his knees, hard enough to have sliced his tendons if my blade had been sharpened. And he knew it, because he let himself fall backward, but he caught me by the shoulders and dragged me down with him.

My head bounced off the wall of his chest as he crashed

into the floor, nearly making me bite my tongue in half. I ripped my arm back and jammed the knife against his side, satisfied by the whoosh of his breath at the impact. He elbowed me hard in the shoulder, numbing my arm and hand. The knife fell from my grip, and he reached for it, but I elbowed him in the upper thigh. He twisted instinctively to protect his soft spots, which put the knife momentarily out of his reach. With my still-tingling right hand, I knocked that knife away from his scrabbling fingers and braced myself as I arched over him and drove my knee into the back of his raised leg, keeping him off balance.

My free left hand yanked a second knife from under my shirt as I threw myself on top of him. He grabbed my wrist with an iron grip and rolled with me, trying to pin me down. All I felt were his hard edges and my desperation to win. To prove to him that I could do this. That he didn't have to worry about protecting me, that we could be together even though—I pushed that stupid thought out of my head and kicked my legs out and over. There was no way I was going to allow him to get on top of me again.

As we twisted, I let him control my left hand and managed to draw a third knife with my right. The moment I felt gravity working for me, I shoved off with my foot and burst upward with all my strength.

Malachi's eyes were bright as his gaze darted down to

my hand, which now held a blade against his throat. "You've killed me," he whispered.

The deep rise and fall of his chest carried me like a wave. I stared into his eyes, completely caught, storm-tossed and disoriented. Before I could think about it, the knife had fallen from my hand and my fingers were sliding greedily along his neck, up to his jaw. His hands tightened around my elbows while his eyes fluttered shut. His chin lifted, exposing his throat, where his pulse beat heavy and hard, where his skin was soft and smooth and *waiting*. I wanted to close my mouth around that pulse. I wanted to feel it tick against my tongue. I wanted to taste his skin and hear him moan. But . . . what if that tilt of his chin was to avoid my touch? What if the *waiting* was for me to get the hell away from him and stop invading his space?

I rolled off him and stood up. "I think that's a first," I said, driving the tremble out of my voice with sheer volume.

Malachi didn't get up, nor did he open his eyes.

I chuckled and nudged his hip with my toe, desperate to wrench this moment back from the abyss of awkward into which it had fallen. But also, wanting him to *notice*. I'd beaten him. I wasn't helpless. He didn't have to worry about me or protect me. "Are you playing dead?"

"No," he said quietly. "I'm recovering." His body was sprawled out, one leg straight, one bent, his arms out to his sides, palms upward, fingers curled. His chin was still raised, his throat vulnerable.

I took a few steps back to keep myself from touching him again. "Not bad, right? You didn't let me win, did you?"

"No."

"So . . ." I bit my lip, hoping for some response. But he just lay there, completely still. "You gonna be okay down there?"

"Eventually." His lips were barely moving.

I shuffled my feet as the moment stretched, leaving me more confused with every passing second. "Want me to help you up?"

"Lela, just go. Please. I need you to leave now."

Every word hit me like a bullet. I'd done something right, but it was *still* wrong. I wanted to scream *Just punch me already!* I wanted to rewind, to be a different girl, one he would love, one he would reach for. But I couldn't fix it. I didn't even know what was *wrong*, not really. So I bit the inside of my cheek as my chest throbbed, stripped off the dull knives that decorated my body, and left my victim lying where he'd fallen.

FIFTEEN

HENRY AND I TROMPED into the camp around ten, after dropping off Malachi and Jim near one of the winter homeless shelters. We'd said our terse good-byes and good huntings, and I drove away, silently determined to prove myself to all of them—especially my Lieutenant. Now my head buzzed with a heavily caffeinated and highly explosive mixture of anticipation and anxiety.

Our boots crunched in the stiff, overgrown grass as we hiked off the sidewalk. We swung our stuff over a useless chain-link fence and wiggled through the ragged man-sized hole that had been cut through it. The traffic of I-95 roared above us, even at this time of night. It echoed in the chill, punctuated by gusts of wind that knifed right through my three layers of clothes. I'd straightened my hair and knotted it tight, and then pulled that thick woolen hat over it. Henry had a bright-red ski mask shoved up on his forehead, which made him look a little like a demented garden gnome. In addition to his own backpack, he'd insisted on carrying our tent, which Raphael had had to bring at the last minute to replace the one Malachi and I had killed.

"Heyheyhey," called a rough voice gouged away by what sounded like decades of heavy smoking, "get the fuck out." A head popped out of one of the bedraggled tents nestled behind a crumbling rock wall at the base of the overpass. The person climbed out of the tent, holding a baseball bat.

I held my hands up in the air, and Henry dropped the tent and did the same. "Looking for a safe place to bed down," Henry called. "My girl and I won't cause no trouble. We just need a place to sleep."

The individual with the baseball bat stepped into the light from a highway lamp far above us. He looked like an Eskimo, completely bundled up except for his eyes, nose, and mouth. He put the bat to his shoulder, his gloved fists tight around its base.

I stepped forward. This guy would back down easily; I could tell by the twitch of his eyes between me and Henry. He was scared. "Dude, we're not going to hurt you," I said as Henry edged up close next to me. He'd probably sensed the same fear in the guy. "And this isn't private property. We can be here same as you."

The guy let out a harsh, hoarse laugh. "Guess that's true, as long as you keep yourselves to yourselves. You heard about the attacks?"

"Yeah," said Henry. "We were at another camp when they came through the other night. Tried the shelters, but they won't let us stay together, so we came here." He put his arm around my shoulders, and I leaned against his wiry frame, trying to look romantically inclined.

The bundled guy pointed with the tip of his bat. "There's a good space over there by the water if you want it. Don't make too much noise, though. Harriet won't like it. She likes folks to keep it clean."

I muscled down a shudder. "Harriet?"

Bundled Guy grunted. "Ex-nun. She's got a bat, too."

Henry laughed. "We'll try not to offend Sister Harriet. And we got supplies we'll share." He pointed to our discarded backpack.

Bundled Guy's eyes shone softly. "We keep collective supplies over there. Thanks for that."

He left us alone while we set up camp on a rocky patch of gravel near the slap and splash of the bay just a few yards and a thin strip of grass away. When we got it up, we added our cans and a loaf of bread to the strange collection of supplies on a dirty white table set up under one of the lights. As we did, a few more people came out to introduce themselves.

There was one couple, Mike and Liz, who said they were just passing through, trying to get to Georgia from Maine. There was a skinny unemployed waitress who'd lost her home, and a guy who seriously resembled a walrus and said he did drywall. He was the only one without a tent, and had built himself a lean-to from corrugated metal and cardboard. He also reeked of booze and kept giving the waitress hungry looks until she fled back to her tent and zipped it up tight.

Two of the camp residents were kids, lanky teenage boys with loose, stretched-out cuffs on their sleeves and a hollow look in their eyes, making me wonder how many tricks they'd turned today and how recently they'd shot up their earnings. I thought of Nick and wondered if they knew him, if he'd shared a mattress or a needle with them. These boys, these *people*, were perfect targets for the Mazikin. No one would know or care if they were missing. Hell, they were *already* missing and no one cared. When they died, people would cluck their tongues and say what a waste it was. They wouldn't look too hard for a cause, for a killer. And if a Mazikin possessed them, no one would know the difference.

I sent Henry back to the tent and patrolled around the edge of the camp, getting a sense of its layout and where it would be most vulnerable to an attack. It would be difficult to hear the approach of footsteps because of the highway noise, and that was a major disadvantage. The tents nearest the water were likely to get hit first, seeing as the others were against a wall. The easiest escape was along the grass, which extended up into a park area, or back toward the neighborhood we'd just walked through. We'd parked about four blocks away in a neighborhood full of people who didn't raise their eyes from the sidewalk as they passed, but I knew they were watching us all the same. Not the safest place to leave a vehicle. Our Guard car was a twelve-year-old Taurus, though, and I doubted anyone would want to jack it.

Around midnight, I joined Henry in the tent, keeping the flashlight aimed at his feet and not his face. He was sitting there in the dark, casually fitting iron-tipped bolts to the long, narrow crossbow he'd assembled from a jumble of components he'd carried in his backpack. "I can't hear anything with this noise," he complained. "I *hate* this noise."

"I know. Me too. I need to go back out there to keep an eye out, but . . ." I hated to admit it, but I was freezing.

"Oh, I forgot," he said. He pulled a pair of heavy black gloves from his pack, and then chuckled as he handed them to me. "'Make sure you give these to the Captain,' he said to me." His imitation of Malachi's accent was hilariously bad. "'She will not remember them herself.'" He nodded at my bare, red-fingered hands clutching the flashlight. "Guess he was right."

I sat down heavily, set the flashlight between us, and took

the gloves from him. They were leather, lined with soft, thick fleece. I slid them over my hands and sighed. They fit perfectly. I wasn't sure what made me feel warmer—the gloves themselves or the fact that Malachi had thought about me being out here in the cold. I just wished he'd given them to me in person.

"Captain, have you talked to him about what happened? At the nest, I mean."

I peered at Henry, trying to read his expression in the mostly dark. "Not since the day it happened." *Right before he tore my heart out.*

Henry scratched at a spot on his neck. "Well . . . I think he took it kinda hard. I don't think he's sleeping well. He's up all hours after we get home from patrols, training in the basement. And when he does sleep . . ." He shook his head. "Maybe I shouldn't be telling you this."

I kept my expression neutral, even though my chest was aching fiercely. "It's my job to help him, Henry."

He nodded and gave me a cautious look. "I think he's been having nightmares, is all."

I wrapped my arms around my knees, curling into a ball around the hurt caused by Malachi's pain. "I'll try to talk to him." *Try* being the operative word.

Henry shrugged and pulled a musty blanket from his pack. "It's my turn to patrol."

"Where will you be?"

"Concealed spot with a clear shot at the path leading to this tent. How we used to do in the Wasteland." His brow creased like a memory had hit him sideways. "It wasn't ever safe, but we could protect each other."

"We?" I met his gaze. "You had a partner."

"I did," he said in a strained voice. "And we were good together. I didn't want to leave him."

The way he said it, the pain in his eyes . . . I could tell the partnership was more than professional. "Did you have a choice? To come here, I mean."

Henry bowed his head. "There's always a choice, I suppose, but it seemed like a chance I shouldn't turn down. When I'm done here, though, I'm going back for him."

"You want to go back to the Wasteland?"

"If I have to. I guess I hoped that doing good on this mission would give me some credit with the Judge, maybe enough to get Sascha out, even if it means I have to stay." He gave me a sheepish look. "That probably sounds dumb to you."

"Not at all. It makes total sense." I spoke past the lump in my throat. "Let's get this done so that you can find him again."

His flickering smile whispered his gratitude. He tugged his ski mask down over his face, tucked the crossbow against his body, and pulled the blanket around him like a cape. "You can rest. I won't be far."

I tucked the smelly sleeping bag around me, leaving it unzipped in case I needed to get out in a hurry. I switched off the flashlight and lay there in the dark, thinking about Henry. His situation reminded me of Ana and Takeshi, who had dared to fall in love in the dark city, and who had been separated tragically when Takeshi had been possessed by a Mazikin. Hopefully, Ana was in the Countryside now, and they'd found each other again, but I knew well enough now that giving one's heart to another Guard was just asking to have it crushed.

To get my mind back on track, I practiced drawing the knives from their sheaths and striking at an invisible attacker. This afternoon, I hadn't been wearing gloves, so it took me awhile to get used to the feel of my fingers being thicker and less sensitive, protected but not as nimble. As I worked, I couldn't help the little spark of pride as I thought about what I'd learned, and how fast I'd learned it.

I rolled over, wincing at the feel of gravel through our thin, moldy pad, still fingering the handles of the knives holstered against my body. I flinched at a distant sound, sudden and high. A shout? Or was that just more traffic noise? Before I figured it out, a hooting laugh only a few feet from the tent brought me out of the sleeping bag. I crouched low in the inky darkness, sniffing at the air, straining to hear anything but the white noise of traffic. A few seconds later, I heard it again.

And then someone screamed.

Suddenly, the camp was full of screeches and clangs and heavy thuds and ripping fabric. I shot out of the tent and into the night, knife in one hand and flashlight in the other, and was immediately tackled by a hissing ball of rags reeking of incense. I hit the ground, rolled, and kicked the thing toward the water. I shoved myself to my feet. The camp was a battleground, sheer chaos. Someone was shouting to call 911. Someone else was sobbing. I couldn't tell what the hell was going on because it was all bobbing flashlights and running, screaming people.

A figure on all fours ran into the beam of my flashlight and looked in my direction. It had white, scraggly hair, broad shoulders, and shockingly long arms. The Mazikin rose up on its feet and came toward me on bowed legs. It had a severe underbite, revealing chipped and broken bottom teeth. "Perfect!" it snarled, and then leaped at me.

I knocked its jagged fingernails away with my coat sleeve and bashed it across the face with my flashlight. Its head tilted to the side with the impact, but then it steadied itself with its thick legs. It lunged toward me with a low growl, and in that moment I realized how hard it was going to be to actually capture one of these things. I pivoted around and plunged the knife into its side, driving it through bone and muscle as an animalistic cry rolled from my throat. As the creature doubled over, its face met my waiting knee with a wet crunch. The Mazikin's eyes bugged out and a string of bloody saliva flew from its mouth as it fell to the ground.

Another Mazikin jumped on my back, making me gag with the stench. It bit my shoulder, but its teeth didn't penetrate all the layers of clothing. I bent over sharply, and it flew off my back and hit the gravel. Before it could get up, I landed on its chest with both my knees and cut its throat; then I scrambled up, grateful I'd dropped my flashlight and couldn't see what I'd done. Grateful I couldn't see the blood soaking my new gloves.

As I was turning to get my bearings, a shock of pain blasted my upper arm, and I couldn't hold the scream inside. White-red pinpricks glittered in front of my eyes as I fell to my side and used my legs to push my attacker away from me, straight into the light from the highway lamps.

"You can't have my camp," the bat-wielding, white-haired woman screeched. Sister Harriet to the rescue.

"I don't want your camp, lady!" I clutched at my left arm, which was pulsing with agony and felt like it had already swelled to the approximate size and weight of a baby hippo. I turned on my stomach and retched from the pain. "I'm trying to protect it!"

Gravel shrapnel hit the embankment over my head, and Harriet the nun let out a shriek and stumbled back, which kept her from swinging at me again. One of the street boys screamed in pain or fear, and he sounded so much like Nick that I actually called out his name. But my voice was only one among many, drowned in the chaos. Where was Henry? Had they already gotten him?

Through a haze of pain, I staggered to my feet and drew another knife, letting my broken left arm dangle uselessly at my side. I pointed the blade at Harriet, and the look on my face made her hug the bat to her chest. "If it smells like incense, hit it hard," I ordered, "and don't let them drag you away, no matter what."

Her face was as white as her hair. She nodded.

"Now get your back against a wall!" I did the same as I squinted into the darkness. Harriet pressed her stout little body to the concrete embankment behind us, and I scooted to give her a wider berth for fear of getting smacked upside the head. A movement in the grass and a low moan near the water drew my attention. Keeping my shoulder to the wall and Harriet at my back, I crept toward it.

Footsteps pounded and skidded in the darkness a few feet away, and I whirled around to meet the attack, adrenaline numbing my white-hot arm. Before it reached me, the oncoming Mazikin let out an airless yip and fell at my feet, a crossbow bolt protruding from the center of its back. Relief flowed through me. Henry was here. He was shooting in the dark.

And I couldn't argue with the results. Now if only we could corner one and take it alive.

Eager and unhinged laughter to my left drew my eyes back toward the waterfront. It was coming from the bundle of hair and rags that had tackled me when I first came from the tent. It was a woman, with a wild mass of dark curls tangled every which way around her. Her hair must have been at least two feet long, full of braids and beads and leaves and twigs. The light from the high moon revealed she was trying to drag the skinny waitress along the narrow patch of grass by the water.

"Hey there." I stepped out from the darkness of the overpass, shoving the pain from my arm into the deep recesses of my mind. "Let her go, and you can have me."

The waitress, whose neck was bleeding all over her pink flannel shirt, whimpered and struggled, but the small female Mazikin jerked her close.

"No, ella es perfecta," the thing snapped, her hair obscuring her face and making her seem more animal than human.

"She's kinda skinny," I commented, stalking closer. Behind me, Harriet grunted, and someone's growl turned into a shriek as the bat hit its mark. The female Mazikin's head shot up, looking toward the sound. I ran for her, hoping this would be a short fight. She dropped the waitress and stood up straight, revealing she was actually about as tall as I was. With long, broken fingernails, she clawed her hair away from her face and met my eyes.

I stopped dead, swaying in place, and stared at her.

She did the same. Her expression melted, from bared teeth to parted lips, from eyes full of fury to full of tears. "*Tú has crecido,*" she said, her voice trembling and high. She took a step closer to me and blinked, sending tears spilling down her face. "*Oh oh oh.* So . . . pretty."

I took a step back, stomach twisting, skull caving in, vision sparking. "No." I raised the knife. She flinched but kept moving, closing the distance between us with tiny, shuffling steps.

"*Mija,*" she crooned, reaching for me with those filthy, jagged nails grasping.

I couldn't move. I was paralyzed with pain from inside and out, making me see red and black and soft hands and curly hair and sad smile and golden-brown eyes now dull with someone else's soul.

"No, nononono," I babbled, stumbling back.

"*Lela,*" the Mazikin whispered.

"No!" I screamed, leaping at her. "You don't know me!"

I hit her hard, but I was desperate and off-balance. She shoved me to the side, and I crashed into the trunk of a tree, crying out as my broken arm caught my weight. The knife fell from my hands as my whole body spasmed with pain. Hunched over, I pivoted around to see her backing up quickly, looking behind her, toward her escape route.

She beckoned to me. "Come," she said. "*Come. Ven conmigo. Lela.*"

A gust of wind lifted her hair from her face again, revealing hollow cheeks, skin wrinkled and sagging, tired and used. But those golden-brown eyes . . . I knew them.

I saw them every day. Whenever I looked in the mirror.

Out of the corner of my eye, I saw another figure step onto the grass, lit up by the bright moon.

Henry raised his crossbow and took aim.

At my mother.

SIXTEEN

IT ALL HAPPENED SO fast, but it felt like forever. Set to an old movie in my head, memories dredged up from the well of time: She pressed a blue teddy bear to my chest and tucked a frayed blanket around me. She sang a song too raspy to make me sleep. She let tears fall down her face in the dark, and they landed hot on my cheeks and made me think it was raining.

I moved with instinct, all impulse and no thought, throwing myself in front of her. The Mazikin inside her watched with wide amber eyes, mouth open, hands flying up to shield herself. The bolt went through me like I was made of nothing, puncturing me like a balloon of skin. The ground caught me. In my sideways world, I watched her sprint away on two legs, and then pitch forward and dive into a four-legged gallop that carried her up a hill and out of sight.

I closed my eyes, drowning in the acid pain, inhaling sick lungfuls of it.

"Captain! Goddammit," Henry blurted as he reached me. "*Goddammit.*"

"I'm sorry," I said, my voice high and small. I sounded like a child.

"I had that Mazikin dead to rights. And now you're—" He let out a long string of curses.

"Are there any alive? Any we can take?" I let out a shivery breath, feeling sleepy and stupid. Half of me was on fire, but the other half was encased in ice.

"Are you crazy?" he shouted. "Forget taking a prisoner, Captain. I have to get you out of here before the police arrive!"

A siren split the night, jerking me into action. "Then get your bolts, Henry. And my knife—by the tree. Don't leave a single one. Finish any Mazikin that are wounded, but make sure by the smell before you cut. Go."

Henry disappeared from my side for what seemed like forever, leaving me in a sea of shock, surrounded by destruction. Then he was back. He leaned over me and folded my broken left arm over my stomach, wrenching a groan from between my clenched teeth. The crossbow bolt stuck out of my chest below my left shoulder. "Can you pull it out?" I gasped. I was certain all the pain would end if he pulled the arrow out. "Get it out. Please."

He didn't answer, just threw a blanket over me and scooped me from the ground, surprisingly strong for such a thin man. He clutched me close to his chest as he carried me away from the camp. In the distance the sirens wailed closer. Henry began to run, making me certain I was going to die with every step.

A million years later, a car door opened, and I was laid across the backseat of our Taurus, which smelled of animal crackers and juice. "Lean forward and keep still," commanded Henry, flipping me onto my side. "I'm strapping you down."

"Excellent," I mumbled as he coiled the seat belts around my body. "Call Malachi and—"

"Already have, Captain," he replied, making me wonder at what point along the way I'd blacked out, and leaving me hoping that I could do it again. Like, right now . . .

Strong, warm hands lifted me, and somehow, it didn't hurt, even though I was still at sea with no boat. "We have to remove the bolt," said Raphael. "I'm assuming you'd like to sleep through that part."

"Right you are," I answered, finding myself on my side again, this time on a bed. I turned my head and inhaled hopefully.

No. Not Malachi's bed. "Where is he?" I whispered before I could stop myself.

Raphael ran his blazing hands over my neck. "He is aware that you are injured and requested to be pulled from the field. Henry is leaving shortly to retrieve him."

"No. Tell Henry to call him. He and Jim should finish their patrol." I wanted him so badly, but if he was my Lieutenant and nothing else, that meant he shouldn't come running when I was injured. So I wouldn't ask him to.

Raphael gave me a questioning look, but nodded.

"I really messed up. Henry doesn't feel bad, does he?"

Raphael unbuckled my leather holster and slid it off my arm, pausing every few moments to allow me to catch my breath. "He is unhappy you got in the way of his bolt. He is happy it didn't kill you."

"Me too."

"He still wants to know why. He said it looked like you were protecting a Mazikin."

Her face flashed in my mind. Her eyes. My eyes. *Lela*, she said. *Ven conmigo.*

I sighed, exhaling shards of pain that cut me to ribbons from the inside out. *My mom*, I tried to say, but nothing came out. *Mom mommommommom.*

It capsized me. Thirteen years of buried longing crashed over my body, crushing me. All those years, all those wishes, those fantasies that she'd come get me, that she would *rescue* me. Only to find out that she was trapped in oblivion, a place I couldn't find on any map.

And now she was trapped somewhere else, just as unreachable.

Raphael bent over me, and from him flowed a golden sheet of light, radiating outward, spreading around us. *Wings.* Arching over me, shielding me while I cried and cried and cried, tossed by the waves in my mind. Within our shimmering shelter, he bowed his head and put his hand on my forehead.

"I'm sorry," I gasped. "I can't stop."

"Take as long as you need," he murmured. "I'll wait for you."

He sat motionless, eyes closed, anchoring me to *now* so that my memories couldn't trap me *then*. His golden wings covered us, glittering diamond-bright, so beautiful it hurt, until I cried myself dry. And when my last sob fell silent, the glow around us retreated, rolling back into his body and fading away. He opened his eyes and looked into mine. "I'm going to let you sleep now, because I have to heal your body."

I nodded, and he lifted the world from my shoulders.

My body was like a stranger's. A warrior's. Strong but scarred. My wet hair dripped rivers down my back as I let the towel fall to the ground and stared into the mirror. A starburst pink-silver scar marked my chest, hovering below my collarbone. My stomach was lined with Sil's claw marks, silver-white. My dead best friend's face was etched onto my forearm.

The marks of battle.

My skin was knitted together, smooth and decorated with scars that proved I'd fought back. And survived, unbroken. My mind was a different story. It was an open, tender wound, raw and throbbing, clamoring with the battle of *now* and *then*. I lifted my chin and glared into my own eyes, seeing nothing but her face. "The next time I see you," I whispered, "I'm going to kill you. I won't hesitate."

I turned away and finished getting ready for school. I'd awakened a few hours ago from Raphael's special brand of dreamless sleep, healed and well rested, at least on the outside. The Guard house was dark and silent. Malachi, Jim, and Henry were still in the field, and I slipped away in the night, too ashamed to see them.

Some Captain I was. They were better off without me.

Which is why I was so surprised when I found them parked outside Diane's house as I left for school. Jim hopped out of the passenger seat. Malachi sat in the back. His eyes slid over me for an electric second, but his gaze didn't reach my face before he turned away. Henry kept his eyes trained on the street in front of him.

"Captain," Jim said as he joined me on Diane's front steps. His hair was combed, and he'd shaved. He looked

like the all-American poster boy. His blue eyes skimmed up
and down my body. Not in a checking-me-out way, though.
More in an I-heard-you-were-mortally-wounded way.
When he was finished with his assessment, he squared his
shoulders. "I wanted to ask you something. Can I . . ." He
looked down at himself, and that was when I noticed he had
a backpack slung over his shoulder. "Can I go to school with
you?"

"Sure," I said, watching Henry pull away from the curb,
carrying Malachi away from me. "It's a good idea, since the
Mazikin may be after some of our classmates. What kind of
school were you in before you . . . you know." *Before you died.*

He frowned. "I've never been to a school."

"How come?" He'd never talked about the life he led
before he became a Guard. Neither had Henry, actually,
and I hadn't wanted to pry. But if he was going to join me
at school, I needed to know he wasn't going to cause more
trouble than he was worth. "Were you raised in a time when
there weren't schools or something?"

"No, I was raised in a *place* where there aren't schools."

"And where's that?"

He looked squarely at me. "I grew up in the Countryside."

My mouth dropped open. "Huh?"

Jim clutched the strap of his backpack. "What do you
think happens to those who die in childhood? Or as babies?"

"I never really thought about it," I said quietly. "You died . . . young, then?"

"I was pretty much born dead," he replied in a hollow voice. "I was alive for a few minutes, long enough to get a name, but that was it. And then I was raised in the Countryside with a bunch of other kids like me. They turn us loose when we reach maturity, and we stay . . . like this. Forever." He gestured at his body and then raised his head. "I can read. I bet I can keep up."

"Okay," I murmured, pushing back all the billions of questions I had about what he'd just told me. "We'd better go or we'll be late."

"The incident at the homeless camp is big news this morning," he explained as I backed out of the drive. "Only one survivor was found. A woman."

"How old?" I asked. Had Harriet made it out all right? Was it the waitress? Or maybe that woman who'd traveled with her boyfriend from Maine? Or a Mazikin?

"They didn't say. She's in critical condition, and the news said the police are hoping to question her about what happened today, since she's the only surviving witness."

"How many dead?" My heart hammered. My brain tumbled with calculations.

"Four. Henry said he got two with his crossbow. Not counting you, of course."

I stopped at a traffic light and sucked a quick breath

through my nose, absorbing the impact of Jim's little dig. "I killed two, I think."

"That's what he said. So no humans killed."

My hands tightened over the steering wheel. "Maybe. We don't know how many Mazikin were in that raiding party, and we don't know if they were able to drag any of the campers away."

"Which is what Malachi said."

I turned into the school parking lot. "And what else did he say?"

Jim gave me a sidelong glance. "Not much."

I pulled the keys from the ignition. My eyes drifted to the front of the school, where a huge pile of flowers, candles, and pictures marked the spot where Aden Matthews had been sacrificed in our private war. Ian and Greg trudged by it on their way in. Greg was talking a mile a minute while Ian's bloodshot eyes slid over the makeshift memorial. He looked like he'd been up all night, and I felt awful for him. I sighed. "Did you and Malachi find anything on patrol last night?"

Jim shifted in his seat. "Sort of. All of the shelters were full and wouldn't let us in. But at the one on Willard, we smelled them." He shrugged. "Actually, the Lieutenant smelled them."

"And?"

"He told me to cover the front door, climbed up a fire

escape, and broke in through a second-floor window."

At least he hadn't gone crashing through the lobby, knives out.

"He didn't find anything, though," Jim added. "We think the Mazikin were creeping around outside at some point last night, maybe looking for recruits."

I nodded. "They're building their numbers by possessing people no one will miss. No one's going to raise the alarm until their numbers are so huge that it's too late to stop them."

"Your classmate was different, though. He was missed."

I closed my eyes. "Yeah. He was a victim of opportunity. They grabbed him because he was chasing them, trying to expose them. And he turned out to be much more valuable than they anticipated, I'm sure."

Jim's eyes followed Tegan as she and Laney walked up to Aden's memorial, carrying a huge bouquet of flowers and a set of pom-poms. "They could try to do it again."

"They will. They'll be cautious because I'm sure they don't want to be caught any more than we do, but we have to keep an eye on everybody just in case. Do you have a cover story for being here?"

"Raphael got me some papers. He said I could use them if you gave me the okay. I'm a transfer from Bishop Mac-Donald Prep." His cheeks turned pink. "I was suspended for fighting and drinking on school grounds."

I chuckled. "Sometimes I think Raphael actually does have a sense of humor. No offense."

He rewarded me with a sheepish smile. "None taken." He pointed at Tegan. "Um . . . who's that? Did she know Aden?"

"Yeah, they dated for a while." I glanced at him and caught the look of interest on his face. "Hey. Don't get distracted, okay? Keep your focus on your *job*."

The eager glint in his eye dimmed but didn't quite die. "Yes, Captain."

I pushed my door open and raised my head to see Malachi staring at me from the front of the school, his face a blank mask. I tore my eyes from him and muttered, "None of us can afford to be distracted right now."

SEVENTEEN

MY FIRST FEW CLASSES passed in a blur. During lit class, I stared at the back of Malachi's neck without blinking. He didn't glance at me once. But as I headed for biology, his fingers closed hard around my arm and dragged me into the hallway next to the gym.

His face was in front of mine before I could protest. And it was no longer unreadable. His frustration showed in the firm set of his mouth. "Why?"

I didn't want to know what he was really asking, because then I'd have to really answer. Why hadn't I captured a Mazikin to interrogate? Why had I nearly gotten myself killed? Why had I kept him in the field instead of letting him come back? Why was I such a screwup? There didn't seem to be any safe ground between us. Every inch was laced with the mines of my mistakes and shortcomings. I fixed my eyes on his shoulder, on a tiny flaw in the stitching at his collar.

A group of guys walked by, throwing curious glances our way. I faked a smile. "We have to decide if we're going to pretend like we're together or not," I said. "I'll let you choose, but either way, I'd like to avoid drama that might distract from our mission." My voice was robotic; I was reciting lines from a script I'd practiced this morning as I got ready.

"I don't care about that." His palms were flat against the wall on either side of my head. His scent, the warmth of him, both drew me in and filled me with the desperate need to escape. "I want to know what happened last night, Captain," he said in a low voice. "Henry told me that you dove in front of an arrow to *protect* a Mazikin. I need to know why."

I gritted my teeth. If I talked about my mother now, I would fall apart completely. The raw, tender wound inside my heart would break open again and leave me spilled out and ruined right in the middle of the hallway.

"I need to focus on getting through the school day, and so do you," I snapped, staring at the now bulging tendon that joined his neck and shoulder. "I will brief you at the Guard house. *Later.* Now. Back. Off. *Lieutenant.*" The words shot from my mouth like bullets.

They hit their intended target. His hands fell away, and

he drew himself up to his full height. I wanted to suck my poisonous words back into my mouth. I wanted to throw myself across the minefield, hoping he would catch me and carry me the rest of the way. I almost believed he would. Until I saw the trembling clench of his fists.

"Yes, Captain." He backed away slowly. "And in answer to your original question: It will be easier if we do not pretend."

And then he walked away from me.

I set down my nearly empty tray and slid onto the bench next to Tegan, who was staring blankly at her plate of lettuce. "Hey," I said softly. "How are you?"

"Hanging in," she said. "They called me down to talk to Ketzler, so I got to skip lit. She thought I might be suicidal or something."

I glanced over at her. She wasn't wearing any makeup and looked like she might shatter. "Are you?"

Her gaze turned sharp. "Of course not. I just—" Her chin trembled, and her fingers scrabbled for her napkin.

A loaded tray landed on the table, and Jim lowered himself into the seat next to hers. He reached into his pocket and pulled out a little packet of tissues. "Need another one?" he asked softly, holding them out to her.

She sniffled and accepted his offering. "Thanks. Did you survive your first lit class without me? Sorry I got pulled out." She nudged him with her thin shoulder as she dabbed at her eyes.

"I barely made it," he said, keeping his voice light. "I think Mrs. Peterson's already decided I'm a lost cause."

Tegan let out a raspy laugh. "I can help you out there. She loves me. I won't abandon you again."

I looked at Jim over her bowed head, and he raised his eyebrows, a silent *What else did you expect from me?* I gave him a warning glare and turned my attention to my apple as Jim and Tegan talked about the afternoon classes they had together. Laney set her tray down across from mine. She was pale, as usual, but her eyes were bright. She didn't even say hi—she was too busy scanning the cafeteria. And I knew the moment she spotted her target, too, because her expression changed, becoming all gooey. She grinned and waved as Malachi seated himself at the end of the table. Laney and Tegan both zeroed in on the six feet and several open seats he'd put between us. Amazing how one little gesture gave everything away; how, with one simple decision about where to sit, he'd practically shouted that he was done with me to the entire student body.

Laney wore the tiniest of sly smiles as she slid her tray closer to his and sat down next to him. "Hey you," she said.

He rewarded her with a killer smile that ripped me open. "I was hoping to see you," he said to her. "Do you think you could help me with that web design assignment?"

Ian blocked my view of them a second later, thank God. With practiced movements, he pulled his milk and a bottle of juice off his tray, setting them down at ten and two around his plate. On autopilot, he sat down, and then paused for a moment, pulled from the everyday ritual. He looked over at Malachi and then at me, his eyebrows raised. I lowered my head and grabbed my apple, my stomach churning.

When Malachi and Laney started to make plans to go to the computer lab during their free period, my legs moved by themselves, carrying me out of the cafeteria, past Evan "Dirty Jeans" Crociere, who was handing a baggie to a pimpled stoner; past Greg leaning against the wall, texting it up on his shiny iPhone; past Jillian and Levi, sneaking in a make-out session behind the double doors; and out into the cool air in front of the school. I sucked it in, driving the scream down deep.

"Slow down, Lela, wait up," Ian shouted as he came through the doors, leaving them to crash shut.

I jolted to a stop, glancing with longing at my car. There was no way I could leave now. Nancy the probation officer would be after me in a second, accusing me of truancy or worse. Ian drew level with me. He clutched his juice in one hand and a sandwich in the other. Mayonnaise was smeared in the crease between his thumb and pointer finger. He held up the food and chuckled. "Want to have a picnic?"

It was such a lame invitation, but unless I wanted to go

back inside and watch Malachi flirt with Laney, I didn't have any other options. We trudged over to the low wall that separated shrubs from concrete and sat down, facing the Aden memorial. I rolled my apple in my hands. "How are you doing?"

He sighed. "I don't know."

"I'm sorry, Ian. I know it hurts."

He turned to me, his chestnut-brown hair falling over green eyes full of sadness he seemed too young to bear. Green eyes that reminded me a little of Nick's, that tugged at my heart. "I know you understand," he said. "You were close to Nadia."

I swallowed hard. "Yeah."

"Two of them within a month." He blinked and bowed his head. "What's going on?"

"I don't know. Nadia had issues for a long time. She tried to hide them from all of us, and finally she just couldn't deal with them anymore."

"Do you think it was that way with Aden? Do you think he'd been feeling this way for a while?" He cursed under his breath. "I was his best friend. I'm supposed to know that kind of thing, so I don't know why the hell I'm asking you."

He glanced down at his sandwich, cursed again, and tossed it into the garbage bin a few feet away. "Sorry," he muttered. "That was an asshole thing to say."

I twisted the stem off my apple. "No, it wasn't. You said

it because it's that confusing. Because it doesn't make sense."

"Yeah. He just—it's like he became this different person in the space of a few hours. He was clean. I know he was. I mean, he'd been drinking that night, but you know. Nothing serious. And then he runs off, and we find him at a freaking meth house? It's like he went crazy. But I never thought—I never even considered that he'd—" His gaze traveled up the wall of the school, to the place the Mazikin had jumped. "*Fuuuuck*," he said, his voice shaking.

At the edge of the memorial was a picture of Aden on the pitching mound. He looked like a teenage god—strong and flawless, one of the luckiest, the angel-kissed—destined for a perfect life. I hoped he was living that perfect life in the Countryside now, free of pain and worry and missing all that he'd had to leave behind.

"I don't think he was in his right mind," I said quietly. "I don't think he chose it."

"What are you talking about?"

I bit my lip. "I don't know, really." Though I did. And I wished I could explain because Ian was blinking tears away again. It didn't fit. He was one of the angel-kissed, too, lucky in so many ways he didn't even recognize. Rich. Loved. Good grades. Ace batting average. Pretty girlfriends. Nice car. But the look in his eyes was that of a confused and hurt little boy. "I just meant that *your* best friend, *that* Aden, didn't make the choice to kill himself. He wouldn't have.

Couldn't have. This isn't the same thing that happened to Nadia."

"You think so?"

I nodded.

"If that meth house hadn't already burned to the ground, I'd do it myself," he said. "I want to find the freaks who gave him whatever ruined him, and I want to kill them with my bare hands." A tear slipped from his cheek and landed on the sleeve of his shirt, and he swiped the backs of his hands across his face and turned his back to me. His shoulders started to shake.

Crap. Was it what I'd said? Hesitantly, ready for him to shrug me off, I reached out. My hand hovered close to his back, not knowing if it should land or circle a few times. Then he gulped in a deep breath, and my palm collided with his body. He relaxed, the knotted muscles of his back going loose under my touch.

"Thanks, Lela," he whispered.

I left my hand there, scared to keep touching him, scared to pull away, until the bell rang and yanked us back into the churning routine of our day.

The call to Ketzler's office came during sixth period. I guessed they'd already run through the cheerleaders and baseball players and were now hitting the third-stringers, the kids who weren't close to Aden but who were there when it happened. When the note arrived and the teacher nodded at me, I knew my turn had come.

Too much was happening. I still had the growing infestation to deal with, and that was my first priority. The Mazikin were attacking the most vulnerable people around, and they were building their numbers. They'd even gotten my mothe—no. I shoved the thought down and crushed it beneath my heels as I stalked toward Ketzler's lair.

The Mazikin were recruiting the homeless. On top of that, I was willing to bet they'd make a play for another one of my innocent classmates. Tegan. Ian. Greg. Someone who had been important to Aden. Important enough for Ibram to tell Sil about. Someone they could use to get to me and Malachi. I had to protect them. I couldn't live with myself if the Mazikin got any of them.

As if all that weren't enough . . . I couldn't figure out how to deal with Malachi. Or how to think about him. But he had been so right: letting emotion interfere was compromising the mission in multiple ways. I needed to let him go and look at him the same way I looked at Jim and Henry. A colleague. A fellow Guard. If only it were that easy.

"Oh, Lela," said the gray-haired secretary, giving me a tremulous smile. "They're waiting for you in there." She pointed to the little conference room next to Ketzler's office.

"I'm here to see Ketzler?" I said, thinking maybe she'd made a mistake. The conference room was where they cornered students. Confronted them and ganged up on them. It had happened to me a few times. Nancy had done it once or twice, teaming up with Ketzler to let me know they "all worked as a team" and were "here to support me." Translation: Ketzler would tattle if I put even a toe out of line, and Nancy would see I got court-ordered back to the RITS.

The secretary nodded. "She's in there, honey. Your foster mother's here, too."

What the heck? My dread mounting, I crossed the room. The door swung open before I got my hand on the knob. Ms. Ketzler, mascara-free today, greeted me with a softly serious expression on her face, like I was about to be executed and she felt kinda sorry for me. I craned my neck and saw Diane, who looked the same way.

"Diane," I said as I walked into the room, my heart thumping heavily. "What's up?"

My eyes scanned the room. My child welfare social worker, Jen Pierce, was sitting in the corner with a thick file in her hands. Nancy wasn't there. A horrible thought occurred to me, one I'd never considered before now. *Oh God oh God.* My lungs stopped working. I sank into the nearest chair, staring at the pained look on Diane's face. "You're giving me up, aren't you? You're ten-daying me."

It had happened to me so many times before. But I'd started to believe it wouldn't happen with Diane, that her house was where I belonged. I should have been prepared for this, though.

It was easy to give me up.

It wouldn't even be the first time this week that it had happened.

After a moment where everyone seemed frozen in place, Diane got up so fast her chair tipped over. She made it across the room quickly, and her arms were around me in the next second. For once, I welcomed them. "No way, baby. How could you think that?" she asked fiercely as I came undone, the pressure and sorrow bubbling up and leaking around my welded defenses.

My hands shook as she clutched at them. She tilted my chin up and looked down at me. "You're mine as long as you want to be. That's not what this is about. I'm so sorry you thought it was."

I blinked up at her, still absorbing the moment. She'd said I was hers. "Okay," I said stupidly.

My social worker righted Diane's chair. The thick folder sat on the tabletop. Ketzler set a box of tissues on the table. Diane withdrew her arms and took a seat next to me.

Jen put her hand on the folder. "Lela, you've been in substitute care for a long time, I know. You've been in a lot of different placements. We wanted permanency for you a long time ago, but things never quite worked out . . ."

Her eyes darted up to Ketzler's, and the counselor's hand closed over my shoulder. I clenched my teeth and slowly leaned away. She didn't take the hint.

Jen cleared her throat. "Anyway, I know you've been through a lot, and that you have stability here with Diane. You've become one of our success stories. We don't want to mess that up."

I glanced over at Diane. "Me neither." If Diane wasn't giving me up, were they taking me away from her?

Jen fiddled with her watch long enough for me to want to reach across the table and rip it off her. Her eyes lingered on the folder again, a catalog of all the places I'd been, all the things that had happened to me. All the things she had *allowed* to happen to me. Maybe that was why she looked so stricken.

"Come on, Jen, you're killing me. What's going on?"

Finally, she met my eyes. "Your mother came to my office today. She's filed a request to see you."

EIGHTEEN

THE MAZIKIN WANTED TO talk. And they were going to use the body of my mother as their mouthpiece. That well of pain at the core of me turned cold, a column of ice along my spine.

Jen squinted at me. "Are you all right?"

Ketzler dove for the tissues and waved them beneath my chin. I looked up at her with dry eyes, and she cradled the box against her chest like she was personally offended by my rejection of them. Or convinced I was an emotionless psychopath. Diane's warm hand closed around mine, which was chilled to the bone.

"Yeah," I heard myself saying. "I should see her."

Jen's mouth dropped open. "Lela, just so you know, you

don't have to. You have every right to refuse. Rita Santos's parental rights were terminated years ago, but we were legally obligated to let you know she'd made the request."

And the Mazikin would have known that, because by taking over her body they had gained access to all my mother's memories. They probably wouldn't have cared about her past—until she recognized me last night. Until Rita Santos's memories betrayed her own lost daughter. Now they knew they had something important, and they were going to try to use her against me.

I wouldn't allow that to happen. I smiled at Jen. "I know, and I'm glad you told me. I want to see her."

Diane squeezed my hand, but her eyes were locked on Jen's. "Was Rita . . . all right?" She knew that my mom had been diagnosed long ago with schizophrenia.

I held myself back from replying. No, Rita Santos definitely wasn't all right. She was trapped in the Mazikin realm—*a place of fire and death*—and I couldn't get to her. I couldn't do anything for her except try to liberate her soul by cutting the throat of the Mazikin occupying her body. *Probably I shouldn't do that during our first visit, though.*

Jen grimaced. "Well, you know she has profound mental health issues, and that doesn't seem to have changed. Lela, I don't know if you remember her—"

I didn't want to talk about this. It was irrelevant anyway, because the person who wanted to visit me wasn't my

mother. My mother, when she was alive, had never asked
to visit me, as far as I knew. She'd never come for me. She
hadn't shown up to any of the planned visits. And finally,
she'd just disappeared. Into oblivion.

"I remember enough," I said. "And I'd like to plan the
visit with her."

I looked over at Diane. "It's okay," I reassured her,
because she looked almost as worried as when Nadia died.
"You know what they say: Closure is healthy."

After fleeing from Ketzler and saying good-bye to Diane, I
endured the rest of my classes. I'd just reached my car when
I heard panting behind me. Ian jogged toward me, his backpack over one shoulder and his tanned cheeks ruddy. "I feel
like I'm making a habit of running after you," he called out.

I tossed my backpack into my front seat, and then kept
the car door between us like a shield. "I'm not that hard to
catch." As soon as the words were out of my mouth, I realized how bad they sounded. "I mean—"

He laughed. "I know what you meant. But yeah, you are."
He'd stopped running, but his cheeks were still ruddy, and
now the red was creeping toward his neck. He bowed his
head. "I just wanted to . . . um."

"Are you all right?"

He nodded. "Are you?"

I frowned. "Sure. I mean, I'm sad like everyone else." *And overwhelmed and wrecked and worried and feeling like the weight of the world is crushing me.*

"No, I mean—about Malachi?"

"Oh." My throat tightened.

"So I guess you guys aren't together."

"I'd only known him a few days. It's not like it was a big deal." Every word was a lie.

Ian nodded. "But it seemed like you liked each other. A lot."

I let out a humph. "Yeah. Well. That craziness is over."

"And what about that blond guy you were with last Friday? I saw him in the cafeteria earlier." He gave me a cautious look. "He seemed kind of into Tegan."

I rolled my eyes. "Don't worry about it. I'm good. I just want things to get back to normal."

He tilted his head to the side. "Normal?"

"What—I'm normal. Sort of." Boy, I was full of lies today.

His mouth curled at one corner, like he was biting the inside of his cheek, but then he said, "You've been at this school for over a year and haven't gone out with a single guy. Not even once. Is that the normal you're referring to?"

"I go out," I protested. Not really. I had followed Nadia to parties and driven her home.

He raised his hands in surrender. "Okay. I didn't mean to give you a hard time about it. I was just—thought maybe you might want to hang out sometime?"

All the blood in my head drained to my feet. Ian Moseley, jock extraordinaire, wanted to *hang out*. I looked up at him, and his lips twisted up into this rueful half smile. Only one dimple showing.

"Hey, I didn't want to make it a big deal," he said. "With everything that's going on, I thought . . ." He scratched at his chin and let out a quiet laugh. "I don't know what I was thinking, actually. You just seem cool. Bullshit-free, if that makes sense."

I rubbed my clammy hands on my jeans. "I guess it does."

If I got to know him better, I could make sure he was protected from the Mazikin, who would almost certainly come after him. Young guy. Strong. With resources. Embedded deeply in Aden's memories. The Mazikin probably knew *all* about Ian.

I smiled at him. "And yeah, we can hang out. I'd like that." And this time, I realized, I *wasn't* lying.

We exchanged numbers but didn't make any plans. I told him I would be at the wake and the funeral, and he gave me a brave smile and said he'd see me there.

I drove to the Guard house in a fog. The sleep deprivation was catching up with me. I couldn't go on like this forever, and neither could the other Guards. We were all human, after all, and our bodies were frail. None of us would be able to make good decisions or fight well if we tried to subsist on two hours of sleep a night. The only time

I got any rest these days was when Raphael put me under so that he could heal me.

I didn't bother knocking when I got to the Guard house, just walked in, only to find all three of them waiting for me in the entryway, their arms crossed over their chests. I laughed. "Hey guys. Is this an intervention? Do you have a therapist tucked away in the corner?"

Identical looks of puzzlement crossed their very different facial features. "You said you would brief us," Malachi said solemnly.

Henry's eyes were locked on my boots as he spoke. "I wanted to give you a chance to explain yourself before I took my concerns elsewhere."

I stalked into the parlor and sat down. "You mean before you call Raphael in here. What do you think he's going to do? Demote me? At this moment, Henry, that sounds fucking awesome."

Henry took a seat across from me. "Last night. You were *talking* to the wild-haired Mazikin. It didn't look like you were trying to capture her."

"Sorry, my arm was kind of shattered at the time," I snapped.

"Which was why I shot at her," growled Henry. "I was trying to protect you."

I looked away from him, and my gaze landed on Jim, who was still in the entryway, watching us warily. "See, Jim?" I called. "I'm a screwup, too. We should start a club."

He gave me a small smile but said nothing. Henry glanced at Malachi and then leaned forward, recapturing my attention. "This isn't funny, Captain. We need to know why you jumped in front of my bolt to save that Mazikin." His expression changed, like a mask falling away, and in that instant, he allowed me to see the true effect of whatever horror and tragedy he carried inside his head. "I could have *killed* you. Do you know what that would have been like for me?"

"I understand," I said calmly, determined not to take this out on him and make his suffering worse. I got to my feet, needing to move. "You don't know me, Henry. So I get why you might be confused, why you might think I'd protect the creatures we've come here to exterminate." I glared at Malachi. "But you know me better than that."

Malachi didn't flinch. "Did you think she was human? Because then—"

I shook my head. "I knew she was a Mazikin."

His dark eyes bored into mine. "You could have told Henry to stand down."

"There wasn't time. Henry can verify that."

Malachi rubbed the back of his neck. "Then you could have captured a different one. Unless perhaps you thought this Mazikin had special knowledge about Sil and his plans?"

"No. I had no reason to believe the female Mazikin had

special knowledge of their strategy." In fact, I'd had every reason to believe she had special knowledge about *me*, and still I'd risked my life to keep her alive.

Malachi's fists clenched. "You took an arrow to the *chest* for this creature, Lela! And I don't—" He stopped short, some realization dawning, and swept the other Guards with an authoritative glance. "I will talk to the Captain alone."

Jim shrugged. "Fine with me. I've got homework." He turned and walked up the stairs.

Henry stood up slowly, looking me over. I could tell that whatever fragile trust he'd had in me was shattered the moment I'd forced him to shoot me, and it would take a while to rebuild, if that was even possible. But it was clear by the way he looked at Malachi that he trusted *him*. After a few seconds, he turned on his heel and headed for the basement.

"Why didn't you just tell us you knew her?" Malachi asked quietly as soon as the basement door clicked shut. He closed the distance between us slowly. "That's it, isn't it?"

Of course he'd figured it out. I shouldn't have expected anything different. "I didn't want to talk about it. I *still* don't want to talk about it." I crumpled onto the couch and bowed my head, letting my hair fall around my face as my misery finally bubbled up to drown me. "In fact, I almost wish that bolt had hit me a few inches to the right. Then you wouldn't have to deal with me, and I wouldn't have to deal with this."

Malachi sank to his knees in front of me like someone had punched the air out of his lungs. "Don't say that, Lela," he whispered. His hands moved forward, reaching for me. I jerked backward and slid sideways along the couch, away from him. I couldn't take him halfway. I had to have it all—or nothing. "Don't touch me. You're the one who wanted distance."

My boots hit the floor, and I was up. Rage singed me on the inside, turning all my edges black and brittle. With my fists balled up tight against my sides, I whipped around, ready to loose some of my fury on him—because the alternative was to collapse on the floor and cry, and I wasn't sure I'd be able to stop once it started.

Malachi was still on his knees in front of the couch, his head bowed, like he was comforting the ghost of me.

I spoke to his back, hurling words like knives. "I'll tell you the deal, and then you can decide if you'd like to request my removal as your Captain. Are you ready for this? Because the irony here is beautiful. That Mazikin was my *mother*."

Malachi raised his head.

"Yeah. You see now. My mom must have been living on the streets. And they got her." It was so much easier to do this when I couldn't see his eyes, when I didn't have to deal with what they might reflect. "Think how you would feel if you hadn't seen your mother since you were a small child. If you were too young when she left you, too young to remember her face, too young to remember if she really cared for you. But when she shows up, when she looks at you with your own eyes, it all comes back. The way she sang to you and loved you once, before she couldn't do it anymore. All of those memories, buried deep in your head. For years. Waiting to ambush you."

My fingers had crept into my hair and were tugging at it. My voice had thinned, small and high again, the voice of me from a long time ago. "I wish I could rip those images from my mind. I wish I could dig them out. For years, I assumed I didn't have them. That would have been so much easier. But when she was right there in front of me, all of a sudden, so were all those memories. All at once. When Henry took aim at her, I didn't think about it. I acted."

Malachi stood up slowly, but did not turn around.

"Yes!" I shouted, anticipating what he might say before he had a chance to open his mouth. "I know what you believe! I know you think I missed my chance to liberate my mother's soul, all because I protected her body! I get it now. I see how hard it is to kill a Mazikin when it's wearing the skin of a person you care about. I *get* it. You must love that."

"Of course I don't," he said, so softly I almost missed it.

I tore my fingers through my hair and headed for the door. "Now they're using her to get to us. They've set up a meeting, using the pretense that my long-lost mother wants to see me again. You're coming with me. To translate. See,

I can't even understand what she says." Bitterness broke my voice, leaving it hoarse. "I assume you can, though. You couldn't have spent all those years with Ana without learning some Spanish."

"You're right," he said, finally turning to me, his eyes ebony pools of sorrow. I almost screamed at him to stop looking at me that way. It wasn't fair, and I needed to get away before I made a fool of myself by collapsing into his arms and begging him to never let me go.

I groped for the doorknob, desperate for my escape. "I'll let you know when it's all set up. It should be great fun." I welcomed the cool air on my burning skin as I swung the door open. "I'll be back tonight. We have less than a week before the city's emergency shelters close for the season. We need to locate the new Mazikin nest, and Sil in particular, before they start picking off those folks—as well as our friends—one by one. So study your maps, and tell the others to get ready. We'll be patrolling heavily, but probably in shifts from now on. The objective is still to find a Mazikin and track it back to the nest or capture one and force it to tell us where they are. Does that sound like an acceptable plan to you?"

His eyes lingered on my face, and he opened his mouth to say something. But then he swallowed whatever it was and drew himself up straight. "Yes, Captain."

NINETEEN

WE DIDN'T FIND THE nest by the end of the week, but not for lack of trying. I mapped out routes, including all four of the shelters, to be patrolled by two Guards each night. The third Guard on duty was assigned to monitor Facebook and connect with our friends in an effort to keep tabs and make sure they weren't doing anything crazy. The fourth Guard on the rotating schedule was under strict orders to rest. I designed the schedule so that the guys would have every third night off, with the instruction that they use that time to get at least eight hours of sleep. I . . . did not give myself the same kind of break. I couldn't.

I could barely sleep at all.

Every time I closed my eyes, I saw her beckoning to me.

Ven conmigo, she whispered. *Come.*

I couldn't figure out why she'd said it. Had that been the Mazikin speaking, trying to capture me, or had she said it because, deep inside her, my mother's memories were so strong that the Mazikin *felt* something for me? I didn't know what I wanted the answer to be, but the question dogged me.

The woman hospitalized after the Mazikin attack on the camp died a few days after the incident, never having regained consciousness. She was identified as Marie Clement, a thirty-nine-year-old unemployed waitress from West Warwick. Cause of death was still being determined, but I knew how it had happened. The Mazikin inside my mother had bitten her, and the venom had paralyzed and slowly killed her.

Her death fueled the enthusiasm of the media. The death of one homeless person might not get much attention, but at this point several had been found dead in local parks, and now five people had been slaughtered in a single night. Rumors about how they died were swirling. Homeless advocates were up in arms, demanding justice. It was becoming more difficult to stay under the radar for Guards and Mazikin alike.

I was a Guard and nothing else. I ate mechanically. Did minimal homework on autopilot, enough to keep out of trouble. Stared my way through classes while my brain whirled with patrol strategies and what-ifs. I trained with the other Guards for hours every day after school, turning off all my emotions and facing Malachi down on the mat with fists and knives. He kicked my ass repeatedly, and sometimes I think he enjoyed it a little. I know I did. I needed a place to vent my frustration, and that was it. I couldn't blame him if he did the same thing.

On Friday, the day after Aden's funeral, I arrived at school to find Malachi sitting on the half wall at the front entrance. As soon as I pulled into a spot, he was up and walking toward me. I groaned and leaned my head back against the seat. He knocked on the window.

"Good morning," he said briskly when I opened the door. "I take it your patrol was quiet."

I nodded, savoring the bitterness. "Jim and I caught a scent outside the Broad Street shelter, but we couldn't trace it. I feel like we're so close, but we're missing something. Maybe tonight we'll catch a break."

"All our friends here are accounted for. Greg has decided he would like to be my new best friend and wants to 'party.' Other than that, no unusual activity last night."

"Good. And tonight you're off."

"No, Captain." He leaned down. "Lela, I think you're punishing yourself with this schedule."

"Punishing myself? Look who's talking," I snapped. "I

hear you're up at all hours, training when you should be resting."

Malachi's expression hardened. "What I do with my time off is none of your concern. I'm following your orders. I'm doing my job."

Again, it would have been less painful if he'd punched me. "I never said you weren't," I muttered hoarsely.

He stepped around the door and squatted in front of me. "Take tonight off. Rest. I'll take your place. We need our Captain to have a clear head. You've earned Jim's trust, and you're just starting to regain Henry's after what happened on Monday—do not let them down."

His eyes showed his concern . . . and nothing else. This was how he would have talked to Ana or Takeshi, his Captain from long ago. I should have been happy that his feelings for me weren't interfering, but it hurt like hell.

"All right. I'll take it under advisement. But the shelters close tonight—"

He shook his head. "We checked this morning. Because of the outcry over the attacks, the city announced that the shelters will remain open through the weekend while they try to solve the crime."

I sighed. "Fine. I'll take tonight off."

"Excellent decision, Captain. I will see you in Pre-Calculus." Malachi stood up, shouldered his backpack, and

walked away, looking unfairly amazing in the morning sun-
light. Laney came skipping up to him, wearing a skirt so
short it had to be in violation of the dress code. Together,
they walked into the school. I jammed my keys in the ignition, ready to attempt escape.

But Diane, Jen, Ketzler, and Nancy the evil probation
officer had all been hovering the past few days. I had to show
up for school. If I showed any signs of "emotional distress,"
as Ketzler had called it, they might cancel my visit with my
mom, which was scheduled for Monday. I ripped my keys
out of the ignition and shoved them in my backpack.

By lunchtime, I had drawn up a new plan to make the
most of the extra days we'd been given, listing new places
to patrol, new neighborhoods to cover. I also wanted to cul-
tivate a few contacts within the homeless community, just
to see what we could find. Feeling a little more energized, I
headed to lunch.

Tegan and Jim were already at the table. Over the past
few days, he'd been glued to her side during school hours. I
was still worried about him losing his focus, but he'd been
totally sober and completely professional as a Guard every
night, so whatever he had going on with her was either helping him . . . or motivating him. Plus, Tegan looked better
than she had a few days ago, and I was relieved that she was
turning to someone other than me for support.

"We're changing the theme," I heard her say to him. "It

was *Tangled in the Stars*, but in honor of Aden and Nadia, it's going to be *Memories and Moments*. Laney and I thought it was important to make them part of it."

I was pretty sure Jim had no idea what she was talking about, but he nodded along while he stared at her mouth. I set my tray down and elbowed him hard in the side.

"I guess they didn't have proms at Bishop MacDonald?" I commented.

Tegan laughed. "Poor boy. No girls! This must be a nice change of speed for you."

Jim grinned. "You have no idea."

Jillian set her tray down and smiled over her shoulder at Levi, who was laughing with Ian about something as they piled their trays with bread and pasta. "Oh! Is that the new poster? I'm surprised it came so fast."

Tegan held the glossy paper up for her to see. "Yeah, they were really nice about letting us change the theme so late in the year. They're going to rush the order as soon as we okay this sample."

Ian dropped into the seat next to mine and glanced at the poster she was now waving in his direction. "Shiny."

Tegan scowled. "You have zero appreciation for art, Ian Moseley."

Malachi and Laney arrived as Levi squeezed himself next to Jillian and kissed her cheek. "It looks great," he said, but he was looking at her, not the poster. "Greg reserved a stretch SUV yesterday. He knows a guy and got us a huge discount. Anyway, we're all set."

Laney smiled up at Malachi and scooted closer as he sat down. "Do you know what prom is?" she asked him.

"No," he answered, looking over at the poster.

I turned toward Ian, in dire need of distraction. "You have a game this afternoon, right?"

He set his milk and orange juice at ten and two. "Yeah. First one without Aden." His voice was sad. "We haven't practiced all week, either, what with the wake and funeral."

"You're worried."

He nodded. "Greg is good on the mound, but the Veterans team has a lot of good hitters this year." He pushed his messy hair out of his eyes. "I don't really even want to play," he said quietly. "It won't be the same without Aden in the dugout. But I want to win. For him." He fiddled nervously with his milk carton. "Hey, can you come?"

My mouth dropped open to refuse, but then I remembered Malachi had insisted I take the night off. Maybe I'd take the afternoon off, too. "Yeah. I'll try."

His dimples were really kind of stunning. "Awesome. Maybe we can meet up after the game?"

I turned my head to see Malachi staring at me while Laney yapped on about tuxes and after-parties. She laid her hand on his arm, and that made my decision for me.

"I'm free," I said to Ian, savagely hoping that my next words hit my Lieutenant like an elbow to the gut. "And I'd love to."

After a terse meeting with Malachi and Henry in the parking lot after school to go over the new patrol routes, I headed for the baseball field. If not for Malachi's insistence that I take a night off, I'd be on the streets tonight, hunting the Mazikin. It was where I was supposed to be. But then I reminded myself that the Mazikin knew exactly where to find me, and where to find my classmates, and that being here might be just as important.

I sat in the stands with Tegan, Jillian, and Laney, scanning for threats or suspicious characters, following their cues for when to cheer and keep silent. I'd been to plenty of games with Nadia last year, because she'd been dating Greg at the time. Sitting on the hard metal benches as the chilly breeze tied my hair in knots made me miss her so much it hurt.

Tegan had her slender fingers wrapped around a hot chocolate. She got me one, too, and handed it over with a calculating look. She leaned around me. "Hey, Laney. Did he say yes?"

Laney gave me a sour glance before she answered. "He said he'd think about it, not that it's any of your business. I think he had to ask his host father."

Oh, God. Laney had asked Malachi to prom. I took a quick gulp of hot chocolate and winced as it burned my tongue and seared its way down my throat.

Tegan giggled as she looked down at her Styrofoam cup. "Did you get him to come out with you tonight?"

Laney sniffed. "He studies really hard. And I think he has some sort of after-school job."

Tegan looked at me out of the corner of her eye. "On a Friday night?"

I hadn't been happy that Malachi would be out patrolling tonight; he hadn't had a night off since Tuesday, and I suspected he hadn't sleaped that night, either. He was incredibly strong, but he was also human. I'd been worried about him, just like I always was when he went out in search of Mazikin. But suddenly I was glad, because it meant he wouldn't be with her. Still, I spent the next five innings picturing him taking Laney in his arms. Kissing her like he'd kissed me. I couldn't shake the urge to snap Laney's skinny arms like twigs.

The Warwick High School Quahogs, only a week ago favorites to take State, lost the game in spectacular fashion, 1–9. Which particularly sucked, since they were dedicating the rest of their season to Aden. Ian hit a home run in the second inning and doubled in the fourth but was left stranded. His face was grim as he and the rest of the team jogged back to the field house.

Tegan drew her coat tightly around her. "Poor Ian," she murmured. "How's he doing?"

I looked up to realize she was talking to me. "Um. Okay, I guess? I'm meeting up with him now."

She gave me the oddest look. "Be gentle, Lela."

I frowned. "Gentle?"

"Don't break his heart! You know Ian's liked you for a long time, right?"

I studied her face, trying to read whether this was a joke. It was hard to tell with Tegan.

She nudged me from behind as we edged along the bleachers toward the concrete steps. "You never looked at any of them, but that doesn't mean they weren't looking at you," she said quietly.

She left me with those words, which bred in my head and multiplied, spreading a thick layer of freak-out over the inside of my skull. I didn't want to hurt Ian. I just wanted . . . to get away. To not have to deal with my life for a few hours. Which was completely selfish because the Mazikin were out there, preying on people. By the time I reached the entrance to the field house to wait for Ian, I'd convinced myself I shouldn't be there. I called Jim.

"Hey, Lela," he said when he answered. "Henry and Malachi just left for the night. They're going to hit those spots you listed."

"Actually, I was thinking of going, too, and—"

He chuckled. "And I'm supposed to tell you to go home and get some rest."

"Huh?"

"The Lieutenant's about six steps ahead of you on this one, Captain. Take a night off, Lela. Things have been quiet."

I gripped the phone hard. "Fine. What are you up to?"

"Tegan called me. She's having a thing tonight at her house. People getting together to share their memories of Aden and the other girl who killed herself."

Jim's job tonight was to monitor and guard our friends. That usually meant phone and Facebook, but today was Friday. "Her name was Nadia," I said. "I might see you there. I'm waiting for Ian."

Jim grunted. "All right. Malachi's not going to be happy. He wanted you to get some sleep."

"It's none of his concern," I said, mimicking Malachi's cold words from earlier. "He needs to focus on patrolling the East Side and making sure no one gets dragged away. Let's leave him to it, okay?"

"Far be it from me to interfere."

"Thanks. And Jim? No drinking. No . . . doing other things. Remember what we talked about."

"Sure, Captain."

Ian came out of the field house carrying a long duffel

bag. His hair was wet from the shower, and he'd changed into jeans and a long-sleeved sweater that was snug across his chest and shoulders.

"Hey," he greeted, his face brightening with his dimpled smile.

I clicked my phone off without saying good-bye to Jim, my mouth suddenly a little too dry as I processed what Tegan had said about Ian. "Hi. I assume we're going to Tegan's?"

He looked down at his feet. "Would you mind if we didn't?"

If we went to Tegan's, I could help Jim guard the others. If we went somewhere else, all I'd have to do was guard Ian, although, looking up at all six feet four inches of him, it didn't really look like he needed it. If we were alone, I might have to worry more about guarding myself.

"Um." I cleared my throat. "What else did you want to do?"

Without raising his head, he said, "Movie? I just . . . don't want to think about anything. I want to do something fun."

He'd echoed my wishes exactly. I didn't want to be a friend in mourning. I didn't want to be a Guard. I wanted to be a girl. A normal girl. One who went to movies and ate popcorn and didn't kill people. For just one night.

"Sounds good," I whispered.

He drove us to the mall, where we stuffed ourselves with burgers and fries. It turned out he was going to URI, too, and so we chatted about majors and classes and base-ball and photography. We didn't talk about Aden or Nadia. We didn't talk about Malachi. I didn't have to think about death or killing or saving the world.

It felt awesome.

He drove us to the movie theater, and we chose a comedy. I was thankful he didn't want to watch the latest zombies-taking-over-the-world thriller, which hit a little too close to home. He insisted on paying for our tickets and bought us a bucket of popcorn. I laughed as he handed it to me. "You're not still hungry, are you?"

He grinned. "Are you kidding? I'm always hungry. I also eat when I'm nervous."

"Are you nervous?"

He gave me a look that said I should be able to figure it out. "Come on. I love the previews."

We were the first people in the theater and had our pick of seats. We settled in, my stomach knotting. I was alone. In the dark. With a guy who was not Malachi.

I grabbed a handful of popcorn and shoved it in my mouth.

Ian chuckled. "Do you eat when you're nervous, too?" he whispered, his eyes full of mischief.

People trickled steadily into the theater, which cut the tension a little. We even recognized a few of them. "I hope you're ready for the gossip on Facebook," I muttered, watching Caroline from my lit class, tap-tap-tapping away on her phone as she shot us curious glances every few seconds.

"Are you embarrassed to be seen with me?" he asked, slouching down and nudging me with his shoulder. "Should we have worn disguises?"

I nudged him back. "That might have been smart." I couldn't help but lean in. His smile was so inviting. His face was only a few inches from mine. His green eyes were bright, even in the semidark of the theater. His breath smelled like popcorn.

And incense.

TWENTY

I JERKED BACK. HIS eyes grew wide as he registered the look on my face. "What's wrong, Lela?"

The lights dimmed and thunderous music filled the theater as the previews started. I leaned forward and inhaled, and he stayed still for me, his expression frozen in a lopsided smile. But I'd been with him all evening, and the scent wasn't coming from him. Which meant it was someone else inside this theater, maybe many someone elses. My fingers drifted toward my waist, where I kept my knife. *Shit.* I couldn't take it to school with me, and I hadn't gone home before the baseball game. I bowed my head, near enough that his hair brushed my cheek, and whispered in his ear, "Do you recognize that smell?"

Ian's eyes strayed to the screen, but he wasn't watching. He inhaled deeply, and then every line of his body went tense. He nodded, like I thought he might. It would have been how Aden smelled the night he became a Mazikin.

As the previews played on, I looked around the theater. I couldn't see very well, but I could still make out a few of our classmates staring at us from a few rows back. Caroline and her friends. Could they be . . . ?

A few guys walked into the theater, buckets of popcorn in hand. A guy sitting in our row half-stood up, waving at them, and then he turned his head and looked at me. I nearly flinched . . . and when I heard the low coughing and grunting coming from behind us, I did, swinging my head around as my fingers burrowed into Ian's sleeve. From the far left side of the room came a clicking canine laughter.

Someone brushed the back of my neck.

I jumped to my feet. The startled couple behind me stared at me like they were too scared to ask me to sit down. Ian tugged on my sleeve. "Are you okay?"

I dropped back into my seat, scanning the crowd. We were surrounded by Mazikin. I grabbed his hand. "We have to go, all right?"

"What?" he whispered. "The smell isn't that strong. Just because there's a stoner—"

I was nose to nose with him before he finished his sentence.

"Ian, get your ass up out of that chair and come with me. Right. Now."

He looked at me like I was insane, but he let me pull him out of his seat and drag him along the row, stumbling over people's feet. I was barely watching where I was going—I was too busy looking behind me to see if anyone was following us. Caroline and her girlfriends stared and whispered, but stayed in their seats. When we got to the aisle, I pushed Ian in front of me. "Watch your step. Come on. The emergency exit."

Ian had parked around the side of the theater because it had been so crowded. His SUV had to be close to this exit. All we had to do was get to it.

A woman wearing a high ponytail and heavy black eye makeup stood up and stepped into the middle aisle, and I recognized her—she was the Mazikin that Jim had chased to the gas station. With her gaze on Ian, she descended the steps in parallel with us. My hand settled on Ian's waist as I urged him forward. We would make it to the door before she did. Then I caught a sudden movement in my periphery. Holy crap. Two scruffy teenagers were now on the aisle steps behind us, coming down from one of the back rows.

Ian stopped suddenly, and I ran into his back. "Excuse me," he said to someone in front of him as a dizzying wall of scent washed over us. I grabbed a handful of his shirt to pull him back.

"Hey!" he shouted, ducking to avoid the swipe of a clawed hand. The girls in the row next to us screamed as Ian jerked his arm forward and punched the Mazikin in front of him, a skinny gray-haired guy who went flying into the laps of the girls.

"Go go go!" I barked, but it was unnecessary. Ian's hand closed around mine, and he pulled me toward the exit. We reached it a few steps ahead of the ponytailed woman. I kicked her away as Ian ripped the door open and yanked me through it.

"What the fuck?" he yelled, spinning around to face the woman and the two teens who had followed us out.

The three of them had taken a few steps toward us when an usher from the theater poked his head out the door. "I'm calling the police!" he said in a tremulous voice.

The ponytailed Mazikin turned around and crouched low, hissing at him. The usher gave me a quick, scared glance before he pulled the door shut, locking us out.

"You heard the guy," I said to the Mazikin. "The police are coming. You better get out of here."

The Mazikin tilted their heads. "No sirens," said one of the teenage guys, his shirt stretched tightly over his protruding belly. "Boy," he said, pointing at Ian. "We are here to retrieve you."

"This one. She's one of *them*," rasped Ponytail, pointing at me. She looked over at her comrades and began to cough and grunt in that hideous Mazikin language.

I cursed as three more Mazikin rounded the corner of the theater and assembled themselves on our right flank. This was a full-scale ambush. They'd been watching. They'd followed us, not knowing I was a Guard at first; their eyes were on Ian. Just as I'd suspected, Ibram had made him a target.

"Ian," I said softly. "I want you to run. Get to your car."

His hand tightened over mine as he backed up toward the parking lot. "You're kidding, right?"

I squeezed his hand and then let it go. "I'm sorry about this."

The skinny gray-haired guy burst out of the theater, wiping blood from his face. He bared his teeth, revealing that they had been filed to sharp points. "Girl with the hair," he snarled at me, recognition burning in his eyes, "I didn't realize you were protecting this one, but I'm glad." He swept his clawed hands in our direction.

The Mazikin all charged at once, and Ian took off, sprinting away with incredible speed. Two of the Mazikin went after him. I only had time to feel a flash of fear for him before Ponytail was on me. I kicked her in the stomach and elbowed her in the neck, and then caught her arm and swung her into her chubby pal. Another Mazikin jumped on my back, so I bent forward sharply and dumped him on the ground, where I stomped on his neck and punched another oncoming Mazikin in the face.

My knuckles split. My fingers throbbed. I heard Malachi's voice in my head, calm and sure, reminding me to use my elbows and knees. To keep my movements short and quick to avoid giving them anything to hold on to.

But the odds weren't good. I was weaponless, facing down a bunch of able-bodied Mazikin. I might have made several of them bleed, but there was no way I was going to win. I pivoted on my heel and took off toward the road, weaving in and out of the parked cars, followed by the heavy pants and hard pelting sound of a Mazikin's four-legged lope, getting closer by the second.

Its weight slammed into my back and its sharpened fangs tore through my sleeve and into my flailing forearm, sending me crashing into a median lined with square green shrubs. A few people screamed, and I knew we had an audience. Which was a shame. Because I was ready to kill this Mazikin with my bare hands. I suspected I knew who he was—I'd only met one Mazikin that filed its teeth. My arm was held tight in his jaws, so I rolled over on him and pressed down with all my weight. "Is that you, Clarence?" I huffed, determined to knock his fangs down his throat. "Did you think we'd make it easy?"

His eyes bugged out—but they also sparked at the mention of his name. He tried to close his teeth and take a hunk of my flesh, but I punched him in the side. He let go of my arm.

Tires screeched. Another Mazikin landed on my back. "Stupid girl," Clarence hissed as his friend began to yank me up. "Now you're ours. Sil will be thrilled that I caught you." The Mazikin on top of me grabbed a handful of my hair, but then it shrieked and jerked as something hit it with enough force to crunch bone. Clarence's eyes grew wide as he watched over my shoulder.

I scrambled to my feet and turned, ready to face whatever new threat was coming my way, only to see Ian standing between me and the rest of the Mazikin, who were coming around his SUV but looking extremely wary.

Ian was holding a baseball bat, swinging it with threatening precision. His first victim—the Mazikin that had jumped on my back—lay groaning at my feet.

The wail of a siren cut through the momentary silence. Clarence screeched at the others. As if they shared one mind, the horde of Mazikin, several of whom were bleeding and limping, threw themselves into four-legged mode and sprinted toward the far side of the parking lot.

"We have to get out of here," Ian said as he grabbed my hand. He tossed his bat into the open back door of his SUV and helped me in after it. He hopped in the driver's seat. The engine was already running.

But instead of peeling out, he calmly put the thing into gear and slowly drove out of the parking lot. I stayed low as we drove past curious bystanders, but realized that we had been hidden behind the SUV when he'd used the bat. If they'd seen anything, it was me running from a bunch of four-legged freaks.

"The windows are tinted," Ian said, still a bit out of breath. "You don't have to hide."

I straightened up and peered out the window. At the far end of the parking lot, an old blue van swerved out of its spot, jumped the curb, and drove over the sidewalk, narrowly missing a couple who'd been walking hand in hand. To the soundtrack of at least a dozen car horns, the van plowed into traffic, swerved, and was out of sight almost instantly.

Ian took a more subtle approach. He drove to the main exit, never missing a turn signal, slowing at every speed bump, stopping at the yellow light. He turned onto the road and accelerated neatly to exactly five miles over the speed limit. I watched out the back window as two police cruisers zipped past us into the theater parking lot, too late to do anything but gather statements. Fortunately, the Mazikin had put on the big show. We were the forgettable ones.

My mauled forearm throbbed, and I gritted my teeth. "Thanks for the rescue."

He glanced into the backseat when he heard my voice. "They hurt you."

I looked down at my arm, examining it in the dim light. "It's not bad."

"Should I drive you to the hospital?"

"No. It's fine." I needed to get to Raphael, but I probably had an hour or so before it got really bad. I hoped. I'd never been bitten before.

Ian laughed dryly and shook his head; then he took a sharp right turn. He pulled into the school parking lot and stopped next to my car. His hands stayed on ten and two, but his knuckles were white on the steering wheel. His shoulders lifted as he took a single deep breath. Then he turned around to face me.

"So," Ian said, his voice completely level. "Want to tell me what's going on?"

I put my hand over the bite wound, wincing as I felt the sticky warmth of my own blood beneath my palm and the hot throb of the venom now being carried through my veins. Fortunately, my brain was fully functional, enough to let the lies flow. "You know these were the folks who sold to Aden, right?"

Ian nodded. "Same smell. Aden reeked of it that night. But they were after me. And they seemed to know you."

"They knew . . . of me. Come on, Ian. You didn't think I was a prep school girl, did you?" I prayed he'd back down easily, as soon as he was challenged. Rumors about me had swirled ever since I'd arrived at school, so why not use that to my advantage?

He let out a short breath. "No, Lela, I didn't, but—are

you saying you're like a gang member or something?"

Never. But I couldn't think of any other explanation. I shrugged. "Aden certainly seemed to think so . . ." I tried to move my fingers, but my entire left hand was numb. I needed to get home. "I'm sorry, really."

Ian shook his head. "You're lying. I know you're lying. There's something else going on."

"Look, um . . . I guess my past kind of caught up with me," I said, wishing that killing Clarence only once had been enough. "But I'm going to try to make sure no one bothers you again, all right?"

He cursed under his breath and threw his door open. A second later, he wrenched open the rear door and climbed in next to me. I instinctively reached for the opposite door handle.

"Who's going to make sure no one bothers *you* again?" he snapped. "Look at you. Your arm's bleeding. They would have done serious damage if I hadn't been there."

Suddenly exhausted, I leaned against the seat, curling my bitten arm against my body as my hand hung limp. "I can take care of myself."

He laughed. "No kidding. It's part of why I like you. But we were attacked by seven drugged-out freaks tonight, Lela. You may be able to kick ass, but you're not a superhero."

"Never said I was. I'm just saying I'd feel awful if you got wrapped up in this."

"Too late. You're bleeding in my backseat."

I opened the door and stumbled out onto the blacktop, clumsily pulling my keys from my pocket. Already my legs were tingling, as was my right arm. Malachi had been able to run for over an hour when he'd been bitten by Juri in the dark city, so I prayed I could hang on as long.

"Lela, wait!" Ian hopped out of the backseat after me. "I wasn't telling you to leave!"

"I need to get home," I said. "I'm tired, and this could get infected or something." I waved my arm at him.

"Call me tomorrow," he said firmly. But the question in his eyes gave him away.

"I will. Please be careful, all right? Keep an eye out for their van, and call me if you see it."

His mouth lifted into this bemused kind of smile. "What would you do about it?"

I sighed. "Fine. Then call the police. Whatever. Just—be careful."

He took a step closer. "You're worried about me?"

With hesitant fingers, he touched my chin, trying to lift my face. I let him, even though he was standing too close, making my heart thump with panic. "I'm worried about *you*," he said softly.

"Good-bye," I whispered, turning to open my car door.

"Let me drive you home."

"Not necessary, I promise."

"Lela . . ." He sighed. "Fine. But I'm following you to make sure you get home safely."

I squeezed my eyes shut and tried not to scream. I didn't have time for this, even though he was being incredibly sweet—after being totally badass back at the theater. "Waste of gas, but if it'll make you feel better . . ."

I opened my car with my right hand. Once behind the wheel, I focused everything I had on driving slowly and smoothly to Diane's. I pulled into the driveway, got out, and waved to Ian as he drove away.

Then I got back in the car and headed to the Guard house. Raphael was waiting for me when I arrived and staggered haltingly up the front steps. Fortunately, no one else was home, so there was a minimum of drama. I let him send me into peaceful nothing and woke up a few hours later to the sound of distant thuds.

A light was on in the hallway, so I padded over to the basement and listened. Grunting breaths, shuffling feet. The memory of Henry telling me that Malachi trained at all hours when he couldn't sleep. As quietly as I could, I descended a few steps and peered through the wooden railing.

His skin shined with sweat under the lights, every muscle defined as he trained. Each of his movements was completely controlled, and it made me instantly jealous. Malachi's hand shot out, loose at first, deceptively fluid. But as it moved forward, it compacted into a fist that struck a dummy in the chest, leaving a deep dent in the frame. He pivoted in place and kneed the dummy three times before elbowing it into oblivion. It fell to the floor, bent in half, its head almost completely detached. He pivoted to destroy another dummy, and I saw that his expression was distant, unfocused. It was like he was on autopilot, like his body was here, but his mind was far away.

Only a week ago, I would have joined him. I would have put my arms around him, and he would have welcomed my touch. Even this dangerous mission had felt possible because we were together, and no one and nothing could get between us. And now . . . there were so many things blocking my path to him, and I had no idea how to get around them, or if it was possible at all. Watching him there, so close yet so far away, the loneliness of it hurt like an open wound. I crept back up the stairs and drove myself home.

TWENTY-ONE

MONDAY DAWNED GRAY AND wet, fat rain-
drops streaming down windowpanes and into flowerbeds,
where the tiniest green shoots were starting to appear. It
was a professional development day for the teachers, so
Jim, Malachi, and I spent our free hours training, and
tracking our friends while trying not to seem creepy. The
baseball players had a long practice and were headed for an
away game that afternoon, so I had an extremely uncomfortable phone call with Ian about keeping an eye out for
the van and warning his teammates to do the same. He
kept trying to ask me how I was, and I kept deflecting him.
I think we spent more time in awkward pauses than actual
conversation.

At lunch, my Guards hit upon the topic I'd tried to avoid thinking about for the past few days: my visit that afternoon with my "mother." It was the best chance we'd had in a while to track the Mazikin back to their new nest. While Malachi and I were meeting with her, Jim and Henry would patrol outside. We'd text them at the end so that they could follow her when she left. As far as we knew, the Mazikin only knew about me and Malachi, so they wouldn't recognize the other Guards. If all went well, we might be finishing this thing tonight. The guys seemed grimly determined as usual, but Malachi kept giving me these cautious looks every time I mentioned my mom. Knowing he might be worried I'd do something emotional again set my teeth on edge, and I spent an extra half hour in the training room, beating on one of the wire-and-cloth mannequins to get my frustration out.

When Malachi and I arrived at the Department of Children, Youth and Families building, Jen Pierce was waiting on the front steps, huddled all frumpy and frizzy under a broken umbrella. "Lela," she called out as we approached. "I wanted to check in with you before you went inside."

Jen gave Malachi—who looked even more imposing than usual because he had the hood of his black jacket pulled low over his face—a somewhat wide-eyed look, and then shook his hand. I introduced him as a friend who would be translating.

"Rita is already here," she said. "She's been here for almost two hours, actually."

Malachi scowled. Jim and Henry were already posted on corners around this block, but apparently we hadn't gotten here early enough to see how she'd arrived. I wondered how many Mazikin were watching us right now. The rain made it impossible to pick up their scent.

Jen led us inside, down a long hallway lined with closed doors. "Because you're seventeen and almost an adult, this meeting will be unsupervised, but you call if you need help, all right? You're not obligated to meet with her, so you can leave anytime you want."

"It's okay, Jen," I said, shoving my shaking hands into my jacket pockets. "It's no big deal."

She threw me a pitying look as we stopped in front of Conference Room 113. The Rita Santos–Mazikin was perched on one of the swiveling chairs, her fingers curled around its armrests. Her wild hair was brushed today. Just a few braids and beads, but she'd managed to comb the leaves and twigs out. She wore an ill-fitting light-blue suit with a stained cream-colored shirt underneath, and I wondered if she'd stolen the outfit from one of the Mazikin victims. Her gold-brown gaze scanned our faces and then fixed on me. She leaned forward suddenly, looking like she might fling herself through the glass wall separating us. I flinched. Malachi whispered something under his breath and shifted closer to me. Jen sighed, and then knocked briskly on the door and opened it. The hallway filled with the faint scent of incense.

"*Hola*, Rita," Jen said, "*Ella está* . . . here." She stood back and looked at me. "I'll be right down the hall, all right? My door will be open."

I nodded, not sparing her a glance, too busy staring at my mother, who was whispering my name over and over again. Drawing in a lungful of hallway air, I strode into the room and seated myself at the opposite end of the table from Rita. A stranger. My mother. My enemy. A Mazikin. I didn't know what label to use, what name. She was all of those things to me. She rose from her chair, but at that moment Malachi entered the room and positioned himself between us.

"*Quédate sentada*," he said firmly, pointing to her chair. "*No voy a permitir que te acerques a ella.*"

Rita grimaced, revealing dark yellow teeth. "I . . . not hurt . . . her."

Malachi looked over his shoulder at me. "This is your meeting," he said, his expression revealing his tension. It was nearly impossible for him to resist killing a Mazikin who was sitting within arm's reach.

Despite the suit and the hair combing, Rita's fingernails were black-tipped and ragged. She watched me with pure hunger in her eyes as I gripped my chair tightly and said, "Tell us why you wanted to meet."

She listened while Malachi translated, never losing her focus on my face. Her Spanish was rapid and sharp as she responded, and I could have sworn it sounded like she'd memorized what she was supposed to say. When she was finished, Malachi turned to me.

"She says the Mazikin are interested in making peace with us. Their numbers are growing, and they could crush us whenever they please, but they see no reason for us all to die if we meet their terms."

I laughed, even as dread bubbled in my stomach. "If we're so easy to crush, you would have done it by now," I said to her.

Rita tilted her head to the side as she listened to Malachi's clipped response. She nodded, like she'd expected to hear something like that. "One-five-zero Briarcliff," she said to me, enunciating every syllable.

It was Tegan's address.

"Twenty-nine Broadway."

Didn't Ian live on Broadway?

Her eyes glinted with something dark and intense. "Five-oh-three-one Kingston Court."

Malachi shot up from his chair as she recited my address, but I grabbed his arm before he managed to reach her.

They might not have gotten Ian or any of the others over the weekend, but it was clear the threat was still very real. I leaned forward as Malachi slowly sank back into his chair, my fingers curling into the sleeve of his raincoat. "Don't you dare touch them," I said to the Rita-Mazikin in a low voice, anger heating my skin. My friends. *Diane.* Now my hand on Malachi's arm was more of an anchor—I needed him to hold *me* in place.

Her tight smile told me she didn't need translation. She chuckled softly and looked at Malachi. "*No podrás impedírnos. Los dejaremos en paz solo si nos dés un sacrificio.*"

Malachi's shoulders tensed.

"Did she just say they want a sacrifice?" I whispered.

He nodded. "In exchange for leaving the others alone."

"What do you want?" I asked her.

Rita's face was the strangest mix of excitement and sadness. "*Tú, mija.*"

Malachi tore his arm from my grip. "*Eso nunca pasará,*" he growled, rising from his chair again.

"Hey, what did you say?" I asked.

I might as well have been invisible. He advanced on Rita with single-minded purpose, sending her scrambling back, rolling the chair along the floor until it hit the wall.

"*Debería de matarte ahora mismo,*" he said quietly.

Rita squawked as he drew near, plaintive, hoarse cries that got louder by the second. I wanted to clamp my hands over my ears to block out the noise.

"Malachi, back off. People are going to come running. *Malachi.*" I suddenly wondered if he was armed. Not that he needed a weapon. And from the way Rita was screeching, she knew it.

Malachi's fists were clenched. "We should take her now, Lela. We can get her back to the Guard house. Interrogate her. We could find out where the nest is. And then we can kill this body and release your mother's soul."

He was almost pleading with me, and I couldn't understand why. Something she'd said had made him desperate, though, and willing to stray from the careful plan we'd laid out. One in which he didn't kill my mother in the middle of the DCYF building.

"We can't take her," I answered. "Listen to her. She'll pitch a fit, and we'll get ourselves in trouble." I glared at him, willing him to remember the freaking plan—to follow her back to the nest.

Malachi stepped back as a few social workers walked by and cast anxious glances into the room.

"Lela," Rita said, edging around the opposite side of the table. "Sil say you come to him, he let you friends live. We go . . . away."

"You're saying that if I go to Sil, you guys will leave my friends alone and, what? Just disappear?" It was a ridiculous offer. Wherever they went, we'd have to hunt them.

She nodded, her eyes darting across the table to Malachi, who looked like he was about to lose it as she inched closer to me. "*Podrías estar con tu mamá.*"

"Shut up," Malachi snapped. "*Cuando te matamos, quedará libre el alma de su madre.*"

Rita's eyes grew wide, and her mouth dropped into an O-shape. And then she started to laugh, this high-pitched, hooting giggle. "*No,*" she said. "*Nunca será libre. Una vez que el alma de un humano se atrape, no tiene ninguna salida de la ciudad de los Maziquines.*"

Malachi froze. "You're lying."

"Translate," I said. "Now!"

He ignored me and stalked around the table, sending Rita scurrying toward me. Words I didn't understand flew from his mouth while he followed her. She wasn't paying attention to him, though; she was whispering to me.

"Sil say you come to him," she kept saying. "You friends. He kill them if you don't come. He take them. Make them us."

"And if I come?" I asked, my heart hammering as she got close, my stomach roiling as I inhaled her sweet, sick scent.

"Lela, do not *dare* consider this." The urgency in Malachi's voice was impossible to miss.

"Translate," I said from between clenched teeth, refusing to look at him.

He obeyed. Rita smiled and replied in Spanish, and whatever she said was the last straw. Malachi lunged for her, and she pitched onto all fours and scuttled around by my feet, pulling me in front of her. She grabbed my hand and

kissed it, and then tossed a crumpled piece of paper onto the
table and ripped the door open.

"He wait for you," she said to me. "But not forever."

She jumped into the hall, slammed the door behind her,
and sprinted toward the front of the building before suddenly turning a corner. Malachi scooped the paper from
the table and started after her, but I grabbed him as he
wrenched the door open, throwing my arms around his
waist. "You can't run," I said, wishing we could. "It'll draw
too much attention."

As I walked quickly into the hall, I pried my cell from my
pocket and texted Jim and Henry that she was on her way
out of the building—and not by the main entrance. "Please
see her," I whispered, knowing they weren't expecting the
meeting to end this quickly. "Or we're going to lose her."

As we got to the front of the building, the sky was steely
dark, and the rain was so heavy I could barely see the street.
There was no sign of Rita. My phone buzzed with texts
from Jim and Henry that came in almost simultaneously:

By side entrance didnt see her come out

*One block down. Saw someone come out fire exit but unable to follow
in car*

We'd failed.

I slammed my way through the first set of double doors
and stood in the damp, tiled space, gazing out the last set of
glass doors at the pouring rain. Malachi joined me a second

later. He handed me the piece of paper, on which was written a phone number. I crammed it into my pocket.

"Nice translating," I snarled at him. "I still don't know half of what she said."

Malachi stared out at the rain, his face a carefully disciplined blank mask. "I'm sorry."

"I don't need your sorry. I needed you to do your job, Malachi! What the hell was that?"

He inhaled a slow, strained breath. "She said Sil wants you in exchange for the promise that they will not possess the people you care most about."

"Got that part. What else?"

"She said that if you go to them, you can be with your mother."

I squinted at him. "What?"

He didn't look at me, and his words were controlled, like he was fighting to keep his voice steady. "She meant they will take your body and send your soul to the Mazikin city, where your mother is."

I crossed my arms over my chest. "She won't be there long. We're going to kill that body and set my mom free."

Malachi turned to me. "Lela . . . she said that nothing, even killing the human body, can set a human soul free once it's trapped in the Mazikin city."

"That's when you said she was lying." I put a hand on my stomach. If what she'd said was the truth, then that meant every soul the Mazikin had ever possessed was still trapped in their realm. Takeshi, Malachi's mentor and friend, who'd been taken by the Mazikin years earlier. Aden. My mother. Thousands, maybe millions of others. It also meant that by killing the bodies they possessed, we gave the Mazikin more chances, since the evil spirits could come back and possess others.

Looking into Malachi's eyes, I could see this idea was destroying him. All these years, he'd thought he was freeing people, and so he'd executed countless Mazikin with his blades and grenades and God knew what else. But if Rita had told the truth, all those souls were still trapped, and there was nothing, not now and not ever, that he could do to save them.

I couldn't stand for him to suffer like that, so I moved on. "Did she say anything else?"

Malachi's black stare went straight through me. "Yes," he said in a hollow voice. "She told me why Sil wants you."

"And?" I mouthed the word more than said it.

Malachi blinked and looked at the floor. "The Mazikin think you are—" He paused, mouth half-open, like he couldn't quite force the next words out. The silence stretched between us until I wanted to scream. Finally, he said, "The Mazikin believe your body is the perfect vessel to house the spirit of their Queen."

TWENTY-TWO

THE RAIN LET UP by the time I got home, where Diane was waiting for me. The smell of my favorite Chinese takeout nearly brought tears to my eyes, as did the anxious once-over she gave me as I walked in the door.

"How'd it go, baby?" she asked.

"Didn't Jen call you?"

She shrugged as she set two plates on the table. "Yeah, she said Rita . . . she said it wasn't a long visit."

It had felt a lot longer than it actually was. I hung up my jacket and walked toward the table, looking over the ridiculous amount of takeout she'd ordered. "Either you're worried about me or you think I haven't eaten yet this week."

She chuckled. "I'll let you guess which one." She pushed a

plate toward me. "Did she say anything? What did she want?"

My gaze settled on Diane's face, on the kind, concerned look in her eyes. Just the thought of the Mazikin threatening her made me want to go on a killing rampage. "She wants to be part of my life, but I'm not so into that."

Diane frowned. "I guess I understand a mother's need to be in her child's life, but she put you through a lot. You do what you think is right, baby." She leaned forward. "I never had kids of my own, but you know I love my foster kids. And you will always have a place in this family if you want it, no matter where you go from here."

"Thanks, Diane," I said, blinking back tears. "Hey. Have you, um, seen anybody unusual hanging out in the neighborhood?"

Her eyes narrowed. "Why? Is someone threatening you?"

"Nothing too bad. And I'm not getting into any trouble," I said quickly, trying to walk the fine line between raising her alertness and sending her into full-on freak-out mode. "But if you . . . if you see anyone, let me know, okay?"

"Mm-mm-mm." She shook her head. "You know we're a tight neighborhood around here. Nobody's mentioned anything, but I'll ask around and tell folks to keep a lookout. You never can be too careful these days. Especially with all that craziness up in Providence."

"Yeah." I sat down at the table and dished rice onto our plates. "Exactly."

I ate a few pounds of Chinese food while Diane told me about the latest drama down at the lockup, and the whole time I stared at her, wondering what my life would have been like if she were my real mom, if I'd had her to protect me all along. It was pointless to ponder, but I couldn't help but think it might have been kind of nice, even now, to let her be that person for me. So many things were like that since I'd returned to the land of the living—my weird friendship with Tegan and going out with Ian, a normal guy who actually seemed to like me—real connections that were nothing more than could-have-beens, because I wasn't here to have a life. I was here to be a Guard.

After such a heavy meal—and maybe some of Raphael's help—Diane fell asleep early, and I crept out of the house after checking to make sure that every single window and door in the split-level was locked. I walked around the neighborhood, trying to detect the scent of incense or anything unusual. Nothing. I drove to the Guard house and waded through ankle-deep puddles to get to the front steps. Jim and Henry were waiting for me in the entryway.

Even though it was his night off, I looked around for Malachi. We had parted ways in silence this afternoon. Every topic of conversation was too painful, and he'd been more withdrawn than ever.

"He's not here," said Jim. "Laney picked him up a few minutes ago."

"Great," I said in a voice that revealed I thought it was anything but. "Let's get going." After our failure this afternoon, I'd decided that Henry needed to go undercover. Tracking the Mazikin wasn't working, but if he could get himself recruited . . .

Henry hefted a ragged pack on his back and adjusted the cap on his head. "Ready."

I drove us to Roger Williams Park at the south end of the city. We'd agreed Henry should walk from there, as we didn't want him seen with me and Jim. I parked at the very edge of the lot.

"Thank you for doing this," I said, suddenly worried for him. I'd been forcing myself not to think too much about what I was asking of him, focused entirely on being a strong Captain, but now that wasn't so easy. What if I was condemning him to an eternity of suffering in the Mazikin city? After what Rita said today, that seemed like a distinct possibility. And knowing Henry had someone who was waiting for him to return, someone he was desperate to get back to, made this even harder.

Henry gave me a ghost of a smile. "Malachi told me what that wild-haired Mazikin said to you. I won't let it happen to me, Captain."

I nodded. If he got trapped in their nest, he'd be hopelessly outnumbered. In the dark city, the Mazikin had been on foot, and it was much easier there to peel off and escape them after being led to their nest. But here, they were driving around, and I was betting they were picking up victims in that van or other vehicles. Sneaking away would be difficult—especially if they were parking in a garage near the nest.

I swallowed and tried not to fidget. "You take care of yourself. Stay alert."

Henry stared at me, his face half in darkness, half lit up by the streetlamp above us. "I spent over sixty years in the Wasteland, Captain."

He let that sink in for a few seconds, the idea that he had been there, that he had belonged there. But it also meant that he had survived there, and if he was a Guard, the Judge must have seen something in him, something beyond a corrupted, evil soul. Henry read my thoughts in my expression. "Don't think I'm soft because of what I told you. And don't think I'm better than I am."

"You don't want to kill. You said it yourself."

"That doesn't mean I'm not capable of it. Or that I haven't done it willingly, many times."

"We're all capable of it, Henry. That's why we're here."

Something like respect glinted in his eyes. "Fair enough, but I'd venture to say I have a little more experience with it than you do. I was a professional killer during my life on Earth. I earned my spot in the Wasteland. And in both places, I learned never to lose my awareness of my surroundings."

"Even when you're in a safe place?"

Henry laughed, a hollow, husky sound. "No such thing, Captain."

"So are you sure you want to do this?"

"No wanting about it," he said firmly. "I'm a convict, Captain. A conscript. It's all I am, and I got used to that a long time ago. Fighting it does nothing." He cast a knowing glance over his shoulder at Jim, who answered with stony silence.

I got out of the car, wondering if in fifty years I would be as emptied out and hopeless as Henry. But . . . Malachi wasn't like that, and he had been a Guard for a decade before Henry died. He seemed to have a sense of hope. At least, he had until recently. Now I was starting to wonder.

Henry closed his own door quietly and stood facing us. He took his phone out of his pocket. "Malachi got me all charged up this afternoon. He said the battery should last for several days if I'm not talking on it."

"Text if you have new information."

Jim stepped forward. "Good luck, man."

Henry seemed to think that was funny. "Same to you. Happy hunting. You'll hear from me soon."

He turned and strode away, looking like a walking scarecrow, scraggly and skinny. But he was strong—strong enough to run for blocks while carrying me, and I wasn't exactly a waif. He could take care of himself.

"Ready?" Jim asked.

"Yeah." I twirled my keys around my fingers and got back in the car. Jim joined me in the front seat. "We'll go downtown tonight." The air was definitely warmer now that April had caught up with us, and people would be out on the streets. Tonight was also the first night the homeless were without the winter shelters to protect them.

We parked in a narrow alley between buildings, fully expecting to return to a ticket. I lowered the hood of my sweatshirt over my face and took Jim's hand. We looked like an ordinary young couple, with our weapons nicely concealed under our baggy clothes. This would become more difficult when summer arrived. I had hoped to complete this mission by the time I graduated, but now Henry's words were echoing in my head, and I realized that even if I did complete the mission, that didn't mean I was free to live my life. I might spend the rest of my existence as a Guard.

Unless the Mazikin caught me and used my body to house their Queen, of course.

"You're hurting my hand," Jim said, annoyed. "I might need it later."

I released him from my death grip. "Sorry."

"You all right, Captain? Did that Mazikin get to you this afternoon? Certainly seemed to have Malachi on edge. And he wasn't even related to it."

"I wasn't related to it, either," I said through gritted teeth.

"You know what I mean." He pulled his ringing phone from his pocket. "Hold up. It's Tegan."

He stepped over by a storefront and answered, and I watched the grim expression on his face transform, softening with . . . I didn't even know what it was. Hope? Happiness? His eyes met mine, and then his smile evaporated. He was on duty. "I'll call you later, okay? No, definitely. *Definitely.*"

He hung up and turned toward me. "What's a prom like?"

I laughed as we started to walk again. "Do I look like a girl who's been to a prom?"

He shrugged. "Can I go?"

"Tegan asked you?" This was an interesting development.

"I want to look out for her. But I'm afraid I'm going to mess it up, not understanding these local customs."

We crossed a busy street, with neon lights from the clubs streaking our faces, turning our skin purple and pink. I kept my eyes open for that dark-blue van or any other suspicious, slow-moving vehicle.

"I guess a lot of this stuff must seem weird." I waved my hand at the HOT GIRLZ marquee above our heads.

"No, the Blinding City looks a little like this. Only much brighter. Much more . . . extreme."

"So kind of like Las Vegas?"

He gave me a blank look.

"How did you end up in the Blinding City, anyway? I

thought the Countryside was heaven. Like, a final resting place."

"Only if you want it to be," he said, pulling his own hood up so that I couldn't see his face.

"I've been there. I've felt it. Why wouldn't you want that?"

"How would you know to want it if you'd never felt anything else?" His voice was hard. "I spent my whole existence there. There were always people around to take care of me, to teach me. I had everything I needed. But like I told you . . . when I reached a certain age, I stopped getting older. Sort of."

"Sort of?"

"My body stopped changing when it reached maturity. But people keep changing, even if their bodies don't. I started to want things. I didn't even know what, but it was this ache inside me. A hunger. And slowly, the Countryside became a prison to me."

"A prison? Are you serious? I don't get that at all. Every person I met in the afterlife would have given anything to end up there."

He snorted. "Come on, Captain. You know that's not true. Didn't you spend some time in the dark city? Are you telling me *every* person wanted to leave?"

He was right. A lot of people had wanted to get out, but a few seemed determined to stay where they were, growing themselves houses, collecting junk, pouring drugs and booze into their bodies, anything to fill the empty spaces inside them that had led them to kill themselves in the first place.

"The human capacity for self-delusion is limitless," he said, seeing that I wasn't going to argue. "That's what she said to me. The Judge. After I tried to sneak into the Blinding City."

"You tried to sneak in? To a place where people get *punished*?" I nearly tripped as my shoe snagged on the jutting, cracked sidewalk.

"You don't understand. One day, it just . . . appeared. No one around me seemed to see it, but I could. Everywhere I turned, it was there at the horizon. From the outside, it looks like a playground. Anything you want. It was *everything* I wanted. So when the Guards caught me scaling the wall and took me to the Sanctum, the Judge said I could have it. She assigned me to Guard it."

"Did you actually like it there?"

"Yes, absolutely." He chuckled. "And no, not at all. It's a terrible place." He ran his hand along a brick wall. "The diamond-encrusted walls will cut you. The luscious food turns to ashes in your mouth. Every alley caters to a different addiction, but it all turns to shit as soon as you touch it. Or snort it. Or inject it. After a moment of pleasure, it does nothing but hurt." He shuddered. "It's a gorgeous, perfect kind of torture, and the citizens inflict it on themselves every day. I was no different. I couldn't stop. I punished myself over and over again."

"Do you like it better here?"

He looked up at the sky, where wispy clouds obscured the fingernail moon. "Yes, but it's still torture. There are things I want here, too. *Real* things. But I can't have them because of what I am."

"A Guard." *This* I understood. I felt the same way.

Jim pulled up short and poked my arm. "Check it out. Two blocks up."

An ancient, enormous Cadillac pulled slowly up to the curb where a solitary woman leaned against a darkened storefront. As the car's window rolled down, she pushed herself away from the wall and walked forward, wearing a lazy smile.

"Probably a prostitute," I said quietly to Jim, already sniffing the air. "Crap. Do you smell that?"

The woman leaned against the door of the car, and a hand reached out from the open window and stroked her mane of curly blonde hair. Jim and I both broke into a jog at the same time.

"If they get her in that car, that's the end of her," I said.

"They won't." Jim sprinted ahead of me, his powerful legs carrying him up the street. But the driver of the car must have spotted him, because he gunned the engine and peeled out, nearly sideswiping an SUV, which honked long and loud.

Jim kept running, ducking his head to get a look in the vehicle, but he stopped as it blew through a busy intersection and sped away.

"What the hell are you doing?" shrieked the prostitute.

"I'm sorry," I said as I approached her. "My friend thought that was someone he knew."

She backed up several steps as I approached. I held up my hands, not wanting to freak her out. "Hey," I said. "We don't mean any harm."

She snorted. By the look of her, she had a lot of years of experience with people more menacing than me. The Mazikin scent still hung in the air, so I said, "You smell that? That kind of incense smell? Don't ever get in a car if you smell it. Warn your friends, too."

The woman inhaled. "I don't smell anything."

"Captain—" Jim called out, eyeing the prostitute as he approached her from the other direction.

She whirled around to face him, and as she did, the breeze carried the overwhelming stench of body odor, perfume, and incense to me. "Pretty clever," I said, drawing her attention back to me. "You nearly had that guy." I pushed my hood away from my face.

Her eyes went wide, like maybe she recognized me.

Jim met my gaze, and I nodded. He stepped up right next to her. "Hi, sweetheart," he said as she flinched in surprise. She'd been so fixated on me that she'd forgotten he was there. "Sorry I chased off your date. Can I make it up to you?"

The Mazikin's eyes darted back and forth between me and Jim. A low hiss came from her mouth. Jim had one arm around her and a hand covering her mouth before she could make another sound. With abrupt and brutal efficiency, he hustled her into the adjacent alleyway. I looked around quickly, but no one seemed to have seen us. "Under control?" I asked the entwined dark shadows in the alley.

"Get the car," Jim said.

I took off, both terrified and exhilarated. Finally, a Mazikin to interrogate, one who might be the key to helping us locate the nest. I reached my car, yanked the orange parking ticket from the windshield, and pulled onto the street, forcing myself not to speed as I drove the five blocks to where Jim was waiting with our prisoner. I pulled into the alley, rolling to a stop a few feet from Jim and the struggling blonde Mazikin. Jim's expression was rigid and cold as he shoved her forward. He'd ripped her shirt and tied one of her sleeves over her mouth. His fingers were a bloody, mangled mess.

She'd bitten him. Our clock was ticking.

I popped the locks, and he wrenched the door open and pushed her inside, holding his injured hand over her mouth and using the other to hold her arms behind her back.

"Malachi put some rope in my pack," I said, reaching for it, thinking I would need to ask Raphael for some zip ties.

The Mazikin growled, the sound muffled by the fabric and Jim's hand but no less creepy for it.

I leaned between the seats, the rope in my hand. "Hold her tight."

Jim moved his hand from her mouth to further secure her arms, but the Mazikin bucked in his grip and lunged at me, slamming her forehead into mine. With my ears ringing and vision blurred, and Jim's curses and the Mazikin's screeches filling my head, I fell back against the steering wheel. Her hands were around my throat in the next instant, sharp fingernails digging in. The horn beeped as we struggled, sending the needle on my panic gauge into the red zone. We'd be lucky if someone didn't call the cops.

The Mazikin jerked back as Jim got an arm around her waist, her stiletto heels narrowly missing my face as she kicked and clawed. I grabbed for her legs but couldn't get a grip as Jim wrestled with her. He was trying to flip her over on her stomach, but now her hands were free, red claws slashing through the air. Jim grunted in pain as a few drops of blood splattered on the window next to his face.

"Control her!" I shouted.

"Trying!" He kicked her hard against the closed door as she threw herself back at him, a ball of animal fury. "Dammit!"

From beneath his shirt, he drew a knife.

He meant to threaten her, I had no doubt, but the Mazikin's eyes lit up as the silhouette of the blade came into view. I opened my mouth to scream at him, to tell him to put it away, but it was too late.

The Mazikin flashed a surprisingly beautiful smile at me. And then she threw herself at Jim and impaled herself on his knife.

TWENTY-THREE

THE MAZIKIN GRUNTED AS the knife plunged in at an upward angle, just below her ribs. Jim shouted in surprise and jerked back, ripping it from her body in a way that probably did more damage than good. She gave a gurgling sigh and slumped over while blood poured over the backseat.

"Put pressure on that wound!" I shouted, turning around to start the car.

Jim felt for a pulse. "I think she's dead. I'm sorry, Captain."

I exhaled a sharp breath through my nose. Now we had a dead hooker in our car. Awesome. For a few seconds I debated dumping her, but the physical evidence . . . our skin was under her fingernails. Our fingerprints were all over her. And mine, at least, were on record. "Take off your sweatshirt and cover her," I ordered. "Get her on the floor. We're going back to the Guard house."

Jim obeyed wordlessly, blood oozing lazily from the claw marks on the left side of his handsome face. I stripped off my own sweatshirt and handed it back to him. "Cover that wound on your face, at least while we drive through the city. And pray we don't get stopped by the cops."

We made it back to the Guard house less than twenty minutes later. Raphael was waiting for us. He looked entirely undisturbed as Jim slowly and clumsily climbed out of the backseat, his shirt and pants soaked and sticky with the Mazikin's blood.

"Go inside, Jim," he said. "Get washed up quickly, and then I'll heal you. The scarring won't be bad if we do it soon."

Jim walked into the house while Raphael peered into the backseat. "Why did you bring it back here?" he asked casually.

"Because it died in the car. And I was afraid there would be too much evidence if we left it behind. You might be able to protect me from indictment for something I didn't do, but I don't see how you can protect me if they find my skin under her fingernails."

Raphael shrugged. "I can dispose of bodies." He stood up and closed the car door, like the dead woman in the backseat was of as much concern as a bag of dirty laundry. "You need healing." He nodded toward my neck.

"Jim goes first. His hand is pretty mangled, and he's already feeling the effects of the venom."

I followed Raphael into the house. The sound of the pipes told me that Jim was taking a shower, so I went to the kitchen and got myself a drink of water, and then joined Raphael in the parlor. "So . . . we met with a Mazikin this afternoon. She had some interesting things to say."

Raphael gave me a small yet dazzling smile. "What a lovely way of putting it."

"Was she telling the truth?"

"Only what you need, Lela."

My fists clenched. "I'm not asking because *I* need it," I blurted.

Raphael's gray eyes met mine. "Malachi has not asked me for this information. Ever. He has had over seventy years to question me about what happens when a human is possessed by Mazikin. Why do you think he hasn't?"

He was giving me such a knowing look, and I wanted to run from it. Or maybe punch it off his face. But it was a damn good question. "Maybe he knew you'd give him that bullshit not-what-you-want-only-what-you-need line."

The smile didn't leave his face. "But you said you thought he did need the answer. If that's true, I would give him the information he needs. But only if he asks."

Suddenly tired, I sank into the chair in front of the computer. "I don't know why he hasn't asked. I think it's because . . . because he wanted to believe he was saving people. In his life here on Earth, he was powerless as everyone around him suffered and died, as his brother was killed in front of him. When he became a Guard, it gave him the chance to protect others. Even the ones taken by Mazikin. Even though they were lost and far away, he wanted to reach them. Do something for them. Help them."

Raphael nodded. "Yes, I believe that's what he *wanted*."

Jim leaned in the doorway, his wounds standing out stark and grisly against his pale skin. "The human capacity for self-delusion is limitless," he said softly.

Raphael turned to him. "Isn't it, though?"

I went out to the front porch and sat on the swing to wait for my turn to be healed. Self-delusion. Jim was saying that Malachi had closed his eyes to the truth. My Lieutenant had chosen to trust in a lie to allow himself the luxurious belief that he was rescuing people.

That way, he didn't have to face the alternative, which was that he was helpless in the face of all that evil.

It was a costly mistake. By killing the bodies Mazikin inhabited, he was giving them second chances. And third and fourth and fifth chances. If he'd only imprisoned them in the dark tower, or even in a cell at the Guard Station, he could have saved a few people. Maybe. The Mazikin would have sent more, but it still would have prevented their most powerful spirits from returning. Like Sil, Ibram, Juri. All of whom were either already here or had a chance to be, in part because Malachi hadn't imprisoned them when he had the chance.

I scuffed my boots against the wooden slats of the porch, ignoring the throbbing sting radiating up and down the sides of my neck. Headlights turned into the driveway, and I recognized Laney's car. She pulled to a stop behind the Taurus.

The one containing the dead hooker in the backseat.

I started to get up, but then looked down at the blood smeared across my sweatshirt. I pulled my knees to my chest and stayed where I was. This could get very bad very quickly.

It was dark inside her car, but I could see that their heads were close together. Too close. He didn't emerge from the car for a full minute.

I knew, because I silently counted the seconds, my heart beating a sick, hard rhythm against my ribs. Malachi finally opened the passenger door and got out, his questioning gaze landing on mine immediately. I shot a fierce glance at the Guard car and shook my head, my eyes growing wide as Laney got out of her car.

I gritted my teeth and didn't move. She was less than fifteen feet from where the dead woman was poorly hidden, where dark-red stains covered the backseat. Laney tossed her long hair over her shoulder and glared at me. "Hey, Lela," she said. "Fancy meeting you here."

"I had to ask Malachi a question," I answered in the friendliest voice I could muster. "He's ace at pre-calc."

Laney made a deeply skeptical noise in her throat as Malachi walked swiftly around the front of her car and met her before she could step forward. He stood close and bowed his head, speaking soft words meant only for her, and it hurt me more than the Mazikin claw marks on my neck. After a few minutes, Laney reached out and touched his arm, and he let her. Then she got back in her car and pulled out of the driveway, stopping long enough to wave to him and blow a kiss.

Malachi watched her go and then turned slowly to me. As he walked past the Guard car, he paused to look inside. With no discernible change of expression, he took the steps and sat down next to me on the swing.

"Who is she?"

"We caught a Mazikin. Tried to bring her back to interrogate her. It didn't quite work out."

He hooked an ankle over his knee and leaned back, staring out at the yard. "You were injured. How bad is it?"

"Just a scratch."

"You've said that to me before."

"This time it's true. Most of this blood is hers. Jim was

worse. Raphael is healing him now. How was your night?"
I shouldn't have asked, but some masochistic part of me
needed to know.

"Pleasant," he said, his voice giving nothing away.

"She likes you a lot." I cleared my throat. Why did my
voice have to shake like that?

"She also believes my heart belongs to another."
He let the words fall like bombs into the space between
us. My heart, already thumping hard, now beat double-
time. I turned to look at him, his severe profile—a hard,
dangerous kind of beauty. I waited for him to say more, but
he didn't. He sat in silence, his gaze on the budding trees in
front of us, and I hung on to those words with everything
I had, wondering if what Laney believed was actually true.
Was he trying to tell me it was? Was this an invitation, a
hint, or just a report of the facts?

And could I be any more selfish, thinking about dumb
high school stuff when everything Malachi believed might
be crashing down around him? "We haven't talked about
what that Mazikin inside my mom told us today," I said quietly.

"What is there to say?" he replied. His gaze was unfocused again, far away. It filled me with a savage ache, so much
worse than the stupid jealousy that had been there before,
especially as he added, "I have made yet another foolish,
disastrous error, and in doing so have condemned countless

innocents to eternal suffering." The muscles of his shoulders were tight, shaking with tension and emotion. "At least the Mazikin that possessed your mother was too addled or ignorant to keep up the ruse. I'm quite sure Sil will be furious at her when he discovers that she's corrected my idiotic misconceptions. Now," he said as he stood up abruptly, "we should retrieve that body from the car."

He rose and went into the house, and then emerged a moment later with a tarp. Together we tugged the body of the blonde prostitute out of the car and laid her on the starchy plastic. As we did, a small change purse fell from beneath her blouse. I picked it up and opened it.

Among a few neatly folded bills was her driver's license. "Her name was Andrea," I murmured, looking down at her beautiful smile in the picture, lit up by the sliver of moon above us, and then down at her white, bloodless face. Her eyes were still half-open. Her lipstick was smeared and smudged around her parted lips. I'd never taken the chance to really look at a person I had killed, too busy fighting or fleeing. Andrea. Did she have a family? A daughter? Had someone loved her? Was someone missing her right now?

"Malachi? What's that thing you say over their bodies? You know, after you've killed one of them?"

He gave me a wary look. "It's *El Male Rachamim*. A prayer for the dead."

I bit my lip and knelt by Andrea's head. With the tips of

my fingers, I closed her eyes. I wiped her lipstick with the cuff of my sleeve. "Can you say it?" Maybe this would be what both of us needed.

He knelt next to me. "I cannot promise a perfect translation." After a long pause, he said, "Ah . . . God who is full of compassion, who dwells on high . . ." He spoke slowly, carefully, with sadness and reverence in his voice. "Grant true rest on the wings of the Divine Presence, in the exalted spheres of the holy and pure, who shine like the stars, to the soul of . . . Andrea, who . . . who . . ."

He cursed and stood up suddenly. "I can't do this." He leaned over and rolled Andrea's body into the tarp.

I slowly got to my feet, heavy with new understanding. Every time he'd chanted over the body of someone he'd killed, he hadn't been praying for the Mazikin, or even for the body. He'd been praying for the human soul he thought he was freeing, far away in the Mazikin realm, unreachable except for the wishful words of his heart.

What did he have to pray for now?

His usually steady hands were trembling as he pulled the edges of the tarp tight. "I will take her to the basement. They'll send someone to come and get her." He picked up the wrapped body, slung it over his shoulder, and turned his back to me. "I'm glad you weren't badly hurt," he said, and then marched up the stairs and into the house.

TWENTY-FOUR

I DIDN'T MAKE IT home until four, and suffered through a few hours of dreams in which I stared at the world through a stranger's eyes, wearing skin that wasn't my own. Filled with hunger, an insatiable craving for one thing. Something I couldn't have.

My alarm was almost a relief, but that keen sense of need followed me right out of sleep. I ran to the bathroom and stood in front of the mirror, just to make sure I was still me. I slipped out early and drove to the Guard house, because with Henry gone, I was the only one who could drive Jim and Malachi to school. It seemed beneath Raphael to have to do it.

When I arrived, only Jim was waiting for me. I glanced

at his face. Raphael had done a pretty good job—the scarring was faint, and only when Jim turned his head could I see the narrow, silvery tracks crossing his pale, otherwise perfect skin.

He gave me a look I couldn't decipher but that seemed to fall somewhere between pity and amusement. "Laney showed up this morning and offered to drive Malachi to school."

We drove in silence. Jim folded his arms over his chest and leaned his head back with his eyes closed. Shutting me out. Or maybe catching a few moments of sleep, which was hard for all of us to come by these days.

Prom posters were plastered on all the glass doors at the front of the school. Just a simple lacy font, white on navy blue. *Memories and Moments.* It was a reminder of what we'd lost—and also that my senior year was rapidly coming to a close. I'd barely noticed. Prom was in three weeks, and graduation was only a month after that. It was hard to believe that a few months ago, I'd assumed I'd be here with Nadia, enjoying all of this. Now that Nadia was gone, I had nothing to look forward to except the hope that I could prevent a bunch of evil spirits from overrunning Rhode Island.

The cafeteria was packed with the before-school crowd. Tegan and Laney were sitting at a table under a row of prom posters, selling tickets to the big party. Jim peeled off to say hi to Tegan, whose face lit up when she spotted him.

She tilted her head and frowned as her gaze lingered on his cheek, and when he reached her, she put her fingers up to touch the faint silver streaks on his skin. He pressed her hand to his face and said something that made her expression brighten again, and then both of them were laughing and leaning in close. As I watched the two of them head for their lockers hand in hand, I was glad I'd told him he could take her to prom.

I sank onto the hard cafeteria bench and put my backpack in front of me so that I could use it as a pillow. I'd just lowered my head onto it when someone sat down next to me.

"We won last night," Ian said. "And no van sightings."

I raised my head. Ian had his eyes on his large hands, which were gripping his knees in a way that looked painful. "Congratulations?"

His eyes met mine, and he gave me a quick smile; then pivoted so that he was facing me. "Do anything fun yesterday?"

"Hell no," I said, and was rewarded with dimples.

I wondered if he'd wanted me to go to his game, if his halting silences on the phone yesterday had been him trying to figure out a way to ask me. I was overcome with this sense of want, for this kind of normal thing. Of having a guy ask me to watch his baseball game, of wondering if he liked me, of wondering what it might mean. But now I was a Guard, and on top of that, I'd managed to fall for a guy caught in the same trap. I scanned the cafeteria for Malachi, surprised he wasn't at the prom ticket table with Laney. I finally spotted him at a table next to the cafeteria line, his back to the crowd, shoulders slumped. He looked . . . defeated.

"Still with me here?" Ian asked.

"Yeah. Sorry. I'm kind of in a haze this morning. I didn't sleep well last night."

He looked over at the prom ticket table. "Me neither."

"How come?"

He laughed. "Nervous again. I got up in the middle of the night and ate my way through the kitchen. My mom was all over me this morning because I scarfed some stuff she was supposed to take to her book group."

A chuckle escaped from my mouth, despite my horrible mood. "What did you eat, exactly?"

He shrugged. "They were these little cakes. Really good. I should have known better, though. I mean, they looked kind of fancy. She doesn't usually buy that stuff for us." He shook his head, still laughing. "I woke up to her screams. 'My petit fours! My petit fours!' I had no idea what was wrong until she barged into my room and waved the empty tray at me. I thought she'd be happy I put it in the dishwasher for her."

"So a petit four is a cake? That's what she was talking about?"

His smile brightened his whole face. "Best thing I've ever put in my mouth. When she stopped yelling at me, I asked her where she'd gotten them."

"And she actually told you?"

He raised an eyebrow. "I can be persuasive. There's a bakery in Barrington."

"That's a long drive for a little cake." It was hard to feel down when he was with me. I looked him over, all carelessly graceful and long-limbed, and wondered how I had managed *not* to notice him in the last year.

"Long drive, yes. But worth it. Maybe we should go sometime." He gave me a sidelong glance.

I sighed. "I don't think I belong in Barrington." It was the wealthiest town in the state.

Hesitantly, Ian slid the tip of his finger along a lock of my hair. I didn't move away or flinch. I let him, astounded at the warmth in his gaze. "You belong anywhere you want to be, Lela."

I rolled my eyes. "And a few places I don't."

"Will you go to the prom with me?" he blurted, and then looked kind of stunned that he'd actually said it.

I let out a shaky laugh. "You want to go to prom with *me*?" I searched his face for a joke that I rapidly realized wasn't there.

He gave me a lopsided smile. "Badly enough to eat my mother out of house and home, just to control the nerves. Are you going to turn me down?"

I stared into his bright green eyes and was overcome with the same feeling I'd had last Friday—I wanted this. I wanted this ordinary, normal life. No heartache, no death or killing, no misery. "No."

He leaned a little closer. "No, you don't want to go with me, or no, you're not turning me down?"

"I'm not turning you down," I said.

He grinned. "Really?"

"Yeah. No promises about my dancing skills, though."

Ian stood up. "This is awesome. I'm going to buy our tickets, all right? I'll see you at lunch?"

I nodded mutely, already wondering if I'd made a mistake. What the hell did I think I was doing? But then I looked over at Laney, who was twirling her hair around her finger while she stared at Malachi.

Then she screamed.

I whipped my head around in the direction she was looking and nearly screamed myself. Evan Crociere, that gangly, disheveled drug dealer, was behind Malachi, whose head was still bowed over his book.

In Evan's hand was a ballpoint pen.

I was in motion before it descended, but it was too late. With utter ferocity, Evan drove the pen right into the side of Malachi's neck.

Everything in my world narrowed to a point, and the only thing that mattered was Malachi. I vaulted over the cafeteria table where I'd been sitting and sprinted along an aisle, grabbing a tray from the stacks as I ran.

With a crazy glint in his eye, Evan yanked the pen out of Malachi's neck, painting the wall beside them with a spray of Malachi's blood. Despite the wound in his neck, I would have expected Malachi to respond more quickly, but he seemed so caught off guard by the attack that he barely had time to lean away before Evan buried the pen in the junction of his neck and shoulder again.

A sound of pain and rage came from Malachi as the pen was ripped from his flesh again, and he began to rise from the table. Blood was streaming down the back of his shirt, droplets splattering onto the floor. And as I got close, I smelled it: incense.

Malachi didn't get a chance to strike at his attacker. Because I was already there. I leaped onto the table where Malachi had been sitting and blocked the next stab of the pen with the tray. Evan's eyes popped with surprise as his blow was deflected. Before he had a chance to recover, I drew the tray back and swung it down with all the force of my fury, hitting him in the throat with the edge of it. He stumbled back, coughing, as I caught a handful of his greasy hair and slammed his face into the painted cinder-block wall.

He crumpled to the floor, blood gushing from his nose, eyelids fluttering. But then he raised his head and looked right at Malachi, who was leaning against the wall with his hand pressed to his neck, blood seeping between his fingers.

"You can't protect her, Captain," the Mazikin inside Evan said quietly, mocking. "She has to protect *you*."

I cut off Malachi as he took a step forward, and the Mazikin's eyes glinted as his gaze slid to me. "You'd better call Sil, Lela," he whispered, grinning with bloody teeth. "Or what happens next is your fault."

TWENTY-FIVE

I STOOD IN FRONT of the full-length mirror. "This is not going to work."

Tegan appeared at my shoulder, looking like a pixie. Her frilly red tutu-like skirt scraped against the back of my hand as she looked me up and down. "What's wrong? You look beautiful."

I snorted. "I can't move." I shifted uncomfortably. The strapless pink-satin straitjacket she'd stuffed me into clung to every inch of my torso and legs, all the way down to my knees. "I don't think I can sit down." And I didn't think I could run or fight, which was most important. Judging by what the Evan-Mazikin had said before he'd been carted away by the police, none of us could afford a night off, and unless I gave myself up, the Mazikin had every intention of attacking my classmates every chance they got. Prom seemed like the ideal target for them, so here I was, shopping with Tegan, when all I wanted to do was drive to the Guard house and check on my Lieutenant. Raphael had shown up at school, playing the role of Malachi's host father and promising to take him straight to the emergency room, so I knew he was okay. Physically, at least. But when I thought about how he'd looked this morning, how miserable and hopeless . . .

Tegan sighed. "I'll get you something else." She'd been amazingly patient with me. This dress was like the eighteenth one I'd tried on.

"I'm sorry," I muttered.

She nudged me with her hip. "Why? This was my idea. I just wish you were having more fun with it. Aren't you excited? You didn't go to prom last year. And this year you're going with Ian freaking Moseley. He's probably going to be elected prom king, for God's sake."

I reached for the zipper on my dress as I shuffled back to the changing room. "You're making me feel sorry for Ian, that he's going with me."

Tegan scoffed. "Oh my God, Lela, you are so blind. You should have seen him at lunch. He's so excited to go with you—and so nervous that you're going to change your mind—that I think he ate about four trays of food in less than twenty minutes as he told us about how you'd said yes. It was bizarre."

"He eats when he's nervous," I said quietly. I'd skipped lunch because I couldn't get my mind off Malachi and hadn't wanted to face Ian like that.

Tegan raised an eyebrow at me. "And since you started noticing that he exists, he's probably eating ten thousand calories a day. Good thing he works out."

"He doesn't have to be nervous around me. I'm not going to hurt him or anything." Actually, I was starting to feel really protective of him. If the Mazikin got him, I'd never forgive myself.

She turned her back on me to root through another rack of sequins and satin. "Yeah? We all saw the way you reacted to Malachi's stabbing this morning."

I hid myself in the changing stall. "Malachi was hurt, Teg. I had to help him. If Ian was hurt, I'd want to help him, too."

"Okay," she said, her voice dripping with skepticism. "I'm going to hand you a few more possibilities, all right? We're going to go short. Your legs are totally ripped, and you seem to harbor some kind of grudge against the longer dresses."

The long dresses seemed destined to trip me up and get tangled at the wrong moment. They made me feel clumsy and slow. I looked down at my legs. I never wore short skirts, or any type of skirt. I wasn't keen on the idea of people looking at me, and so my clothes tended to be an afterthought. Which made this whole prom dress thing feel really weird. It felt like I was trying to wear some kind of disguise.

Tegan flopped a wine-red dress over the top of the door. "This is the one. Get that on, and get out here."

I tugged the dress down and examined it. Unlike so many of the others, this one didn't have a plunging neckline. It was a halter-style neck, with thin silvery straps that circled around and crisscrossed in the back. Feeling hopeful for the first time this afternoon, I pulled it on, carefully untangling my crazy hair as it got caught on the zipper. The front of the dress mostly covered the starburst scar from Henry's crossbow bolt. Once I had myself decent, I walked into the mirrored vestibule where Tegan was waiting, wearing a cap-sleeved, skintight black dress that made her hip bones look scary sharp. When she saw me, her eyes lit up. "I knew it!" She clapped a few times.

I stared into the mirror. The waistline was high and tight, just below my breasts, and the skirt was flowing and loose over my hips and legs, ending at midthigh. I turned in place. It was actually comfortable. The color looked good against my light-brown skin and eyes, too. I . . . kind of looked pretty. And I could run in it. "This is the one."

Tegan's grin was huge as she skipped over to me. With both hands, she gathered the curly mass of my hair, twisted it, and piled it on top of my head. "I'll do your hair and nails. You're going to look incredible. Ian won't know what hit him." Her expression changed, uncertainty clouding her eyes. "I'm kind of feeling sorry for both Ian *and* Laney. Because when Malachi sees you in this—"

My eyes met hers in the mirror. "What?"

She bit her lip. "Malachi is going with Laney to prom. They're riding with all of us in that stretch SUV Greg rented."

I squirmed to pull my hair away from Tegan's hands. It fell over my shoulders and down my back, and I leaned forward so that it hid my face from her. "I knew she'd asked him." But I had selfishly hoped he'd say no. "I'm glad he said yes." *So glad that it feels like my heart is being crushed in a vice.*

Tegan chuckled. "She texted me half an hour ago. I've never seen so many exclamation points in my life." She pulled a lock of my hair out from under the strap of my dress. "She said he looked good, by the way. I guess it seemed worse this morning, what with all the blood."

I pretended to fiddle with the silvery waistline of the dress. "That's good."

"The timing was interesting, wasn't it?" said Tegan. "A few hours after you say yes to Ian, Malachi finally gives Laney the answer she wanted?"

"Coincidence." And even if it wasn't, I couldn't afford to

think too hard about it. I raised my head and turned to her. "Thanks for this."

Her gaze strayed down my arm and lit on the tattoo there, on the beautiful face of Nadia inked on the inside of my forearm. Tegan had been shocked when she saw it as I tried on my first dress. She'd stared at it for a long minute, looking like she was about to cry.

That was her, she whispered. *That's how she looked.* And then she'd changed the subject.

Now, she touched it lightly with the tip of her finger. "I laughed at Nadia when she said I would like you if I ever gave it a chance." She smiled sadly and then shook her head, like she was trying to shed the grief. "Anyway, she was right."

I stared at her jaggedly stylish dark hair, her fragile smile. Nadia had told me the same thing, that I would like Tegan if I gave her a chance. I still found her kind of hard to take, but it was difficult not to enjoy her at the same time. She was clever and funny and understood things about people that I just didn't get. With all my heart, I wished Nadia were with us right then, because I knew it would have made her happy. I wished I could have done this when she was alive. "Yeah, she was."

I ate dinner with Diane and indulged in a little modeling session to show her I'd picked a dress that didn't make me look like a streetwalker. When we were done, I went around the house to check all the locks and then waited in my room until she fell asleep. Most of that time was spent on Facebook, punishing myself by reading Laney's ecstatic status updates from the past few hours. Malachi's page was much more reined in, but his status had been changed to say he was headed to prom with Laney. It wasn't like him to say something like that, more like a part he was playing. But then again, I wasn't sure I knew the real him anymore.

After reading that, I spent some time in the bathroom feeling nauseated. I managed to hold it together somewhat, and wandered back to my room to check Ian's status. His most recent update was also about prom, and I read it over a few times, wondering if he really meant it.

Going to the big party with a beautiful girl. Love my life.

It made me feel warm and shivery at the same time. I marveled at his simple, sweet enthusiasm for things. I wanted to slip into it, hide inside it, and forget my responsibilities.

But now I could hear Diane snoring down the hall, which meant it was time to go and face them instead. I drove to the Guard house, checking myself in the visor mirror every once in a while, just to make sure I had my game face on.

Malachi and I were patrolling together tonight.

He was waiting on the porch when I arrived, sitting in the swing with his long legs stretched out in front of him, wearing cargo pants and a loose hoodie. As I pulled to a stop next to the Guard car, he stood up, shouldering his own pack, and tromped down the stairs. Malachi had an excellent game face.

I got into the Guard car and so did he, settling his pack between his feet, and then staring straight out the windshield. "Where are we going tonight?" he asked.

I faced the front, too, my stomach aching. "I figured we could hunt around downtown. The Mazikin are trying to pick people up, and they've gone beyond the homeless. I think they're trying to lure people who have cash. And cars."

"All right." He put on his seat belt.

I waited, my hands on the steering wheel, until I couldn't stand it any longer. "Are you okay? From this morning, I mean."

"Raphael did as well as he always does. It's like it never happened."

Bullshit. "That kid hit you pretty hard. He caught you by surprise. That doesn't happen often."

He shifted impatiently in his seat. "I was slow. But I could have handled him."

I flinched. I wasn't used to this edge from him, this irritation. "I know. But if you're feeling depressed or something, we should talk about it. I mean—"

He squeezed his eyes shut. "Thank you. Is that what you want to hear?"

"No, I want to hear that you'll stop punishing yourself for accidentally killing Nick! I want you to snap out of this funk, because I'm afraid you're going to get yourself killed!" My heart pounded with frustration. I wanted to shake him.

"Duly noted, Captain," he said in that overly formal tone that told me he was shutting me out completely.

I gritted my teeth and drove us to Providence. "When was the last time you heard from Henry?" I finally asked. He'd been texting every few days since he'd headed out alone, just to let us know he was alive. But I knew that he sometimes called Malachi, and part of me wondered what on earth they talked about.

"He checked in this afternoon. He hasn't had any luck."

"I wish I knew what the Mazikin were up to," I said as I exited the highway and headed for downtown. "I mean, is it a mistake, patrolling the streets? Should we be focusing more on our school? They got Evan. Who will they try to take next?"

"I don't know. But if we can keep them busy here rather than at school, our friends will be safer."

I decided to say what I'd been thinking ever since realizing the Mazikin had possessed yet another of our classmates. "I know one thing that could draw their attention. Me. That's what they said they wanted anyway. Evan confirmed it this morning."

Malachi grimaced. "You can't be serious. I understand

the value of bait, Lela. Ana and I used that tactic many times. But only when we knew what we were facing and had a strategy to get her out. She was too important to sacrifice. And so are you."

I found a spot in an alley and edged the car in, deciding to drop the argument for the moment. There, in the dark, Malachi handed me my knife belt. He slid a baton into a holster on his back, hidden under his shirt. Our movements were practiced. We didn't need the light. I barely needed to think. He'd trained me like this, in the dark of the basement of the Guard house, so now my fingers moved on their own to check the knives and secure them along my waist, to make sure they were in exactly the right position in order for me to draw them quickly. Wordlessly, we got out of the car and walked down the street, side by side.

The cool breeze blew my hair around my face as we walked block by block, keeping an eye out for alley dwellers and hookers, anyone looking like they were seeking company for the evening. Up near one of the massage parlors, I spotted a familiar face. It was one of the two boys I'd seen the night Henry and I stayed in the homeless camp. "Hang back," I said to Malachi.

He slowed his pace and let me walk ahead, sniffing the air. The kid, lanky and narrow-faced, watched me approach with wary curiosity, probably wondering whether I wanted drugs or sex or both. Which seemed incredibly sad, because he looked no older than fifteen. He crossed his arms while his fingers fiddled with the loose cuffs of his long-sleeved shirt.

"Hey," he said quietly. "How's it going?"

"I was going to ask you the same question. Do you remember me? We met a few weeks ago, out at the camp by the interstate."

He took a cautious step back. "Don't know what you're talking about."

"Yes, you do. Where's your friend?"

His brows drew together. But he didn't run.

"The camp was attacked that night. I never got to see who got away. I heard you and your friend screaming."

He looked at the ground at my feet and tugged at a greasy curl of hair on his forehead.

"I'm not a narc," I said.

"Is he?" The kid raised his head and stared at Malachi, who must have been standing behind me.

"No. He's here to make sure no one gets dragged off. Is that what happened to your friend?"

The kid's gaze darted back to mine. "He wasn't my friend. We were just hanging out."

He and I took a step away from each other as a cop car cruised by. "Have you seen him since then?" I asked.

He nodded. "A few times. There's some kind of new

weed on the street, and he's deep into it. Selling it, I think. They've got some kind of crazy scene going on in this abandoned warehouse down in the Jewelry District. I think it's off Eddy Street?"

"You been there?"

With another quick shake of his head, he backed up so that he could lean against the brick storefront behind him. "I've heard they're like a cult. Rumor is some of them were victims of those attacks, you know? Like what happened in our camp. And now they've sort of gone in together and have their own thing going."

Or, more likely, those victims of the attacks were Mazikin now. They'd become the bad guys. And there were enough Mazikin at this point that they were being noticed by others. It was both good and bad—people knew they existed now, though they had no idea what the Mazikin were. They would assume a cult or gang, when the truth was much more terrible. I looked over my shoulder at Malachi, who was watching the kid with a predator's concentration. His gaze slid over to me, and he inclined his head in the direction of the Jewelry District. I nodded.

I pulled a ten-dollar bill from my pocket and held it out to the kid. "Nice talking to you."

He wiped his nose with his sleeve and took the cash with a silent bob of his head. Something about the vulnerability of that movement caught me, and suddenly I wondered where this kid's mom was. Was she worried about him? Had she thrown him out? Or was she like my mom, stuck in oblivion?

"Take care of yourself," I murmured, pivoting on my heel, now headed to scope out the Jewelry District. How easily I could have been just like that kid. How close I had been.

"Are you all right, Captain?"

I let out a long, slow breath, wishing he would say my name. I needed to hear it now. "It's fine. I wish I could have done more for him than just giving him some cash. He'll probably be shooting it into his arm within the hour."

"You know a lot about what happens out here," he said. He put a careless, heavy arm around my shoulders as another cop drove by. We were supposed to be a couple, out for a stroll, and it made me ache.

"I lived a different kind of life than the kids we hang out with at school, that's for sure," I said. "I come from a completely different place."

"I can see that. They are quite privileged, I think." His arm dropped away from me.

My chuckle was bitter. "Yeah, that's a nice way of putting it."

We were walking along Friendship Street, past apartment buildings and parking lots, and I held out my hand and lightly slapped it flat against each parking meter we passed. Malachi was not nearly so loose, as usual. His line of vision zigzagged up and down the street, lingering on each person we passed. His intensity freaked people out, often causing them to avert their eyes and scoot to the far edge of the sidewalk. A few even crossed the street to avoid us.

"My family had money," Malachi commented. "For a time, at least. Before everything fell apart. We never wanted for anything."

"Maybe that's why you fit in so well." It slipped out before I could stop it.

He stiffened. "I fit in because it's my job to fit in."

"Come on. This is more than a job for you." I slapped my hand hard against the cold metal of the last parking meter on the block, remembering his Facebook status and all of Laney's little heart symbols after her announcement that he was her prom date.

He stopped at the curb. "Of course it's more than a job." His eyes glittered darkly, and the edge had returned to his voice. "Just like it is for you."

And then a high, wavering scream pierced the quiet, sending both of us into action.

TWENTY-SIX

WE MADE IT TO the end of the block and stopped short, listening. Nearby, rapid-fire footsteps pelted through the darkness, followed by another shriek.

"I'm looping around," Malachi said, and then he took off, hurdling the low fence blocking an alley between two warehouses.

I sprinted toward the sounds of scuffling feet and muffled shrieks. Up ahead, in the half shadow of a dim streetlight, two figures were struggling, one on top of the other. "Hey!" I shouted.

The figure on top whipped around and bared his teeth. His victim used the opportunity I'd given her, and she scrambled to her feet and took off again, her dark hair streaming behind her. The attacker growled at me as I ran toward him, but then he dove onto all fours to chase after the girl. *Damn.*

I ran across a street, ignoring the squeal of tires and the honks of a horn pounded by the driver who'd almost hit me. We were in the Jewelry District now, desolate streets and abandoned buildings interspersed with funky little shops and restaurants now closed for the evening. Scraggly patches of weeds reached out to trip me as I chased the Mazikin across an empty lot. The girl he was after was almost too far ahead to see, but I caught the flash of something reflective as she disappeared into one of the buildings at the end of the block, a rambling low structure with a realtor's sign out front, planted in the weedy gravel next to a chain-link fence.

From the corner of my eye, I could see Malachi coming up the block, cell phone in one hand and baton in the other. Determined to do my part, I put on the speed and closed the distance between me and the Mazikin as it reached the building where the girl had fled. Behind me, Malachi called my name, but I had too much momentum—I caught the door the Mazikin had ripped open and followed him in.

I was slammed against the door in the next second and assaulted by the stench of incense and rot. Blinded by the inky darkness. Deafened by the roar of the Mazikin as he barreled into me. With a rending crash, I was thrown to the floor as Malachi thrust himself against the door from the other side. I turned on the writhing, growling Mazikin knife-first. A warm gush flowed over my fist as my blade sank into the Mazikin's side and it wheezed wetly.

"Lela," Malachi whispered. His hand closed over my ankle. "Get up."

I wrenched my foot away from him. "Doing my best."

From deep within the darkness came a soft, hooting laugh. I froze, still on my hands and knees, as the door Malachi had just come through was slammed shut. "Malachi?"

His fingers wrapped around my ankle again, and he squeezed, silently letting me know where he was. Next to me, the Mazikin I'd stabbed groaned. Several feet ahead of me, something growled, and then hissed. I scooted backward quickly, right into Malachi's arms. He pulled me to my feet.

"Can they see in the dark?" I whispered.

"Better than we can," he breathed.

Another cooing laugh, this one higher-pitched. Coming from the other side of the room. I tensed at the soft shuffle of feet and palms on concrete. They were everywhere, all around us. Right next to me, a swishing sound told me that Malachi was sliding his hand over the door, and then tugging on the handle.

"They've barred it from the outside," he muttered at the same time a Mazikin growled from a few feet away. But instead of attacking, it retreated, its footsteps growing fainter. It coughed and grunted in what I now recognized as the Mazikin language.

"He's calling to his friends," Malachi said against my ear. "He said he smells your fear."

"You can understand them?"

He didn't answer. Instead, he drew a knife from beneath his shirt and whipped it into the darkness. There was a high yip followed by the sound of a body hitting the floor. And then . . . snarling and growling all around us. It sounded like there were at least two dozen of them. My heart lodged in my throat, choking me.

A light flickered on in a hallway at the far side of the space, revealing a few people standing in a corridor, huddled in the archway leading to the long warehouse room where we stood. One of them was the girl I'd been trying to protect, the one who'd been running from the Mazikin. She grinned at me as she twirled her hair around her fingers.

I had led us into a trap. "Malachi, I'm sor—"

"*Shhhh.*" His hand found mine. I absorbed the warm pressure of his fingers through my skin and drew my strength from it. "Focus."

We were going to have to fight our way out of here, and I was his only backup.

I held my breath and tuned in to the tiniest of sounds around me, the barest wheeze, the lightest footfall. Malachi extended his baton, and I drew a knife. If we walked

into the center of the room in an effort to get to that hallway, we would be surrounded. It was probably what they
were waiting for. A chance to come at us from all sides. A
memory echoed in my head, from my time in the dark city.
Ana, talking to me about how the Mazikin were afraid of
Malachi. How they'd never attack him unless they had him
greatly outnumbered. I grabbed his sleeve and pulled us
back against the door.

Malachi didn't resist. With our backs against the wall,
I slid to the side, out of the intermittent light coming from
the far hall. I closed my eyes, picturing this building as I
had seen it from the outside. It was a two-story, not huge.
Probably not the nest, since it was right in the middle of
a neighborhood that was pretty busy during the day. That
hallway light provided the only illumination, but I remembered seeing windows as I approached the building. They
were probably painted from the inside, but they hadn't been
boarded. There were three of them, located to our right
along the wall.

Skin slapped concrete, the sound of a Mazikin charging—
from three sides at once. In the thick, oppressive darkness,
we only had our ears and the stirrings in the air around us
to tell us from where they were coming. I squatted low as
Malachi pivoted and stepped backward, and then we were
back to back, with the wall of the building blocking their
access to my right flank and his left.

"We'll have to get to the hallway," he said over his shoulder. "No. There are windows in front of me." Then I had no time for words, because the scrape and slap of hands and feet was way too close. I slashed my knife through the air and the thing yelped and rolled away, only to be replaced by another, who used its friend as a springboard to jump on me. I plunged my knife up, hitting something hard, and then soft. Bone and gut. The Mazikin landed at my feet, shrieking.

I kicked it out of the way and tugged at Malachi's belt to let him know he could take a step back, closer to the windows that were our best chance of escape. All the Mazikin started to hoot and shriek, and against my shoulder blades I felt Malachi's muscles flex as he wielded his staff with deadly efficiency. The emergency lights in the warehouse all flicked on at once, controlled by the female Mazikin in the hallway. She snarled something in the Mazikin language and pointed at us. "Take them!" she screamed.

I crouched as Malachi's staff whirled over my head and then pulled my second blade. Slashing out with a knife in each hand, I inched forward as the Mazikin descended. With vicious stabs and slices, I protected Malachi's back as he sent one Mazikin after another flying with fierce blows from his staff. Two young men with a maniacal glint in their eyes ran at us from the side, and I threw myself out of the way to give Malachi room. His boot smashed into the face of one while he jabbed his staff into the other's throat, and they both fell to the floor, where I finished them without hesitation, with the brutal descent of my blades through vital organs, unwilling to let them rise again and attack.

Something slammed on my back right as I ripped my blade out of a Mazikin's neck, sending me down on top of him. From above me, I heard Malachi shout, and then his legs were on either side of mine, shielding me. Another Mazikin dropped, and another stumbled out of my reach. The pipe I'd been clocked with rolled away with a clatter. Malachi called my name, and even though my ears were ringing, I still picked up the note of desperation in his voice.

"I'm fine!" I yelled, though my back and ribs were radiating hot waves of pain. My arms were buzzing. I had dropped one of the knives. Instead of reaching for another, I lunged and grabbed the pipe, and then bashed an oncoming white-haired Mazikin across the knees with it. Malachi nailed her hard in the head with his staff, knocking her out cold. And when she fell just a few feet away, I recognized her. Harriet. I guess her bat hadn't protected her after all, and neither had I.

I slammed the pipe down on her head and got to my feet. I kept low, swinging hard, cracking knees and shins, breaking ankles and a few hands that reached down to try to stop me. My bones vibrated from fingertip to spine every time I made solid contact, and I clenched my teeth and hoped for the soft crunch that told me I had disabled another one.

Above me, defending my left side and my back, Malachi jabbed and deflected, kicked and punched, crushed and dropped anything that came at him. He was an unstoppable force, smooth and invulnerable. Above the ruckus, I could hear the rapid but steady rush of his breath as he did his thing. Never once did it falter. We inched toward the windows, now only a few feet away, leaving a trail of broken and bleeding Mazikin behind us.

"The hall," barked Malachi. "More coming."

I didn't turn to look. I smacked a skinny girl Mazikin away from me and lunged for the nearest window. Behind us, I could hear the thunder of footsteps as the second wave of Mazikin pushed out of the hallway. With my heart pounding against my aching ribs, I raised the pipe and smashed the window glass, which exploded outward, sending a rain of shards tinkling to the sidewalk below. I leaped up on the windowsill and grabbed Malachi's shoulder as a siren sounded in the distance. His dark eyes met mine, and he nodded. I jumped onto the walkway, only a four-foot drop, ready to take on the Mazikin who had barred the door. But there was no one outside, only the wail of a siren coming closer. From across the street, tires screeched as a car peeled out. Someone had called the police.

Malachi grunted and stumbled against the window as the mob of Mazikin attacked. He swung his staff in an arcing blur, giving himself a pocket of space in which he could move. Then he squatted down and threw himself shoulders-first out the window, still slicing his staff through the air. He hit the ground and pushed himself to his feet as a few Mazikin came scrambling out of the window after us.

"We have to get out of here," I huffed, my fingers scrabbling along Malachi's waist as he stabbed the end of his staff into the neck of a skeletal middle-aged guy with inch-long fingernails. Dread rolled over me as I realized how bad this was. "I think we just killed at least eight of them. And they have plenty of witnesses."

"That won't be an issue, Captain," came a voice from behind me. I whirled to see Henry, a crossbow in his hands, wearing the same clothes he'd left the Guard house in. He shot the skeletal dude in the heart, and then leaned over and yanked the bolt from the guy's chest as soon as he collapsed. He nodded at Malachi. "Glad you texted. Run along now. I'll clean up."

I opened my mouth to argue, but Malachi grabbed my arm and pushed me into the lot while Henry leaped onto the windowsill and took aim.

"Grab any blades we left behind," Malachi called out as he started to run, collapsing his staff without breaking stride.

A flash of red light told me the cops had found our block. My feet slid in the gravel as I sprinted for the nearest alley, trying to get off the street. I barreled into it without even slowing down; then I tripped and went sprawling, hitting the cement hard. Stars appeared in my vision, but I scrambled forward, desperate to hide myself. If they caught us here, that would be it for me. They would probably charge me as an adult, would never let me go, would put me in a—

Warm hands skimmed across my ribs, and I let out a gasping breath. Malachi moved in close behind me and hooked his fingers beneath me, tugging me up. Like me, he was breathing hard, but unlike me, he seemed calm and determined as he guided me into a shallow alcove, a side entrance to the building next to us, concealing us as three police cruisers roared into the empty lot across the street.

My back was to the splintery wood of a door, and my face was pressed to Malachi's chest, my ear to his heart. I wrapped my arms around his waist and held on, taking unfair advantage of the chance to steal his warmth and strength, to pretend for a moment that he was still mine and wanted me to touch him. His earthy scent filled me up and left me starving. The drum of his heart both soothed me and called to me, until I was sure mine was beating in the same rhythm. The weight of his body against mine as he hid us from view both settled me and drove me crazy.

As we listened to the police using their bullhorn to demand that anyone left in the building come out with their hands up, Malachi's arms slid around me, steadying us as we tried to remain flat against the wall, buried in darkness.

"Are you hurt?" he whispered.

"Not really. My ribs ache from where I got hit with that pipe."

"Broken?"

"I don't think so. You?"

"My hands are bleeding." I tried to twist to see them, but he only held me tighter to keep us both from falling backward into the alley again. "I'm fine. It was just the glass. Nothing Raphael can't handle. You were right about the window. It was the smartest point of exit." His voice was gentle and soft. Reassuring. Like it used to be.

I never wanted to leave that alleyway.

"Did you notice how the Mazikin didn't try to bite or claw you?" he asked. "They were trying to subdue you. Not kill you."

"The one who hit me with the pipe must have missed that memo."

He shook his head. "They wanted us alive. They wanted *you*." His arms coiled around me, like he was still trying to keep them from getting me, and it was the best thing I'd felt all night. All week. All month.

"It's possible they wanted the police to catch us," I said. "This whole thing was a setup. They were waiting for us. They might have even paid that kid to feed us information."

"I realized that a little too late. They've never been this organized before. They've never come after us like this before."

"In the dark city, you had hordes of those enormous Guards watching your back. And even then, by the end they'd started picking off the Guards, one by one, right? We only have each other here. There are different rules, too. And they've realized that." My fingers curled into the fabric of his shirt. It should have been all professional, two Guards trying to survive, but it was hard to concentrate with him so close to me.

He only made it harder when he rested his chin on the top of my head. "Then I'm glad I have you. You are an excellent Guard, Lela. And a good partner."

"I'm not—"

"You fought well. Ana could not have done better. I had no fear for my back in there. I knew you would protect me."

"Well, you're the one who trained me."

"I never trained you to wield a pipe like that."

"Okay. I might have some moves of my own." I turned so that my forehead rested in the curve of his neck. This was not allowed. It was a shade too close, skin to skin, and I waited for him to pull away, but he didn't. He stayed very still while I inhaled, drawing the scent of him into my lungs.

The sound of footsteps across the street froze me in place. Malachi's heart picked up a fast, heavy rhythm, and he braced himself in the doorframe, pressing harder against me, making sure no part of us was visible from the mouth of the alley. From over his shoulder, I watched the beam of a flashlight skitter back and forth across the bricks, and I held my breath until it finally disappeared. Crunching gravel told me the cop was headed back to the cruisers.

I looked up to see Malachi, his face in shadow, gazing down at me. "I think they're gone," I whispered stupidly.

He nodded. I could barely see his face, had no idea what his expression would tell me if I could. But I knew it so well, had long since memorized every plane, every angle. If I could have, I would have run my fingers across his skin and read him with my fingertips. I knew that was off-limits, though, so I settled for staring, hoping he couldn't see my face either.

I drew in a shaky breath. "Do you think Henry got away?"

"I don't know," he said, his even tone giving way, turning ragged.

"Should we go?"

He didn't answer for a long time, just kept staring down at me, unreadable and unmovable. "I'm sorry," he finally said. "For being harsh to you earlier. You didn't deserve that."

"It's all right," I breathed.

"No, it's not."

As if it had a will of its own, my hand rose between us and rested against his cheek. When I realized what I was doing, I pulled it away, but Malachi caught it and held it to his face. Every part of my body came alive as the stubble on his cheek abraded my palm, and I stroked my thumb over his mouth. The hitch in his breath almost made my knees buckle. It nearly made me forget everything. But then . . . he cleared his throat and stepped back into the alley.

"There's a passage back here between the buildings," he said, all business again, leaving me wondering if that moment between us had been a figment of my fevered imagination. "Now that they've checked back here, we can probably make it out unnoticed."

We crept through the narrow alley, and then along a gap between two rusty chain-link fences, emerging about a block from the lot. I poked out my head to make sure we weren't emerging at the exact wrong time and peered back at the abandoned lot, now full of official vehicles and lit by spotlights. Detective DiNapoli was standing outside the building, watching over the swarm of activity with an impassive expression. The sight of him made my stomach hurt. I hoped Henry was okay—and that he'd gotten the knives we'd lost in the fight.

Knowing that if I had been caught there, I'd have some serious explaining to do, we stuck to the alleys until we were several blocks away and then turned toward downtown. We had survived, and we had eliminated several Mazikin, without being arrested or taken. It sent a message to the Mazikin—we could take a lot of them out, even if there were only a few of us. It should have felt like victory, but to me, it felt like the opposite. If the Mazikin numbers kept growing, if they kept coming at us like this, it was only a matter of time before our lucky streak snapped. We were running out of time to root them out. They were winning.

I glanced over at Malachi, who was walking with a slight limp. His hands were in the pocket of his hoodie. And his faraway, sorrowful expression told me he was probably thinking along similar lines, especially because he felt responsible for some of it. Defeat did not sit well with him.

My phone buzzed. I pulled it out and looked at the screen. A text. From Henry.

Pick up at Eddy and Bay. Prisoner to deliver.

I held up my phone so that Malachi could see. "Looks like Henry got out in time. And our evening is far from over."

It was the first time I'd seen Malachi smile in a long time.

TWENTY-SEVEN

THE MAZIKIN STARED AT me from across the mat, with his teeth bared, revealing filed, nasty little points. It was Clarence. His skinny thighs sported identical crossbow wounds, small round holes that oozed blood through the fabric of his filthy pants. I had tied his arms and calves to the heavy chair while Jim and Malachi held him down, but as we watched our enemy strain against the ropes, none of us let down our guard.

Henry had handed Clarence off to us in the alley and then disappeared into the darkness again, saying he hoped the thing would tell us where the nest was, because he hadn't been able to track any of them back to it yet. He'd told me enough to confirm my suspicions that the street kid had played us. The Mazikin had recruited human allies, which filled me with dread. It would be so much easier to get to us that way. We wouldn't be able to see them coming. We wouldn't be able to trust anyone.

Malachi walked over to the side table. Not thirty minutes before, he'd refused to summon Raphael to heal him, saying it would take too long. So I'd explained who our prisoner was while I tweezed slivers of glass from the palms of both his hands and bandaged them, leaving his fingers free. Now he was running them over the array of knives in front of him. "That was a nasty little ambush at the warehouse, Clarence."

The old Mazikin laughed, a quiet, hooting chuckle. His lips were cracked, and his skin was deeply weathered. His smile created a maze of wrinkles on his cheeks and brow. "Wait until you see what we do next," he snarled.

Malachi flipped a serrated knife into his bandaged palm with a single deft movement, his expression betraying nothing, though I'm sure it must have hurt. "We have no intention of waiting. You're going to tell us."

"It doesn't have to go this way." The Mazikin inclined his head in my direction. "If you give us what we want."

Next to me, Jim shifted restlessly. I gave him a sidelong glance, and he took a few steps back to lean against the wall, his face a bland mask.

Clarence was still staring at me, ignoring Malachi. "You haven't called Sil yet. He waits for you. He's getting tired of waiting."

Malachi stepped in front of me. "He needs a lesson in patience, then."

"Malachi," I said softly. He stiffened, but then moved out of the way.

Clarence watched the exchange with amusement. "How things have changed. This girl with the hair is your master now?"

I shook my head before I remembered we didn't owe him any answers. I wanted to apologize to Malachi but forced myself to save that for a private moment. "If we let you go tonight, Clarence, where would you run?"

His eye twitched, like I'd poked him with a needle. "I wouldn't run. I'm yours to kill now."

I took a few steps forward, close enough for me to smell the sweat and incense on his clothes and skin. "We're not going to kill you," I whispered.

He sat back a little, and his lips formed a tight line.

"You were counting on death, weren't you?"

He didn't answer.

I walked a slow circle around him and managed not to flinch when he stretched his neck toward me as I came near. "Do you miss your family, Clarence?"

He dropped his top teeth over his bottom lip while he stared at me, no doubt imagining the things he'd do if his hands were free.

"We could hold you here for a long time."

"He could be like our pet," Jim added, and then laughed to himself when everyone else responded with silence.

"We'd have to disable him," Malachi added. "I could amputate his hands and feet if you like."

Malachi's cold, utterly sincere words reminded me that he had decades of experience interrogating Mazikin in the dark city. He always killed them in the end, but he'd tried to get information from them as well. It was probably out of desperation and fear that a Mazikin prisoner had told him that story about how killing a Mazikin liberated the soul of its victim. Better to die quickly than be held indefinitely at the mercy of the Captain of the Guard.

I raised my head and met Malachi's eyes. There was no apology there. Only a brutal calm. If I told him to do terrible things to Clarence, he would. Without hesitation.

Clarence obviously knew it, too. He hissed at Malachi and then squealed when my Lieutenant feinted toward him and pulled back just as quickly. I would have had to use a scimitar to cut the thick haze of hatred between them. Clarence's fingers curled into fists as he glared at Malachi. He opened his mouth and closed it again, clamping down on whatever words he was about to spew. Then he hitched a hideous grin onto his face and looked at me.

"You can do what you want with me, girl, but we won't leave your friends alone unless you come to us. You can't stop us. You can only postpone the inevitable. But the longer you wait, the worse it will be."

This time, I stepped in front of Malachi before he reached Clarence, who started to giggle. "Oh, dear, things have changed, haven't they? Is it her soul, Captain? Or her body? Will you miss her when she's gone? Or will you still crave her when the Queen is wearing her skin?"

The knife zinged over my shoulder before Clarence finished his sentence. He shrieked and threw his head back. His left ear plopped to the ground next to him. I spun around and stared at Malachi, whose gaze was riveted on Clarence.

"Do that again, and you're going upstairs," I said quietly. I firmly reminded myself that Malachi was protective because I was his Captain, and for no other reason, and then turned to face Clarence again. "Sorry, dude. Here you go." I picked up the ear and dropped it in his lap, trying to make it look like it was all part of the plan.

"When you're in our city, I will return this favor," he growled, staring at his bloody ear.

"You're not going back there," I said. "Ever."

His head jerked up. "Humans are so stupid. This body won't hold up." He chuckled grimly. "It won't last long at all. Your idea of forever is very limited."

I talked directly to the monster hiding behind his gray eyes. "At first, you don't know what's happening. The dark tower is only a building, after all."

Clarence's eyes narrowed.

"It seems simple enough. Just walk through the lobby. It shouldn't take more than a minute, right?" I closed my eyes and tensed against the shudder. "But then the doors disappear. It's the funniest thing."

I listened to the snuffle of his breath as it became rapid and shallow. "You still think you can make it through. Until the first memory comes at you. It's the smell. Or, at least, it was for me. The scent of it. The feel of it. All around you. Inside you. And then it all hits you at once. Your pain, your humiliation, your fear. The memories you've spent your entire existence trying to scrub from your mind. Before you can fight them off, they're crawling up your spine. Into your brain."

I opened my eyes and looked down at him. He was paper-white. "And you get to fight not only *your* memories, but the memories of everyone you've ever possessed. Isn't that right?" I smiled. "It's okay, Clarence. You won't face it alone. They're all around you, the other people who didn't make it out. Some of them have probably been there for centuries. Maybe longer. It eats them, see. It sucks them down, holds on tight, and digests them slowly."

There was a solid ring of white around the irises of his

eyes. "You're right," I said softly. "Forever is a long time."

"The dark tower is not in this realm," he snapped, blinking quickly.

He was right. I was kind of bluffing, but what the hell. "You're mistaken if you think we're alone here," I said.

"The angels will not interfere. They are not allowed to." But now he was sweating. It beaded on his brow, dripped through the blood crusting on the side of his face.

I looked over my shoulder at Malachi. "Call Raphael. Get him to open a door to the dark city."

Malachi's expression was stony, and his face was pale, probably because he knew the terrors of the dark tower intimately. But he immediately pulled his phone out of his pocket.

"No!" squawked Clarence. "No!"

"Then give me what I need!" I shouted at him.

"No!"

"Malachi, dial! Tell Raphael I need him to summon two Guards from the dark city!"

Clarence strained against the ropes, the tendons in his neck making his throat look webbed. Poisonous spit flew from his mouth as he screamed, "We will destroy you, girl! If you think you have bad memories now, they are nothing compared to what we will do to you!"

With a hard shove, I upended Clarence's chair and sent him crashing to the floor; then I nudged his head with my boot. "What about your memories, Clarence? Got any good ones in there? How about the time I *killed* you?"

Clarence groaned and struggled as I lowered my knee onto his chest. "Where's the nest?"

He glared at me. "If I tell you that, it's better if you send me to the tower. If you destroy the nest, they will know I am a traitor. The Queen will eat my heart in the square."

"Then give me something else. Information I can use." I glanced back at Malachi again. He had the phone to his ear. "He's talking to Raphael now. You'd be amazed at how quickly angels get from place to place." I had no idea if Malachi was actually talking to Raphael or not.

Clarence tore his eyes from me to stare at Malachi. His chest was heaving. I could feel his fear through the soles of my boots. He believed my threat. And he feared the tower more than death or torture. He looked back up at me and flinched when he saw me glaring down at him.

"Your dance," he whispered. "This 'prom.' That is when we will strike. When we will take you and all your friends."

"How do you know about that?" I snapped.

His smile was wistful, with a serial killer edge. "You look so perfect in your dress. The Queen likes dresses."

Out of the corner of my eye, I saw Malachi's head jerk up. The Mazikin must have been tracking Tegan and me when we went shopping, and the thought made me want to scream.

Clarence's breath wheezed out of him, and I realized I was leaning all my weight on his rib cage. "I'm not going to prom, so don't bother," I said automatically.

Clarence shook his head. "Doesn't matter. We'll be there anyway. Such beautiful young people. Perfect." He rolled his eyes like he was savoring the idea. "Sil promised me I could have a new body. Maybe the tall one with the shoulders and the green eyes, the one with the bat."

Ian. I stood up and kicked Clarence in the side before I could stop myself. Waves of nausea rolled over me. They knew too much about us. Way too much. How the hell did they know so much?

I sucked in a deep breath and took a step back from the wheezing, bug-eyed Clarence before I made another mistake and kicked him again. He blinked up at me. "I think you broke me, girl. Good for you. Do it again."

"Give me more information."

"Captain," Jim said quietly.

Clarence grinned. "Captain, girl? You are the Captain?" The laugh boiled up from inside him, phlegmy and thick, and rolled out hysterical and shrill. "The mighty Guards of the Shadowlands, led by the girl with the hair." He could barely get the words out through peals of wild laughter.

I sank down next to him, feeling ice crystals form along my spine. "I know. It's hilarious, isn't it?" I nudged his leg with my elbow. "There. See what I did for you? Try to hold on to that funny memory when you're sitting in the mouth of the dark tower. I'm sure it'll help."

His laughter cut off like I'd chopped him in the windpipe. "I gave you information," he squeaked. "Important information."

I got to my feet. "*Meh*. Not enough. I need to know how you guys know so much about us. Now *that* would be worth something. Maybe even a quick death."

His eyes glinted with eagerness. "We have many ways."

"You're going to have to be a lot more specific than that, Clarence. Do you guys have anyone else at our school?"

He nodded, smiling, his pointy teeth sticking out over his bottom lip.

"Who? Who is watching us?"

He winced and shook his head. "She would know. She would eat my heart."

I gritted my teeth. "Then what can you tell me?"

He lifted his head off the mat. "Your mother misses you. Rita wants you so badly, girl. You are deeply in her head. So deep that my poor sister cannot get her mind off you."

"Shut up." I took a step back.

"Your mother didn't even scream when we took her. No struggle. Her soul slipped free like it had been hanging by a thread. I wonder if your eyes will look like Rita's did as the Queen takes hold of you. So wide. So perfect."

"Enough!" Malachi roared.

I snapped to, realizing with disgust that there were tears on my face. I couldn't stop thinking about it, how they had tied my mother to a table and torn her soul away from her. I couldn't shake that vision of her wide gold-brown eyes, of the ropes around her wrists.

Jim touched my arm. "Raphael's here."

I opened my mouth, gasping in a shuddering breath. I brushed my sleeves over my cheeks and turned around. Raphael stood against the wall. "Do you know why I called you here?" I asked.

He nodded.

"Will you open the doorway?"

His eyes lingered on my face, solemn, unreadable. He nodded again.

Without looking away from me, he ran the flat of his palm along the concrete wall of the basement, and a door appeared. He turned the knob and opened it, and beyond the threshold I could see one of the stone corridors of the Guard Station in the dark city, lined with gas lamps giving off that melancholy greenish light. Malachi's gaze flitted toward it, and then he turned away, like it hurt him to think about going back there. In the distance, I could see two of the enormous, inhuman Guards striding toward us. One of them was carrying the thick leather muzzle and mittens made especially to protect from Mazikin teeth and claws.

"Tell them to take him straight to the dark tower," I said

to Malachi, my voice hard and cold and frighteningly steady.

As Clarence began to shriek and writhe, I headed to the stairs, seeing nothing in front of my face but my mother's eyes, feeling nothing but a restless tug in my chest, making me wonder if my soul was fastened as tightly as it needed to be to get me through whatever was coming.

TWENTY-EIGHT

FOR A SINGLE DAY, I wondered if we could cancel prom, avoid the whole thing, but then I realized that the Mazikin were watching, and that no matter what we did, they would know. Better they come after us in a way we could plan for than to come up with something we couldn't anticipate.

I talked to Henry once or twice over the next few weeks. He was lying low after the Jewelry District Massacre, in which twelve individuals were murdered in what was thought to be some sort of turf fight between vigilante groups. The police were apparently seeking connections between these killings and the attacks on the homeless camps, seeing as some of the individuals killed in the warehouse had been survivors of the earlier raids. Nancy, my PO, and her pals on the force came to talk to me informally a few times, but seeing as there were no witnesses, no physical evidence, and about a million other, more plausible perps, they eventually decided to leave me alone and spend the taxpayers' dollars elsewhere.

The Mazikin were lying low, too, though we weren't sure if it was because they didn't want to draw more attention to themselves or because they were busy planning something horrific. We patrolled every night, but the streets were eerily quiet. We began to wonder if human informants were alerting the Mazikin to our movements, making it easier for them to avoid us and more human attention.

Along with Jim and Malachi, I obsessively watched every student at Warwick High, wondering which of them was on the wrong side. But whenever I could, I avoided the cafeteria, preferring to eat outside with Ian and let him distract me for a half hour each day. Seeing Laney with Malachi made me want to hurt her. Even the idea of them together added fuel to my training sessions with my Lieutenant, which left us both spent and aching. More than once, I hit him harder than I should have. More than once, he made me pay for it. More than once, Raphael had to be called in to fix us up afterward so we didn't go to school the next day looking like we'd participated in a prison riot.

My times with Ian were the only moments I felt normal

and even the slightest bit happy. Seeing him smile reminded me why all the vigilance and training was worth it and helped ease the ache of missing Malachi a little. I hung out with him at a party one night when it was my turn to guard our friends and realized how much I enjoyed his company. I even attended a few of his home games, though I spent the time staring at the spectators, trying to figure out which of them were Mazikin spies. Time was running out.

A week before the prom, I showed up at the Guard house after school and slid out of my car, yanking the garment bag from the passenger seat. I stood at the top of the stairs to the basement and listened. Judging from the clang and sizzle of a blacksmith's forge coming from below, Michael was already waiting for me. I went to the bathroom and changed. I put my hair up as best I could, in a semblance of the style that Tegan had selected for me. I strapped on the shoes with two-inch heels. Shimmering, floating, I descended the stairs.

"*Bhebha*, Lela, I've been waiting!" his gravelly voice called from below, followed by three sharp clangs.

"Coming!" I shouted. "Trying not to fall down the stairs."

"If that's what we're dealing with, I'm not sure I can help you, my darling *iqaqa*."

I reached the bottom step and wobbled onto the mat. Waves of heat coursed over my face. In front of me, half the basement appeared to be connected to another realm.

Specifically, to the vast workshop inhabited by the only person I figured could equip me properly without getting too personal about it. Unless calling me an *iqaqa* was personal. "Look, Michael. I know Malachi tolerated the name calling, but I'm a totally different—*whoa*. Are you all right?"

Though I was sure he was an angel, Michael didn't look any more like one than Raphael did, and certainly never acted in any way angelic. He was staring at me with his mouth hanging open, a red-hot column of metal in one hand and a hammer in the other. He looked like he was having a stroke. I'd already made it halfway across the mat before he snapped out of it, dropping the half-forged scimitar into a barrel of water and wiping his hand across his mouth. He cleared his throat. "Sorry. Er. Captain." His gaze moved to my chest. "*Amabele*," he mumbled, tossing the hammer over his shoulder.

"I see we've moved on from the British slang."

His gaze lifted a bit, almost making it to my face before being dragged back down. "Zulu. I needed a change."

"Are you going to be able to keep your eyes off my boobs long enough to help me?"

His eyes snapped up to mine. "I'm an excellent multitasker."

I shook my head. "I guess I look all right, then. Like a normal girl."

The chortle rolled out of him like an ocean wave, causing

his enormous belly to undulate, shaking the floor. "*Uyah-lanya*, Lela, if you think you could ever look like a normal girl." He squeezed his eyes shut and a lone tear leaked out as he tried to control his laughter.

I scowled, and then silently counted to ten. Malachi and Ana tolerated this for decades. I could tolerate it for one afternoon. "I hope that's a compliment."

"Get over here," he said, motioning me around his forge, into the sweltering open space between a workbench piled with tools and half-completed weapons, and that huge, steaming barrel of water. "I made something just for you." He held up two silky loops of material in his chubby fingers. "Behold!"

"And that is—"

"Your garters, my dear." He leaned forward. "May I help you put them on?"

I snatched them from his hand. "How about you watch? That enough for you?" I'd learned the first time we met that Michael could be handled with one part charm and one part sass. Ana had been a master of it, and that made me miss her more than ever. She would have handled this situation beautifully. It made my chest ache to think of her.

Michael leaned back against the barrel. "Don't let me stop you."

I lifted my foot to set it on the workbench, and then pulled my skirt high on my thigh, leaning forward to try to keep Michael from seeing too much. Judging from his sharp intake of breath, I wasn't doing a good enough job. As quickly as I could, I strapped the circle of silky material to my upper thigh and set my foot on the ground. It remained secure, even though it seemed like it should come sliding down. "This will stay in place?"

"Eh?" he grunted, still staring at my legs. "Oh. Yes. Specially designed. Here you go." He handed me three small knives. "The blades have a forward drop like all the rest. Your Lieutenant said they fit your style—slash and slice. Hang 'em high, or everyone will know you're armed when you shake your *nqe* on the dance floor." His eyes glazed over.

I took the knives from him, cringing at the creepy half grin on his face. "You're picturing me doing that right now, aren't you?"

He nodded, his eyes still dreamy.

"Thanks for your . . . thoughtfulness." I tucked the blades into the sheaths along the outer curve of my thigh and then repeated the process on the other side. Malachi was right: thanks to his endless drills, I'd gotten pretty good with these knives over the past few weeks and could fight efficiently with one in each hand. I would just have to practice drawing from the thigh instead of the waist. "Anything else you can do for me?"

He whipped out a long, slinky pair of silver gloves. "I made these just for you. Lightweight sap gloves."

I took them from him and raised my eyebrows, surprised by the weight of the silky material. I turned them over to see the delicate stitching along the backs, extending halfway along the fingers. "Is there something sewn into these?"

"Steel shot. You'll be able to punch through concrete boards."

"For real?"

"Trust me."

Damn. I slipped them on and examined the effect. Beautiful but badass. I smiled, something that felt almost foreign these days. "Anything else?"

He motioned for me to turn in place. I obeyed, ignoring the low whistle as he took in the rear view. After I'd completed a full revolution, he pointed at my feet. "Off with the shoes."

I did as he asked, handing over my heels and enjoying having my feet flat on the ground again. He held the shoes in front of his eyes, making a sour face. "You really going to wear these things?"

"It's not an occasion for boots."

His brows lowered, and he shooed me away. "Go play, and let me work."

I took my bare feet over to the unoccupied side of the training room, where I practiced drawing my knives from my new thigh sheaths, thinking this was not really what I pictured when I got asked to prom. Still, if it was going to prepare me to protect Ian and Tegan and Greg and Levi and Jillian and, *yes*, Laney, then I was all—

"Michael, are you ready for us?" a voice called from the top of the stairs.

My heart did an uncomfortable little flip.

"You're early, *umdidi!*" Michael roared, pausing in the middle of using a tiny mallet to hammer at a small metal spike on the forge.

I scrambled back against the wall as hard soles tromped down the stairs.

"Yes, but I thought maybe we could talk about what Lel—" Malachi froze at the bottom of the stairs. He was wearing a tux. The top few buttons of his shirt were undone, and he held a tie in his hand. His black hair was disheveled, like he'd just changed. And his dark eyes were on me.

His mouth opened and closed a few times. "Lela," he said in a strained voice. "I didn't know you would be . . . here."

"My car is in the driveway."

He swallowed hard, nodded, and tried again. "I didn't know you'd be . . ." He gave up and gestured at my dress.

A red-faced Michael plunged something into his barrel of water, sending a thick cloud of steam rolling across the space, curling my hair with the humidity. "Did ya think I'd make two trips?" he yelled at Malachi. "*Tsa mor kaka!*"

Malachi gave me a questioning glance. I shrugged. "Zulu."

Jim trudged down the stairs, his tux jacket slung over one shoulder. "Hey, Captain. We came to get outfitted for the party." He looked me up and down. "You look good. No idea where you'll put your weapons, though."

I slid my hand down my thigh and teasingly tugged up my skirt, just far enough to reveal the lower tips of my wickedly sharp blades. "I have my ways."

Jim smiled appreciatively, but Malachi frowned. "It's a start," he said to me. "I was going to talk to Michael about your—"

"But I decided to take care of it myself." I turned back to Michael. "How are we doing there?" I was suddenly desperate to leave the basement.

Michael raised his head, sweat dripping from the fat folds on his forehead. He held up my shoes. "Titanium coating and tips for the heels. Weaponized sexiness, *gugu*." He winked at me, leaving a few drops of perspiration clinging to his lashes.

I strode forward and took the shiny-heeled shoes from his hands. "Cool. So basically, I should try not to step on anyone's foot unless I want to sever some toes?"

He grinned. "Bravo, lovely. You got it in one."

I braced my palm on the edge of his table and slipped the shoes onto my feet. When I straightened, Malachi was watching me. "You'll need to practice with those. They'll be heavier than your regular shoes, and you want to make sure you don't turn your ankle. I'll get more dummies down here for tomorrow so that you can work on it."

"Okay. Thanks." I waited, wondering if maybe he would say more, hoping he might comment on how I looked, but after a few seconds of watching him fiddle with his tie, it was obvious that wasn't going to happen.

Not wanting to make a fool of myself, I carefully slid my shoes off and walked toward the stairs. Jim hopped off the bottom step and strode forward to bump fists with Michael, and then immediately started arguing with him about how many knives he could conceal in his vest and still be able to slow dance with Tegan.

Malachi brushed his fingers against my arm as I passed, and then immediately drew back when I turned to him. "Are you sure about this?" he asked me. "You are wearing so much . . . less than Jim and I." He glanced down at my shoes. "And your footgear—"

"You don't think I can handle myself?"

He gave me a warning look. "I *know* you can handle yourself. But you are at an automatic disadvantage because you are wearing what appears to be underclothes and little more."

"*Underclothes?* You think I look cheap or something? What do you think Laney will be wearing, Malachi? Has she modeled it for you?"

He raked a hand through his hair and looked over my

shoulder at the forge. "She is irrelevant to this conversation."

"Except she can wear nice dresses, but I can't?" I pictured Laney, her pale, skinny arms and bony shoulders, her slender hips and long legs. She'd wear something designer, something made for her. She'd look like she stepped from the pages of a catalog. I looked down at myself and saw the truth. I was never meant to wear dresses. I was meant to wear fucking *armor*. The only thing right about this stupid outfit was the lethal blades strapped to my thighs. My heart hammering, I whipped two of them from their sheaths and struck like a snake, whirling before he could get his guard up. In a fraction of a second, I ducked to avoid his grasping hand and drove him back into the wall with my shoulder.

My seriously toned, decidedly non-bony shoulder.

Malachi's gaze traveled slowly from one knife, the blade of which was less than an inch from his throat, to the other, the tip of which was positioned at an upward angle between his legs. Something dark and dangerous stirred in his eyes, a look that startled me in its familiarity—he'd looked at me this way the day he'd kissed me on the training mat. Fragile hope mixed with the boiling anger in my chest, stealing my breath, riveting my eyes to his face.

So I got to watch while his expression smoothed into a blank mask. "Was that necessary?" he asked.

I retreated as quickly as I'd attacked, my cheeks hot as Michael's forge. My fists were clenched so hard over my knives that my knuckles felt like they were about to splinter.

No, it wasn't necessary.

And if I didn't get out of here, I was going to do it again.

Malachi reached out to touch my arm again, but I jerked away. He sighed. "Lela, please—"

"I'm going to get changed for patrol." Without looking at him again, I ran up the stairs.

TWENTY-NINE

IAN HAD BEEN RIGHT—petit fours kicked ass.

When he'd called on the morning of prom, I'd already been up for hours, practicing with my knives, knowing today would probably bring the biggest fight of my life, one I hoped wouldn't end with my soul being ripped from my body. I'd been so close to saying no to him, but then realized this might be my last chance to just . . . have *fun*. Simple, easy fun. So there we were, walking out of this boutique bakery in Barrington with our mouths full.

He unlocked his SUV and opened the door for me; then he handed me the flat box containing a dozen more of the beautiful little iced cakes. "What you expected?"

"Better."

He shut my door and went around to the driver's side. He gave me a nervous glance as he fastened his seat belt. "Which part?"

"All of it." I looked away from him, focusing on my hands clutching the ribbon-wrapped box.

He twisted the key in the ignition and pulled out of the lot, heading south past quaint shops and treelined walkways. "Up for a hike?"

"Sure," I murmured, glad we would be doing something active, something that would keep me moving.

Ian brushed the tips of his fingers along the top of the box while he kept his eyes on the road. "Did you notice?"

I watched his tanned hand, keeping my own very still. "Notice what?"

He smiled. "The way nobody looked at you cross-eyed. The way your money was just as good as anyone else's."

I shifted in my seat so that my back was to the window. "Are you suggesting," I said slowly, "that my feelings about not belonging in Barrington were wrong?"

He shrugged. "I'm only saying that if you give people a chance, they might not disappoint you *all* the time."

I fiddled with the gold-and-red ribbon, suddenly wishing for an escape route. The dark shape on my forearm caught my eye again. Nadia's face. She and I had come from different places, too, and like Ian, it hadn't mattered to her, either. I'd dreamed of her last night, of walking with her by a clear stream, of hearing her laugh, watching her grin as the silver scales of fish caught the light of the summer sun. I'd wanted to ask her how she was, but found I didn't have a voice, didn't have words. Or maybe words were unnecessary. She was past that kind of thing, deep within a peace so *full* that there was no room for anything else. When I'd gasped myself awake, the envy almost choked me.

After letting me drift in my thoughts for a good long while, Ian pulled over. "Come on. We're here."

I looked around, and thought of Nadia again. "The Cliff Walk?" We were at the place I'd died. And come back to life.

"I've got a few favorite spots. I think we're early enough to avoid the wedding picture crowd."

He hopped out of the car, and together we picked our way along the rocky start of the trail, leading to the path along the ledges overhanging the ocean. My heart skittered with the memories of the night I'd followed this trail straight over the edge.

Ian led the way past that high, shrub-covered hill, to a spot where the rocks became boulders and the sun sent diamond shards of light off the surface of the ocean. He climbed up on one and sat down, and I joined him, leaning my head back to feel the late-spring sun on my face.

"Have you been here before?"

"I came here with Nadia a few times. She loved this place, too."

"Damn. I was hoping I'd be the first to bring you here."

I glanced over at him, startled to see real disappointment there. "Why is that important?"

He chuckled and shook his head. The breeze blew his shaggy brown hair away from his face, letting me watch as his expression changed from smiling to serious. "If I ask you something, Lela, will you promise to tell me the truth?"

My heart dropped into my stomach. "You have a way with the ominous, you know that?" His green eyes met mine, and they pulled the words right out of me. "All right," I said, my voice choked.

He leaned forward very slowly, his gaze sliding from my eyes to my mouth. The heat of it caught me completely by surprise. His playful, nervous mask had dropped away, revealing a hunger that crackled along my skin and made me shiver.

"Hanging out with you is the only time I don't think about everything that's happened," he said. "I could talk to you for hours, and I could stare at you for longer than that. But no matter how much I do, I can't figure one thing out." His face was inches from mine. I could smell the strawberry filling on his breath. "Do I have a real shot here?"

And then his lips were on mine, warm and soft and sweet, paralyzing me. His hand slipped around the back of my neck and held me while he slid closer, blocking out the sun. And my heart . . . it ached. Because this was everything

I could have hoped for, everything I might have wanted in a moment like this. Because he was missing *nothing*.

But I was.

I laid my palm on his chest, over his heart. And gently pushed.

Ian pulled away, and when I saw the hurt in his expression, I closed my eyes. "Okay," he said quietly. "At least I know. So will you answer another question for me?"

I nodded.

"Is it me? Or is it that I'm not him?"

My eyes flew open. "Does it matter?"

He rubbed his chest, right over the spot where my hand had been a second earlier. "Yeah, actually."

What the hell. "It's not you. This would have been different if—"

"If Malachi Sokol hadn't decided Warwick High was the perfect place for him to experience American culture," he said bitterly. "That dude's timing *sucks*." He stared out across the water. "Or maybe mine does."

I drew my knees to my chest. "Ian, I—"

"No. You've done me a favor. Don't worry about it."

"A favor?"

"Yeah. It's been killing me, wondering if it was me. If I'm just not . . ." he sighed. "But you said this would have been different if he hadn't shown up. Do you mean that?"

I squeezed my arms tighter around my legs. "I think . . .

yeah." It might have helped if I could have told him how I met Malachi, how he'd saved me, how he made me better than I was, and how he sacrificed a peace he'd earned with decades of suffering and service, all for me. How he was the first and only person who had ever told me he loved me. And even if that wasn't true anymore, it had changed the shape of my heart and carved itself into the marrow of my bones. It had created a space in which my own feelings could grow, and they had, and that couldn't be changed now, no matter how beautiful and good the boy in front of me was.

"He's going to prom with Laney. I think they're together." His words were quiet but deadly.

"I know." A thought occurred to me, vaulted into the front of my brain by the pain in his voice. "That's not why I'm here, Ian, and it's not why I said I'd go to prom with you. No matter what we do now, I need you to know that. I'm here because of you. And I never wanted to hurt you."

"It's okay. You love who you love." His smile was laced with sadness. "We all do."

"You're amazing, Ian." I meant it.

"That's what all the ladies tell me." He grinned in this devastating, fake-cocky way and snagged a petit four from the box.

I laughed and grabbed one for myself. The bittersweet chocolate provided an endorphin rush I badly needed. "So," I said when I'd finally swallowed it. "What now?"

He leaned back and rested his elbows against the rough stone. "I drive you home, and I pick you up tonight, and then we have an awesome time at our senior prom."

I frowned. "You still want to go?" I realized that I'd half-hoped this would get him to stay home. If I had to break his heart, I wanted to at least keep him safe.

He looked at me like I was crazy. "It's senior prom. Party. After-party. You expect me to stay home and cry into a plate of spaghetti?"

"Okay, then." I paused. "Hey, listen. I've heard some rumors. Nothing too specific. Only that there might be some party crashers."

"Are you talking about those meth freaks who jumped us at the theater?" His gaze sharpened. "There'll be security. They'll only allow students in."

I bit my lip. "Okay. Just, I don't know. Be ready."

He raised an eyebrow. "All right," he said slowly. "Does Malachi know? 'Cause Laney's been my friend since elementary school, and she's a nice girl. She shouldn't get mixed up—"

"Malachi would never let anything happen to her. And believe me, he can protect her. She's probably safer than anyone."

"And who's going to protect you if anything goes down?" Ian sat up straight, brushing off his palms.

"I don't need anyone to protect me, all right? Trust me

on that one, too."

He mumbled something under his breath, and then stood up and held out his hand to help me to my feet. "It's after noon. I should get you home."

I followed him back the way we had come, drawing slow, steady breaths of ocean air into my lungs and taking measured, sure-footed steps over wobbly rocks and loose gravel. Time to get ready for tonight . . . and maybe squeeze in another hour of knife practice, too. There was no way the Mazikin were getting my friends. I was just getting my head right when my phone buzzed with a text from Henry.

Tonight we won't be so gentle.

While I tried to make sense of the words, my phone buzzed again. It was a picture. A man, lying in a pool of blood, his face a pulpy, unrecognizable mess. But even so, I knew him by the scarecrow limbs, the thinning gray hair.

And the crossbow lying at his side.

THIRTY

"STOP FIDGETING, FOR GOD'S sake, Lela. Do you have ADHD or something?" Tegan was about to lose it on me. I'd arrived an hour late at her house, having spent the entire afternoon in an intense planning session with Malachi and Jim, waiting to hear word from Raphael.

Henry was in the hospital, under heavy police guard. The Mazikin had somehow figured out who he was, beaten him nearly to death, and called in the cops. We didn't know if they'd possessed him before they dumped him. We didn't know if he would survive. All we knew was that he was the prime suspect in the homeless murders, and in his head he carried all the necessary knowledge to bring the earthly Guard unit down. Raphael had gone in to do damage control, however he saw fit, but if Henry was a Mazikin now, one of us would have to put him down. That knowledge, along with my rage that they'd hurt one of my Guards, almost made me look forward to fighting them face-to-face. I wanted to hurt them. Especially Sil. I had no doubt he was responsible.

Tegan pinned another curl into position. Her own hair was slicked into place, and her makeup was shimmery and perfect. I had a feeling Jim was going to have a hard time holding himself together when he saw her. With the stakes so high and the danger so clear, all his protective instincts would go into overdrive.

"You and I haven't talked about Jim," I said, wishing I were better at girl talk.

Her look softened. "I've never met anyone like him."

"That makes sense," I mumbled.

"He's . . . he's so sweet. Innocent, kind of. Like when he experiences stuff, it's for the first time. But then, there's a part of him that's all been-there-done-that." She shrugged. "He's a bit of a mystery. I've never even been to his house."

"But you like him?"

Her mouth twisted up at one corner. "Well. He's hot as hell, so how could I not?"

"It's more than that."

I felt her quiet burst of laughter on the back of my neck. Most of my hair was piled on top of my head in what she called "a messy updo." It was organized chaos, but she insisted it looked good. She slid in a final hairpin and stepped back. "It's a lot more than that," she agreed. "But we're taking it slow."

I couldn't hide my surprise. She saw the look on my face and slapped my arm. "I'm not a slut. Jeez. But also, he's kind of old-fashioned. He said we should make sure what we have is 'real' before we . . . he said this was important to him. Too important to rush." With a hopeful smile, she turned her face away. "We'll see what happens tonight."

Indeed we would. Right now, Jim and Malachi were probably strapping weapons to their battle-hard bodies, getting ready to defend the senior class from Mazikin attack. I glanced over at my backpack. Time to add a few critical finishing touches to my own outfit.

I stood up. "I'd better get changed, I guess."

"Go ahead. Greg said they'd get here at seven."

I grabbed my backpack and went into Tegan's enormous bathroom, all marble and brushed nickel. The mirror reflected a stranger, a shimmery-lipped, bronze-cheeked girl. Apart from the scars, a pretty girl.

A girl who would kick serious ass if anyone threatened the people she cared about.

My fist tightened over the strap of my backpack. I pulled out my phone and called Raphael, who answered before the phone had a chance to ring.

"They didn't possess him," he said to me by way of greeting. "Henry is himself."

I exhaled with relief. "How is he?"

"They hurt him very badly. Tortured him, by the looks of it. I'm impersonating a doctor here at the hospital this afternoon, so I'm healing him in spurts. I'll remove him from their custody later, once I'm sure he won't die while I'm moving him from place to place."

"Okay," I whispered.

"Enjoy your evening," he said, his tone changing completely, turning bright and casual, sending a chill down my back. "I'll call you if anything changes. Be careful tonight." He hung up.

I dropped my phone into my pack and pulled out my garters, gloves, and shoes. I stripped down, avoiding the sight of myself in the mirror, of the claw marks across my stomach that Sil had given me the last time we met. He'd been small and weaselly, but fast. Deadly fast. And merciless. I'd barely gotten away, and even then, I would have died if Raphael hadn't healed me.

The flowing fabric of my burgundy dress slid over my skin, light and comfortable, fitting me perfectly. The matching garters were snug at the tops of my thighs; the narrow, sharpened blades, their curves catching the light, slid snugly into their sheaths and were concealed completely by the skirt. I pulled on my weaponized shoes and put on the gloves. Ready.

A knock at the door. "Lela? They're here early. So is Diane. She and my mom are dying to take pictures, so you'd better get out here."

I looked down at my beautiful disguise. "Coming."

With my heart beating a rolling rhythm against my ribs, I walked down the long hallway and entered Tegan's living room, which could have comfortably housed Diane's entire split-level. Jillian and Levi were by the window, their heads together, breathing on each other. Tegan was introducing a nervous-looking Jim to her parents, Mr. and Mrs. Murray. Alexis and Greg were lounging against the piano, where Tegan's little sister, Greta, a ten-year-old prodigy, was showing off.

Laney was on the couch, looking luminous and angelic and fragile in deep-green silk, jabbering at Malachi, who was standing next to her and staring at the arm of the couch like he was about to kill it. He looked up as I walked in, and our eyes met, long enough for me to feel it like a rusty poker through my chest. His posture changed subtly as we stared at each other, like some of the air had leaked from his tires, but he kept a straight face. I fought to as well, but it was hard. He always looked good, but tonight he looked amazing. Like a young, olive-skinned James Bond or something.

I'd never seen anyone look so good in simple black.

Then Ian came out of the kitchen with a sandwich in his hand, which he raised in Mrs. Murray's direction with a smile. She nodded back indulgently; clearly, she was no stranger to Ian's compulsive eating habits.

He took a few steps into the living room, and then stopped dead. "Whoa," he mouthed, his green eyes sliding from the top of my head down to my feet. He looked down at his sandwich like he had no idea how it had come into his possession, swallowed hard, and then set it on an end table. "Hey," he said, walking toward me, wiping his hands on the side of his tux. "So Tegan wasn't kidding about this dress."

I grinned because, *Goddammit*, this felt good. Much better than Malachi's perfect professionalism, the ease with which he turned away from me to attend to his gorgeous date. To have a guy as hot as Ian look at me like I was some sort of goddess wiped a little of the pain away.

"I'm glad you approve." I reached out and took his offered hand, and he pulled me toward him. I narrowly missed stepping on his foot, and reminded myself to be careful. He probably needed his toes.

"*Approve* is a mild way of putting it," he said quietly. "You're killing me. Can we pretend like our conversation this morning didn't happen?" His easy smile told me he was kidding. Mostly.

My cheeks warmed, and the way his eyes stroked over my

face, I knew he hadn't missed it. "I've got an idea," he said, leaning over me. His lips brushed my ear. Out of the corner of my eye, I saw Malachi's head turn quickly. "Use me to make him jealous. Please?"

I pulled back, looking into his handsome face. "Even if that were possible, I'd never do that to you." I reached up and touched his cheek. "We'll have fun tonight, all right?" *And hopefully, we'll all come out of this alive.*

He put his arm around my waist, and the heat I'd seen this morning had returned to his expression. "I want you to know something, Lela. Sooner or later, Malachi will go back to wherever he came from, but I'll be here. And I can be *very* patient." He bowed his head over mine, staring into my eyes until I blinked. Then he grinned, and the fire in his eyes was gone—or maybe hidden. "I just needed to say that. But for tonight, good clean fun, coming right up." He kissed my temple. "You look beautiful."

A flash startled me, and I looked up to see Diane wipe a tear from her face and aim the camera at us once again. I smiled as Ian threw a casual arm around me, still a little stunned by the way he could switch that intensity on and off. He turned on his easy charm as Diane took a few more pictures, stopping between each to wipe her streaming eyes. It was totally embarrassing—but in an awesome way. She was here. I mattered to her, and everyone knew it. Before she left for her night shift at the prison, she pulled me into a tight hug. "You deserve this happiness, baby," she said quietly before she let me go.

I squeezed my eyes shut and willed myself not to cry. For a moment, and despite everything that was going on, I *was* happy, wrapped in the arms of my foster mom and feeling no desire to pull away.

After Diane left for work, Mrs. Murray took a few pictures of all of us together, me and the people who had become my friends, people who I'd thought were as two-dimensional as a snapshot, but who'd turned out to be so much more once I actually got to know them. The irony was a little painful—I hadn't known that when I was alive and had a life to live. Only now, when I had no right to any of it, could I see it clearly, all this possibility.

God, I wanted Nadia to be there so badly. I wanted her to see this and know she'd been right, to thank her for burrowing a tiny tunnel through the miles of defenses I'd built, enough to let the light in.

"I know you're missing her," Tegan said. I turned to see her standing at my shoulder. She gave me a sad smile. "I am too."

I nodded, struggling to speak around the enormous lump that had formed in my throat. "I think we're all missing people tonight. I know Ian's missing Aden."

Our eyes traveled across the room, to where Ian was now lounging on the couch, laughing with Levi. There was a conspicuous space between them, and I got the sense that they'd unconsciously left a seat for Aden there, not yet having reshaped around his absence. I shuddered, thinking about where Aden really was, hoping he wasn't suffering too much.

"We'd better get going, folks," Greg finally hollered, tapping at a new watch worth more than my car. "The bus leaves for the restaurant in five! Load up your overnight bags because we're not coming back!"

The girls all filed down to the bathroom for final lip glossings and cleavage boostings and whatever else, while the guys started carting bags to the SUV. Ian hoisted his long duffle over his shoulder, as well as my smaller backpack. It looked like he'd packed enough clothes for a whole week. Levi had also packed a massive duffle, but it was clear he and Jillian were sharing. I stood there, watching everyone file out to the SUV to start the evening, feeling there but not there, with them but alone.

I promise, I thought. *I promise I'll keep you all safe.*

As we walked into the civic center, I was happy to see security guards hanging around. It made it seem less likely that we'd have a horde of vagrant-looking Mazikin descending upon us. Pictures of Aden and Nadia graced the lobby, reminding us that they should have been here. Ian slowed as he walked by, and I took his hand and squeezed when his jaw tensed and his eyes got shiny.

Malachi, Jim, and I took turns patrolling the perimeter so that we didn't leave our group of friends unguarded. Raphael had texted during dinner to say that Henry had regained consciousness, and I was hoping he'd slipped him out of the hospital by now. I was also hoping Henry would be able to tell us what happened—and maybe the location of the Mazikin nest. I circled the ballroom with my phone in my hand, waiting.

As the hours dragged and nothing bad happened, apart from the agony of having to watch Laney and Malachi slow dance, which, thankfully, they only did once, I actually found myself getting impatient. Had Clarence's threat been a total ruse? Had the Mazikin changed their plans? And if they had, what had that text—*Tonight we won't be so gentle*—meant?

I returned from my final perimeter watch just in time to hear the announcements for prom king and queen—Ian was king, as expected.

And Laney was queen.

Her face lit up, but then fell as she looked at Tegan, who I'd thought would have a lock on it. But Tegan only gave Laney a sly smile and shooed her away, making me wonder if she'd stuffed the ballot box. Levi and Jillian were named prince and princess. I stood behind Malachi's chair and watched as the four of them were crowned on the stage and descended to the dance floor. They seemed . . . right where they should be. The angel-kissed, ready to go on and have fabulous, happy lives. It didn't hurt to watch as much as it felt disconnected somehow, like I was already a step removed from this place, from these people.

Tegan and Jim got up to join, followed by Greg and Alexis, leaving Malachi and me alone at the table. It was Jim's turn to patrol, but he deserved a break, and he looked so happy with Tegan in his arms that I couldn't hold it against him.

Warm fingers brushed over mine, and I looked up to find Malachi standing next to me. He held out his hand, but the look in his eyes was surprisingly uncertain.

"I'm sure Ian wouldn't begrudge me one dance with you," he said quietly.

"Would Laney?"

He sighed. "If I thought it was improper, you know I wouldn't do it."

"That was an amazing nonanswer," I mumbled as I watched my hand rise without my permission and take his.

And then I was in his arms, and it overwhelmed my circuitry, making the rest of the room go dim around me. I missed being that close to him, at least, during a time when we weren't trying to kill each other.

Malachi must have been thinking along similar lines. He used one arm to hold me close, and then took my hand and tucked our entwined fingers against his chest. "This way," he said with a devastating smile, "I can be sure you won't draw with your strongest hand, which greatly increases my chances of survival."

I laughed. "Good thinking." I was surprised I could actually get the words out; the feel of his body against mine was rapidly turning my bones and brain to jelly. It took everything I had not to lean my head against his chest, not to stare without blinking at the harsh beauty of his face.

We were barely moving, barely swaying, but under my skin, there were earthquakes, tidal waves. Solar flares. I'd danced with Ian a few times tonight, and it had been fun, but it hadn't felt like this. No one else could affect me like this. No one else could simultaneously terrify me and fill me with this kind of warmth. I didn't want it to be this way. I didn't like the idea that anyone had that firm a grip on my heart, especially someone who had made it clear he didn't want anything to do with said heart. But I'd fought it for so long, and there was nothing to do now but admit defeat. Whether he wanted me or not, I was his. Only his.

My rebellious fingers rose from his shoulder to the back of his neck, seeking skin-to-skin contact. And when it happened, his eyes fell shut for a moment before his expression shifted into playful and casual once again. Was I making that up, that I'd affected him like that? Was I imagining that the steely arm around my back tightened, pulling me even closer? Was I the only one who felt the electricity as his fingers slid up to brush the bare skin of my back?

"Are you having a good time?" I asked, hating the way it came out breathless and halting.

He shrugged. "It's been a complicated evening. You? Is he treating you well?" His eyes looked black in the low lights, and they were focused on mine, waiting for my answer.

"Ian is totally nice. I don't think he has a mean bone in his body."

"I'm glad to hear it," he said, his eyes honing in on where Ian and Laney were dancing.

I glanced over, too, to see Ian pull Laney close and guide her head to his shoulder. He cradled her tenderly, stroking her silky red hair as they swayed to the music. Fear for him zipped through me at the frightening image of him facing off with Malachi, a matchup that wouldn't last more than a few seconds. "They've been friends since elementary school," I said quickly. "I'm sure he's just—"

"He's comforting her," Malachi said quietly, turning back to me.

A million questions flashed into my head, but I never had the chance to ask them.

Because at that exact moment, the Mazikin came crashing into the Warwick High prom.

THIRTY-ONE

A RAIL-THIN TEENAGER WEARING a stained suit and skinny tie vaulted onto one of the tables, kicking aside the centerpiece. He squinted at the dance floor, and as soon as his eyes landed on me, he was in motion. Diving onto all fours, he threw himself onto another table, sliding on the tablecloth before taking another leap on his way to me. Kids lunged out of the way, screaming as a second Mazikin bounded into the room, a muscular guy whose blond dreads looked like a lion's mane. He, too, was wearing a suit. A bow tie, even.

The two of them had eyes only for me. Snarling, they made their way across the huge room, punching and knocking aside anyone unfortunate enough to be in their way.

Malachi released me, and both of us were reaching for our knives when Levi nailed the thin Mazikin midair—with a chair. The impact sent the Mazikin to the ground, bleeding and dazed.

The other Mazikin roared when he saw his friend go down, and he lunged for Levi, but Jim shoved Levi away and shot a hard punch to the Mazikin's stomach before leaping into the air and performing the most acrobatic kick I'd ever seen. He landed on his hands. The Mazikin landed face-down. The kids nearest Jim gave him a round of applause.

Neither of the invaders had made it to the dance floor. Not even close. Two security guards ran in a second later, having heard the commotion. I could only assume they'd let these guys in thinking they were students. One of them lifted a phone to his ear as he leaned over the skinny Mazikin. A bunch of our classmates crowded around the guards, all talking at once about how these guys had crashed our prom.

"I'm calling the police," one security guard finally said in a loud voice.

The other security guard held up his hands. "We've got this under control, kids." He stood over the blond Mazikin like he'd been the one to take the guy down.

Levi chuckled between heavy breaths. He turned to catch Jillian in his arms, grinning as she practically wrapped herself around him. Jim straightened up, not yet ready to relax. He cast a sidelong glance at Malachi and me while he ran his hand up his rib cage, probably wishing he could pull the knife I knew was hidden under his jacket. A security guard shooed him away, and he backed up reluctantly, dripping aggression. His posture didn't loosen until he felt Tegan's hands on his back.

The music switched off as a song ended, and the DJ didn't seem sure he should load up another track. Most of the kids on the dance floor were staring at the crowd around the Mazikin.

Malachi looked over at me. "That was too easy."

"I know." We stood close as we watched the two Mazikin, who were now handcuffed but conscious, each with an over-weight security guard sitting on his back. Out of the corner of my eye, I caught a flash of emerald silk—Laney. I turned my head to see her standing next to Ian. She glared at me while he glared at Malachi. I cleared my throat and stepped away from my Lieutenant.

Greg turned to Ian. "Hey, your majesty," he called. "How do you feel about cutting out for the after-party early?"

"Fine with me." Ian put his arm around Laney's shoulders and spoke too softly to her for me to hear what he was say-ing. She nodded, directing her gaze at the floor. Somewhere along the line, I had missed something. Malachi had said Ian was comforting Laney—had they broken up? I shut my eyes and gave myself a hard mental shake, stomping down any stupid hope trying to take root in my brain.

The failed Mazikin attack had killed the party mood, and everyone trailed out to their cars, some of them stopping to give police their names to follow up with statements. I eagerly sidestepped them, leaving them to cart away our attackers and keep them off the streets for at least one night. My mind was focused on where the next attack would be coming from.

Our crew climbed into the stretch SUV to head to the after-party at an all-ages club in Providence. Malachi, Jim, and I had already checked it out, in case the Mazikin decided that would be a better place to attack. I scooted onto the leather seat of the vehicle, making sure my skirt didn't ride up and reveal the weaponry strapped to my thighs.

Ian gave me a sad smile and took a seat across from me, next to Tegan and Jim, who seemed only aware of each other. Levi was in a fabulous mood, and I couldn't blame him; Jillian was looking at him like he was some kind of superhero. They were like the opposite of Laney and Malachi, who sat several inches from each other, stone-faced. Greg and Alexis seemed to have gotten into some kind of tiff as well; she had her back to him while Greg kept glancing at his watch, like this was the last place he wanted to be. I sympathized. Then my purse started to vibrate. I pulled my buzzing phone from my clutch.

"I've been trying to call," Raphael said when I picked up.

"Sorry. We had an incident at prom."

"Anyone hurt?"

"No, it's fine. How is he?"

"That's why I was calling. He's awake, and we're at the Guard house. He knows the location of the nest."

My head shot up, and I met Malachi's steady gaze and nodded. This was it. If we could make it there and attack preemptively, our friends might be safe. "Can you come get us at the Phase Three Club?" I asked quietly, looking apologetically at Jim. He didn't notice, though. He had his tongue halfway down Tegan's throat. So much for taking it slow.

I hung up. Malachi pulled his phone from his pocket and checked the time; then he reached over to pry Jim off Tegan. Duty called.

The SUV braked suddenly, and then lurched over a landscaped median, tossing Laney right off the seat. Alexis screamed, and Tegan and Jim jerked apart. Greg's fingers curled over the edge of the seat, his face and knuckles white. Levi banged on the thick plastic barrier separating us from the driver, but there was no response from the front.

The SUV veered, and one wheel bumped up on the sidewalk, sending off sparks as it took out a parking meter. Malachi lunged forward and drove his fist against the barrier. It cracked but didn't give. The SUV accelerated sharply to the shrill of horns and the sounds of screeching tires as a few cars swerved out of the way. It jumped the curb completely and skidded onto a dark, narrow side street.

Malachi punched at the barrier again, leaving a smear of blood across the thick plastic, but the thing didn't give. As the SUV swerved into the parking lot behind some old brick building, I looked down at my hands, at the thin pockets of steel shot sewn into my silvery gloves. Then I drew back my fist—and drove it straight through the barrier, shattering it completely.

A wall of scent hit us, turning my stomach. Our driver was Mazikin. But it was too late for us to do a thing about it. He was driving straight for the side of the building. The only thing we had time to do was throw ourselves down as the thunderous impact raised the back end of the stretch SUV high into the air before sending it crashing to earth again. The front end crumpled, and bricks tumbled through the destroyed windshield. I was thrown against the seat and then fell to the floor on top of several of my classmates as glass and metal crunched and popped, as everyone around me screamed. And despite all that noise, I still managed to hear the animal howls coming from outside the vehicle.

I raised my head and saw them, closing in on us from both sides of the lot, eyes bright and feral, hands curled into claws, with dirty faces and wild hair, old and young. They had found the perfect moment, when all of us had our guard down, when we thought we were safe, and they'd set up their ambush. And one thing was very clear: they had no intention of being gentle.

Hands grasped my face, and I jerked away, but they held me fast. "Lela. Look at me. Are you hurt?" Malachi asked. His face appeared in front of mine after I blinked a few times.

"Not hurt."

His expression was grim, but his eyes were soft. "Good. Get up. And stay close to me."

"But I can—"

His hands tightened. "They're here to take *you*. Stay behind me." All I could do was nod. His hands fell away from me, and he whirled around to face the threat.

The tinted windows of the SUV were spiderwebbed with cracks, but not yet shattered—until one of the Mazikin slammed a crowbar through the glass. Another did the same on the other side. With crashing blows, they hammered their way from the rear of the vehicle to the front, turning glass into shrapnel as screams once again filled the cramped space.

Malachi and Jim pushed our stunned, disoriented friends to the floor and hunched over them awkwardly, their shoulders pressed to the low ceiling. Malachi had taken off his jacket and thrown it over Laney and Tegan's heads, revealing the full extent of his preparations for the evening. He drew two throwing knives from the holsters that ran down his sides, but had to close his eyes as he was pelted with shards of glass. As soon as there was an opening, though, his knives were flying to thin the crowd outside. With my ears still ringing, I leaped onto the seat and lunged for the crowbar as it came bashing through the window in front of me, ripping it from the Mazikin's hands and stomping my shoe right onto the creature's arm. He yowled and fell away.

"Lela!" Malachi shouted.

"I'm right here!"

I crawled along the glass-strewn seat, slicing my knees to ribbons but terrified to step on my friends with my titanium shoes. All the girls except for me were crouched on the floor, practically in the fetal position, whimpering and flinching. I couldn't blame them, and I was actually glad they weren't watching as Malachi hurled the last of his throwing knives at our attackers just beyond the windows. The noise was overwhelming: crunching, rending, shrieking—and growling. Snarling. Snapping. It was like being attacked by a pack of wild dogs, except they were smarter and could wield crowbars.

A hand grabbed for mine from the floor: Laney. She stared up at me with wide doe eyes. "Can you get us out?"

"We will, but if you have a phone, you might want to call the police," I said as a pair of arms reached for me from the outside. Before I could get away, they coiled around my waist and yanked, slamming my hips and shoulders against the side of the SUV.

"I've got the girl with the hair!" the owner of the arms called, and the answering hoots of excitement told me they were all coming on the run. I reached for one of my knives, but a second pair of arms joined the first, and then I could barely move at all. I was bracing myself to be pulled into the night air and surrounded by Mazikin when a bat slammed down on my attacker, breaking bone with a dull snap. I turned my head to see Ian hunched behind me with a baseball bat, his eyes blazing.

"You told me to be ready," he huffed, and then raised the bat and smacked another Mazikin dead in the face.

The rear doors of the SUV flew open as we were attacked on all sides. Mazikin tried to crawl through the shattered windows, but apparently Ian had warned Levi, too, because the guy was standing protectively over Jillian as he pulled a bat from his overstuffed duffel. He and Ian each took a side, swinging with deadly precision, temporarily holding the Mazikin off. With that cover, Malachi tugged his backpack from under a seat, and from it he pulled his baton, and handed another to Jim. We'd hidden extra supplies in our overnight bags in case the fight ended up in the parking lot. Malachi and Jim pushed out the back of the SUV, extending their batons into staffs and driving back the Mazikin mob waiting outside.

From over Malachi's shoulder, I could see we'd already cut their numbers. We were now facing off with fewer than twenty, but they all seemed determined to get to me. Rage burned in my chest, shooting strength to my hands and fingers. I tugged my gloves up my arms, reassured by the weight along my knuckles, knowing Michael hadn't been kidding when he'd said I could punch through concrete. I drew a knife in each hand and got ready to jump from the back and carve my way through our enemies.

A shout of pain from behind me was all the warning I had before arms wrapped around my waist, dragging me back into the depths of the SUV. A hand clamped over my mouth, and something metal scraped against my cheek. A heavy gold watch. I screamed against his palm as I realized who had been giving the Mazikin so much information about us. Greg. I didn't know when or how they'd enticed him. Judging by the Hugo Boss tux and the watch, they'd paid him well to be their spy, and they'd certainly gotten their money's worth.

Struggling bodies were all around me, and I couldn't lash out with knives or heels because I was terrified of hurting or killing one of my friends. I tried to shout for Malachi. He was fighting for his life—and mine—just a few feet away, thinking I was safe inside the vehicle. Like it was all going down in slow motion, I watched his clipped, precise, and devastating swings as he drove the Mazikin off. Jim had dropped his staff and was resorting to hand-to-hand combat, staying just outside of the deadly arc of Malachi's staff. I was failing them. With a desperate wrench, I drew one of my knives and plunged it into Greg's arm.

He cursed and caught my fist in midair as it descended again, stripping me of the knife with a brutal twist of my wrist. His hand stifled my shriek as the white-hot pain shot up my arm. As he dragged me farther from the rear doors of the SUV, I saw both Ian and Levi struggling with Mazikin, barely keeping the creatures' jaws away from their faces. I was thrown onto my stomach on one of the seats, and Greg crashed down on top of me.

"She's really strong. You'll need more than one," Greg called as he fought to keep me beneath him, mostly by squeezing my broken wrist, grinding the splinters of my bones together, making me fight to keep from passing out. Finally, he hoisted me up and shoved me shoulders-first out the shattered window, cutting up my side and shredding my dress. A body reeking of incense grabbed my arms and began to tug, pulling me out of the SUV. I kicked out at the last second, nailing Greg in the chest with the deadly heel of my shoe. His mouth dropped open in stupid surprise, and he fell backward into the SUV.

The Mazikin dropped me, and I landed on my hands and knees on the asphalt, and then collapsed onto my chest as my broken wrist failed me completely. Rough hands ripped my garters off, stripping me of my knives. I kicked out again and again, and then lunged under the SUV, but one of them grabbed my legs and dragged me back. Once again, I tried to call out, but all that came from my mouth were wordless cries. I didn't know if I wanted Malachi to hear those.

Two Mazikin, a balding man who looked like he should have been behind a desk and a woman with most of her teeth missing, gripped my arms and yanked me up, while another Mazikin wrapped himself around my legs.

"We've got her!" the woman called to someone over her shoulder.

I fought wildly, even as my wrist bent at a horribly unnatural angle and made me see stars. I opened my mouth to scream, but another hand closed over my face. This time, I bucked forward, caught a finger between my teeth, and bit down hard, choking on blood as a roar of pain filled my ears. I spit blood and flesh onto the asphalt. Teeth sank into my neck in the next moment, and I was lurched backward away from the others by the enraged Mazikin whose finger I'd just amputated.

"No!" shouted a voice behind me.

It wasn't Malachi. Or Jim. Or Ian.

It was my mother. Or, at least, the Mazikin who wore her skin.

She tackled the Mazikin who'd chomped on me, and I fell to the ground, my neck and shoulder throbbing and buzzing. I lifted my head to see the Rita Santos–Mazikin struggling with one of the men from the homeless camp, the burly drywall guy who'd been putting the moves on the skinny waitress. He stumbled away from my mother, scowling. She leaped to her feet and threw her head back, meeting my eyes. Her wild hair flew around her face. She put out her hand. "Come."

"No fucking way," I snarled, rolling clumsily to my feet. The sounds of battle were still coming from the back of the SUV. Only twenty feet or so away. Most of the Mazikin were focusing their efforts there, probably to distract Malachi and Jim from what was happening. I drew a sharp breath into my lungs.

"Guards!" I yelled.

"*Estúpido!*" she screeched, and then lunged for me, grunting and growling in the Mazikin language at her pals, who leaped on me like a hungry wolf pack. I kicked out with my heels, jabbing, throwing hard punches with my good hand. Nearby, I could hear Malachi shouting something, but I couldn't make out his words over the snarls of my attackers.

And then—I had an opening. I hit the Rita-Mazikin's chin with a blow hard enough to send her head snapping back, jerked my knee up and struck the drywaller in the balls, and head-butted the toothless woman. I staggered away from them, my chest heaving, trying to summon the strength for their next strike.

The sound of squealing tires drew my head up.

The Mazikin van didn't have time to stop.

It hit me head-on.

THIRTY-TWO

MY WORLD EXPLODED IN a nuclear blast of pain, and then it all went away. I didn't remember hitting the asphalt. All I knew was it didn't hurt. When I opened my eyes, my mother was leaning over me, stroking my face, tears falling from her cheeks, making me think it was raining.

"*Lo siento, mija*," she whispered. And then she squeezed her eyes shut and shook her head, like she was trying to jar something loose. She stood up, grunting in that grating, harsh Mazikin language and pointing at something.

Tegan screamed.

A sound must have come from my throat, because my mother looked down at me again. "I take her. Good enough for Sil."

The van door slammed, cutting off Tegan's shrill cry. All around me, grunts and snarls receded, followed by more doors slamming. The van's engine roared, and then wheels crunched nearby. I didn't know how far, exactly. I couldn't turn my head.

Malachi's face appeared over mine a few moments later, cutting through the noise and the chaos all around me. His expression was filled with emotions I couldn't understand. He leaned down, closed his eyes, and touched his forehead to mine, just for a fraction of a second. And then he sat back on his knees as Ian and Levi arrived. They stood over me, staring in horror. I wished I knew why. Or maybe, I should have been glad I didn't.

"Is anyone else hurt? Bitten or scratched?" Malachi asked.

Levi shook his head. "They grabbed Tegan and went running as soon as Lela got hit. The girls are kind of shaken up. Alexis might have a broken ankle. But everyone else seems fine . . . except for Greg." He put a trembling hand to a bleeding gash at his temple. "He hit me. And then he grabbed Lela. He was *helping* those guys."

"Laney said she called the police, and I just called an ambulance," Ian said, his voice shaking as he moved closer. "They'll be here soon."

"Lela's not going to the hospital," said Malachi calmly.

"What? She's still alive!" Ian shouted, his face turning red. "They might be able to save her!"

"She needs more than a doctor. Please go take care of the others. Tell Laney I'm sorry," Malachi said. "I'm taking Lela."

He started to lean over me again, but Ian shoved him away, his palm hitting Malachi's chest with a solid thump. Malachi was on his feet with terrifying speed. His hand shot out and grabbed a fistful of Ian's shirt, and he wrenched him close, so the two of them were nose to nose above me.

Malachi spoke through clenched teeth, his accent emphasized by the cold rage in his voice. "You are very, *very* fortunate that Lela said you treated her well. If it weren't for that, I would gladly hurt you. Now. You'll have her back soon, and I will not stand in your way. But tonight, I am taking care of her, and you will not stand in *my* way."

Ian's jaw ridged with tension, and to his credit, he looked more pissed than scared. "You are a clueless *idiot*, Malachi. If I didn't know it would upset her, I'd have caught you upside the head with a bat ages ago." He bunched his fists in Malachi's shirt. "And if she dies, you can count on it. I don't care how long it takes me to catch you off guard. It's going to happen, asshole."

Malachi pushed him away, and Ian stumbled back, only to be caught by Levi. Malachi's breaths were sawing in and out, and he looked like Ian *had* caught him upside the head with a bat. A choked sound bubbled from my mouth, and Malachi was on his knees again instantly, blocking out everything else.

"Henry is picking us up," he said in my ear. "He'll be here any minute. You're going to be fine." His voice was soft. And laced with fear.

"Tegan," I whispered.

His eyes searched my face. "Jim is going after her. He's

called Henry to find out where the nest is, and he'll do reconnaissance, but he promised not to go in alone. I'll join him as soon as I know you're going to be all right."

Jim must have been going crazy, knowing what might happen to her. "Go . . . now."

Malachi's expression twisted with pain. "Lela, please. Don't make me leave you."

I couldn't argue. In that moment, I was relatively sure his presence was the only thing that kept me from letting go, from drifting away. I tried to thank him, but all that came out was a wheezing breath.

"*Shhh*," he soothed, lightly caressing my cheeks with his warm fingers. Over his head, I watched the red and blue lights flashing, signaling the arrival of the police. Malachi ignored them. He touched his nose to mine, and I was amazed to see tears glittering in his eyes. "Don't leave. I know it hurts. Just don't leave."

Actually, it didn't hurt at all. I felt like I was encased in a block of ice, immobile and frozen, nothing working except my brain, which couldn't quite make it past the pain on Malachi's face, past the lump in my throat as he whispered to me, telling me to stay with him.

I love you, I wanted to say. *I would never leave you.*

Darkness licked at the edges of my consciousness, tugging my thoughts away and drowning them. Raphael's face appeared in front of mine. "I'll get her to the car," he said quietly as his gaze shifted to Malachi's. "No one will notice us leaving. And I'll start working on her immediately."

I fought very hard to bring one word to my lips, to push it off my tongue. "Awake."

I didn't want him to make me sleep, to plunge me into darkness. I didn't want to leave Malachi. I didn't want to leave Jim without Tegan. I would be healed, and then I would get up fighting.

Raphael leaned forward. "It will hurt, Lela. More than you think."

"Faster?" I whispered.

He nodded. "You'll be on your feet faster. Is it worth it?"

"Yes."

He lifted me in his arms, and set me in the backseat of the Guard car as we were serenaded by the peal of ambulance sirens. "Most of your friends are all right. The police will assume this is gang-related violence. No one will think to ask where you are."

My head was cradled in Malachi's lap. "Drive away slowly, but go now," he said to the person in the front seat, who I could only assume was Henry.

Raphael locked eyes with Malachi. "She requested to remain awake while I heal her."

Malachi's eyes grew wide. "No. It's too much, too painful. She's been through enough."

"It's her choice, not yours, Lieutenant. The only choice

you have is whether you'll stay with her."

Malachi's jaw started to tick. "That's not a choice."

Raphael chuckled. "There's always a choice." He bowed his head over me. "Your neck is broken, Lela. That's why you can't feel anything. Once I fix that, you're going to feel everything. And you have a lot of injuries that I need to heal very quickly. We're not going to do this slow and easy. Are you ready?"

He took the blink of my eyes as a yes. "Very well."

And then . . . nothing happened. I stared up at Malachi's face, feeling warm and drifty, and he stared down at me, looking like he was feeling all the pain. In seemingly no time, we were back at the Guard house.

"You can carry her to your room," Raphael said. "I'll finish there."

Malachi's arms closed around me, and I was conscious enough to be horrified as my wounds smeared blood over his black tuxedo shirt. He didn't seem to care, though. With an almost painful tenderness, he scooped me up and ascended the stairs, nodding as Raphael announced he was going to check in with Henry before joining us.

I watched Malachi's face as he clutched me against his chest. I wanted to tell him I needed him to keep touching me, to keep looking at me with dark eyes filled with emotions that had burned all the cool indifference away. He laid me down on his bed, and I inhaled deeply because all of it smelled like him, more than his pressed and cologned tux, his pillowcase and sheets, his room . . . they smelled like the real Malachi, earth and sun.

He knelt beside the bed, looking like he was at war with himself, torn between two agonizing extremes. Finally, he closed his eyes and sighed, and when he opened them, it was clear he had made his decision.

"You looked so beautiful tonight," he said with a sad smile. "It was devastating, you know." His fingers smoothed over my cheek. "Once again, I have been such a fool."

I tried to turn my head, but still couldn't. I think he picked up my efforts, because he leaned over so that I could see him better. "I'm going to tell you something," he said, "because I can't go on like this. And I'm going to do it now because you don't have the strength to argue or fight me or walk away. It seems like that's all we do lately, and it's killing me."

I stared at him, and deep in my numb chest, I felt the tremors of my unsteady heart.

"From the moment I met you, nothing has been the same. You were a burst of color and fire after decades of gray. All my wishes and wants, wrapped up in the most frustratingly lovely package." His eyes stroked over my face. "But when I said I could let you go, when I said I could stop loving you, I meant every word. And since that moment, I've tried very hard to do just that. To turn it off, cut it out . . ." He bowed his head. "To try to feel something for someone else, hoping it would make what I feel for *you* fade away."

Something warm streaked down my face, and Malachi followed it with his gaze, his expression turning pained as he caught the tear with his finger.

"I believed I would be a better Guard if I felt nothing for you. I was good before I met you, and I wanted that back. It didn't matter how much it hurt me. I believed I had earned every moment of unhappiness with all my mistakes." He lifted his fingertip, gazing at the crystal drop in the light. "I'm so sorry for causing you pain, Lela. I've missed you every second . . . the things we had, that we could have had. All the times I could have comforted you. Encouraged you. Touched you." His lips curled up at one corner, all bitterness. "As it turns out, after pushing you away, I'm *not* a better Guard. Quite the opposite. And despite my best efforts, I don't feel any less for you than I did before. In fact, as I've watched you shoulder your responsibilities, as I've felt you grow stronger with every fight, as I've seen how all these things hurt you and yet somehow cannot defeat you, I've only fallen deeper."

His eyes met mine. "I cannot undo my mistakes, all the lives lost because of me. I have to find some way to atone for that, and I have no idea how long it will take. I know I will have to be stronger and smarter than I have been if I want to succeed. But perhaps I will think more clearly if I am honest with myself—and with you—about one thing." His lips, warm and soft, touched my temple, and then my forehead. "And so," he whispered, "you can slap me when you regain the use of your arms."

He carefully stripped one of my gloves off and pressed my palm against his chest. He looked down at my fingers, my painted wine-red nails spread across his shirt, over his heart. Then he raised his head to look at me. "This beats for you. It has for some time. And it always will. No matter what happens now, no matter how you feel, that's how it is for me."

He winced and gently placed my hand at my side again. "No, Lela, please don't cry." He wiped the fresh tears from my cheeks, which flowed as my throat closed too tightly for me to draw breath. "I don't expect anything from you. I won't stand between you and Ian. I want you to be happy. I just . . . I couldn't lie about it anymore. You deserve better from me."

"Wise choice, Lieutenant," said Raphael as he strode into the room. "Henry has decided to join Jim at the nest. But they'll await Lela's orders before they move."

Malachi sat back on his knees, his fingers withdrawing from my face and leaving me stunned and choking on my own emotions. I barely heard anything else Raphael said as he sat down on the edge of the bed; I was too busy replaying Malachi's words in my mind, trying to make sure I hadn't imagined them. I needed to tell him how much I loved him, how I forgave him, how—

It was like being cut open, like a red-hot scimitar sliced down my spine, from neck to tail, shooting agony along the stalks of my arms and legs, sending me arching all the way off the bed. The real healing had begun, reconnecting nerve to nerve, muscle to muscle, bone to bone, and it crushed my thoughts, stole my words. Fire curled along the walls of my chest, and then caught and exploded, pumped by my blistered heart through each of my arteries, turning me to ash.

I know I must have screamed because Malachi's arms closed around me. He buried his face in my neck.

"I've got you," he said in my ear. "I won't let you go. This will be over soon. Just hold onto me."

And I did. As the agony continued, as my body knitted itself back together, leaving only silver scars and bad memories, I coiled my newly unbroken bones around his body and used it as my anchor, let him hold me down as I shuddered and seized, let him bind me to the present with his words in my ear and his hands on my skin. I might have hurt him; I was holding on tight enough to turn bones to pulp. But he was so strong; he took it all and then offered more of himself. I clung to it, eagerly, and as the pain began to subside and my vision cleared, I stared at his face and knew he'd felt it all along with me.

"You're hurting," I whispered between hot jolts from Raphael's hands as he put the finishing touches on my healing, making my body strong and ready for what was coming.

Malachi looked into my eyes. "I'm hurting because I love you. But not being with you is infinitely more painful."

"All done," Raphael announced.

Malachi loosened his grip on me immediately. He got to his feet, taking a few uncoordinated steps back before steadying himself with a deep breath. I lay very still for a few moments as the pain evaporated, becoming an unreachable, distant memory, like my mind was wrapping it up tight, walling it off. I sat up, my eyes on Malachi, desperate to tell him everything, to give him my love in return for taking his. But we had to get through this first. I couldn't let Tegan down by having a heart-to-heart with Malachi while the Mazikin strapped her to a table and ripped her soul out of her body. She'd become my friend, and I don't walk away from my friends.

"Call Jim and Henry," I said to him, swinging my legs over the side of the bed. "Tell them we're coming."

"What's your plan?" asked Malachi, already reaching for his phone.

"I'm going to give myself up to the Mazikin."

THIRTY-THREE

MALACHI DIDN'T ARGUE WITH me. He
called Jim and Henry, told them we were on our way, quietly asked Raphael to procure us a car and some clothes for
me, and then shut his bedroom door. "You are the Captain.
But I need a few more details apart from 'I'm giving myself
up.'"

He crossed to his closet and pulled out a long-sleeved
shirt and pants, which he tossed onto his bed, along with a
pair of combat boots. He kicked off his patent leather shoes
and yanked at the tie around his neck. And then he unbut-
toned his shirt and stripped it off.

I turned my back and inhaled a shaky breath. "I'm going
to let them know I'm offering myself to them, as long as

they don't hurt Tegan or possess her. And then I'm going to go in alone and unarmed to keep Sil distracted. You, Jim, and Henry will get in some other way, and it'll be your job to get Tegan out so that I can escape without worrying about her."

"Jim and Henry better have some intelligence for us when we get there, then," he said. "And you can turn around."

I did, to see him lacing his boots. He was wearing bracers over his shirtsleeves, the leather cuffs that protected his forearms from Mazikin claws and teeth. He'd also strapped on his vest. When he saw me eyeing him, he said, "I won't be trying to blend in, and I figured I could use the extra protection."

True enough. I looked down at myself, at my shredded dress, at the dried blood on my skin, wishing I had some armor of my own. I couldn't wear any because Sil had to believe I hadn't gone there to fight. If I could play my part, it would give the other Guards a chance. Still, I wanted to cover myself in thick plates of molded leather, anything to keep those fingernails, those teeth, those hands away from me. Then Malachi stood up, and the look in his eye gave me everything I needed. Without thinking much about it, I walked into his arms. He wrapped them around me, placing his hand on the back of my head and holding me against his armor-plated chest. I put my arms around his waist and held on.

"I won't fail you," he said.

"I know. I'm only worried about failing *you*."

"You won't . . . Captain."

I smiled. For the first time in a long time, it didn't feel like he was using the word to put distance between us. I tightened my grip on him and closed my eyes. "When we're done kicking their asses, you and I are going to talk, all right?"

Even through his leather armor, I felt his heart speed. "Because I was out of line."

Of course he would think that. I slid my hand over his chest and around the back of his neck. "Did you hear what Ian said to you, how you were a—"

"Clueless idiot. Yes, I caught that, thank you." But there was hope in his voice.

"Here's a clue." I got up on my tiptoes and pulled his face to mine. Our lips met for the briefest moment, unbearably sweet and tender, full of promise. I sank back onto my heels. "Tonight, okay?"

He stared down at me, looking like I'd just hit him over the head, but then the most gorgeous, wolfish smile spread across his face. "Tonight."

I nodded, and then went to open the door for Raphael before he could knock. I took the jeans, T-shirt, and boots from his hands. "Thanks for healing me. You did an awesome job."

He gave me a faint yet blinding smile. "My pleasure. I'm

glad to see you on your feet. Your car is waiting. Good luck."
He nodded at Malachi and disappeared.

I changed my clothes and pulled any remaining hair-
pins from my hair, letting it fall in loose curls around my
shoulders. With Malachi on my heels, I went downstairs,
retrieved my phone from the ruined clutch Malachi had
been smart enough to remove from the SUV, and sent a
text to the number scribbled on the crumpled paper my
mother had given me at our meeting at the child welfare
building.

I'm coming. Alone. In exchange for the girl.

The response was instant. *You know where to find us. She will
be released when we have you.*

I gripped the phone hard. "They know we know where
the nest is."

Malachi followed me as I stalked out to the car, a black
Hyundai that looked like it had seen better days. "I suspect
they allowed Henry to survive on purpose. If they'd wanted
to kill him, they could have."

"Why didn't they possess him?"

Malachi's dark eyes glinted with anger. "You know why.
They've set their sights on you, and they won't give up until
they have you."

"Why me, though? It doesn't make sense."

"It makes perfect sense to me. You were everything they
want in a human."

I bristled as I backed along the driveway. "Because I look like an animal?"

"Because you look like exactly what you are. Wild and fierce and strong. Unstoppable and unbreakable. Beautiful and dangerous." He laughed quietly to himself and touched a loose lock of my hair. "You're everything *I* want in a human, too."

I drove toward Providence. The latest nest was apparently in an abandoned nightclub down by the river. Malachi silently stared out the window as we got off the interstate and threaded our way along the city streets, toward the waterfront. I parked several blocks away and texted Jim, letting him know we were close.

By the water meet you in five, came his response.

It took us slightly longer than that to reach them, as we stuck close to the buildings and kept a careful eye out for scouts who might spot us together. Henry and Jim were crouched behind a concrete wall at the edge of the property. Above us loomed the nightclub, three stories high, ramshackle steps leading down to the pier below. Jagged shards clinging like loose teeth to their frames were all that remained of the once huge windows. A dim, flickering glow emanated from the upper floor. A candle. And, of course, a thick haze of incense hung over the place.

"The Mazikin held me on the bottom floor," said Henry,

staring up at the building with hatred. He was completely healed, but his face now bore the scars of his beating, the marks of torture.

"That's where they're holding Tegan," said Jim, gripping the knife in his hand with white knuckles. "I saw them carry her in."

Henry pointed to the lower patio, strewn with overturned beach chairs and chunks of rotted wood that had fallen from the collapsed deck above. "There, right? That's the main entrance." His arm swung to the right, and I followed the line of his finger to a corner window, busted out like all the others. "That's where we can go in. There's a bathroom down there, and no one's guarding it. But it's like a maze once you're inside. A bunch of rooms, and they've got prisoners in every one. It's like they've been collecting them. I could hear them crying the whole time I was in there."

"How many Mazikin?" I asked. "Were you able to get a sense?"

"The one named Sil worked on me." Henry grimaced. "Other than that, maybe a few dozen? Some in front of each room guarding those prisoners."

"There may be fewer than that now," said Malachi. "We terminated at least fifteen this evening. And two were arrested."

Henry grunted. "Assuming they haven't turned more in the past hour," he said.

"They couldn't have turned them all. It takes too long." Even the thought of it made me shudder, though. Malachi scooted in a little closer, offering me the solid warmth of his body, the armor of his touch. This seemed possible—three of my Guards against a few dozen Mazikin was actually decent odds—*if* I could keep Sil busy. "I want you guys to get in there. Find a way to free their captives. Get to Tegan and get her out."

I typed a text and sent it off, proud that my fingers didn't tremble as I hit send. *I'm here. Where do you want me?*

Top floor street entrance open welcome lela girl

I clenched my teeth and stood up. "I'm going to go around the front. Give me two minutes. Then you go in. But be quiet. I'll keep whoever's up top with Sil occupied as long as I can. Text me when she's safe, and come get me if I haven't come down. Then we'll burn it out." I touched the tip of my finger to Malachi's backpack, which held the deadly and powerful grenades that would blow this place into the next dimension. "With any luck, this will be it." I raised my head and looked at each of them. "Kill all of them. We'll clean up the stragglers tomorrow."

My battle-hardened Guards nodded their heads. I drew the humid night air into my lungs, turned quickly, and took a few steps toward the street, only to be caught and whirled around. Malachi's arms wrapped around me, pulling me close.

"You will kill whoever comes at you," he said fiercely, his breath hot against my cheek. "You will do whatever it takes. But you will *not* let them take you."

I put my arms around his neck and held on tight. I knew this was his worst fear, and this wasn't the first time I'd made him live it.

"I won't let them take me," I whispered. "I promise."

He gave me an iron-edged kiss. "Then I'll see you when this is over." He let me go, and I headed for the street before I had a chance to change my mind.

I looped around the block, coming at the club from a completely different direction. From the street, the building appeared completely dark and deserted, except for the smell of incense that permeated the entire area. Broken glass crunched under my boots as I approached the steel front door covered in a thick layer of graffiti. As promised, it wasn't locked. It swung open easily as soon as I tugged on it. I poked my head in.

The distant spotlights of boats roved the river, and the indirect glow of dock and streetlamps shone through the shattered windows. I stepped inside and pulled the door shut behind me. Like a cold hand on the back of my neck, I suddenly had the worst feeling, like I wouldn't make it out of this place alive.

I closed my eyes tight and shook my head, begging my

thoughts not to turn on me now. *Keep walking, Lela. Time to put on a show.*

I followed a wide corridor to the main room, and as I walked, that dim, flickering candlelight came into view. A thick pillar candle. Weirdly enough, apricot-scented. Sitting on the U-shaped bar next to the dance floor. The panoramic view of the river, with the water glinting darkly under the stars, was breathtaking.

"You live," came the choked whisper. I whirled around to see two figures at the edge of the rotting, splintered parquet floor.

My mother. No. The Mazikin who'd taken my mother's body.

And Sil. The Mazikin who wanted to take everything else.

He grinned as he stroked a hand over my mother's wild mane. "She told me you were dying. I guess she was wrong."

"Wouldn't be the first time."

"I haven't seen you in a very long time, girl. You look better here than you did in the dark city. This is where you belong."

"It's the makeup," I said, gesturing at my face. Tegan was an artist. It hadn't budged, despite the fact that I'd been savagely attacked and hit by a van.

Sil threw back his head and laughed, revealing his brown

and jagged teeth. I might have looked better, but he looked worse. Less like a Japanese businessman, and more like an animal. More savage. And more crazy, if that was possible. "It's more than paint on your face. You never belonged in that dead place. You are completely alive."

His hand closed over a fistful of my mother's hair, and he jerked her close, rubbing his nose along the edge of her face. She made this pathetic mewling sound and put her arms around his waist, turning my stomach as she tilted her head up and allowed him to give her a kiss so deep that he must have been licking her tonsils. Then he wrenched her head away, and his eyes swept back to mine. "I was so happy to find Rita here. She reminded me of you immediately. That's why I took her, actually. I had no idea how you were linked. Such a nice surprise." His hand slithered across her chest, squeezing and pinching, making me clench my fists.

"Where's Tegan?" I asked, taking a step forward.

"They'll bring her up when I have you secured." He nodded across the room, where a table had been set up in the open space on the other side of the bar. Ropes had been tied to each of the table legs, and incense smoked up from four pots set at each of the corners. "But I wanted a chance for us to have a family chat first."

"She's not my family," I snapped. "She hasn't been my family for a long time. Nice try, though."

He buried his face in my mother's hair, but raised his head when he heard the glass crunch beneath my soles as I took another step toward him. "Ah, but you're wrong. You risked your life to save hers. You took an arrow meant for her. You betray yourself, Lela girl. And our Rita . . . she cannot get her mind off you, no matter how hard she tries."

The Rita-Mazikin gave me a tremulous, tender smile. "*Mija*," she whispered.

Sil giggled, running his hands over her in a way that said one thing: he owned her. "You see? This Rita is bad," he said, his voice soft and gentle as he nuzzled her neck. "She is bad and weak. This is her first time away from our Mazikin realm. And this body . . . its brain is rotten. It has made her very confused. She has lost touch with who she really is." He snorted. "She forgets where her loyalties lie."

Rita, unable to understand his words, purred at his touch. Sil wrapped an arm around her waist. "She said she understood how this place works. She insisted she could bring you in without drawing the attention of the authorities here, and so we allowed her to try. So many plans she suggested, and because she claimed to know you, I listened to her. Until I realized she was lost in this brain, in scattered and broken old memories, and she doesn't know you at all. Tonight she was dispatched with final orders to bring you in, and she failed *again*. Instead, she brought me that skinny little thing, thinking that would satisfy me. It turns out Rita is mostly useless to me." He pressed himself against her from behind. "Mostly."

My cheeks burned as I watched, wishing my phone would buzz with a text, letting me know they had Tegan, that she was safe, that I could attack and then get myself out of here. But it lay silent in my pocket. "Sorry to hear that she hasn't lived up to your expectations," I said. "She never lived up to mine, either."

He chuckled. "So hostile, girl with the hair. Is that where all your anger comes from? Did this woman hurt you?" He fisted her hair and gave her a shake, drawing a little cry of protest from her.

"She never hurt me. She just . . . left me. A long time ago. I barely remember her." *Let her go. I don't like the look in her eyes.*

"Your memories are in there somewhere. But I bet you wish they weren't," Sil said.

"Sometimes," I admitted.

"I'll give you new memories. You'll thank me. You'll be with her again. Don't you want another chance?" He leaned forward eagerly. "Your bodies can be together here, and your souls can be together in the Mazikin realm. It's perfect!"

"Your idea of perfect is vastly different from mine."

He frowned and tilted his head. "You, a discarded girl, don't wish to be our Queen?" His expression hardened.

"You're ungrateful."

My phone buzzed in my pocket. I clenched my jaw. "Oh, I'm grateful." I took a step forward.

"Me too," he said. And then he drew a knife from his waist and slit my mother's throat.

THIRTY-FOUR

HER AMBER-BROWN EYES CAUGHT the candlelight and flickered, allowing me to witness the moment life left her body. Blood flowed down the front of her shirt. Sil abruptly let her go, and she crumpled to the floor. He wiped the knife on his pant leg.

"Wouldn't want her trying to help you at the worst moment," he muttered, nudging her body with his toe.

Somewhere below us came a chorus of animal howling followed by a muffled explosion. In the far corner of the room, part of the dance floor caved in, crashing downward.

Sil's eyes brightened with anger. "Explosives or not, they will never win. When Rita failed to capture you, we made other plans."

Fear encased my heart, burbling up like acid in my throat. He knew I wasn't alone. He wasn't even surprised by it. "I wouldn't underestimate them. We could go down and join the fun if you want."

His eyes narrowed. "You are a stupid girl. Don't make me damage you."

"You're going to have to. Unless you're going to stand there and let me kill you."

I feinted to the right, and then to the left, herding him backward toward the jagged, yawning mouths of the empty window frames. I kept my arms close to my sides, but loose. My newly healed wrist felt stronger than ever. I felt like I could snap him in half.

He held up his knife and laughed nervously. "I should have brought something bigger, probably." He tossed the knife out the open window, ruining my hopes of stripping it from him and gutting him with it. His fingers curled into claws, revealing his filthy, serrated nails.

My phone buzzed again.

Sil's gaze zipped straight down to the bulge in my jeans pocket. "You should check that. It might be important."

"It can wait." And then I attacked.

Sil was fast as ever and took off running. He dove onto all fours, and then bounded up on the bar, grabbing one of the few remaining light fixtures and throwing it at me in an effort to slow me down. I skirted the bar and ended up by the table with the ropes, the place they'd planned to tie me up and sacrifice me. Sil watched me with half-lidded eyes, waiting for me to attack again. I dipped a toe in one of the pots and stirred quickly, sending a thick haze up around me. I took a few steps back and did it again, hiding behind the thick fog, and then pulled my phone from my pocket and held it close to my face to check the newest text.

I have Tegan

It was from Jim. My knees nearly buckled with my relief. My head jerked up as Sil roared and charged, flying from the bar to the tabletop in a single wild leap. He didn't slow down as he crashed into me, curling his steely fingers around my arms and trying to flip me onto the table. I brought my knee up, driving the breath from him with a blow to the stomach, and then leaned back and slammed my fist into his weaselly, dirt-smeared face.

The floor shook with another tremor from below, throwing Sil and me both off balance. If Malachi and Henry kept this up, the place was going to collapse. Sil took advantage of the moment to wrap one of the ends of the rope around my wrist, catching it in the noose-like loop and tethering me to the table.

"One down, three to go," he whispered, and then cackled like he'd made a hilarious joke.

I clawed at the rope around my wrist, but had to give it up as he charged again. I ducked to the side and then used the rope to clothesline him as he spun around, knocking him back onto the table. Then I crouched and flung myself over him, flattening him back onto the table as I straddled him, pinning his skinny shoulders with my knees. All rage and fear, I jerked my hand down and around, drawing the rope tight around his neck. With my free hand, I held his forehead to the table, and with my other, I pulled.

And pulled.

And pulled.

Until spots flashed in my vision. Until they coalesced and became my mother's eyes, staring at me from beyond, condemning me, loving me, forgiving me, I had no idea.

Fierce animalistic howls from below yanked me out of my trance. I looked down at Sil. His eyes, bright red with burst blood vessels, were half-closed. His face was frozen in an eerie smile. I leaned forward and put my fingers on his sweaty throat. Nothing.

I rolled away from him, untied my wrist, and climbed off the table, wiping my hands on my pants. I'd done it. It had been easier than I'd thought. Now I needed to figure out what the hell was happening below. I checked my phone and read the text that had come first. From Malachi.

Freeing prisoners now will be up soon

But that text had come in several minutes ago, and none of my Guards had come up. With my pulse pounding in my temples, I jogged over to the window and climbed carefully onto the collapsed deck to retrieve Sil's discarded knife. Even though I'd killed Sil, I still couldn't shake the bad feeling I'd had when I came in here. With the knife in my hand, I reentered the club and crept across the dance floor, which was unstable and soft beneath my boots, rotten nearly all the way through. As I neared the caved-in area, I heard a sound that made my stomach knot with fear: chanting.

The Mazikin weren't supposed to be chanting. They were supposed to be running for their lives.

I got down on hands and knees and crawled toward the collapsed section. Dusty light was filtering up from the lower level, revealing the smoky swirls of incense floating and breaking apart just above the hole. I inched forward on my belly, not wanting to fall through the floor and land right in the middle of them. Finally, I hooked my fingers over the edge and looked down, squinting through the haze and trying not to cough as I inhaled the sickly sweet fumes.

About fifteen feet below me, through the crisscross of splintered floorboards, I could see one end of another altar. Pots of incense at the corners. A group of Mazikin massed, leaning over a struggling figure tied to the table. I could see his chest and shoulders straining against the ropes. And when one of the Mazikin dropped to her knees to stir the incense, their victim's face was revealed.

Malachi.

THIRTY-FIVE

PARALYZED BY DISBELIEF AND horror, I stared down at the boy I loved, unable to fathom how they could have caught him. He was so strong, so invulnerable, so unstoppable. But now he'd been stripped to the waist. His armor had been tossed to the floor next to the table. Blood coated one shoulder and flowed from a wound in his neck, a clean cut rather than a bite mark. His jaw was ridged, and his eyes were clamped shut as he fought to free himself from the ropes; his wrists were torn and raw from his efforts.

Several of them were touching him, running their hands over his body, exploring their prize. One of the Mazikin, a young woman standing near his shoulder, slid her fingers along his chest. She bent to lick his cheek, her pink tongue seeking his skin. His eyes flew open as he jerked his face away.

And that's when he saw me. His chest heaved, and his eyes grew wide. In them I saw too many things to name. Love. Regret. Fear. And pleading. It was a look I'd never seen before, and my throat closed as I translated it. He knew what was about to happen to him, and he didn't want me to watch.

It jolted me out of my paralysis. My fingers clenched around the knife as fiery rage swept through me, more powerful than anything I'd ever felt before, disintegrating any terror or hesitation, sending wave after wave of determination and strength through my body.

Malachi was going to get his wish. I had no intention of watching. I was going to kill. Them. *All.*

I plunged through that hole with a rending crash as my boots collided with rotting boards, and was in the open air for a split second before landing with a crunch on the Mazikin that had just tried to taste his skin. I grabbed her hair and wrenched her head back; then I drew my knife across her throat as the rest of the Mazikin roared with surprise and stumbled away from the table Malachi was tied to. With my blade dripping red, I dropped my first victim and spun around. There were at least twenty Mazikin in the dimly lit rectangular chamber, which looked like it had once been a private party room. A lot more than we'd anticipated.

I dove for one of the ropes holding Malachi's wrists and began to slice at it frantically, but a muscular arm looped around my waist and yanked me away before I could cut all the way through. As I was carried backward, I stabbed my captor in the wrist. The arm let me go, and I turned to see a stocky male stagger back. I buried my blade in his neck, splattering blood on a group of Mazikin closing in on me. Malachi was shouting, but I couldn't hear his words over the snarls and grunts of the Mazikin.

Smoke burned my eyes; one of them was stirring up the incense, filling the room with its heavy haze. Above the table, a dense shape began to coalesce, and then was blocked out as several Mazikin launched themselves at me at once, driving me into a wall. My head bounced off its upholstered surface as my legs kicked at them. I drove my knife upward into the gut of the fat Mazikin directly in front of me, and it doubled over, allowing me to see the ghostly shape near the ceiling turn in the air . . . and dive into Malachi's body.

His shoulders slammed into the table, and then he arched up, his head snapping back. His face twisted with agony, his mouth opened in a silent scream. And my whole world shattered. Dimly, I felt the Mazikin grasping at me, trying to wrestle me to the floor, but my heart was with Malachi on that table. Every muscle in his body was rigid as he fought with the smoke beast trying to pry his soul loose, trying to send him to hell.

And if he was still fighting, I would, too. I had to get to him. I had to save him.

My existence shrank to the two feet in front of me. Nothing could slow or stop the slash of my blade, fueled by deadly rage and fierce love. Blood flowed sticky over my hands as I stabbed and withdrew, stabbed and withdrew, planning to kill every single Mazikin who had dared to touch him, dared to hurt him, dared to stand between the two of us. I was beyond reason or rational thought. Beyond pain. Beyond doubt.

Teeth bared and snapping, nails jagged and clawing, the Mazikin lunged. But they couldn't stop or subdue me. I cut off fingers. Noses. Jammed my knife into eye sockets and necks and guts. Cracked my elbows against mouths and cheekbones and slammed my knee into groins and bellies. They fell onto each other, leaking crimson into a giant puddle on the floor, and it wasn't enough. I wanted them to drown in their own blood. Red was the only color I could see. I was sure I was bleeding and breaking beneath the assault, but I couldn't feel it. I knew eventually I'd go down, but I fought for the next moment, the next satisfying vibration as metal sank through flesh and collided with bone. The coppery scent filled my nose, blocking out the stench of incense. All I could hear was the roar of my own heart beating in my ears.

Until one voice cut through all of it. "Get away from her!"

It was so loud, so powerful and authoritative, that all the surviving Mazikin went still for a moment, and then turned away from me to look at the voice's owner. It was Malachi. The severed ropes dangled from his wrists. One of his razor-sharp throwing knives was dangling from his clenched fist. Blood was smeared along his chest from the wound in his neck, but he stood on the table, unbroken and strong.

Before I could figure out what had happened, the Mazikin next to me growled and clamped his clawed hand around my throat.

Malachi's knife sliced through the air and plunged into the Mazikin's back with a hollow thud, and it dropped to the floor without a sound. The creatures around me snarled, and I sank against the wall under the weight of my relief. I'd cut through that rope enough for him to get his hand free, and that had been all he needed. He'd freed himself. Somehow, he'd fought off the smoke beast.

His predator's gaze slid over a few Mazikin who had pressed themselves against the far walls of the room and were watching him with stunned expressions, and then over to the small group of living Mazikin and the several dead or dying ones all around me. His mouth quirked up at one corner, and then his eyes met mine. They were no longer filled with regret or fear or pleading. Now they were filled with a quiet pride that felt like a caress.

Malachi jumped to the floor and stepped casually over

the body of a fallen Mazikin. The remaining creatures appeared too frozen with fear to move. The six or so still around me crouched as Malachi came toward us, like they weren't sure if they wanted to attack or run.

He feinted toward them, and they squealed and flattened themselves against the wall, sliding out of his reach. Smiling, he leaned over and yanked his throwing knife from the body of the Mazikin who'd tried to grab me. He wiped the knife on his pants but didn't sheath it.

"It's okay," he said, offering his other hand. "It's me."

"How did you do it?" I asked hoarsely.

He raised his eyebrow. "I was stronger than he was."

All the Mazikin in the room nervously eyed the closed doors at either side of the room, their escape routes, but they seemed afraid to move, because that would make them targets. Malachi's fingers closed around mine, and he helped me climb over the low wall of bodies separating us. I fell into his arms, wrapping myself around him as tears stung my eyes. He held me tightly against him as I started to shake. I had been so close to losing him, and suddenly I couldn't wait anymore to say how I felt. I had been saving this for our conversation tonight, but the words bubbled out on the current of my happiness. "I love you," I breathed. "I love you so much."

His face was buried in the crook of my neck, and I felt him smile against my skin. "Say it again." His lips moved against my throat, turning my knees to jelly.

"I love you," I said with a laugh.

"I've missed you so much, Lela," he said, his voice rough. "I had no idea I'd miss you this much."

"Are you all right?" I whispered. "That looked so painful."

"It was." A warm huff of laughter skated across my skin. "But now I'm fine. Better than fine, actually. Now I'm perfect."

And then his teeth sank into my neck.

I screamed as the truth crashed through my mind like a tsunami, laying waste, washing all my strength away and replacing it with bitter, ragged grief. I'd been so stupid. Too hopeful, too desperate to have him back. Too ready to believe it was him, simply because I wanted it so badly.

But as the rending pain in my shoulder and neck became a deep, penetrating agony, I knew . . .

Malachi was gone.

They'd killed him.

The boy I loved had been defeated. A monster had taken his place.

And now it was going to kill me, too.

With his mouth clamped at the junction of my neck and shoulder, he pressed me up against the wall, a twisted embrace. I kicked and struggled feebly, but he caught my wrist and squeezed at just the right place, making me drop my knife.

I could barely fight him. I didn't *want* to fight him. I was too destroyed by the idea that this body that had touched me with such tenderness, that had caressed me, protected me . . . was now tearing my flesh, sending hot venom into my bloodstream. All the Mazikin snarled and hooted, enjoying the show. My vision blurred with tears as black memories blossomed in my head: being held down with no ability to defend myself. That someone I had loved and trusted was doing this to me now drowned me in that darkness, sapping my will to survive. I slapped at his shoulders with my free hand, but it was a pathetic effort. Even with everything that had happened to me, I'd never felt this weak. Losing Malachi had sucked the fight right out of me.

Something crashed against one of the doors, and from outside came the unmistakable sounds of a struggle. "Malachi! Are you—" Henry shouted, but the rest of his words were cut off by a muffled explosion.

The creature inside Malachi released my neck. "There are two of them," he said to the others as my blood trickled down his chin. "Kill them both. And don't disturb me again." Then he barked something in their growling language, the sounds foreign and horrifying coming from Malachi's mouth. He nodded toward the exit behind the altar, on the opposite side of the room. The Mazikin whooped at him as eager grins spread across their faces, and too late it occurred to me that they hadn't been scared of Malachi when he rose from the table—they'd been scared of this Mazikin. It had to be one of their leaders. As if to prove my theory, they all jumped for the door at once and tumbled through it, ready to join the fight in progress.

When they were gone, the monster behind Malachi's black-brown eyes looked down at me with the strangest expression, an odd tenderness mixed with savagery. "I don't know what to do with you, Lela Santos."

"You killed him," I whispered, staring at the face I knew so well and loved so much.

He grinned and licked my blood from his lips. "Not really, but he'll regret that I didn't. He's in our city now. They were waiting for him. I wish I could see them celebrating."

I closed my eyes, not wanting to imagine how a city full of Mazikin would treat the Guard who had terrorized them for the last seventy years.

"Look at me, Lela. Your eyes are so beautiful." He set his forehead on mine. "He loved them, too, you know. Your eyes. Your mouth. Your body. Your spirit. *Most of me wants to protect you . . .*"

My heart stuttered as he recited Malachi's words from that day on the training mat.

He pulled back a little, and I opened my eyes. "He never told you the rest of it," he said quietly. "It's all in here—" He tapped his temple lightly with the blade of his knife. "All his memories. So I'll tell you the rest, because he never would have."

Tears streaked down my face as he leaned in. "Most of him wanted to protect you, but the rest of him just *wanted* you. You have no idea what's in this head." He closed his eyes, like he was savoring it. With a laugh, he stepped away from me, and I slid boneless to the floor, sobbing at everything I'd lost.

"All his fantasies are in here," he continued. "Poor Malachi. He makes so much more sense to me now. All that frustration, bottled up tight." His mouth twisted into a wry smile. "Did you know he died a virgin, Lela?" His laughter rang out, cruel and hard. "Twice!"

A tiny spark ignited inside me. "Don't talk about him like that," I said, my voice cracking.

"Oh? Should I show some respect? Maybe so. He's killed me several times, after all." He tilted his head as he looked me over. "You've only killed me once, but you did quite a job of it. And with only a hunk of cement. I underestimated you."

Dread welled up, choking me. "Juri."

His smile widened, and he drew his tongue along his bottom lip. "Say it louder, Lela. I want to hear you scream it."

"Fuck you," I whispered, the spark flaring.

He grinned and gestured at his neck. "I think both of us need to patch ourselves up before we get to that. I've lost a lot of blood. When the esteemed Captain realized it was a trap, he tried to cut his own throat to keep us from taking him."

I rolled onto my hands and knees, rage becoming an inferno in my chest. Pure, simple hatred. Enough to heat my muscles and jump-start my fractured heart. All focused on Juri. He watched me with a lazy smile as he leaned on the pool table and used his knife to cut away the ropes from his wrists.

I looked away because the sight of Malachi's gorgeous face threatened to pull me under again. I focused on the sounds coming from outside the room. Crashes, growls. Would Jim and Henry come back? Did they know we were in here?

"We designed the trap especially for him, knowing of his eagerness to save lost human souls," Juri said, gazing at his reflection in the blade of his knife and wiping the blood from his chin. "It was worth the wait, and all the weeks of planning and collecting. When he came into this room, all he saw were dozens of frightened young faces. All tied up, helpless and desperate to be rescued." His eyes glinted, and I knew he was seeing all of it through Malachi's memories. "As soon as he freed them, they turned on him. At first, he had no idea they were all Mazikin. And even once his situation became clear, he . . . hesitated. He was afraid some of them might be human."

Juri looked down at his bare chest, the curves and ridges

of muscle he now controlled, and then sauntered over to Malachi's armor and clothes. He pulled the shirt over his head and secured the baton to his belt. "They were gentle, even though he killed many of them," he said softly, gesturing toward the far wall.

For the first time, I noticed the huge booth in the farthest corner of the room, where the shadows were deep. It had obviously been meant for VIPs. But now bodies were piled onto the seats and stashed under the table like human trash, used and tossed away by demons from hell. "I'll reward them for their sacrifice," Juri said.

He wasn't talking about the humans. They were only shells to him. He was talking about his Mazikin family. He'd reward them by bringing them back and letting them possess others. By killing more people. Suddenly, it blazed all the way through me like a wildfire, the fight that had been torn away by grief. Malachi had died trying to save innocents. The Mazikin had exploited his selflessness, his courage, his determination. They'd taken his goodness and turned it to weakness. They'd used his compassion as a weapon against him. "I'm going to kill you," I breathed, my eyes scanning the floor and spotting my knife.

I lunged for it, but he was on me before I reached it, crushing me to the floor. He grabbed a handful of my hair and ran his nose along my cheek. "I love your fire, Lela. I don't think I'll ever be able to bring myself to turn you."

He caught the confusion in my eyes. "Did you really think we wanted you for our Queen?" He laughed, the deep vibrations humming against my back as he held me tight, half lover, half enemy. "No, don't be insulted. You would be a perfect vessel, but the Queen will not leave the realm until all her children are here."

"Why, then?" I whispered, fighting furious, helpless tears as he ground himself against me.

"You still don't understand? There was no way to get to Captain Malachi, until you came along. His love for you made him careless. To him, you were everything, so it was easy for him to believe you'd be everything to us, too. The more we threatened you, the more single-minded he became, until he did not give his own safety—or importance—a moment of thought. And now that we have Malachi's mind and his body, the Guards of the Shadowlands are nothing. We will wipe you from this realm and make it ours."

It took him only a second to roll me over. He held my wrists over my head in a punishing grip while he settled himself on top of me. I jerked my head up to try to smash his nose, but he caught my hair and pulled me back down; then he licked at the bite wound he'd left on my throat, sending waves of painful buzzing electricity along my limbs.

Of course the Mazikin hadn't wanted me. Because who was I next to Malachi? A stupid girl, pretending to be in charge. Malachi had been a Guard for seventy years. And for all those years, he had been merciless, efficient, and deadly. Inside his head, he carried knowledge of the Guard, of Raphael and his powers, of Michael and his weaponry, of the Judge. Of our strategies. Our backgrounds. Our weaknesses. And the Mazikin now controlling him was one of the most vicious and dominant in existence. The combination would be unstoppable.

And meanwhile, Malachi's soul was at the mercy of these creatures, trapped forever in a place of fire and death. The broken, enraged scream that came from my throat startled Juri, and he raised his head and lowered his guard just enough. I jerked my hips up and bucked him off me; then I scrambled to my feet and darted across the room.

"Jim! Henry!" I shrieked.

Juri hit me like a freight train, flattening me against the wall. "Don't be like that, Lela. Don't you want to know the animal side of Malachi? I can show you."

"Get off me!" I screeched, driving my elbow back into his stomach.

He huffed and took a few lazy steps back, but then caught my wrist and spun me into the wall of his body. "He always enjoyed fighting with you, and I can see why. It's rather . . . stimulating."

He ducked his head to kiss me, but I hit him with a knee strike to the thigh. His grip on me loosened, and he growled, baring his teeth. For the first time, he didn't look like Malachi at all.

Which made it easier to smash my fist into his face. My knuckles split on his teeth, and he roared, throwing me to the ground. Outside the door, a man called my name.

Juri turned his head toward the noise and cursed. "Now we're done playing."

"You're right about that," I said, and extended the baton I'd just stripped from his waist.

He laughed. "Really, Lela? If you can land a blow, I might consider letting you go. See if your angel can't clean you up and send you back to me looking a little less damaged. Go ahead." He gave me a little come-on gesture with his hands, a perfect imitation of Malachi in a playful mood. "Show me how much you've learned, Captain."

I jabbed at his left side, and then reversed course and thwacked him in the knees. He grinned. "That almost hurt. Very nice. You'll live through tonight. Want to try for another day?"

"Captain! Is that you?" Someone pounded against the door, hard enough to splinter it. Jim.

"Here!" was all I was able to scream before Juri hit me, punching all the air from my lungs. The staff fell from my numb hands and I dropped as if my legs had been ripped out from under me. Wheezing, with darkness swirling at the edges of my vision, I curled into a ball and tried to keep drawing breath, which seemed too difficult to master.

Juri lifted me from the ground and cradled me to his chest. "Keep your mouth shut, or I'll kill them in front of you."

Then he kissed my cheek and raised his head. "Jim! We're in here. Sil's dead, and I've got Lela." The moment he said it, I realized that that had been the plan all along. Sil had let me kill him, to keep me busy while they took Malachi. He'd known Juri would be taking over.

Jim burst into the room, Tegan folded against his side. Her pale, bare arms were wrapped around his neck. She looked ready to faint, so scared, like Jim was the only thing keeping her from screaming. He had dark smudges on his face and a cut over his eye, but other than that, seemed unhurt. His blue eyes widened as he took in the scene in front of him, bodies piled high, blood smeared over the floor, me bleeding and dazed. "Weren't you upstairs, Captain?"

Juri nodded toward the ceiling. "She jumped through. We fought off the ones in here, but she was bitten. Let's get out of here." He strode toward the door, and Jim scooped Tegan into his arms and stepped out of the way to let us by. As Juri crossed the threshold, I caught Jim's eye. Only for a moment, but enough to make his brow furrow with confusion. Juri's scent wouldn't help him figure it out—the whole freaking place was hazy with it, and the sickening smell had seeped into our clothes, our hair, our skin.

Juri carried me into an open room connected to a wide patio and the decrepit dock beyond it. We were at the back of the club, the part hidden from street level, visible only from the water. It seemed like most of the walls on this level had been blasted away by grenades. Bodies were everywhere. Henry jogged across the patio, and the sight of his scarecrow silhouette made Juri tense.

"Couldn't catch 'em," Henry panted as he vaulted through the gaping hole where a picture window had once been. He stopped dead when he saw us standing there. "A bunch of them got away," he said to us, looking disgusted. "They'd turned every single prisoner, except for her." He nodded at Tegan. "We'll definitely have cleanup to do tomorrow." He inclined his head toward me, squinting in the darkness. "You okay, Captain?"

Juri's fingers curled into my side, a warning. "I'm all right," I said. "I'll be better once Raphael works on me a little."

Henry locked eyes with Jim over my shoulder. "Maybe we should summon him now," he said, taking a step forward.

"You'll be fine, won't you?" Juri asked me, looking at me in a way that told me my answer had better be yes.

"I'll live," I whispered.

Jim chuckled and squeezed Tegan. "Look at us acting like such cavemen. Can you walk, baby?"

Tegan looked up at Jim and nodded shakily. He set her

on her feet, kissed her with aching tenderness, and then nodded at me. "Don't be such a girl, Captain."

I laughed airlessly. "Sorry about that." I straightened my legs.

Juri gave me a tight smile and allowed my feet to slide to the ground. "We should get to the car. I have no doubt one of the escaped hostages will have called the police by now." He sounded so much like Malachi that I winced.

His fingers closed around my upper arm. "Lead the way, Captain," he said smoothly, giving me a gentle push toward the gaping picture window that would be our exit.

I turned to Tegan. "Let's go."

She gave me a frightened look as we walked toward the windows. Well, she walked. I hobbled. One of my legs was starting to go numb. From behind us, Jim's easy, friendly voice called, "Hey, Malachi. You forgot your staff."

I turned in time to see Juri look over his shoulder.

Right as Jim slammed the staff into his face.

The enraged roar that came from Juri betrayed him for what he was. He covered his face and stumbled back, and Henry lunged forward and grabbed Tegan, nearly tossing her waifish body over the windowsill.

"Run," he said. "Get to the street."

He boosted me up next, dumping me in an uncoordinated sprawl on the other side. Then he jumped over behind me. He shoved me toward the stairs to the upper

level, but the sounds of the struggle were too much for me.
I didn't want to leave Jim. He and Juri were locked in bone-
crunching combat: Jim's acrobatic yet devastating kicks and
punches against Malachi's clipped and efficient style. Each
of them had a knife clutched in one hand. Their movements
were almost a blur.

Juri faked to the left and then whirled before Jim could
recover, slashing his blade along Jim's ribs and soaking his
white tux shirt with blood.

Tegan screamed.

Jim flinched as his gaze darted over to us. "Get out of
here!" he shouted, his voice cracking in desperation. "Henry,
get them out of here!"

Henry stepped up behind Tegan and wrapped his arm
around her waist. But her shriek had shaken Jim, pulled him
from his zone. With a quick, brutal punch, Juri had him
doubled over and staggering. He pressed his advantage by
kneeing Jim in the face, sending his head snapping back.
The look of evil delight on Juri's face tore at my heart.

Henry and I stepped forward at the same time, determined to help Jim, but that was the moment Juri grabbed
Jim's hair and wrenched him to his knees. He yanked Jim's
head up, letting us see his wide blue eyes, full of pleading.

"Run," he whispered.

And then Juri plunged the knife into his neck.

Henry whirled around as Tegan shrieked and dove

toward the window. It took the two of us to drag her back while Juri finished off Jim, allowing his limp, twitching body to fall to the dirty floor. Juri lifted his head and met my eyes.

"Soon," he mouthed.

Henry grabbed my arm, and we ran.

THIRTY-SIX

HENRY DROVE US STRAIGHT to the Guard house. It had taken all of my rapidly fading strength to hold Tegan down on the way. She was completely hysterical, screaming for Jim, and the sounds that ripped from her throat harmonized perfectly with the shrieks for Malachi in my own head.

We pulled into the driveway of the Guard house just after three in the morning. Raphael was waiting on the steps, grim-faced. Henry got out of the car as I struggled with Tegan.

Raphael walked slowly down the steps, his eyes resting on Tegan, who was alternating between hitting me and hugging me. Deep, wrenching sobs rolled from her tiny frame. He opened the passenger door, focused entirely on her.

"Look at me, Tegan," he said. His voice flowed over me, golden and warm.

Tegan stopped struggling and obeyed him.

He squatted in front of her and looked into her eyes. His expression was so compassionate, so intimate. I scrambled out of the car to get away from it.

"Do you want me to make you forget him?" he asked. "You'll feel better."

She blinked at him. "You can do that?" she whispered.

"I can. You won't remember watching him die."

"Will I remember . . . anything?"

Raphael frowned. "What do you want to remember?"

"He said he loved me." Her eyes filled with tears again. "Tonight. He told me he loved me."

I closed my eyes.

"If you like," said Raphael, "I can make you think he's left here, that he's merely moved away. Would that be better?"

"Anything would be better than seeing him die over and over again. Anything would be better than that."

I stepped back into the yard, my neck throbbing and aching, the numbness buzzing down my arm and up the side of my face, anger throbbing in my heart. Raphael wasn't doing this for Tegan. He'd refused to take away my hurt, my heartbreak. And he'd never healed a human, never stepped in to save an innocent. He'd always let things run their course—unless they interfered with our ability to complete our mission. So now he was pretending to be compassionate, but only because Tegan could tell people about Juri, about Jim's murder, about our involvement in all of it. Raphael was doing his *job*—covering for the Guard so that we could get on with business, just like always.

Tegan nodded, blindly accepting this offer of forgetting because she was too destroyed by grief and terror to question it. Her new reality would be that Jim took off without saying good-bye. Instead of sorrow, she'd have outrage. Instead of terror, she'd have bitterness. And I had to wonder—if I had the choice, would I want to believe Malachi had chosen to leave? Or would I want to know what had actually happened to him?

The noise inside my brain was endless and overpowering as I remembered him in his final moments, head thrown back, fighting a frenzied losing battle. It sent me to my knees, doubled over and nerveless. From my toes to my legs to my gut to my chest to my head, there was nothing but a rupturing wail, nothing but the pain of what I'd lost, and how thoroughly I'd lost it. I would never recover from this, even if I did live through it. Which I didn't want. Not at all. I didn't want to live through it.

I rose to my feet. I shouldered my way past Raphael as he carried Tegan to the Guard house. I trudged up to Henry, knowing I was about to fail him completely. But when Henry's dust-colored eyes met mine, all I saw was understanding.

"I got to know Malachi pretty well," he said. "He never told me in so many words, but I could tell how he felt about you."

I opened my mouth, but I couldn't push the words out. *I love him. And I can't stay here when he's not.*

He saw the look on my face and nodded. "I know what it's like to be torn away from someone you love," he said. "Do what you have to do."

"Juri knows all about us, Henry. He could show up at any second."

"But he won't find me. I need to lie low, anyway, being a fugitive from justice and all that." He looked over his shoulder at Raphael, and then back at me. "Go, Lela. I'll hold down the fort and protect your friends until you come back."

I stared into the haunted depths of his eyes. None of my well-meaning lies or promises made it past the shriek caught in my throat, so I walked away from him and got into my car. I twisted my key in the ignition and backed out of the driveway.

By the time I got onto the highway, the wailing in my mind had declared its rhythm and settled in to stay like an old friend, one who wanted to torture me before he killed me. I didn't need another friend like that. But there was no shaking this agony planting itself on the inside of my skull, portraying images of Malachi's stern, gorgeous face, replaying moments, like the one in which he'd told me that being with me when I was hurting was much less painful than being away from me and knowing he couldn't help.

"I feel the same way," I whispered to myself as I drove over the bridges to Newport.

I motored all the way to the start of the Cliff Walk, and then headed out on foot, in the dark. I closed my eyes and let the vision plow its way to the front of my brain, just like I knew it would, just like it had with Nadia. But this time the vision—the *bait*—was Malachi, ripped free of his body, hurtling down a deep black hole.

And when he opened his eyes, they were waiting for him. The monsters were more than happy to welcome him. They would keep him in their realm, torturing him for all the things he'd done to them, for eternity.

I reeled a little as the sea breeze swirled around me.

"I'm surprised you can still walk," said Raphael, appearing at my side. "You're going to collapse soon, though. Would you like to come back to the car and let me drive you back to the house?"

I gave him the finger. "Don't pretend to be worried about me. You want to patch me up and send me back into the fight."

"I'm not sure what I said to make you think I'm worried about you. I do my duty, and so should you."

I turned to him, my rage pulsing red with every beat of my heart. "Yeah? Is that what I *need*, Raphael? Was that what Jim needed? He needed to die on his knees, knowing he'd failed?" I shouted.

"Jim didn't fail, Lela," he said gently, not fazed at all. "Quite the opposite. He gave his life for his comrades. It was the first utterly selfless thing he's ever done."

I clenched my fists. Whether he was right or not, I couldn't get past the desperate yearning in Jim's eyes as he looked at Tegan for the last time, knowing he was about to lose her, about to lose the life he wanted, the real things he'd finally found.

Raphael tilted his head. "What do you think *you* need, Lela?"

"I need Malachi." It came from me automatically.

"No, you *want* Malachi."

The rage exploded, crimson and iron, burning all the way through me. I shoved Raphael with all my strength, and he stumbled back, but his mild expression didn't change as he regained his footing on the rocks. It sent me straight over the edge. "Did Malachi *need* to have his soul torn from his body? Did he need to be tortured?" I screamed, hot tears streaming down my face. "Because that's what's happening! Right. Now. After seventy years in the service of the Judge, *this* is what he fucking needed?"

Raphael took my shoulders in his warm grasp, his face glowing with that otherworldly light, like it always did when he started to get pissed off. I tried to wrench myself away, but his grip was too strong. "The Mazikin are not under the authority of the Judge, Lela. Surely you don't think—"

"Oh, I do," I spat. "She's thrilled, isn't she? This is what she wanted all along. She wants him there. This whole thing was a setup, for him and for me. So let's get this fucking show on the road. I need to see the Judge. Now."

He smiled. "She hasn't invited you to her chambers yet."

"I'm inviting myself *now*. I have an offer for her. And she knows it. You guys think the strings are invisible, but I can see you pulling them."

"How clever of you, little human." His face had transformed from ordinary to blinding, but I didn't look away. "You've got us all figured out."

"Not all of it. Just what I'm going to do. And you're going to help me."

He let me go, chuckling. "Oh, really?"

"I think so." I backtracked until my heels were right at the precipice of the rock and teetered on the edge, sticking my arms out for balance. "Tell me, Raphael, are you going to let me end up at the Suicide Gates? Is that what I *need*?"

His eyes narrowed, but he didn't say a word. He wasn't chuckling anymore, though.

"Are you going to stop me, archangel? Do I need to stay here and grieve while I wait patiently for my summons to the Sanctum? And in the meantime, do I need to have my throat cut by the psycho who stole the body of the best

Guard you have? Tell me," I shrieked. "What. Do. I. Need?"

I didn't wait for him to reply. I didn't care what his answer was. I was ready to take the biggest gamble I ever had, because I only cared about one thing. One thought. One person. Beyond reason, beyond duty.

Beyond my fear of dying again.

I took a quick backward step and threw myself off the cliff.

Tumbling, falling, I only had time to mark the glitter of moonlight on water, the soft lap of waves I could finally hear, because the wailing in my head had gone silent the moment I accepted what I had to do.

I was going to find my way to the Mazikin realm.

And I was going to get Malachi out.

ACKNOWLEDGMENTS

SO MANY PEOPLE HAD a hand in making this book what it is: the Amazon Children's Publishing team, especially Margery Cuyler, Tim Ditlow, Deborah Bass, Jenny Parnow, and, of course, Courtney Miller, my amazing editor, who has shepherded it through the process, advocating for it every step of the way. My developmental editor, Leslie Miller, whose positivity, patience, and understanding of the story and characters made the revision process a true pleasure. I would like to thank my copyeditors, Jennifer Williams and Carrie Wicks, and my proofreader, Ruth Strother, for seriously excellent nitpicking and detail work. Thank you to Tony Sahara, for designing a cover that perfectly captured the emotional intensity in the story.

I want to thank the team at New Leaf Literary—most notably Joanna Volpe, Danielle Barthel, Jaida Temperly, and Pouya Shahbazian—for supporting both this series and my career in general. Most importantly, I want to thank Kathleen Ortiz, my agent, for managing all details big and small, for understanding the intersection between intellect and emotion, for keeping things in perspective, and for talking me off the ledge whenever necessary.

My intrepid beta readers: Justine Dell, Jaime Lawrence, Leah Block, and Stina Lindenblatt, thank you a thousand times for both criticism and encouragement. My dear friends, Jennifer R., Lydia Kang, and Brigid Kemmerer, for listening—my day is made every time I see your names in my inbox. My patient and understanding boss, Paul Block, for making it possible to balance two worlds, and my incredible colleagues: Liz Cantor, Catherine Allen, Kim Bennett, Heather Drever, Anne-Marie Bora, Yerissa Mago, and the entire CCBS staff, for understanding the weirdness of my double life, for being excellent, and making my "day" job easy. And Petra (Safari Poet), for reaching out from across the ocean to support suicide prevention, a cause I hold dear.

Book bloggers, especially Alexa, Lili, Bethzaida, Maja, Heidi, Keertana, Rachel, Nicole, Christy, and Ali: your enthusiasm and insight made my introduction to the online world of readers and reviewers much more fun and rewarding. And to all my readers! I could never have anticipated how inspiring it would be to interact with you. It's an honor, and I'm grateful. And if you ever crave more from the Guards of the Shadowlands world, look for Malachi's journal entries at GuardsOfTheShadowlands.tumblr.com, which is also where you can ask questions and look for news about the series.

Finally and most fundamentally: my family. I sincerely hope you know what you mean to me, and that I could not do anything if not for you. My parents, Jerry and Julie Fine; my sisters, Cathryn and Robin; my husband, Joey; and my babies, Asher and Alma (okay, I know: you're not babies; you're BIG). Nothing else to say except you bring me joy.